WHERE HONOR DWELLS

GILBERT MORRIS

Tyndale House Publishers, Inc.
Wheaton, Illinois

Living Books is a registered trademark of Tyndale House Publishers, Inc.

Published in association with the literary agency of Alive Communications, Inc
7680 Goddard Street, Suite 200, Colorado Springs, CO 80920.

Scripture quotations are taken from the *Holy Bible*, King James Version.

ISBN 0-8423-4274-5

Printed in the United States of America

05   04   03   02   01
7   6   5   4   3   2   1

CONTENTS

✤ GENEALOGY OF

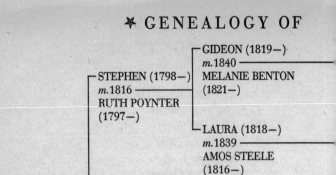

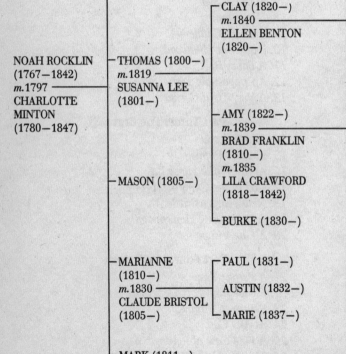

STEPHEN (1798—)
*m.*1816 ——————
RUTH POYNTER
(1797—)

GIDEON (1819—)
*m.*1840 ——————
MELANIE BENTON
(1821—)

LAURA (1818—)
*m.*1839 ——————
AMOS STEELE
(1816—)

NOAH ROCKLIN
(1767—1842)
*m.*1797 ——————
CHARLOTTE
MINTON
(1780—1847)

THOMAS (1800—)
*m.*1819 ——————
SUSANNA LEE
(1801—)

CLAY (1820—)
*m.*1840 ——————
ELLEN BENTON
(1820—)

AMY (1822—)
*m.*1839 ——————
BRAD FRANKLIN
(1810—)
*m.*1835
LILA CRAWFORD
(1818—1842)

MASON (1805—)

BURKE (1830—)

MARIANNE
(1810—)
*m.*1830 ——————
CLAUDE BRISTOL
(1805—)

PAUL (1831—)

AUSTIN (1832—)

MARIE (1837—)

MARK (1811—)

THE ROCKLINS ✳

TYLER (1841—)
ROBERT (1842—)
FRANK (1843—)

PATRICK (1840—)
COLIN (1841—)
DEBORAH (1842—)
CLINTON (1843—)

DENTON (1842—)
DAVID (1842—)
LOWELL (1843—)
RENA (1846—)

GRANT (1840—)
RACHEL (1842—)
LES (1844—)
VINCENT (1837—) ½ BROTHER

✶ GENEALOGY OF THE YANCYS ✶

— ROYAL (1832—)

— MELORA (1834—)

— ZACK (1836—)

— CORA (1837—)

BUFORD YANCY
(1807—)
*m.*1829 ————————— LONNIE (1843—)
MATTIE SATTERFIELD
(1813-1851)

— BOBBY (1844—)

— ROSE (1845—)

— JOSH (1847—)

— MARTHA (1849—)

— TOBY (1851—)

***

PART ONE
THE COWARD

***

CHAPTER ONE

BRAND OF A COWARD

"RACHEL!" Les Franklin grabbed his sister's arm and pointed toward the street. "Look, here comes Vince—and he's so drunk he can hardly sit on his horse!"

Rachel Franklin turned at once to see her half brother, Vince Franklin, dismount by almost falling off of his horse, then stagger into the arms of Bruno, a white-haired slave. She bit her lip in vexation, watching as Bruno caught Vince and kept him from falling, only to be rewarded by Vince's shoving him away roughly. Vince then turned to look across the crowd that had gathered for the wedding of Dent Rocklin and Raimey Reed. He laughed loudly and moved toward the massive steps of the Congregational church, shoving his way through the crowd.

Rachel moved quickly to where her great-uncle Mark Rocklin stood. "Uncle Mark, Vince is drunk. He'll ruin the wedding if someone doesn't stop him!"

Mark Rocklin was a tall, lean man of fifty with a pair of dark eyes that few men cared to face when they burned with anger. He had been a misfit among the children of Noah Rocklin, who was the patriarch of the Rocklin family in Virginia. Mark had never been interested in farming, as were his brother Thomas or his sister, Marianne. Mark's brothers Stephen and Mason had not cared for farming either, but they had found worthwhile occupations: Mason had been a professional soldier in the Union Army for years; Stephen owned a prosperous ironworks in Washington.

Mark, however, had been a wanderer, a gambler with no roots. He came back to visit Richmond only on rare occasions, finding little there to draw him. Little, that is, except his great-niece Rachel, for the two of them had a similar temperament and so had formed a close and warm bond. Now he smiled at her, his face lighting with an uncharacteristic tenderness.

"I'll see to him, Rachel." Mark's voice was low and even, but there was purpose in his face as he moved down the steps and halted right in front of Vincent Franklin. "Hello, Vince," he said casually.

Vince stopped abruptly, almost falling. He caught himself, looked up, blinked owlishly, then said thickly, "Oh . . . Uncle Mark . . ."

"I need some company, Nephew. Come and sit with me for the wedding."

Vince reddened and an angry reply rose to his lips, but he was not too drunk to realize he had no choice. Mark Rocklin was a man of easy manners, but there was something dangerous about him. As Vince peered at his great-uncle, he suddenly remembered some of the things he'd heard about the man's past. "Why . . . sure," he muttered. He licked his lips, then said, "Maybe I'd better sit down. I don't feel so good."

"Let's sit in the balcony, Vince," Mark said, taking his arm and leading him firmly toward a side door. "We can see more from there."

As the two men disappeared inside the church, Rachel turned to her younger brother Les. "He'll behave now," she said, then added, "I wish he hadn't come."

"I'll get him to leave after it's over, Rachel," Les said. At seventeen he was almost an exact copy of his father, with the same fair skin and reddish hair. But as he moved away from her, Rachel knew that Les could not handle Vince. None of them could.

"Come along, now, Rachel—" She turned to see her father and mother at the front door. She hurried up the steps, hoping her father hadn't noticed the commotion her half brother had created. But her father glanced over her shoulder and asked, "What was the trouble with

Vince? I didn't know he was back." Brad Franklin was attired in the dress uniform of a major in the Confederate Army, sword and all. His rather hungry-looking face was tense, as it usually was whenever Vince was around, and he shook his head angrily. "Why did he come at all?"

Nothing brought as much humiliation to Brad Franklin as the sight of his eldest son. A product of Brad's first marriage, Vince was the image of his mother, Lila Crawford, and this alone was enough to stir painful memories. Lila had been as promiscuous and selfish as she had been pretty, but Brad had been young and in love. He had not discovered his wife's self-centered nature until after they were wed—and then it was too late.

Brad had remained firm in his convictions after their marriage. He had refused to overlook Lila's flirtations and involvements, demanding that she become the wife she had promised in her vows to be. So it was that less than a year after Vince's birth, Lila divorced her husband, took her baby, and ran away with a gambler from Natchez. All of Brad's attempts to reclaim his son had failed. He had seen Vince only a half-dozen times after Lila's departure, and never for more than a few moments. Then, three years after Brad's marriage to Amy Rocklin, he had received word of Lila's death. Hoping to be at last reunited with his son, he had taken five-year-old Vince into his home—but by then the boy was totally spoiled and as selfish as his mother. It hadn't been long before Vince's half brother and half sister, and his father, had little to do with the boy.

Now, staring with distaste in the direction Vince had gone, Brad shook his head again. "Never mind, Father," Rachel said with a smile. She gave his collar a slight pull and said, "My, you look dashing! Doesn't he, Mother? And look at you, in that new dress!"

Amy Franklin, the only daughter of Thomas Rocklin, was not really a beautiful woman, but she made people think she was. She was tall and dark like her father, and her fine dark eyes were her best feature. She smiled indulgently at her daughter. "Nobody looks at old women at weddings, Rachel. Let's go take our seats before somebody else gets them."

"Not much danger of that," Brad said, holding the door open, then following the two women inside. "Sam Reed has got this wedding planned down to the last bouquet. I think you have to have a pass from him to even get in the church."

An usher met them, saying, "This way, sir," and led them to their seats. When they were situated, Rachel said, "Isn't it lovely? I've never seen so many flowers!"

"Too bad the bride can't see them, isn't it?" Brad whispered.

"She can smell them," Rachel said. "And she's gone over every one, I do think, touching them."

"A strange thing—for Dent to marry her," Rachel's father said thoughtfully. "We all thought it'd be that Yankee girl, Deborah Steele, walking down the aisle with that boy." He gave a restless shake to his shoulders, adding, "I guess Dent thought a blind woman wouldn't mind the way he looks with all the scars."

Though he sounded cold, Maj. Franklin was merely voicing what many others had thought. Dent Rocklin had been one of the most handsome men in the city of Richmond, the object of many women's devotion. But a terrible saber cut on his face, which he had received at the battle of Manassas, had left him with a ghastly scar. It was, perhaps, natural that some would leap to the conclusion that he would marry someone such as Raimey Reed, who was lovely, but totally blind.

Rachel shook her head firmly. "No, Daddy, it's not like that. They're really in love. I even heard Dent say that Raimey was the most wonderful gift God has ever given him. If I ever got a husband, I'd want him to love me as much as Dent loves Raimey." Then she said quickly, as if to cover up a slip, "But here I am, the spinster of Lindwood, talking about a husband, just like all the old maids."

"I wish you'd stop calling yourself that ridiculous name, Rachel!" A quick flash of anger flared in Amy Franklin's eyes, and she added, "You could have been married long ago. There are a lot of young men around."

"Lots of gophers and jackrabbits around, too."

"Oh, you drive me mad, Rachel!" her mother said, then lifted her head. "Look, it's starting!"

The organ began to whisper, then grew louder as the members of the wedding party began the old ritual. As it went on, Rachel felt tears gathering in her eyes despite herself. Angrily she blinked them away, hoping no one had seen her. She hated how easily she was moved to tears—though she seldom let them be seen. Long ago she had decided to keep a tight rein on her emotions. Usually she succeeded, but there were times when she could not stem the tide. It never ceased to shame her that she was a young woman who constantly struggled with her emotions. She had been taught from an early age that God had created her as she was, giving her gifts and characteristics that were special to her. Even so, she envied women who were always cool and stately, like her great-aunt Marianne Bristol and her own mother. *I won't cry!* she thought fiercely as the wedding proceeded, but when Dent came out accompanied by his best man—his identical twin, David—she could not ignore the pang of pity that stabbed at her.

Dent and David had always been handsome. Now, as Dent stood with his scarred face turned toward the congregation and waited for his bride, everyone could see the full extent of his injury—and there stood David as a graphic reminder of what Lt. Denton Rocklin once had looked like.

Since Dent's injury, Rachel had instinctively avoided staring at her cousin's scarred face, not wanting to hurt him. Now that he could not see her, though, she lifted her eyes and took in the magnitude of the damage. The cut had caused Dent's left eye to droop, giving him a sinister appearance; the scar pulled the side of his mouth to the left, which only added to that impression. Rachel could not help but glance at David, noting the firm lines of his face—and then she could look no more.

Then, suddenly, the organ began to swell in volume, and Rev. Jeremiah Irons gave a signal with his hand, bringing the congregation to their feet. Rachel turned to see Raimey, her hand resting on her father's arm, coming down the aisle, a vision of loveliness all in white. A smile was on her lips and her blue eyes were clear, fixed in front of her. She moved with such confidence that it would never have occurred to someone who was seeing her for the first time that she was blind.

As she took her place in front of Irons, her father stepped back, and at once she reached out and put her hand on Dent's arm. *She knew he'd be there*, Rachel thought. *She's always sure he'll be there.* The thought pleased her, bringing a softness to her lips. *That's what love is—just knowing that the one you love will always be there! Oh, heavenly Father, that's the kind of love I want.*

Then she listened as Irons read the familiar words and as Dent and Raimey spoke their vows, pledging them-selves to God and to each other. It was quiet and solemn, and their words seemed to hang in the air like the notes of an organ heard from far away.

Finally the ceremony was over, and the Franklins rose. "Well, let's go to the reception," Rachel's father said. "Reed's reserved the ballroom at the Elliot Hotel. It's going to be a dandy." Just then, Rachel glanced up toward the balcony and saw Mark Rocklin sitting there, holding Vince in place with an iron authority. Her fa-ther, following her glance, frowned. "I'm glad Mark's keeping a tight rein on him. He's done enough to hu-miliate this family!"

The Elliot Hotel was not the largest hotel in Rich-mond, but it was the most elaborate and the most expen-sive. The ballroom was decorated with white banners, which picked up the gleam of light thrown by the glitter-ing chandeliers. The dresses of the women added splashes of color to the crowd, and the gray uniforms of many officers, with their gleaming black boots and gold buttons, gave a final touch of stylishness.

Long tables filled with meats, appetizers, candies, and cakes lined one wall, while other tables held crystal bowls of pink punch. The crowd was in a festive mood, and the air was filled with the sound of laughter and the hum of half a hundred conversations. A group of men had gathered in one section of the room, talking about things other than the weather—hunting, crops, horses, and especially the war. Maj. Brad Franklin and Col. James Benton of the Richmond Grays were there in uniform. Clay Rocklin, Thomas's son and Amy's brother, was also in the Grays. However, as a sergeant he had chosen to wear a brown suit, saying, "If I wore a uniform, I'd spend the whole time saluting."

Capt. Taylor Dewitt, also a member of Clay's company—and one of Clay's oldest friends—was there, too. The two of them stood off to one side, drinking punch while Col. Benton spoke of the battle of Bull Run. Most of the soldiers there had been in that battle, and they had not tired of talking of the victory.

"I tell you, the Yankees are whipped!" Benton declared. He was a tall, impressive figure of a man, with white hair and a florid face. "We sent 'em scurrying back to Washington with their tails between their legs!"

It was a common view, spoken every day by many Southerners. They gleefully recounted "the sprightly running" of the Federals as they fled to Washington, and many of the young Confederate soldiers were grieved that it seemed probable that they would never have a chance to see a battle. Capt. Dewitt just shook his head. "With all respects, sir, I think we'll be seeing a lot more action." Taylor was forty, one year younger than Clay Rocklin. He had a lean pale face, light blue eyes, and a clear mind that could not help analyzing things. Now he added, "You saw how they fought, Colonel. I know they broke and ran, but there were a couple of times when we

9

were in about as bad a shape as the Yankees. It could have gone the other way if Smith and Elzey hadn't come at just the right moment."

"Oh, come now, Dewitt! I don't see that at all!" The speaker was Simon Duvall, a thin, dark-skinned man in his late thirties. His French heritage was revealed in his thin face, which he adorned with a narrow black moustache, and a pair of dark eyes that grew hot when anger took him—not a rare thing. He had fought four duels, killing one man, and his temper was a frightful thing when aroused. Now, however, he was merely arguing mildly, adding, "Why, the entire Army of the Potomac is huddled in Washington, and Lincoln fired McDowell and put McClellan in charge."

"I think President Davis was right," Clay said suddenly. He was one of the Black Rocklins, with raven hair, olive skin, and dark eyes. He was six feet two, lean and muscular, and had a temper that few men cared to challenge. His youth had been stormy, but after being away from home for many years, and after encountering the one who had loved him no matter how far he had fallen into degradation, he had returned to try to pick up his life. Sadly, he had been met with great opposition from his children, particularly from Dent, who seemed to burn with resentment toward his father. Still, Clay continued in his efforts to become the kind of man and father he believed God wanted him to be.

For his own reasons, Clay had long opposed the war, and his views had made him an unpopular man. Even so, at the last moment he had joined the Grays as a private. He had won honor by leading a charge in a crucial battle—but more important to Clay than the honor he earned was the fact that the charge had saved Dent's life. Through a course of events following, Clay and Dent had finally reconciled.

"What did the president want to do, Clay?"

The voice came from his right, and Clay turned to see that Vince Franklin, having escaped his great-uncle, had joined the group. Vince was a fine-looking man of twenty-four, with crisply curling brown hair that he wore long and a neat, full beard of the same texture. The beard covered the lower part of his face, giving him a cavalier appearance. He wore an expensive suit of light gray, and the shining boots on his feet cost as much as a good horse. He had a glass in his hand, and everyone in the group could tell by the redness in Vince's deep-set, wide-spaced brown eyes that the glass held more than the harmless punch being served by the ladies at the table.

Clay shrugged his shoulders, saying, "When the Federals ran, President Davis wanted to follow them and take Washington."

"By Harry!" Brad Franklin cried. "We ought to have listened to Davis!"

Clay said thoughtfully, "We may never have another chance like that . . . but we were about as worn down from the battle as the enemy. And they had plenty of fresh reinforcements. I don't think we would have been successful."

Vince Franklin took a drink from the glass in his hand, then grinned rashly. "Why, that would have been a tragedy! If we had taken Washington, the game would be over."

"Game?" Brad Franklin stared at his son with obvious displeasure. "This war is no game, Vince!"

"Looks like it to me! Dressing up in uniforms and playing soldier!"

Vince Franklin could not have made a more insulting remark to a more hostile audience. All of those gathered, in one way or another, were pledging their homes and their hearts in the war. Some of those present had lost family members; all of them had lost close friends at Manassas. The sudden enmity of everyone's glances would have been warning enough to most men, but Vince Franklin seemed to court the kind of encounters that others would do their best to avoid.

Clay saw Vince's father turn pale with anger, but it was Simon Duvall who answered the young man's rash words. "We fight for the honor of our country, Franklin, and I question the courage of any man who stays at home and lets other men do his fighting."

His words made many of the men blink, for it was the equivalent of a challenge. If Duvall had said such a thing to any other man in the group, there would have been a meeting at dawn with pistols. Duvall's smooth face was turned toward Vince, and Clay saw there was a pleasure in his dark eyes. *He loves this!* Clay thought, and disgust ran through him at the thought that any man could find gratification in killing another.

But Vince Franklin felt only amusement at the thought of engaging in a duel over words. He grinned at Duvall, saying, "Why, Simon, somebody has to stay at home and comfort the women while their husbands are away fighting for the Cause."

Duvall sucked in a quick breath, his dark face growing pale, and those gathered around the two waited for his response. Clay glanced at Taylor, and he could tell from the look in his friend's eyes that they shared the same thought: *Duvall already suspects that Vince has been having an affair with his wife—and he knows that every man here is aware of his suspicions.* Black anger leaped into Duvall's eyes and he stepped forward, but before he could strike Vince, the younger man wheeled and walked away, saying, "I'm not a fool, Duvall. Fight your duels with men who have no brains!"

Duvall stood there, his eyes boring into Vince's back, then he turned and stalked away without a word, his body rigid.

For a moment there was silence in the room. Then Col. Benton said, "Vince is a fool, Brad," then turned and left. The others, finding the situation most unpleasant, moved away, leaving Clay and his brother-in-law alone.

"Benton is right, Clay," Brad said bitterly. "Why did Vince come here? His greatest delight seems to be spoiling things for others." When Clay remained silent, he added, "His mother was like that, too."

It was the most revealing thing Brad Franklin had ever said to Clay about his first marriage. It had been a bitter affair for Franklin, a stormy union that had left deep scars on the man. But his second marriage to Amy, Clay's only sister, had been happy. Their children, Grant, Rachel, and Les, were all good youngsters, taking after their mother to a large extent. With a happy and stable home, Brad had had high hopes for Vince when he brought him into his family. But the boy only seemed to grow more wild, undisciplined, and cruel, doing all he could to go his own reckless way. It had been a bitter pill for everyone involved.

Amy, who had loved the wild boy from the first time he entered her home, had prayed for him every day and had done her best to show him she cared for him. But Vince would have none of it. As the years passed, he rebuffed any advances from Amy or his half sister or half brothers and treated his father with impudence. By the time he left home, he had successfully alienated them all. To this day he made no attempt to become a part of the family, seeming instead to enjoy tormenting those who should have been the closest to him.

The reason he was able to torment them so effectively, Clay understood, was partly because of the will that Hiram Franklin, Brad's father, had left. Brad and his father had never gotten along. In Hiram Franklin's opinion, his son was too wild and undisciplined to amount to any good. And so he had cut Brad out of his will, favoring instead his firstborn grandson, Vince. And the will provided for Brad's oldest son in a generous way—a certain amount each year until his twenty-fifth birthday, when he would receive the bulk of the inheritance—and the bulk of the control over Lindwood.

During the years since Vince had left Lindwood, he had done as he pleased and, with plenty of money, he found others to go along with him. He had an unsavory reputation as a womanizer and, since his return, his drinking and gambling habits were no secret to anyone in the county.

Clay drew a deep breath, then said, "Duvall's a dangerous man to cross, Brad. Better try to talk to Vince."

"He's not listened to me for years, Clay. Or to anyone else, for that matter."

The two men were not the only ones interested in Vince Franklin. Even as they were talking, the young Franklin was the subject of yet another conversation. Rachel had been serving punch but took a break to walk around the room with Leighton Semmes. Semmes had spoken of Vince's untimely appearance, saying, "That brother of yours seems to have little in the way of manners, Rachel." A lean man of twenty-six, with dark hair and eyes, Leighton had fine manners and wore the latest fashions, and there was an ease in him that Rachel knew had been developed by his pursuit of women. Semmes, she knew, saw the relationship between the sexes as a game. She liked the man but knew that it was not wise to encourage his interest, for he had broken the hearts of at least two other young women.

"I can't explain Vince, Leighton," she admitted, shrugging. "He's my half brother, but I have no idea what makes him act the way he does."

Semmes studied her, admiration in his dark eyes. He took in the picture she made: a tall young woman with a wealth of honey-colored hair and a pair of blue-green eyes that matched her silk emerald dress. Her eyes were strange, unique; almond-shaped and very large, with thick lashes. As he gazed at her, Semmes thought there was something almost sultry about them, though the girl herself was not aware of that. She had a squarish face, with a wide mouth and a cleft chin, which Semmes knew she hated. Still, it gave her a striking look, one that seemed to suggest that this was a young woman who kept a passionate streak under firm control, covering it with a rather pointed wit. The fact that she called herself the spinster of Lindwood was a sample of that wit, for no woman looked less like a spinster than Rachel Franklin.

Semmes had played a game with her, drawn by her beauty and wit, but sensing that if he tried to press his luck, she would mock him. Now he said, "Your father spoils him, I think. Always has."

"No," Rachel said thoughtfully, "Vince spoils himself. He has never needed Father, you know, because he has money of his own." Then she added with a quirk of a smile, "Did you know the Bible says, 'Money answereth all things'? That's in Ecclesiastes 10:19."

"I didn't know that was in the Bible," Semmes said, "but I believe it. Nothing is stronger than money."

"You're wrong about that, Leighton," Rachel said at once. "Love is stronger than anything in the world."

"You are fortunate, then, for you're made for love, Rachel."

She laughed at the eager look on his face, then shook her head, her heavy mane of hair sweeping across her back. "Never mind all that, Leighton. I know that look. You've used it on too many of my friends. They've all warned me about you!"

"It's not fair!" Semmes exclaimed. "A man smiles at a woman, and she thinks it's a proposal of marriage." He spoke quickly, wanting her to know what he believed. "Love is important, Rachel, but I've never understood the rules. I like women, and some of them have seemed to like me, but they want to draw lines that I can't fathom."

"Oh, you understand the rules well enough, Leighton," Rachel answered. "You just don't like them."

Semmes knew she was laughing at him, which pleased him in a way. Of all the women he had known, only this one could hold him at arm's length and make him almost enjoy it. "You know me too well, Rachel." He smiled. "Maybe you'll be able to reform me."

"I think that would be a difficult job, Mr. Semmes." Rachel's eyes laughed up at him and she decided to change the subject. He was, quite simply, too attractive—and Rachel had begun to think of him far too often. This troubled her greatly, for playing at love with Leighton Semmes was like playing with live ammunition. "Let's go congratulate the bride and groom."

"Has anyone heard about the newlyweds? It's been two weeks now. I hope they're still together."

Rachel smiled at Grant, knowing that her brother loved to tease her. He was wearing his uniform and looked very handsome, and, as the carriage rolled along the dusty road toward Richmond, Rachel was strangely happy. "I expect Dent's worked all the foolishness out of Raimey by now," she said, teasingly. "You know how they say a woman needs a strong hand now and then."

Grant laughed aloud at the idea. "I'd like to see the man who'd have the nerve to try such things with *you*, Sister! You'd give him a thrashing!" He looked at her with real affection, for there was a close bond between the two. He was twenty-one, only two years older than she, and they had always shared things. While he had the fair skin and reddish blond hair of his father, his even temper was that of his mother. Now he added, "But if you marry Semmes, he might be a handful."

"I'll never marry Leighton. He's too much in love with somebody else."

"Who is that?"

"Himself, of course." Rachel laughed at the expression on Grant's face, then sobered. "I'll just keep on being the spinster of Lindwood, Grant. It's safer that way."

"Aw, Rachel, you can't live in a cave and think small," Grant protested. "Marriage works out fine for some. Look at our folks."

"Yes, but look at Uncle Clay and Aunt Ellen." Both of them knew that their uncle's marriage to Ellen Benton had been so stormy that Clay now lived in a summer house on his plantation, Gracefield, to avoid contact with his wife. Ellen, on the other hand, spent most of her time in Richmond, flirting and spending money—when she had it. Rachel, who liked her uncle very much, was turned gloomy by the thought of their troubles and fell silent.

When they pulled up at the livery stable, Grant helped Rachel down, then said, "Let's go get something to eat." She agreed, and they went to French's Restaurant and had fresh veal and corn bread. While they ate, Grant spoke little of the plantation, for it was Les, the younger brother, who was a natural farmer. Grant had been at Manassas, and his whole mind was on the war. He was a second lieutenant in D Company.

Later, as they left the restaurant, Rachel said, "It'll all be over soon, I pray. I hate this war."

Grant said stubbornly, "No, Sister, it won't be—"

"Grant! Hey, Grant!" The two Franklins turned to see their younger brother, Les, dash up and stand before them. His face was flushed and hot anger lit his blue eyes. "It's Vince and Simon Duvall!" he said, speaking so fast he was hard to understand. "Come on, Grant!"

"You wait here," Grant said to Rachel, but as he and Les raced down the street, she grabbed up her skirts and flew after them. When she turned the corner, she saw a crowd of people gathered around Vince and Duvall, who were standing in an open space. There had been an argument, she saw, for Duvall's face was livid.

"Stay away from me, Duvall!" Vince was saying. His eyes, as usual, were red rimmed from drink. As he tried to move away, Duvall reached out and caught him, whirling him around. Though Duvall was much smaller, he was wiry and strong.

"You've sullied my wife's name in public," he snarled in fury, "and now you're going to answer for it!"

Vince, Rachel saw, was pale as paper; fear had washed all the color from his face. He jerked his arm free and wheeled to move away, but Duvall stepped to a buggy tied to the rail, jerked a whip from the socket, then, in one motion, lifted it and brought it down on Vince. It curled around his neck, and when Duvall gave it a pull, Vince was stopped as if he'd run into a wall.

Rachel moved to stand beside Grant, who said, "I've got to stop this."

"Stay out of it!" Rachel took her brother's arm and held him tightly. "You know what kind of man Duvall is! He's likely to shoot anyone who interferes!"

Duvall struck Vince three times, then cried out, "Now will you fight?"

Vince, a red mark from the whip across his brow, gave a sob and broke into a run, pushing men aside. It was a disgusting thing to see, and Grant turned away, shaking his head. "He'll have to leave the country!" he said in a low voice.

Duvall shouted, "You'd better start wearing a gun, Franklin! Next time I see you, I'll kill you!" He tossed the whip down and walked stiffly down the street.

"He'll do it, too," Grant said to his brother and sister as the crowd broke into an excited jumble of voices. "Come on, let's go home."

The three of them got into the buggy, aware that people were staring at them. On the way home, Les said bitterly, "I wouldn't let a man do that to me!"

Grant shrugged. "Vince knew what Duvall was like. He should have left the man's wife alone."

"Do you think he had an affair with Rose?" Rachel asked.

"Doesn't matter much, does it? Duvall will kill him whether he did or not."

They arrived at Lindwood to find that their father was gone with his unit. Even so, they had to tell their mother what had happened. She said nothing at first, then remarked, "We need to get word to your father. Les, will you go tell him?"

"Let's both go," Grant said, and the two got their horses and left. All afternoon Rachel thought of the ugly scene, and even after she went to bed that night, it kept coming back.

Father, she prayed silently, feeling helpless, *please do something about Vince.*

Finally she got up, put on her robe, and went to the kitchen. She was drinking a cup of warm milk when suddenly Vince came through the door, a suitcase in his hand. He was obviously leaving and was shocked to see Rachel, so he stood there uncertainly.

"Well, I guess you're happy about all this," he snapped hatefully.

"No, I'm not," she answered quietly. "Are you running away?" Rachel looked at the suitcase he held in one hand and the small bag in the other.

He stared at her as if she had said something stupid. "Running away? Of course I'm running away! Did you think I'd stay around and let that fool of a duelist kill me?"

Rachel studied Vince, then asked, "Where will you go?"

"I'm taking a little ocean voyage," he said with a nod. "Been wanting to see more of the world. I'll let that hothead cool off, then I'll come back."

"Duvall won't cool off," Rachel said, quiet certainty in her voice. "You can never come home."

"Maybe he'll get killed in this war. I certainly hope so!" He moved to the door, then something prompted him to turn. He stared at Rachel, then said, "Well, good-bye. I don't guess you'll miss me much, will you?"

"Not much, Vince," she said honestly. "We haven't been close, though I've tried since you've been back. You've never thought of anyone but yourself. I can't think of a worse way to live or a quicker way to become a miserable human being." His face darkened in anger as he listened, but Rachel went on. "I will be praying for you, though. And I wish you luck. I think you'll need it."

"Just you wait until I get control of this place, dear sister," he spat at her. "Then we'll see who's miserable!" Whirling, he left the room, and soon she heard him driving his carriage, whipping his horse to a full run down the drive.

Rachel put out the lamp and left the kitchen, disturbed by the scene. She had no love for Vince—he had not opened himself to it—but he was still a part of her family . . . and as the sound of hoofbeats grew dim, a bleak sorrow came to her.

CHAPTER TWO

A MIDNIGHT SWIM

THE HUGE stern paddles of the *Memphis Queen* thrashed the muddy waters of the Mississippi into a white froth as it drove downstream under full power. Capt. Daniel Harness was a bold man to thread the turns of the river at such a clip, but he knew the thousand turns and windings of the river as well as any steamboat captain afloat. In the darkness, Capt. Harness stood with his feet firmly braced against the floor, seeming to feel the snags and sandbars with the soles of his feet. When he had threaded a particularly tricky maneuver that put the *Queen* around a fishhook-shaped bar, he said, "Take her, McClain."

"Yes sir."

"Come along, Jake. Let's get a drink."

Jake Hardin followed the captain out of the pilothouse and, as the two descended to the main deck, he said, "Nice job, Captain. I think sometimes you know every snag on the Mississippi."

"I've had collisions enough to know some of 'em pretty well." Capt. Harness was a short, barrel-shaped man of thirty-five, with a round head and a pair of gimlet hazel eyes. He was temperamental, as all captains were, but now he turned a friendly smile on his companion. "My job is a lot safer than yours, though. You gamblers are the ones who take risks. Most of you wind up either broke or with a bullet in your head."

The two entered the salon of the *Queen*, and a waiter came rushing up. "Yes sir, Captain. Right this way!" He led them to a table, and Harness said, "Bring us some steaks, Phil. Make mine rare."

21

"Well done," Hardin murmured. "And some whiskey." The two waited until the bottle and glasses came, then Hardin poured two drinks. Lifting his glass, Hardin said, "Here's luck, Dan." The two drank, and then Hardin picked up on the captain's words. "I guess you're right about my trade. I've been on the river five years, and most of the captains who were here when I started are still around. A lot of gamblers are gone, though."

He was tall, this man, and he sat loosely in his chair, running his eyes idly over the salon. He was an inch under six feet, and his 180 pounds were so solid that he looked as though he weighed less. He had sharp brown eyes and a long English nose over a wide mouth. Crisp brown hair, slightly curled, could be seen from beneath the black wide-brimmed hat he wore shoved back on his head. His fingers were long, supple, and strong.

Capt. Harness took his drink slowly, studying the tanned face of his companion. He had few friends among the gamblers who traveled on the *Queen*. Indeed, he had a thinly veiled scorn for most of them. In his mind they produced nothing, and he was one who believed that a man should do or make something useful with the strength God gave him. Even so, he had grown fond of Jake Hardin, seeing in him something more than the usual greed and sloth that made up most gamblers.

The two of them had once spent some time together when the *Queen* had hit a submerged tree just out of St. Louis and was forced to lay by while the hole was repaired. Most of the passengers had chosen to take another ship, but Hardin had stayed, and the two of them had met at dinner. Harness had spent his life studying the dangers, both obvious and hidden, of the river—and somehow he had learned to see what was hidden in men, too. As the two had lingered over meals and talked slowly about unimportant things, the captain had decided that there was none of the meanness in this man that he had come to expect from professional gamblers. Since then, Hardin had been on his boat many times, and the two of them kept up a certain brand of friendship.

"You ought to do something else, Jake." Harness squinted his eyes, peering at Hardin as if he were a difficult passage on the river. His comment made the other man shift uneasily.

"Like what? Be a captain on the river?"

"You're too old for that. How old are you, anyway?"

"Twenty-five."

"Got to start at twelve or so to do my job. You got to be responsible, too, which you ain't never been."

Hardin grinned suddenly and took a sip of his drink. "You got that right, Daniel. Got no character at all."

"Oh, you got it," Harness said, "You just ain't never *used* it." As Harness spoke, he seemed to grow somewhat angry. "Makes me mad to see a man wasting what the good Lord gave 'im. Why don't you do something worthwhile?" A thought touched him and he demanded, "Which side you for, North or South?"

"Neither. I'm a citizen of the *Memphis Queen*, Daniel. When they start shooting at her, I'll go to war and start shooting back."

Harness glared at him. "Don't you care about slavery?"

"All men are slaves, Daniel. We just have different masters."

"Now, that ain't so and you know it!"

The two men argued about the war until the food came. It amused Jake to get the captain stirred up. He liked Harness as much as any man he knew, and he knew the captain liked him—which still surprised him—but he was aware that the two of them were miles apart in their outlook on life. When they finished their steaks and were drinking cups of strong black coffee that was stiff with chicory, the gambler tried to explain to his friend how he felt. It was important to him for Harness to know that.

"Daniel, you're what you are because of a few accidents. You were born with whatever genius it is that makes a man able to memorize a river and you happened to be born where there was a river. If you'd been born in Kansas, you'd have been a failure as a farmer because you were born to do one thing. You're for slavery and the South because you were born and raised in Tennessee, but if you'd grown up in Michigan, you'd be for the Union. You're right where you are because of a few chances, Dan. And so am I."

Harness snorted and slapped his hand hard on the table, making the bottle jump. "Jake, that's the dangedest nonsense I ever heard! I made my own decisions! And you've made yours, which is to be a lazy bum of a gambler!"

"Guess you're right. Like I say, I've got no character." He rose, stretched, then grinned down at Harness. "Got to get to the table, Captain. Fellow there named Longley is out to do me. I aim to do the same to him."

"Better stay away from Max Longley. He's a bad 'un, Jake."

"So am I, Daniel. You just said so."

"No, you're just triflin' and lazy. Longley is a real bad 'un."

"Well, he's a rich bad 'un, so I'll just relieve him of some of his cash. See you later, Daniel."

Hardin left the main salon and made his way to the section set apart for gambling. The *Memphis Queen* sported the most ornate gambling establishment on the river, complete with roulette wheels, poker tables, blackjack dealers, and a bar across the rear. Jake went at once to a table where four men sat playing poker and took a seat, saying, "Give me five hundred in chips."

The dealer, a bulky man with a catfish mouth, said, "Where you been, Hardin? I been waiting to take some of your cash."

"Had supper, Max. Had to build up some energy to carry out all that money I'm going to take from you," Hardin answered with a smile. The game went on slowly. Several times men joined the game, others left with their money mostly in front of Max Longley. Longley's brother, a dumpy man everyone called Boog, was in the game as well. He was a sour-faced individual, in contrast to his brother, who was florid and wore a big smile.

Finally Max said, "Blast these small stakes. How about we double up?"

One man dropped out, saying, "Too rich for me," but Hardin, Boog, and two others stayed. The chips flowed across the table, again with Max the big winner. An hour later, he looked across the table, saying, "You game to double again, Jake?"

"All right with me."

It was a big game now, and people came over to watch. Many hands were worth two or three hundred dollars, and slowly the piles grew in front of Hardin and Max Longley. At midnight, only the two of them were in the game. The stakes had swelled to huge sizes.

As always in such games, the two men finally found themselves involved in one huge pot, with each of them sure he had the winning hand. The air was blue with smoke, and there was no sound except for the falling of cards on the felt or the clicking of chips as the two men continued to shove them across to the small mountain that had grown there.

Finally, Longley studied his cards and shoved most of his chips to the center. "Bet two thousand more."

Hardin watched Longley's eyes, thinking, *He expects me to fold.* He had been reading men's eyes for five years and thought he knew Longley well. But he said without emphasis, "Call you."

Longley studied his hand, then said, "I'll stand."

Every eye was on Jake Hardin, and he let the time run on. He knew that pressure could make the sand run out of a man, and he saw the confidence in Longley's eyes fade. Then he puffed his cigar, saying, "Dealer takes two."

A gasp went around the room, and Longley grinned, a savage expression on his face. "Knew you was bluffin',

Jake!" He turned over his hand. "Three aces and two kings," he announced.

Hardin once again let the silence run on, then dealt himself two cards. He picked them up, studied them, then smiled and laid them down. "Royal flush," he murmured.

Several cries went up, one man saying with a curse, "He filled it! I don't believe it!"

Max Longley stared at the cards Hardin had laid down, and his wide face grew even more florid. He stared as Jake reached out and drew in his winnings. Then he said, "You dealt yourself that hand from your sleeve."

The sound of men talking was cut off as if it had been sliced with a knife, and the men sitting behind the two players hastily moved to one side. Longley got to his feet, saying, "You're not taking that pot, Hardin."

Jake sat there, studying Max. There was only one thing to do. If he backed down, he'd be marked all down the river.

"Longley, back off," he said quietly and then got to his feet. "I'm cashing in." He took a small velvet bag from his pocket and filled it with the chips, all the time keeping his eyes fixed on the man across the table. Slipping the bag into his coat pocket, he gave Longley a careful look, then turned and walked away.

He had taken only a few steps when he heard the sound of metal against leather, and at the same time a man yelled, "Look out, Jake!"

Hardin threw himself to one side, drawing his pistol from the shoulder holster. Even as he turned, the crash of Longley's gun rocked the air and he felt a tug on his right arm. He came around as he fell, bringing his gun to bear on Longley, who was drawing down on him again. The gun bucked in Jake's hand, and Longley's second shot went into the ceiling, blowing a chandelier to smithereens. Longley was propelled backward by the bullet, which drove directly into his heart, then fell to the deck and lay still.

"You all saw it," Jake said. "He didn't give me a choice." He turned and walked toward the door, forgetting that Max Longley had a brother. That lapse was a costly mistake, for Boog Longley pulled a gun and let fly one bullet. Jake felt a cold touch, heard the explosion, then was sucked into a soundless sea of black.

There was sound, but no meaning. From far away came the slow thudding of some sluggish machine, and with each beat, a streak of raw pain touched him like a whip of fire. The heavy darkness that enveloped him was broken at the edges by streaks of light, and something seemed to be drawing him out of the warmth and comfort and safety of the darkness. A voice came to him, muffled but insistent. When he tried to draw away, it came again.

"Jake! Come out of it!"

He knew the voice, and now the light came rolling in, but it brought such a slashing pain to his head that he lay still, gasping and waiting for it to go away.

"Wake up, Jake!"

He opened his eyes slowly and saw the dusky shadow of a man's face surrounded by a corona of yellow light. Blinking his eyes, he turned his head carefully, and the outlines of a room began to take shape. He tried to speak, but only a dry croak emerged from his throat.

"Here, have a drink of water."

He heard water being poured, then felt coolness on his lips. Thirstily he drank it down, then gasped, "More!"

"Sure, Jake." Now the man moved, and Jake saw that it was Milo Bender, a steward on the *Memphis Queen*. Bender was a good man who had become well acquainted with Jake—particularly after Jake loaned Milo two hundred dollars when one of his children was sick.

"Now sit up. Not too fast, though. That's a bad gash on the top of your head." Bender let Jake drink the water, then set the glass down. Sitting in a chair beside the bunk, he examined the gambler with a critical eye. "An inch lower and you'd be pushin' up daisies, Jake."

Carefully Hardin reached up and touched the bandage on top of his head. Just the touch brought a sharp stab of pain, and he quickly dropped his hand. He peered at the room around him. "Where is this, Milo? It's not my room."

"No, it ain't," Bender agreed. "You're under arrest for murder, Jake."

His words brought Jake's head upright, a move he instantly regretted. "For murder! Why, that's crazy, Milo! The man tried to kill me."

"Boog Longley says otherwise and he's got two witnesses who say you pulled on his brother and killed him without giving him a chance." Bender hesitated, then said, "I sure wish you'd picked somebody else to plug, Jake. Them Longleys got lots o'.money, and they just about run this county. I know you're telling the truth, but the Longleys are the he-coons. They've had men put in jail for a lot less. Old man Longley was a senator, and he's got every judge in his pocket. It don't look good."

A streak of fear threaded through Jake. "But there were witnesses who *saw* Longley shoot me first!"

"And where will they be when the trial comes? You know well as I do, Jake, that soon as we dock, everybody scatters. You can bet they won't be none of them at your trial 'cept the two Boog done bought and paid for." Milo leaned forward and whispered, "Jake, you got to get away or you'll stretch hemp for sure."

"Is there a guard outside the door?"

"Yeah, but I can get him away for a while. You can get outta this cabin, but what then?"

"Have to swim for it!"

"With that head?"

"It's the only head I've got." Jake was wide awake now and put his feet on the floor. "What about my money?"

"Boog took it. Here, I brought all I could scrape up. Only about thirty dollars."

"Milo, thanks!"

"Aw, it ain't much, Jake. Maybe I can get more against my pay, but there ain't much time."

"This will do. Where are we?"

"'Bout an hour out of Helena. You can swim to shore easy. Cap always hugs the shoreline along here. Get to town and catch a train or another boat. I better run. Good luck, Jake. Write me a note when you get someplace. I'd like to know you made it."

"Sure. And thanks again."

"Here's a knife. You can open the door with it—just slide it along the edge. And don't lose this. It's some matches and grub all wrapped up in oilcloth. I snatched your gun off the floor and it's there, too." Bender got up and picked up the tray. "I'll tell the guard you're still out cold. He'd rather be drinkin' than guardin', so he'll be easy to convince."

Bender knocked on the door and, when it opened, slipped outside. Jake pressed his ear against the door. "He's maybe not gonna live, Charlie. Couldn't get him awake to eat. Come on, let's get some of that bonded stuff I got in my cabin," Bender said.

"Hey, Milo, I can't leave here. I'm guardin' this feller."

"Do as you please," he answered carelessly. "If you'd rather guard a stiff than drink bonded whiskey, it's your say-so."

Jake heard Milo's footsteps as he moved down the hall alone, and his heart sank. Then Charlie said, "Wait up, Milo! I reckon I got time for just one!"

Moving quickly despite the pain in his head, Hardin removed a cord from the curtains, then picked up his boots and tied them together. He checked the loads in his gun, slipped it into the shoulder holster, and stepped to the door. Using the knife he opened it easily, then moved to the stairway leading to the deck and climbed topside.

It was dark, and he could see two figures at the rail, the sound of their voices clear on the night air. Moving to the starboard rail, he peered both ways, then moved to stand beside it. The shore was a mere bulky darkness slipping by rapidly; the trees were ghostly outlines against the night sky.

Thinking of the huge paddle wheel, he moved back to the stern and stepped over the rail. Without a pause he jumped into the water, holding his boots tightly. The water was cold to his touch, sending a chill through his body, and the pounding of the massive paddle wheel throbbed into his head. Then the action of the churning wake turned him over like a doll, and he spun helplessly until he finally came to the surface, gasping in great gulps of air.

The stern lights of the *Queen* glowed like malevolent eyes in the darkness. He only glanced at the boat for an instant, then turned and began to swim for shore. It was not a long swim, but he was weak and confused by his wound, and the weight of his clothes and boots dragged him down. When his feet hit bottom he was about finished. He crawled ashore and lay on his face, gasping for breath.

The fall air was cold, and he got up as soon as he could breathe easily again, looking around. It was too dark to see clearly, so he blundered along through bamboo cane until he came to firm ground. Then, luckily, he ran into a huge tree that had been uprooted. He followed the outline of the tree to the first limb, groped around, and broke off the ends of the dead branches. It was an old tree and the wood was dry. Making a pile of the twigs, Jake dug into the oilcloth package, found the matches, and carefully struck one. It spurted with a blue flame, and when he touched it to the twigs they caught at once. As the tiny fire grew and cast flickering beams around, he scavenged as much sticks and brush as he could find and soon had a large fire going.

As Jake took off his shirt and pants and dried them, he thought of what he had said to Capt. Harness. "'A man's life is made up of accidents,'" he said aloud, then asked, "Wonder if coming ashore here near this dead tree is one of those things? I could have hit a bluff and not been able to climb out." The question troubled him, but he was not a man to spend time or thought on such things.

When his clothes were dry, he put them back on, then used a sharp stick to skewer some of the bacon Milo had put in the sack. He cooked it over the fire and devoured it. He was hungry and wanted more but wrapped the rest back in the oilcloth. "Don't know how long this has to last," he said. Then he piled more sticks on the fire and lay down.

The skies were black, without even a single star. As Jake peered into the darkness, he knew that he was in big trouble. The Longleys would have the alarm out before long, and this was their country. If he stayed, they would find him. Of that he was sure. But the Mississippi River had been his home for the past five years. Where else could he go?

For a long time he lay there, but no answers came. Finally he went to sleep.

Vince Franklin looked around the saloon with distaste. *Should have known better than to come to a dump like this,* he thought. He took a drink of the raw whiskey that seemed to scratch his throat as it went down, then looked over at the woman who was drinking with him. *She looked a lot better in the dark.* He had met her on a side street in Helena and, by lantern light, she had appeared fresh and very pretty. Now he saw her rough skin and the hardened gleam in her red-rimmed eyes and knew he didn't need her.

He had gotten off the riverboat at Helena looking for an old crony, only to find that the man had joined the army. Vince was now forced to wait until the next morning to catch a packet, and so he had made a tour of the dives in the river town. There were quite a few of them, and by the time he met the woman he was both unsteady and surly.

"You like me, honey?" the woman said with a smile,

breaking into his thoughts, the gold in her teeth gleaming in the light. "I love you plenty!"

Vince suddenly came to a decision, but before he could get up, a man dressed in a checked shirt, whose face was all but hidden by a bushy, unkempt beard, came through the door. He scanned the room and, when he spotted Vince and the woman, he growled, "I got you now!"

The woman scrambled to her feet, her face filled with fear. "I was on my way home, Con! Honest I was!"

"'I was on my way home!'" The huge man stood there, filling the doorway, mocking her. Drunk as he was, Vince noticed that customers were carefully moving out of the man's range. He stood up, but the man called Con said, "Where do you think you're going, sonny?"

"I—I'm not involved in this," Vince said quickly. The sight of the man's wild eyes had sobered him up considerably, and he stepped to the side of the table.

"You stand right there!" The burly man pulled a revolver from his pocket and laid it right on Vince's chest. "I'm gonna teach you not to fool around with another man's woman!"

As bad as the moment was, Vince almost burst out laughing. He'd run all the way from Richmond to avoid getting shot by one jealous man and was now about to be killed by another.

Just then there was a movement to his right. A man wearing a ruffled shirt and a pair of black pants stepped to stand beside him. He had on a low-crowned black hat, and his eyes were hidden in the shadow of its brim. "Back off, Con," he said in a husky voice. "My friend and I are getting out of here."

"You'll get, all right—to the cemetery!" Con cocked the revolver, but the man beside Vince had suddenly produced one of his own, and it was aimed right at the big man's forehead. Con looked at the muzzle, blinked, and considered the gun in his hand.

"This ain't yore fight!" Con muttered, trying to see the man's face more clearly.

"Any time I see a man draw on someone who's unarmed, it's my fight," a flat, emotionless voice answered him. "Besides, I've got nothing to lose. So make up your mind. . . . What'll it be?"

Con dropped his gun and threw his hands up. "All right! All right! I ain't got no gun!"

"You about ready?" the man said to Vince. Vince grabbed his hat, nodded, and the two of them left. "We'd better move away from here in case your friend has second thoughts," the man said calmly, holstering his gun.

"Let's go to my room," Vince said. His voice was shaky and, now that the scene was over, he found that the fear made his legs weak. "Come along. I owe you a drink—or maybe more. Name's Vince Franklin, by the way."

After a noticeable silence, the man said, "Jake Hardin."

The name meant nothing to Vince and he hurried along to the hotel. It was late and even the night clerk was gone. Vince led the way to his room, opened the door, then went in and lit the lamp. "Have a seat, Jake," he said. "I've got a bottle here. Good stuff, too." He found the bottle, poured two drinks, then said with a nervous smile, "Here's to you, Jake Hardin. I was never so glad to see anybody in my life!"

"Glad to help, Vince." Jake downed his drink, then said, "Well, guess I'll be going."

"Here now!" Vince said quickly. "You can't run off like that. Sit down, man, and let's talk. I don't get my life saved every day!"

Vince watched the man as he sank back into his chair. "I've got nothing to lose . . . ," he'd said. Vince smiled to himself. *Anyone that desperate could prove most useful.* Soon the two men were talking easily. Vince took in the man's worn clothing, the still-raw wound on his head, and the fact that Hardin was about dead for sleep.

"You from around these parts, Jake?" he asked and sat back to listen, calculating.

Jake had not eaten for two days. He had stayed outside of town as long as he could, then had come in out of desperation. It had not taken him long to find that the Longleys had posted a reward notice for him. He had slept in an alley, sneaking into a store at the outskirts of town to buy crackers and meat, but his limited resources hadn't lasted long and his money was almost gone. He had gone to the saloon to buy a pint. From there, he didn't know what he would do.

Now the warm room and the whiskey made him sleepy—and careless—and he found himself telling Franklin about his life, revealing that he was a riverboat gambler. He broke off abruptly, saying, "I lost all my money and hit rock bottom."

Vince smiled again. The memory of Con's gun looming in front of him was still fresh in his mind, but it wasn't so much gratitude he felt toward Jake as a sense of not letting an opportunity pass by. *Who knows?* Vince thought. *Hardin might even be the answer to my problems. . . .* "I'll stake you, Jake," he said, surprising Jake. "All you need is some good clothes and a little money—plus a little luck. Tell you what, the boat's due to leave in about three hours. Go with me to New Orleans. I'll back you until you've won some money, then you can pay me back."

Jake stared at Vince but said at once, "Well, I'm in no condition to be proud. I'll just take you up on that offer."

"Fine!" Vince said. "Look, we're about the same size. Why don't you wear some of my duds? I've got too many anyhow."

When the boat bound for New Orleans left Helena, the two men got on. Jake saw a man with a sheriff's star standing by the gangplank, along with a deputy. Vince stopped and asked, "What's up, Sheriff?"

"Looking for a killer," the officer said. He looked at Vince and at Jake, noting the expensive clothes, then said, "Watch out, just in case the man gets on this boat. He'll be wearing some fine clothes that've been in the water—and he'll have a fresh bullet gash on top of his head."

Jake resisted an impulse to tug the hat Vince had given him down tighter. Instead he leaned forward, asking the sheriff, "A dangerous fellow?"

"A killer, like I said. Shot Mr. Max Longley dead. Fellow's name is Jake Hardin, but I don't guess he'd be fool enough to use it."

Vince said, "I guess not. Well, come along, Frank. Packet's about to leave."

The two of them went to stand at the rail and, as the hands cast off the lines, Vince said, "I always pay my debts, Jake."

"I figure you paid this one, Vince. Thanks."

They stood there as the paddle wheels began to churn, and soon Helena was lost as they moved down the river.

CHAPTER THREE

JAKE GETS AN OFFER

THE TRIP from Helena to New Orleans should have taken only two days, but the engine developed trouble and they had to dock at a small town. By the time a part had been shipped from Memphis and installed, the *Lightning* was delayed for two more days. For Jake Hardin it was a welcome delay. It gave his nerves time to settle down and the wound in his scalp more time to heal. And, too, he found himself growing more curious about Vince Franklin. Franklin seemed amiable enough, and the two of them played cards, but only for small stakes because Jake had seen at once that Franklin was not in his class as a card player. They strolled through the small town where the ship was docked, sat on the deck during the afternoon, and ate the good food provided by the riverboat's excellent chef.

As for Vince, he felt things were going his way for once. Jake was in his debt—after all, he'd kept him from being arrested and was giving him a new start. And though Vince wasn't sure how, he knew that debt was going to work in his favor. They had just finished a fine lunch on the second day and were walking around the town when they came upon a group of men in a small field beside the blacksmith shop. "Looks like a shooting match," Vince said. The two of them stopped and listened as the men agreed on the terms. A tall man named Harrod was evidently the judge. He had a full beard, which gave him the air of a biblical prophet as he announced in a ringing voice, "Costs one dollar to enter. The three top shooters get the prizes—three jugs of the smoothest whiskey Si Edwards ever made. Now fust of all, we'll have the rifles."

The contest proceeded in a leisurely fashion, with much joking among the contestants. Jake watched the winner of the rifle shoot, saying, "That fellow is good."

Then Harrod said, "Next, pistols at the settin' target." The men lined up and took turns shooting at bottles balanced on a fence, and the winner claimed his jug with a whoop.

"Now the last prize goes to the feller who can hit a target on the fly. How many of you fellers want in?" Only four men volunteered, and Harrod snorted in disgust. "What's wrong with you fellers? Ain't you got no pride?" Then he glanced at Jake and Vince. "How about you two? You look like sportin' men to me."

Jake nudged Vince. "You want to risk a dollar?" Vince grinned and produced the cash. "I'm in," Jake stated and pulled his gun out. "Anybody got any .44 bullets?"

"I'm shootin' a .44," a short, pudgy man with bright blue eyes said. He pulled a handful of shells from his pocket, saying, "If you win, I get first go at the jug, right?"

"Sure," Jake agreed. He loaded his pistol and watched as Harrod said to the first shooter, "Ready, Mac?" When the man nodded, he tossed a glass bottle into the air as high as he could. The contestant took his shot but missed. A hoot went up. He took three more turns, hitting only one bottle.

Two of the other men hit only one in four, but the final contestant hit three. Harrod turned to Jake, saying, "Your turn, I reckon."

Jake looked around at the men, then said, "Anybody here want to bet a little cash?"

"How much?" the one named Mac demanded.

"Much as my friend here wants to cover. But the deal is, Mr. Harrod throws all four glasses at once. If I miss even one, I lose."

"I'll just take ten dollars of that bet," Mac said and began digging in his pocket.

Vince pulled his wallet from his pocket, saying, "Step right up, gents. All bets covered."

Most of the men put a few dollars into the pot, but Harrod shook his head with a grin. "Since I'm doing the throwin' guess I better not git in on this. You ready?"

"Any time."

Harrod had to use both hands, but he tossed the four bottles high, all of them reaching their apex at about the same time. Jake lifted his gun and fired, shattering the first bottle as it paused. The next shot caught one of the bottles that had just started to fall, and the third shattered one a few feet above head level. His last shot took the final bottle just before it hit the ground.

"By gum!" Harrod exclaimed, his eyes wide. "You must be a trick shot for a circus!"

"Just had lots of practice," Jake said with a shrug. "Let's get started on that jug."

When the two men got back on board the *Lightning,* Vince handed Jake a wad of bills. "Here's your share. About thirty dollars." He considered Jake curiously. "Where'd you learn to shoot like that?" he asked.

"Like I said, lots of practice. Always been pretty fair with a handgun. Can't do as good with a rifle."

"Guess if that fellow Max Longley had seen you shoot, he wouldn't have tried to take you."

"I wish he hadn't," Jake said quietly.

"Bothers you, does it, Jake?" Vince asked curiously.

"Sure. Wouldn't it bother you?"

"Not a bit! He was trying to snuff your light, so he got what he asked for."

Jake didn't answer. Sometimes he wasn't sure that he really liked—or trusted—Vince Franklin. The two men went down to supper, and, as they ate, Vince began to talk about himself. "Got a big place outside of Richmond," he said expansively, then went on to describe Lindwood.

"Sounds like a fine place, Vince," Jake commented. "You got a family?" Jake noted with interest that the question obviously disturbed Vince.

"Well, I'm not married. My mother died when I was young. My father married again." He sipped from his wineglass, his brow knitted as he added, "My father and I don't get along too well. Matter of fact, none of the family likes me much."

"Too bad," Jake said. "Never had much of a family myself. Always envied fellows who sat around a big table with their folks. I've always wanted that."

Vince stared at him, then began to relate how little he was a part of the family. He finished by saying bitterly, "They've always shut me out, but they'll sing a different tune pretty soon! All of them!"

"How's that?"

"Why, in a few months, I'll be sitting at the head of the table!" Vince's eyes gleamed and he drank frequently of the wine as he began to speak of his future. "My grandfather Hiram made a pile of money, but my father never got along with him. So when Grandpa made his will, he left the plantation to my pa, but most of his money he put into a trust fund. Then he told my father he'd have to learn to get along with his son. And to make sure, he put it in his will that the oldest son—and that's me!—would inherit the whole fund on his twenty-fifth birthday. 'Course, it hasn't worked out quite the way Grandpa thought it would."

Jake stared at the man sitting across from him, then asked, "What went wrong, Vince?"

"My father went wrong!" Vince broke out angrily, a hardness in his eyes. "He never gave me a chance. All the time it was the others he favored—Grant and Les and Rachel! Maybe I been a little wild, but it was him that drove me to it! Well, that'll change when I get Grandpa's money."

Jake watched him silently, once again feeling uneasy about Vince's bitterness. Then, with a sigh, he shook his head. Maybe he was just overreacting. . . . Vince spoke freely of his family, dwelling on each of them and stressing how they'd have to mind their manners when he took over. It was a side of the man that Jake didn't admire, but he said nothing, as was his custom.

The *Lightning* was refitted, and as it pulled away on the last leg of the journey to New Orleans, Jake was standing at the rail watching the shore. The purser came up behind him, saying, "Mr. Franklin, your clothes are ready. Shall I put them in your cabin?"

Jake turned, and as soon as the purser saw his face, he said, "Oh, I thought you were Mr. Franklin!"

"No, I'm Mr. Franklin." Vince had come up behind the purser and was smiling.

"Why, this gentleman is enough like you to be your twin, sir!"

"He's not nearly as handsome as I am," Vince said, winking at Jake.

But the purser shook his head stubbornly. "You two are as alike as can be. Why, I thought you were brothers the first time you came on board together."

Vince looked at Hardin speculatively. "Well, maybe we do favor each other a little."

"More than that!" the purser insisted. "If you shaved your beard off, you'd look exactly like your friend!"

"Well, since my friend is a nice-looking chap, I can't take offense. Now you can put my suit in my cabin."

"Yes sir."

As the purser left, Vince said with a smile, "How do you feel about that, Jake? Insulted, perhaps?"

"Why, no." Jake smiled. He studied Franklin's face, and as he did so, surprise came to his eyes. "He's right, you know! Your beard covers most of your face, but we've got the same features. Same brown eyes, same color hair—our noses are even shaped the same."

"I always heard that everybody has a double somewhere on earth, but I never expected to find mine," Vince said. "Strange, though, that you and I would encounter each other as we did."

"One good thing about it," Jake said, "we're the same size, so I can wear your clothes. I was looking pretty ragged in my own outfit." He looked down the river and went on, "We'll be in New Orleans tomorrow, I'd venture. Then I can go to work and quit sponging off of you, Vince."

But Vince was not listening. He was studying Hardin's face closely. "What? Oh, yes, I suppose so . . . but we'll stick together for a few days, until you can put a stake together."

"No longer than I can help, Vince," Jake replied and shook his head. "Don't like to be taking from you all the time."

"Well, you saved my life, didn't you?"

"Maybe not. That fellow would probably just have roughed you up a little."

"No, I'm in your debt, Jake." He paused, about to say more, but changed his mind. "We'll have lots of time to talk when we get to New Orleans." He laughed softly, cocked his head as he studied Jake. "Funny thing, how we've gotten together. My sister Rachel would say God did it."

Jake raised his eyebrows. "She's religious?"

"Lord, yes! After me all the time to give up my wicked ways!"

"Well, maybe she's right, but I think it's all luck."

"That's the way a gambler would think, I suppose, but still . . . it's strange. Gives me the creeps in a way! Well, we'll talk about it later." His eyes narrowed and he said slowly, "I've got the fragment of an idea in my head. Might be a good one."

"I owe you, Vince. If you hadn't staked me, I'd be done for. And if you hadn't covered for me with that sheriff when we got on the boat, I'd either be in prison or hung." Jake shrugged. "If I can do something for you, just name it."

"I may do that. I just may indeed!"

New Orleans had always been one of Jake's favorite cities, but caution made him say as he walked down the gangplank of the *Lightning*, "We'd better split up for a time."

"Why? I thought we were going to stay together for a while!"

"We can meet, but there's probably a wanted notice out for me. I'll have to lay low for a while."

"Hadn't thought of that," Vince said slowly, then nodded, "I know just the place. Friend of mine owns a little place in the French Quarter. Got four or five nice rooms. He'll keep his mouth shut, too."

"Well—"

Vince waved his hand at a cab and half shoved Jake toward it. "Get in!" he ordered, then added to the driver, "French Quarter, driver. You know Tony's place on St. Charles Street?"

"Yassah! I does indeed!" The driver flicked his whip, and the team stepped out smartly. He drove from the wharf to the Quarter, then stopped in front of a two-story building on the narrow street. "Tony's place, sah!"

The two men got out of the cab, Vince paid the driver, and they went inside. Tony was a small Italian with a pair of sharp dark eyes, and soon he was leading the pair to the second floor. "Same room you had last time, Vince," he said. "And the one next to it's vacant. You gents make yourselves at home, then come on down and we'll see what we can find to drink."

The rooms were small, but well aired and light. A balcony framed with black wrought iron gave a good view of the street below, and during their stay, Jake spent a good deal of time looking down at the crowds that thronged the street. He went out twice, but on his second time he discovered that there was indeed a warrant out for his arrest. The thought of prison frightened him; he didn't think he could keep his sanity if he were cooped up.

Vince came and went but was always cheerful, saying, "Don't give up, Jake, old boy! Something will turn up."

Finally, on the third day, the two of them stood on the

balcony, smoking cigars after the evening meal. For a time neither of them said anything. Finally, Jake broke the silence. "I've got to get out of the country, Vince. If I stay here I'll be caught and hanged sooner or later. Either that or prison—and I'd rather have the rope."

Vince flicked the ashes from his cigar, seemingly caught in thought. "Hard for a man to hide, Jake. Mexico is pretty tough, too, unless a fellow has lots of cash."

"I'll make out."

"Sure, you're tough, Jake, but I'd like to see you leave with some money. A fellow can live like a king down in the Caribbean if he has just a little money. Nobody will come looking for you there." He puffed three times on his cigar, then tossed it over the railing. "I'd like to help you get a good start, Jake."

"No, you've done enough for me, Vince. I can't take anything more from you."

"Well, Jake, look at it this way—I need some help from you."

Jake said at once, "That's different. What can I do, Vince?"

"You know that will I told you about, the one that lays it out that I get the money when I'm twenty-five?"

"Sure, I remember."

"Well, there's one clause in it that says I don't get the money unless I'm living at Lindwood."

Jake frowned. "I don't see the problem."

"The problem, Jake, is a man named Simon Duvall. If I go back to Richmond, he'll kill me." He looked at Jake, saw that he had his attention, and rapidly sketched the thing out, concluding by saying, "So this fellow Duvall is a dead shot. I wouldn't have a chance, Jake!"

Hardin stared at Vince, then said, "Let me guess what you have in mind. You want me to kill this Duvall."

"That's it," Vince admitted readily. "It's pretty simple. If I go back, I'm dead. If I don't go back, I don't get the money. Now here you are, dead broke and likely to stay that way. You can use a gun. It all adds up, Jake. You take

Duvall out, and I put ten thousand dollars in your hand." He shook his head, adding, "Think what a life you could have down south with ten thousand in your pocket!"

Jake stood there, watching the blue smoke from his cigar curl upward. He owed this man a lot, yet . . . there was something in the thing that went against his grain. Finally he tossed the cigar to the street then said, "I don't like it, Vince. Sure, I've used a gun once or twice—but it was always forced on me. I'm not a hired killer."

"I thought you wanted to help me, Jake! If I'd been caught hiding you, they'd have nailed me for it. Now I'm asking you to risk a little something to get me out of a jam. How about it?"

"You're putting me on the spot, Vince—but I'll think about it."

"Sure!" Vince nodded. "You do that. We'll talk about it later."

For two days neither man mentioned the matter, and finally Vince brought it up. They were sitting in Jake's room drinking café au lait, when suddenly Vince said, "Jake, I was wrong to put you on the spot with my problem. You're not a killer. I should have seen that."

"Vince, I feel rotten—!"

"No," Vince broke in. "I know you pretty well. You're not the type to hide in a dark alley and shoot a man in the back."

Jake felt terrible, for he liked to pay his debts. "Maybe I can teach you to shoot," he offered, knowing it was no use.

"I can shoot straight enough." Vince nodded, then smiled sadly as he added, "But can you teach me to look into a gun that's aimed at me and not run? That's my problem. I'm a coward." He seemed to have no particular shame about admitting that. "Some men have courage; some don't. It's that simple. I just don't have it and you do."

"Not sure that's right."

"Well, anyway—" Vince broke off abruptly and stared blankly across the room. His brow wrinkled in thought, and he whistled softly and then laughed. "Jake, old fellow, I'm not brave, but I'm *smart!*" Reaching over, he slapped Jake on the shoulder, grinning broadly. "It's so brilliant, only I could come up with it!"

Jake gave him a curious look. "What's in your head now, Vince?"

"Why, it's like this. You couldn't kill a man in cold blood. But there's another way."

"I don't see it."

"Duvall loves to duel. He's killed more than one man. So you take my place in the duel! Don't you see it?"

"You mean I go to Richmond and pick a quarrel with Duvall, and—"

"No! No!" Excitement brightened Vince's eyes and he leaned forward and whispered, "You don't have to do that. *You take my place!* Don't you see?" He suddenly slapped his hands together, exclaiming, "Jake, remember what that purser on the boat did? He took you for me! We look that much alike."

"Wait a minute, Vince," Jake protested. "We don't look *that* much alike. I'd be spotted in a minute!"

"No you wouldn't. First, you grow a beard. Then we have the duel at dawn, with almost no light. You'll wear a cloak and a hat pulled down over your eyes. When it's over, I hand you the money, you shave your beard and head south. It's *perfect*, Jake!"

Jake was a quick thinker, but he sat there confused by the suddenness of Vince's plan. There was, he knew, something about the whole business he didn't like, but two things kept rising in his mind: He needed a stake and he owed Vince a lot. If it weren't for Vince, he'd probably be in jail by now. Or dead.

Vince sat there, letting Jake search the thing out in his mind; he was calculating enough to know that the more he tried to pressure the man, the less likely Jake was to respond. Finally he saw a break in Jake's expression and said, "Of course, I'm asking you to lay your life on the line for me. And that's too much for one man to ask of another."

"No, it's not!" Suddenly the issue became very simple to Jake. "I'll do it for you, Vince. I'd do it even without the money. Matter of fact," he said thoughtfully, "I wish there were no money in it. I owe you, and the money means I'm doing it partly for that reason."

"No, that's wrong," Vince said quickly, a sense of exultation running through him. He was sure now that all his problems would be solved in one instant, and if Jake took the bullet instead of Duvall—well, that was the risk the man was taking. "You're helping me as a friend with Duvall, and I'm helping you as a friend with money. So, it's settled?"

"Yes. When do you want to go to Richmond?"

"Have to let your beard grow first. That'll take a month, I guess. We can have some fun in the meantime. I'll tell you all about my family and the people you might run into." The uncertainty that had been eating at Vince since he had left his home was gone, and he laughed loudly. "Now I can sleep better!"

For a week the two of them stayed at Tony's making plans. Actually, there was little to plan, but Vince spent hours telling Jake about his family and his friends—not to mention his enemies. Once he said, "I'm telling you all this like a good Catholic confesses to a priest, Jake. Maybe because I know it's safe. A priest can't tell anything he hears, can he? And I reckon you won't, either!"

"No, I won't tell, Vince."

As Vince had talked about his life, Jake had revised his opinion of the man. At first he had thought of Vince as rather a nice scoundrel, a charming sort of reprobate— but a picture emerged from what he heard that was less pleasant. He learned of Vince's affairs with women, and while Jake was no prude, he disliked the way the man obviously thought of women as toys to be enjoyed and then cast aside. Vince's hatred for his father and his family came out, also, and though he painted them with black colors, Jake realized that it would have been hard for anyone, family or otherwise, no matter how good, to put up with Vincent Franklin.

There seemed to be some sort of rotten streak in the man, and it was far worse than cowardice. Jake knew that if the two of them were together for long, they would have conflicts. Before long he began to think that it would have been better if he had left New Orleans without getting involved. More than once he toyed with the idea of running out, penniless as he was.

But he stayed. *Maybe Vince will do better when this Duvall character is taken care of,* he thought. He knew it was merely a wishful dream, though, and the idea of killing a man grew more and more heavy, like an ominous shadow. It had all sounded logical enough when Vince had explained it, but no matter how Jake tried to think of it, the fact remained that he was going to kill a man for money. He told himself that it was not murder and that he himself could get killed, but it all seemed a feeble excuse for taking a man's life.

Slowly he came to the conclusion that he couldn't do it.

Time ran along, and as Jake tried to find a way to tell Vince what he had decided, Vince continued to talk about his past. Finally, one night, Jake said, "You've told me so much about your family and friends, I swear I'd recognize them if they walked through that door!"

"All right, Jake." It was late, and Vince had been happy all day. "Won't be long now, will it? I'll be master of Lindwood and you'll be living like a king down on a sunny island. Pretty soft, Jake, old boy!"

"Pretty soft, Vince," Jake answered absently. He sat there trying to find some way to put his decision to Vince, but he knew that no matter how he put it, Vince would not like it. Finally he said, "I've got something to tell you."

"What is it?"

"Well . . . I don't like to go back on my word, but it's

just too raw for me, killing Duvall." Jake saw anger spark at once in Vince's eyes and added, "If it was anything else, I'd do it. But—"

"That's pretty small of you!" Vince broke his words off sharply. He pressed the point, trying to convince Jake. When that failed, he began to curse him. Finally he ran out of things to say and stood to his feet. "You'd better get out of here, Jake. I might forget myself and turn you in."

"You could do that, I guess." Jake's voice was quiet, resolved.

Vince started to turn, then paused. With a sigh he shook his head, looking at Jake with a strange, defeated light in his eyes. "No, Jake, I reckon not." He walked to the door, then stopped again. "I've waited all my life for the time when I'd be *somebody*," he said in a low voice without turning around. "Maybe I should have lived better, been more ready to listen to my father or to Rachel." Again he shook his head. "But it's too late for that now. A man's what he makes himself." He turned to look at Jake, a bitter emptiness in his eyes. "I've heard you say the same thing," he added, almost sadly. "Men like you and me, we never change."

He turned, picked his coat up off Jake's bed, and put it on. He started out of the room but paused, turning and saying evenly, "I'll get somebody to put Duvall down, Jake. I'll get the money and I'll get Lindwood. But you know what? I don't really think I'll be happy when I get it. And I don't think you'll be happy on your little island or wherever you land." A sadness such as Jake had never seen in the man came to his eyes. He looked small and even a little lost as he stood there.

Then he summoned up a smile and said, "Well, we have to play what we're dealt, don't we, Jake?" Then he added so quietly that Jake almost missed it, "Somehow I think I knew all along you wouldn't do it—you're just not the type. But I've been thinking, if I'd been dealt a friend like you when I was younger, maybe I wouldn't be the rotten way I am. The one thing I wish, though . . . I sometimes wish my family thought a little better of me."

Then he was gone. Jake made a move toward the door, but stopped. "I'll talk to him tomorrow," he said aloud. He moved to the bed, picked up his coat and started to hang it up. But something fell out of the pocket, and as he picked it up he saw that it was Vince's wallet. Staring at it, he realized, *Vince must have taken my coat by mistake.* He took a step toward the door, then paused. *I'll give it to him tomorrow.*

Jake undressed slowly, thinking of how strangely Vince had behaved. The man's sad words kept echoing in his mind: *I sometimes wish my family thought a little better of me.* Jake lay in bed, but sleep wouldn't come. Restlessly he tossed until he finally dozed off, though his sleep was fitful and he still had flashing thoughts and short dreams. One of the thoughts grew, and he suddenly awakened with the idea fully developed. Getting out of bed, he stood in the middle of the room, thinking hard.

I'll help Vince make it—and without shooting Duvall.

So firm was his resolve that he walked to the table, poured water from the pitcher into the basin, then picked up his shaving brush. Quickly he lathered his face, then shaved the two-week beard with hard, even strokes.

When he was finished, he looked at himself, feeling a satisfaction. Vince would be angry, but it set the timetable back by two weeks. Jake lay down again, looked at his watch and saw that it was only a little after midnight. He lay there thinking. *How does one force a man to face up to his life?*

He could find no answers, but he pinned his hopes on what Vince had said: "I sometimes wish my family thought a little better of me."

Then he went to sleep, determined to stick with Vince and somehow make him see that Vince himself was the only one who could make that come to pass.

CHAPTER FOUR

A MIDNIGHT CALLER

JAKE awoke coughing, almost strangling, and when he sat up, he gagged instantly, for the smoke that filled the room was thick.

In one terrifying moment, the thought came to him: *The hotel's on fire!*

The thought screamed silently in his mind as he rolled off the bed and lay down on the floor. The air was clearer there, but a fit of coughing grabbed him and he had to wait until it passed before he could do any more. Someone was yelling below, and Jake began to crawl toward the door. He reached up to turn the brass knob, only to jerk back when it burned his hand. The door itself was sending off heat waves, and through a crack he saw a yellow glow.

He rolled over and began crawling toward the balcony door. On the way, he stopped and grabbed his pants, which were on the chair, wiggled into them while lying flat, then pulled on his coat.

Keeping as close to the floor as possible, he moved until he got to the balcony door and opened it. As soon as it opened, a flash of light caught his eye, and he turned to see the door leading to the hall burst into flame. Quickly he stepped outside and took a deep breath of the fresh air. It was not really fresh, though, for the flames on top of the building were leaping high into the air, filling the area with thick, acrid smoke.

Time was short.

It was only ten feet to the street level, and men below were motioning to him, yelling, "Jump! Jump!"

Jake threw one leg over the rail, then suddenly paused

and cast a look at the balcony outside of Vince's room. The door was shut, and he hesitated, watching the leaping flames for a moment, then pulled his leg back and ran down the balcony. The two balconies were not joined, so he climbed up on the rail and jumped as hard as he could. The heat of the fire above struck him as he fell sprawling on the other balcony. Instantly he got to his feet and tried the door. It was locked, so he stood back and began to kick at it. His foot went through and he reached inside, turning the lock and swinging the door open.

The interior of the room was filled with black smoke, and the far wall was blazing. Jake took a deep breath, went on his belly, and crawled toward the bed. It was dark in the room, and the smoke was bad, even on the floor. When Jake reached the bed, he raised himself to his knees and threw his arms across it. The smoke blinded him as he groped for Vince. Finally he found Vince's body, inert and motionless.

"Come on, Vince!" he yelled, struggling to his feet, but his mouth and eyes filled with smoke, and he was suddenly choking. Fear came then, and he knew he couldn't stand the smoke much longer. Through weeping eyes, he saw a coat thrown across a chair. Quickly he grabbed it, wrapped it around Vince's head, then reached down and picked him up. Stumbling, he made his way across the room toward the balcony, but before he got to the wall, the ceiling gave a great creaking roar, and he knew it was collapsing.

He reached the door, but blinded by the smoke, missed the opening and ran into the wall. He fell with Vince on top of him, and then the roof came down. He pulled at Vince, but at that moment something struck him a wicked blow across his right foot. The pain was almost unbearable, but he yanked his foot loose and tried again to get Vince out, crawling because he couldn't stand. Overhead the raging flames licked at the sky, and he saw that the entire room was blazing now.

With all his strength he gave a heave and the two of them rolled out onto the balcony—but the outer wall began to lean, and Jake looked up to see that it was toppling. He grabbed Vince in his arms, struggled upright and, though he could put no weight on his right foot, lurched to the rail and simply leaned forward. He flipped over, lost his hold on Vince, and then hit the ground, landing on his back with a force that drove all the breath from his lungs.

Looking up he saw the wall of the building, blazing with yellow fire, slowly coming down on top of him. He rolled over, getting as far on his side as he could. Then something struck him, and he knew no more.

Jake came out of unconsciousness suddenly, with no hint that he had even been in a deep coma.

One moment it was dark and quiet; the next he was awake, pain washing over him. He tried to look around, but there was something over his eyes. A man's voice was saying, ". . . have to keep a close watch on him. I'm afraid that he might have some internal injuries."

Jake spoke, his voice a raw croak. "What's wrong with my eyes?"

The doctor moved to his side at once. "Well, so you're awake. That's good. I need to find out some things. Just answer and tell me where you hurt and then we'll give you something for the pain."

"Right ankle," Jake whispered. "Right hand, too."

"Yes, I know about those. They'll be OK. But do you hurt inside? Chest or stomach?"

"No." Jake was hurting too bad to waste words, but managed to say again, "What's wrong with my eyes?"

"You got them scorched. I want to keep the strong light off of them for a few days. No more injuries?"

"No. Yes—sore throat."

"You took in too much smoke. Now don't try to talk any more. Just relax."

Jake asked, "What about my friend?"

A pinprick touched Jake's arm as he waited for an answer, and suddenly he began sliding into a warm darkness. "What about . . . ?" his voice trailed off.

He woke again, thinking it had been only a few minutes since he drifted off, but suddenly he knew it must have been longer. He was in a dark room, but the bandages were not on his eyes. There was only a table, a chair beside the bed, and a single door. The window across the room was heavily curtained, but he could tell that it was daytime.

Looking down, he saw that his right ankle was bandaged, as were his right wrist and forearm. A raging thirst assailed him and he tried to call, but his throat was too dry. Then he saw a tiny brass bell on the table and rolled over to get it. That simple act awoke the nerves in his ankle, but he rang the bell despite the pain.

Almost at once, a man in a white coat came into the room. "Well now, you're awake! How do you feel?" He was a short man with a fat paunch and light blue eyes. He read the request in Jake's eyes and at once poured a glass of water. "Let's try to get you upright," he said, and Jake almost fainted with the pain but finally was sitting up in bed.

He drank the water greedily, then asked, "Where is this?"

"St. John's Hospital," the man said. "You've been here—let's see, oh, two days. You were hurting pretty bad when you first came."

"I'm hurting pretty bad now!" Jake whispered. His eyes burned and he blinked them. "My eyes are better, though."

"They were scorched, but the doctor says if we keep them medicated and away from strong light for a while they should be all right."

"What else is wrong with me?"

"No bones broken, which is a miracle!" The orderly shook his head and gave Jake an admiring look. "You're a pretty tough fellow! Not many men can have a burning building fall on them and not get killed. The leg is pretty badly strained, and the arm as well. Got some burns, too, which must hurt like the devil. But you're alive, and that's what counts. You drink some more water, and I'll go get the doctor. He'll want to look you over."

Jake lay there, grateful, since he was left-handed, that it was his right that was hurt. Then he realized that he still didn't know about Vince. When the doctor came in a few minutes later, he asked, "How's the man I pulled out?"

The doctor, a very thin man of fifty with a pronounced Adam's apple that moved up and down when he spoke, shook his head. "I'm Dr. Sealy. Sorry to have to tell you, but he didn't make it." He pulled the chair close to the bed and sat down on it. "I think he was dead when you pulled him out. The smoke got him, I'd guess."

A sense of frustration swept over Hardin. He'd known Vince only a short time and recognized that there was something bad in him—but somehow he'd been bound to him, perhaps by the fact that Vince had gone out on a limb for him. Oh, yes, he realized that Vince had actually risked little—nevertheless, he couldn't help thinking he might have been able to help him.

There'd be no way to do that now, Jake realized, and the futility of his efforts and of Vince's death came down hard on him. Dr. Sealy saw it and said briskly, "Well, well, too bad! A young man like that, but you did your best from what I hear. Now then, let's check you over."

Though the man was a good doctor, the examination was painful. Finally he said, "You ought to be dead, but really there's nothing wrong with you that rest won't repair, Mr. Franklin."

The name went off like an alarm bell in Jake's mind.

He thinks I'm Vince! That seemed impossible, but as Sealy continued to talk about his injuries, Jake suddenly remembered the mixed-up coats. *They must have found Vince's papers in the coat I was wearing. But somebody will know better—like Tony. He'll spot me right off.*

Sealy continued, speaking of the fire. "Bad thing, that

fire. Not too many got out. Only three, I think. Building must have gone up like tinder."

"Did Tony make it, the owner?"

"No, he didn't. Friend of yours, I suppose."

"Yes."

Dr. Sealy stood up, his face dim in the dark room. "I sent a wire to your people as soon as I treated you. Thought it best, and there was nobody to ask." He rummaged in his pockets, came out with a slip of paper. "Got an answer this morning. It says, 'Will pick up Vincent Franklin within a week. Will travel home by steamboat.' It's signed 'Rachel Franklin.'"

"Thanks, Doctor."

"Well, you need lots of care, and the family can do it better than we can. It's a good idea, too, to go by boat. You can stay in the stateroom where it's dark during the day. I'd say you can leave as soon as she comes. Is this your mother?"

Jake took a deep breath and, feeling as though he were taking a leap into the dark, he cleared his throat. "No, Rachel is my sister."

"Well, I'll be checking on you. Don't move around too much, and don't let the light get at your eyes. I'll get you some smoked glasses to wear after you leave."

"How long will I be laid up?"

"Oh, if you mean how long till you're fully recovered, quite a while. Say . . . two months. But you'll be able to get around with crutches within a week, maybe. Then a cane. Your eyes, though—be *very* careful of them!" He rose and went to the door, then turned and came back to the bed. "The man you pulled out of the fire, was he a good friend of yours?"

"Just a fellow I met on the boat several weeks ago. I sort of liked him."

Dr. Sealy said slowly, "His name was Jake Hardin."

"Oh?"

"He was wanted for murder. Killed a man on a gambling boat. The sheriff came and identified the body by

the papers the fellow had on him, telling who he was."
Sealy studied his patient carefully, then added, "A bad
way to go, even for a murderer. Well, they buried him in
Potter's Field. He didn't have any money, and nobody
was likely to pay for his funeral."

"He had some good about him, Doctor," Jake said.
"More than some I've met."

"I suppose that's so." Dr. Sealy nodded, then left the
room.

Jake lay there quietly, thinking. He grieved over Vince
Franklin, over the good things about him. All afternoon
he lay there and finally was given a shot when the pain
got bad.

The next morning he found he was able to eat a little.
"Put me in a chair, Rog," he said to the orderly. "I'm sick
of this bed."

"Yeah, sure," the orderly said. He helped Jake into the
chair, then asked, "You want anything? I got stuff to do,
Mr. Franklin."

"Go on, Rog. I'll be all right."

He sat there, relieving the muscles that had stiffened
from his days in bed. Carefully he tried to move his right
foot, but the stab of pain made him catch his breath.
"Going to be a while before I'll stand on that," he murmured. His wrist was not much better, but as he sat there,
he was conscious of how fortunate he was. How had Rog
put it? *Not many men have a burning building fall on them
and live through it!*

Well, he was alive. Battered and burned, but alive.

The future loomed before him, darkly, like a tunnel
whose end he couldn't see. *Maybe there's no end to it,* he
thought. *Maybe all this is just an accident.* He thought of
Capt. Daniel Harness with his rough-hewn theology.
Dan would never think it just happened, Jake mused. *And
Rachel wouldn't either, if what Vince said about her was so.*

He thought then of the girl who was coming to meet
him, to take him home with her to a place he'd never
seen, to live among people he'd never met. And he

thought of the wild plan to reform Vince that had taken form in his mind on the night before the fire. Now, in the quietness of the hospital room, it seemed even more insane than he'd thought possible.

He pictured Vince as he'd seen him for the last time, standing at the door with something like grief in his eyes. *Men like you and me, we never change.*

Something in Jake Hardin rebelled against that. He had knocked around the world quite a bit and had picked up his scars, and he'd seen many a man go down to defeat and ruin. He'd always figured that was just the way the cards had fallen to people. But now . . . now he was starting to wonder if a person couldn't change his hand and make life what he wanted. Maybe all a person had to do was want it bad enough.

Now the memory of the futility in Vince's words rubbed against him, making him uneasy. He didn't want to believe it.

The sun was bright outside, outlining in yellow the blanket someone had pinned over the window. The sun would never shine on Vince Franklin again, that was true enough. But if Vince had lived, he *might* have found his way. At least, Jake tried hard to believe that.

Finally, he took a deep breath, put the thoughts of Vince and the futility of his death away, and forced himself to think on his own danger. "Got to get away before that girl gets here," he muttered. "She'd see in one look that I'm not Vince, and when they find that out, the next question will be 'Who *is* he?' It won't take them long to figure out that Jake Hardin isn't buried in that grave at all."

He lay awake late into the night, and though his injuries pained him, he refused to take the morphine the nurse urged on him. For hours he thought of escape, but it was hopeless. He couldn't walk or see, and he had no money. He assumed that some cash was in Vince's wallet, but he didn't think it was much.

Finally as dawn came to illuminate the cover over his

window, he forced himself to hammer out a plan of sorts. *I'll get the wallet and hire someone to come and take me away the day before the girl arrives. Maybe there'll be enough to get a place to stay and someone to take care of me until I can move around. Have to be a secret place, because they'll be looking for me as soon as Rachel comes and her brother's not here.* He lay there trying to find a better way but could not. Finally he decided. *Got to try it. Not much of a chance, but like Vince said, I have to play the hand I've been dealt.*

For the next five days Jake did everything he could to put some sort of action into his plan. One of the orderlies, a man named Asa Blunt, was not a promising candidate as an accomplice, but he was the only choice. Jake took pains to be friendly toward him and quickly discovered that Blunt was open to making money and was not overly scrupulous. Jake began by mentioning that he would much rather stay in New Orleans than go back to Virginia, adding, "I've got money enough to pay for a place, but I guess my sister would find me no matter where I tried to stay out of her way."

An avaricious light had gleamed in Blunt's muddy brown eyes, and the next day he waited until after dark, then came to Jake's room. "Been thinking 'bout what you said, 'bout a place to stay." He licked his lips, glanced cautiously around, then said, "I mebby got a place, but it'd come high."

Jake nodded, saying, "I'd pay pretty well, but it's not going to be easy. I can't check out of this place. You'd just have to roll me out to a carriage after everyone was off duty."

"Sure, that ain't no problem. Now about the money . . ."

Jake finally agreed to a larcenous figure, but after the man left, Jake was not happy. "He'd turn me over for a reward in a minute—but at least it's a way out of here."

That was on Tuesday. Jake knew he had to be out soon, so he spent every day trying to strengthen himself by eating all he could—but there was nothing he could do about his injuries. His eyes were very sensitive to light, and he could hardly bear the pain when the dressing on his ankle was changed. Still, he had no choice.

Dr. Sealy came in on Friday evening, about six o'clock, and looked him over. Standing back he said, "Well, you're better, but not much. I'll be glad when you get home and can get total care."

"You've been mighty good to me, Doc," Jake said. "Couldn't ask for better treatment."

"Thanks, but it'll be better when you get home. Well, I'll see you in the morning. Good night."

Jake closed his eyes, weary of thinking. For almost an hour he tried to think of a better way, to no avail. Finally he dropped off into a fitful sleep that was more of a twilight affair in which he was neither awake nor completely asleep. He was aware after a time that someone had come into the room and was standing beside the bed. Rousing himself, he whispered, "Blunt?"

"No, not Blunt," the man said. At the sound of his voice, Jake came fully awake with a start that jerked his body. "Easy, Jake!" the voice said, and at the same time, the man shifted around so that the feeble light from the lamp fell on his face.

A shock ran along Jake's nerves, and he lay there for one instant, thinking he was dreaming. Then he said hoarsely, "Vince!"

"It's me, Jake. Just lie still and don't call out." Vince leaned over the bed, peering at Hardin's face. "Sorry to do it this way, but I couldn't figure out any other way of getting to you without anyone knowing."

"But . . . if you're alive, who was that in your room?" Jake demanded, his mind working fast. He sat up painfully with a little assistance from Vince. "They think he was *me*."

"Just a fellow I met in the hotel lobby," Vince said, glancing around. He saw a chair and pulled it to Jake's bedside. "Listen," he whispered. "Here's what happened. When I left your room, I was pretty sick inside. Here I thought everything was all set, and then you backed out on me. I decided to get drunk, so I left and told Tony I was checking out the next day. There was a fellow standing there, and I guess he'd been trying to get a room. Tony said to me, 'OK if this fellow has your room?' I said it was and left to get drunk."

"But you've been gone for—"

"Sure, sure, I know, but just listen," Vince insisted. "I went down to the river and boarded a paddle wheeler. Started drinking, then got in on a card game. There was a woman there, too, and she kept egging me on to drink. Anyway, I passed out and when I woke up, the blasted ship was moving upriver! I was broke, of course, done in by the woman, I guess. I got off at the next town and got a room. Had to wire my bank for money. But it was a bank holiday so I had to wait a day for that, and then I got a copy of the paper."

"And read about the fire?"

"That was the way of it." Vince smiled. "They made me out as quite a hero, going back into a building to save a fellow. Just the dumb sort of stunt a hairpin like you would try to pull off, Jake—and one that a fellow like me would never even think of!"

Jake suddenly felt relieved. "I'm glad you're alive, Vince." He paused, then added, "I've had some bad times, thinking about you."

The words embarrassed Vince and he laughed shortly, still keeping his voice down. "Yeah, well—I'm glad you're alive and kicking, too, Jake."

"Listen, you've got to get me out of here. Your sister will be here any day, maybe tomorrow."

"Get you out?" Vince sounded a little surprised. "Why, I didn't come to get you out!" He saw the look of stunned amazement on Jake's face, then slapped his thigh and made a face. "Well, of course! You would think that!"

"What else is there to think?"

Vince looked over his shoulder, then said quickly,

"I've got it all figured out, Jake. We go through with a little of the plan we had. You go back to Richmond—but you don't shoot Duvall."

"Go back to Richmond! You're crazy!"

"No, I'm not. Just listen and don't argue. I talked with the doctor who's been treating you. Didn't tell him who I was and kept my hat pulled low, so he thinks I'm a friend of yours. Which I am, Jake." Vince paused, then added, "You're still going to get to that island we talked about!"

Jake shook his head, saying, "Vince, it won't work!"

"Yes it will," Vince said, and confidence showed in his eyes. "It's better than the first plan. You're a sick man, Vince Franklin, very ill. So you go back to Virginia and you stay sick until it's time to collect the big money." He saw that Jake was staring at him, then spread his hands apart. "Don't you get it? Duvall can't shoot a helpless man!" He laughed softly, adding, "He's a man of *honor*! And that's the beauty of it all."

Jake shook his head. "It won't work. Your sister will know I'm not you the first time she looks at me."

"Not a chance! Last time she saw me without a beard, I was sixteen. And you've got those burns swelling up your face. We look a lot alike to begin with, and you don't even look like *yourself*, Jake," Vince said.

Jake shook his head stubbornly. "It's hopeless, Vince. Even if they didn't know I wasn't you by looking, they'd find out soon enough. I don't sound like you, and I don't know what you know."

"Your voice is husky from breathing in all that smoke," Vince said, "and your mind's not working very well. Dr. Sealy told me that, and that's what he'll tell Rachel. You can't remember things. Sealy hopes it'll get better, but you can see to it that it doesn't. If you don't remember the name of a cousin, well, it's just that you haven't gotten rid of the effects of your injuries."

For the next twenty minutes the two spoke, Jake arguing and Vince supplying answers. Finally Vince said, "Jake, it's our only chance. All you have to do is go to my home, stick it out for a few months, then go away for a trip after you've met the conditions of the will."

Jake thought hard, but finally a slow smile touched his lips. "Well, I guess it's like you said. We have to play the hand we're dealt!"

Vince beamed at him. "I knew you'd do it, Jake, you old son of a gun! Now you let Rachel take you home. Here's an address. You can reach me there under the name of Bill Underhill. Don't write unless you have to, and if there's trouble, try to explain without giving anything away on paper. I'll write you from time to time, and if you *have* to know something, I'll try to get it across. I don't think anyone will be reading your mail, but we'll take no chances." A thought came to him, and he smiled. "You'll have to send me money, Jake. I can't draw any out, can I?"

Jake smiled back at him. "Maybe I'll let you dangle. You'd only spend it for frivolous affairs and foppish attire anyway."

"Sure! That's what money's for, isn't it?" Then Vince sobered and said slowly, "I guess I'm in your hands, Jake. If this doesn't work, I'm a gone goose—or, even worse, a penniless goose! But you won't let me down." He rose and moved away but paused to add, "Don't say any more than you have to to Rachel. She's sharp, Jake."

"Do my best for you, Vince." And then the door closed softly, and Jake lay there, his mind busy with what lay ahead.

"Guess I'll have to tell Blunt I've changed my mind," he murmured, then tried to think ahead to the next few days. Finally he thought, *No use making a lot of plans. I'll just have to take it a day at a time.* But the hopelessness that had wrapped his mind was gone. He finally believed he had a chance.

"Well, Jake, old man, I like this hand a whale of a lot better than anything I've had lately! The law's not after me anymore, and maybe, just maybe, I can do something to help Vince get his wish." He wiggled his foot, grimaced at the pain, then nodded. "Go on, hurt all you please!" Then he thought of Rachel, of what Vince had said about her, and sobered. "I hope you don't like me much, Rachel. Because the more you dislike me, the farther away from me you'll stay!" The idea pleased him, and he lay back on the bed, his fertile mind spinning one idea after another.

In it all, Jake Hardin was strangely happy.

CHAPTER FIVE

TRIP TO NEW ORLEANS

RACHEL was standing in the kitchen making a caramel cake when the rider came into the yard. Wiping her hands on a damp cloth, she said, "Mother, Roy Delaughter just rode in."

Her mother looked up from the table where she was peeling potatoes, concern coming into her face. Getting to her feet, she came to look out the window. "I never feel good about getting a telegram," she murmured. "I don't think good news ever comes like that."

Rachel knew what her mother was thinking, for she herself had thought instantly of her father and her brother Grant, who had been sent with their company to the Shenandoah Valley. There had been little military action since Manassas, but both women knew that it only took one small action—and one single bullet—to bring tragedy. They watched as Delaughter hitched his horse then came at once down the walk. He had been in charge of the telegraph office in Richmond since it had first been established, and he was a good friend of the Franklins.

Rachel went to the door, calling out, "Over here in the kitchen, Mr. Delaughter." He looked up sharply, then hurried down the walk and came in. Pulling off his hat, he said, "Afternoon, Amy. How are you, Rachel?" He was a small man, neat in dress and feature. "It's not about Brad or Grant," he said, reaching into his pocket and pulling out a sheet of paper.

A wave of relief washed through both women, and Delaughter saw it in their faces. He handed the telegram to Amy Franklin. She read it aloud for Rachel: "Mr. Vincent Franklin seriously injured in hotel fire. Condition not critical. Will need extended home care. Please advise. Dr. Winford Sealy, St. John's Hospital, New Orleans."

Rachel took the telegram, scanned it, then frowned. "He's not going to die, but he must be pretty bad."

"Be a hard trip for a sick man, all the way from New Orleans," Roy Delaughter commented. "Best thing would be by ship, wouldn't it?"

Amy thought hard, then said, "Brad says that the Yankees are going to blockade the coast. It might be hard to get there—or to get back, for that matter."

"Oh, they don't have enough ships for that, Amy!" Roy said at once. "But it wouldn't be a bad idea to do it quick as possible." He pondered a moment, then said, "There's a fast ship making for New Orleans in the morning—the *Jupiter*, with Capt. Maylon Stuart in command. If you want, I can get passage for you when I get back to town."

"Yes, Roy, please do that. And see if you can find out about a return passage."

"Sure, Amy. Anything else I can do, just let me know."

"Thank you, Roy. Now sit down and have something to eat before you go back." She and Rachel fixed the man a good lunch, then went to the study to talk. "I wish Brad were here," Amy said with a worried look. "I hate to send Les, though I'm sure he'd like to go. He's the only man on the place right now, and he's needed here. I'll have to go, Rachel."

"No, you can't leave, Mother," Rachel said firmly. "You're not over the flu yet. I'll go get him."

Amy gave her daughter a doubtful look, then her brow cleared. Though Rachel was only nineteen, Amy knew without a doubt that this daughter of hers was fully capable of such a mission. "Well, I think it'd be best if you did go, Rachel. We'll pack the middle-sized trunk. It's a long voyage, and you'll have to bring back with you whatever medicals Vince will need."

Rachel nodded, and the two women at once began

preparing for the trip. Not knowing the exact departure time of the *Jupiter*, Rachel decided to go to Richmond at once. "I'll take a room for the night," she explained to her mother. "The ship may leave at dawn, and I don't want to miss it."

When Rachel was in the buggy with Les beside her, Amy asked, "Are you sure you have enough money? It's terribly expensive traveling so far."

"I have plenty, Mother." She leaned down, kissed her mother, and added, "Don't worry about me. Just pray for traveling safety."

"Yes, I will. Good-bye, dear!"

Les whipped up the horses; he knew only one speed of travel and that was as fast as the horses could go. He was disappointed because he was not making the trip, but being good-natured he gave over his protests. The horses lined out at a fast gallop, and Rachel said, "For goodness sakes, Les, slow down! You'll wear the horses out!"

"Aw, this ain't really fast," Les protested but pulled the team down to a brisk trot. He looked at her with envy, saying, "Sure wish I could go."

"Mother needs you here, Les. You're the man of the place now." Her words brought a flush to his fair cheeks, and she added, "I'll bring you a present from New Orleans. What'll it be?"

"A picture of some of them fancy Creole gals!"

"Not likely, you scamp!"

"Well, some fancy boots—or maybe a pistol."

"Don't know your size in either," Rachel teased him. "Better let me surprise you." They rode along talking in a lively fashion, but when they got to Richmond and were on their way to the hotel, Rachel grew serious. "I don't relish this trip, Les. You know how Vince is. He's bad enough when he's well."

"Well, if he's hurt bad, he shouldn't be able to stir up too much meanness," Les answered.

"He'll be as unpleasant as he can be, I know that!" Rachel said, frowning. Then she looked up and said,

"There's the hotel. You can dump me off and get back to the house."

Les carried her trunk inside and waited until she had found out from the clerk the departure time of the *Jupiter*. Then the brother and sister walked back to the buggy.

"Be careful, Sister," Les said and awkwardly leaned forward and kissed her cheek. "Don't let the Yankees get you."

"I'll shoot them with the pistol I'm going to get for your present," she said with a smile, then patted his arm. "Take care of things until I get back, Les. Don't let Mother work too hard." He grinned at her, then vaulted into the buggy. She watched as he left, then walked back into the hotel.

She knew that the *Jupiter* left at six the next morning, but feeling too restless to go to bed right away, Rachel walked around the city for an hour. At six o'clock she went to supper and was surprised to see Leighton Semmes sitting at one of the tables. He looked very handsome in his ash gray uniform. He stood at once when she came into the room, saying, "Rachel! I never thought to see you here! Come and bring some light into this lonely man's life."

She was glad to see him, and they had a pleasant meal. Semmes listened as she told him of her mission, as always enjoying the opportunity to watch her. He was a connoisseur of feminine beauty, and in a part of the world noted for beautiful, graceful women, Rachel Franklin held his attention. Quite honestly, this was a puzzle to him; he was a man who either got his own way from the women he pursued or else moved along to easier prey. He had done neither with Rachel.

Now he leaned back, peering at her through the aromatic smoke of his cigar, suddenly amused at himself. *Why do I put up with her rebuffs?* he wondered. *She's a good-looking woman, but there are plenty of those available.* He studied her carefully as she moved her hands from time to time in quick motions. She wore a simple blue dress with a white lace top, and her turquoise earrings reflected the blue-green of her eyes. Her lips were a little too full for true beauty, but not for drawing a man's glance. The smooth sweep of her jaw and the elegant joining of her neck into her shoulders were so strong as to be almost masculine. The deep cleft in her chin added to that impression of strength, yet there was no denying the dainty femininity of her trim figure.

Semmes moved restlessly in his seat and took a sip of his wine. An idea rose in him, and he said idly, "It's a long trip all the way to New Orleans, Rachel. Lots of pretty aggressive men on those ships. I think I can get a leave. Maybe I'd better go along to look after you."

Rachel's eyes suddenly gleamed with mirth and her lips turned up in a smile, followed by a sudden delighted laugh. "That'd be like putting the fox to watch the chickens, Leighton!" The thought amused her greatly, for she knew him very well indeed, but when she saw the expression on his face, she put out her hand and covered one of his. "I didn't mean to hurt your feelings, but you don't know how funny you looked, all innocent and pious!"

Leighton suddenly laughed out loud, his eyes crinkling at the corners and his mobile lips turned up. "I don't know why I keep hanging around you, Rachel!" Shaking his head, he took her hand and held it captive. "Well, you know me pretty well, I suppose. Do you think you'll ever change your opinion of me?"

Rachel considered him thoughtfully, still smiling a little. There always was a strange mixture in her of humor and seriousness, and now the two struggled. Finally she said, "You're not a tame man, Leighton. That's the one thing I couldn't stand."

Her words surprised him greatly. "That's the most revealing thing you've ever said to me, Rachel."

She gave him a half-embarrassed look, for the thought had slipped out—but now that it was spoken, she wanted to express the part of her that had given birth to it. "Many marriages seem to be so dull, don't they,

Leighton? I've watched it since I was a little girl. A marriage is a woman's whole life. A man can do a hundred things. Marriage to most men is usually something they turn to when their real work is done." A look of rebellion touched her bright eyes, and her lips thinned as she shook her head. "It may sound strange, but I believe there should be more to marriage than that!"

Semmes was tremendously interested. He leaned forward, his penetrating eyes on her face. "Do you really think a marriage can be more? I've seen what you're talking about, the way many marriages fall into a habit and convenience. I'm sure they didn't start out that way. What do you think makes men and women lose that magic they feel at first?"

"Women are to blame," Rachel said instantly, then smiled at the expression of surprise that her statement drew. "They grow careless. It's as if they're saying, 'I've got him. Now I don't have to be anything except a dutiful wife.'"

"You don't think wives ought to be dutiful?"

"Wives are to obey their husbands, yes—the Bible says so. But did you know, Leighton, that the Bible *doesn't* say that wives are to love their husbands?"

"No, I didn't know that. Sounds like a mistake to me."

Rachel gave him an arch look, but went on. "The Bible does say that *men* are to love their wives. Women to obey, men to love. And it's easier to obey than it is to love, did you know that?"

Semmes considered her, then shook his head. "I don't see that."

"Why, anyone can obey," Rachel said at once. "But you can't *command* love. Sometimes love doesn't even exist in a marriage, so it's no wonder that two people become more like business partners than lovers. But I will tell you this, Leighton, I will never marry—not unless I am absolutely certain of two things. One, that I love the man enough to give everything to him."

"And the second?"

"Why, that he loves me the same way." Rachel gave a short laugh, then rose to her feet. "How did I ever get to talking like this? Come walk me to my hotel, Mr. Semmes."

He paid the bill, and the two of them walked slowly along the street, speaking lightly of Rachel's upcoming journey. When they got to her hotel, he said, "Let's sit out on the balcony awhile. It's early yet."

"Just for a little while," she agreed, and the two of them went out on the balcony of the second floor. They were alone, and for an hour they sat there talking until Rachel finally rose. "I have to be up early."

Semmes stood and came close to her. A sickle moon hung in the sky, turned butter yellow by a haze in the air. The stars were great wooly crystal masses overhead, and the large magnolia tree that rose beside them gave off a sweet savor.

Rachel stood there quietly, watching Semmes carefully. She knew that he was going to kiss her. She did not turn away, as he half expected; instead, when he put his arms around her, she lifted her face. And when his lips fell on hers, she deliberately leaned forward, meeting him halfway.

The sweetness of her lips and the feel of her as she leaned against him stirred Semmes tremendously. He pulled her closer, his desires beginning to clamor. Rachel was different from any woman he'd known; he sensed that the same emotions that moved him were in Rachel, yet she seemed strangely removed from him.

After a moment, she slid her lips away, and he released her. "Good night, Leighton," she said quietly. But she was shaken. Leighton's kiss had touched something deep within her, some part that she kept buried—and for a moment, as Semmes had held her, she had felt her control slip. That was disturbing enough.

What was even more disturbing was that Rachel was aware that Leighton knew it.

Even so, he made no effort to restrain her as she

moved away, for something had come to him—a sudden knowledge that this woman could not be taken by storm. He wanted to reach out and take hold of her again, but instead he said, "Good night, Rachel. Have a good journey." Then he paused. "You've let me see something different tonight. I didn't know a woman could be so independent." Despite himself, he hungered for some modicum of commitment from her and asked again, "Do you think you could ever change your judgment of me?"

Rachel said, "You've been a woman chaser for most of your life, Leighton. But if you and I ever fell in love, I'd make sure you'd find something better at home than you could find anywhere else."

Her bluntness astonished him, and he laughed ruefully. "By heaven, I believe you would, Rachel! A man would never get tired of you as his wife."

"You and I are not placid people, Leighton," she said, looking at him with a strange smile on her lips. "No, we'd either have heaven together—or we'd explode. But we wouldn't be bored!"

Then she was gone. With a shake of his head, Semmes went to have a drink at the saloon. But he could not shake a restlessness, an awareness that she had stirred him in a way no other woman ever had.

As Rachel tipped the carriage driver and followed the tiled walk toward the entrance to St. John's Hospital, she fought an impulse to turn around and run away. The trip from Richmond had been swift, and she had been thinking of Vince steadily. Now it seemed to her that there were few tasks in the world that appealed to her less than being a nurse to her half brother. But knowing that she had no choice, she squared her shoulders and entered the front door.

A small man dressed in white pants and shirt looked up from the desk that sat to the right of the large reception room. Getting to his feet, he asked, "Yes, miss?"

"My name is Rachel Franklin. I'm here to pick up one of your patients," Rachel said. "Mr. Vincent Franklin."

"Oh, yes. Dr. Sealy left word that he wants to talk with you. Come along and I'll take you to his office."

"Thank you." Rachel followed the man down a long hall, and she could see, through the open doors, patients in the rooms off to each side. At the end of the hall, the orderly knocked on a door. "Dr. Sealy? Miss Franklin is here to get her brother."

The door opened, and a thin man with sparse graying hair and wearing a white suit looked out. "Thank you, Evans. Come in, Miss Franklin." He stepped aside and motioned her to a chair, the only one in the room except the one behind his desk. He waited until she was seated, then settled behind the desk. "You made a quick trip, Miss Franklin. Any trouble with the Federal navy?"

"Two days ago we were sighted by one of their ships, but the *Jupiter* was so much faster that she just ran away."

"That's good. Won't be that way for long, I'm thinking. They'll close in as soon as they build their navy. Well now, how about the voyage back?"

"The *Jupiter* is loading today and tomorrow and will leave the day after that. She'll go back to Richmond with a load of supplies. I've got a stateroom for myself and my brother."

"Good. I think he needs to be taken home right away."

Rachel asked, "How badly is he hurt, Doctor?" She listened carefully as Sealy outlined the injuries, then commented, "So it's mostly just going to take time and good nursing?"

"Exactly right, Miss Franklin," Sealy confirmed, nodding. "Now just two things. First, his physical condition. He doesn't look too good thanks to some rather serious burns on his forehead. Also, he took in so much smoke that it damaged his throat, so we haven't been able to get him to eat much. Mostly liquids and soft foods. When you first see him, don't let him see how you feel if you get a shock. He's not as bad off as he appears, though his eyes need care. Mostly you need to keep him from bright light and apply the ointment—I'll give that to you— twice a day. The burns on his right hand will heal quickly, I hope. Put the dressings on once a day and, as soon as your physician at home thinks it wise, leave the hand open to the air and light. The ankle will be painful for at least a month or more, but only time will help."

"I'll see to him, Doctor."

"Yes . . . well, the other thing isn't quite so easy. He had quite a shock, you understand, and he's not over it yet."

Rachel blinked, then asked directly, "Is his mind affected?"

"I don't like to put it like that," Sealy said quickly. He rubbed his chin, trying to put the thing to her well. "It's almost as if his thinking processes were slowed down. You'll notice that he doesn't respond to questions quickly. Or perhaps that's a way of his?"

"No, Vince has always been very quick with words."

"Well, I don't think it's a permanent thing, but he can't seem to remember very well. Again, I think he just needs rest, but you must be patient with him if he forgets some things."

"I'll do my best. But I assume he won't be seeing too many people at first. Just the family, and I'll tell them what you've said."

"Fine! Now I'm sure you want to see him. I'll take you to his room, then I'll leave you. I wish you'd watch the nurses change the dressings, things like that. We'll take him to the ship in our ambulance day after tomorrow." He rose and left the room, Rachel walking beside him. "This is his room. It'll be darkened, so you'll have to let your eyes get accustomed to that."

Rachel entered the room, and Dr. Sealy said, "Well, Mr. Franklin, your sister is here to take you home. Think you feel up to a sea voyage?"

"Yes, Dr. Sealy." The voice was husky and halting. Rachel would not have recognized it as Vincent's.

"I'll just leave you two alone," Sealy said. When he left,

Rachel moved closer to the man in the bed. One lamp burned on a table, and some dim illumination filtered through from the covering over the window. Her eyes were not adjusted to the murky room, and she stopped when she was a few feet away.

"How do you feel?"

"Pretty well, Rachel. Better than when I first came here."

"Does your throat hurt?" she asked, squinting at him. "You sound so hoarse."

"Still hurts, but not like it did. I couldn't even croak when I first got here."

"Father would have come, or Grant, but the Grays were sent to reinforce Jackson in the Valley." She saw a chair and pulled it next to the bed and sat down. "Dr. Sealy's been telling me about your injuries. He's very hopeful."

"Good man."

Rachel leaned forward and, by the light of the lamp, got her first clear view of the injured man. She let nothing show in her face, but a shock ran through her. She would never have known Vince! She was not prepared for the sight of him without a beard; she hadn't seen him clean-shaven since she was very young. What's more, his face was hollow, much thinner than she had expected, and the raw burns on his forehead were painful just to look at. His hair, which still showed signs of having been singed, was cut short, and he was wearing a pair of smoked glasses so that she couldn't see his eyes at all.

"You look awful," she said frankly. "I hope you don't feel as bad as you look!"

That seemed to amuse him, for his lips turned up and he said in a husky tone, "Just like you to cheer a fellow up, Rachel!" Then he shook his head, adding, "It could have been worse."

"Yes, I suppose so. Well, we'll leave day after tomorrow. I'll get the nurses to teach me how to take care of you."

He said nothing, and she thought, *Just like him. I come all the way around the country to help him and he can't even grunt a thank-you!*

Rachel sat there in the dimly lit room, saying little. Sometimes he would ask a question, but not often. He dropped off to sleep, and Rachel sat there beside him wishing that she had more of a heart for Vince. She knew she should care more, that that was what the Lord would want of her—but the years had not given her the love for Vince that she had for Grant and Les.

After a moment, she squared her shoulders. If she could not love him, she would at least do her duty. *I'll get him home and do what I can to care for him. Then, when he is well, he can shift for himself,* was her final thought as she rose and left the room.

She didn't like the feelings she had and wished that they were milder, more gentle, more loving. But surely even God couldn't expect her to force herself to love a man who'd spent his entire life making himself despicable.

✳ ✳ ✳

PART TWO
THE IMPOSTER

✳ ✳ ✳

CHAPTER SIX

MAN WITHOUT A STAR

RACHEL, holding a straight razor in one hand, had just touched the cold steel to Jake's face. He flinched, and she lifted the blade saying firmly, "Hold still!" Reaching out, she placed her left hand on top of his head, then drew the razor through the thick foam on his right cheek, ignoring the raspy sound it made as it plowed through his whiskers.

"Be careful with that thing," Jake pleaded, then asked, "Did you ever shave anyone before?"

Rachel, biting her lower lip with concentration, did not answer until she made another clean strip appear on Jake's cheek. Wiping the blade on a towel she'd draped over his shoulder, she began work on the other cheek. Only when it was finished did she say, "No. Now put your head back."

As she gripped the crown of his head and forced his head back, Jake decided it was no time for a debate—not with the edge of the blade moving over the taut flesh of his throat. He sat up in the bed, enduring her effort, thinking that Rachel Franklin was not very feminine, at least in her manners.

She had marched into his room at dawn with a pitcher of hot water, shaving equipment, and a determined look on her face. "Sit up," she had greeted him. "I'm going to get you cleaned up." He had wrestled himself to a sitting position, and she had practically ripped the white cotton gown from him, ignoring his startled protests. He kept the sheet pulled up as high as possible, but she had washed his upper body without a flicker in her blue-green eyes.

*She might as well be washing a dish for all the emotion she
shows,* Jake had thought, then had realized that her cold
attitude was what he could expect. She had cleaned his
face carefully, actually causing him much less pain than
any of the orderlies who had performed the same service,
then had picked up a mug and begun working up a lather
with a brush. Without a word, she had lathered his face
and begun shaving him.

Still, despite her brusque and cold manner, there was
nothing mannish about her appearance. Her simply cut
tan dress with a line of white lace at the bodice and
sleeves complemented her trimly rounded figure. As she
shaved him, her face was only inches away from Jake's,
and he could not help admiring the clean sweep of her
jaw and the silky texture of her skin. Her eyes were fixed
on the progress of the razor, so he could study her without fear of being noticed, and he was somehow surprised
to see that she was so pretty. He had expected less, for
some reason. As she held his head firmly and ran the razor over his face, he realized that there was an element in
Rachel Franklin that most women lacked—at least, most
of the women he had known.

It was not, he decided, that she was pretty, even on the
verge of true beauty. It was clear that she was physically
attractive; it would be difficult to ignore the soft round-
ness of her form or the well-shaped eyes and generous
mouth. But there was something more, a reserve in her
eyes, and the shadow of strength, intensity, and control
that intrigued him. That control was evidenced by the
firm line of her lips and the deliberate light of her eyes.
She was, he decided, possessed of a great degree of vital-
ity and imagination—which he guessed were also held
under careful restraint. As she moved the razor over his
upper lip, he observed a hint of her will—or her pride—
in the corners of her eyes and lips.

She finished the shave without speaking, carefully removed the lather with the damp cloth, then stepped
back to study him. Still she didn't speak, and Jake said,

"A good job, better than most barbers. Can't believe you've never shaved anyone."

"I'm going to change the bandage on your arm," she said, ignoring his remark. There was a cold efficiency in her manner, but she did a good job of removing the old bandage, which was the worst part of the job. She had a light touch yet moved firmly as she cleaned the burn, applied the ointment that Dr. Sealy had furnished, then bound the arm up in fresh bandages, saying, "In a week or two, it'll be better to leave the bandages off." She looked at his ankle, pushing at the swollen flesh, then remarked, "Going to take some time before you can get around on this."

"Not too long, I hope." He took the fresh gown she handed him, saying, "Rough on you, having to take care of a sick man."

"No worse than when one of the horses gets injured," she remarked without a change of expression. While he put on the gown, she picked up the shaving equipment and began to clean it. "We'll go down to the ship late this afternoon. The captain said he wants to leave after dark to avoid the blockade ships of the navy."

She left the room, and Jake stared after her. "Not much chance of Miss Rachel finding out I'm not who she thinks," he muttered. "She sure does despise you, Vince, old boy!" It was a relief to him, for he had envisioned having to try to carry on long talks with her, which would be dangerous.

After the noon meal, Dr. Sealy came by to check him, accompanied by Rachel. "You're looking better than I hoped when they brought you in," he said, standing over Jake. "You're a lucky man. If you'd been a few feet closer, they tell me, you'd have been crushed by that building."

"Wasn't my time to go," Jake said with a shrug.

"Well, you mind your sister," Sealy said. "Biggest problem I have with patients like you comes from their own foolishness. Don't try to get up too soon. Do what your nurse tells you."

"Guess I don't have much choice, tied to this chair."
Jake put out his hand and, when Sealy took it, said, "I appreciate what you've done for me, Doctor."

"Well, good-bye then, Vince. Take care of yourself."

As soon as the doctor left Rachel began putting Vince's things into a small bag. There wasn't much, for the fire had destroyed all of Vince's clothing and personal things. "I got you some extra gowns—and plenty of underwear," she said. "You won't need much, and you've got all those clothes at home that you just recently bought."

"Be glad to put some pants on!"

"Well, don't get too glad, because you won't be wearing any for a while," she said calmly. "I've got to get a few things. Anything you want to take on the boat? Whiskey or some special food?"

"No. Guess not."

She was surprised. Turning to stare at him, she said, "That's the first time you ever turned down liquor as far as I can remember." She frowned and wondered for a moment what Vince was up to. Then she brushed her hair back from her forehead and left, saying only, "All right. We'll go to the *Jupiter* about four."

Jake was restless until she returned. Being bound to the care of others was galling, but he forced himself to remain calm. Blunt followed her into the room and, when it was time to get Jake into the wheelchair, he deliberately slammed him down, drawing a sharp gasp of pain from the injured man.

Rachel had been packing, but she had not missed the scene. Anger flared in her eyes, and she moved across the room to give the orderly an abrupt shove that set him back on his heels. "You clumsy ox!" she burst out. "Get out of here!" Blunt glared at her until she said, "Maybe you'd rather I take this up with Dr. Sealy." Then he scurried out of the room, his face reddened with frustrated anger.

Jake watched with interest as Rachel paused, noting

that she was able to regain her composure only after a brief struggle. *She's got a hair-trigger temper—if she gets that mad over somebody she doesn't like, I'd like to see what she'd do if somebody hurt a person she really cared for.*

Something of his thought must have been visible in his face, for Rachel, giving him a sharp glance, flushed slightly. "I hate to see sloppy work," she said, then put the small case in his lap. "Time to go. Put your glasses on."

She waited until he took the smoked glasses out of the single pocket in his loose white shirt and settled them in place. "We're taking the chair with us," she said as they left the room, turning down the hall toward the front of the building. When they passed out into the light, despite the dark glasses, Jake was forced to shut his eyes against the glare of the sun. The wheels grated on the walk, then the chair was stopped, and Rachel said, "You'll have to give him some help."

"Yes, ma'am." Strong hands were placed under Jake's armpits, and he came out of the chair. Opening his eyes to slits, he got a close view of a black face, then he was suddenly lifted from the ground as easily as if he were a baby. "Jest set right down," a deep voice instructed, as he was placed on a padded leather seat. "Now, miss, you get in and I'll load your gear."

"The chair goes, too," Rachel said. She stepped into the coach, and soon the driver was back in the seat. "The *Jupiter* is it, miss?" Being assured, he sent the team down the street at an easy pace.

When they got to the dock, Jake's eyes had adjusted somewhat and he could see the outline of the ship waiting at the wharf. She was, he noted, a clipper-hulled vessel with three masts, which could be hung with canvas in a following wind. The engines sent their power through a big walking beam amidships to huge side paddles. As they pulled up, the driver leaped down, unloaded the chair, then helped Jake into it. "Thanks," Jake said. "Wish you could be on the other end to help me off."

The black man grinned but only shook his head. "You want me to wheel him on, miss?"

"No, I'll do that, but please put all our luggage aboard." Stepping behind the chair, she pushed Jake down to the gangplank, where a purser in a white coat was standing.

"*I'll* do that, miss. My name is Smythe," the purser offered, and soon Jake was in the cabin. It was plain and small—no larger than eight feet by ten feet—with two bunks, some built-in closets, and a small chair. Rachel took some money from her purse and handed it to the black driver, who grinned at her broadly then was gone. Smythe said, "Supper at six, Miss Franklin. Capt. Stuart would like for you and your brother to join him. Shall I come down and help Mr. Franklin to the dining room?"

"No, thank you," Rachel said. "I can manage."

As the door closed, Jake looked around, then said, "Close quarters. This blasted chair of mine takes up all the room."

"You won't be running around much," Rachel said briefly, then began to unpack their clothes. There was nothing for Jake to do but watch. As soon as she had everything put away, she took a small package from her purse and looked around the room. A bronze lamp was fixed to the wall by a bracket attached on the outer bulkhead, exactly in the center of the wall. She took what seemed to be a hoop from the packet, but it proved to be a roll of wire. She fastened one end of it to the lamp bracket, then unwound it and, finding another bracket on the inside wall just to the left of the door, she secured the free end to that. As she returned to one of the bunks where she'd placed the packet, she noticed Jake watching her.

"It's already quite dark in here. I'll cover the windows with some cloth tomorrow. That way you won't have to wear the glasses at all."

"That will be better," he commented, then asked, "What's the wire for?"

"Privacy," she answered briefly, then took some pins

from the small package and began fastening them to the side of what seemed to be a piece of very lightweight canvas. When they were in place, she stood and began slipping them over the taut wire. When the last one was in place, she tested the makeshift screen by pulling at one end. The cloth slid along the wire between the two beds, which were on opposite ends of the small cabin. Satisfied, she pulled the curtain back until it bunched against the wall.

"You're resourceful," Jake conceded. "But wouldn't it be easier to have two cabins?"

Rachel looked at him coldly. "You may have money to waste, Vince. We don't. Cash is scarce now and it's going to get more so. Do you want to lie down?"

"No." He hesitated, then asked with a sarcastic tone, "Would it be too much trouble to push me around the deck?"

Rachel's face flushed for a moment, then she shook her head. "It's almost time for dinner. Let me change, then I guess we can go around the deck a few times." Pulling the curtain, she changed her dress, then emerged and pushed him out of the cabin. For the next half hour she maneuvered him around the deck. There were few passengers there—most had gone to the dining room early—but the loading of the ship was still going on, with sailors wrestling the last of the cargo into the hold. Some of their language was fairly raw, but Jake saw that Rachel was able to ignore it. She was, he considered, the sort of person who would refrain from complaining about things that she could not help. Finally she said, "Let's go to the dining room."

She pushed him into a large room of mahogany, ivory paint, and crystal lamps. Still, though the design of luxury remained and the paint was fresh and the glasswork glittered, the original elegance had quietly vanished with the ship's youth. The same purser who had taken them to their cabin saw them enter. He came across the room to say, "Let me help you, Miss Franklin."

"Thank you, Smythe," Rachel murmured and stepped back to let the man move the wheelchair to the table. Capt. Stuart and the other gentlemen at the table rose gallantly. The captain was a short man and thick as a stump. He had a pair of icy blue eyes, but he said warmly, "Miss Franklin, we're waiting for you. I take it this is your brother?"

"Yes, Captain." Rachel nodded and slipped into her seat while the captain named the guests around the table for the newcomers. Afterward Jake sat silently, listening to the talk that flowed around the table, noting how Rachel drew the attention of the men. She wore a dark blue dress that fit snugly, and her neck and shoulders were coral against the shining of the lamps. The only jewelry she wore was a pair of sapphire earrings, their deep blue accenting her eyes.

The talk was of the war, or the effects of it. One of the men, a tall man named Prince with a startling crop of dundreary whiskers, wore the uniform of a Confederate major. He had been at Manassas and, at the request of Capt. Stuart, gave an account of what his regiment had done there. One of the ladies at the end of the table said, "I suppose it will take another battle or two to convince the Yankees to stay where they belong, Maj. Prince?"

"Well—it'll be a little more difficult than that, Mrs. Lowery," Maj. Prince said. A thought struck him and his lips curved in a smile. "Did you hear about Gen. Anderson? Well, after Fort Sumter fell he became quite a hero in the North. Don't understand why, when all he did was surrender! But in any case, he had a nervous breakdown and had to be replaced." He laughed softly, adding, "His replacement was Gen. William T. Sherman, and the joke is that Sherman's had a nervous breakdown of his own. But you know that new fellow Grant? The one who's in charge in the West? Well, he's had a drinking problem, and Sherman said, 'Grant stood by me when I was crazy, so I'll stand by him when he's drunk!'"

A laugh went around the table, and one of the men

asked, "Is that who we've got coming against us, Major? Drunks and crazy men?"

Prince shook his head, seemingly reluctant to speak, but finally he said slowly, "Lincoln is listening to Gen. Scott. He's old and too fat to ride a horse, but he's got the best military mind in the country, I do think. Scott wants to get control of the Mississippi and blockade the coast. If that happens, there will be no way we can win."

"They don't have enough ships for that, Major," Capt. Stuart commented with a shrug.

"No, but they have the shipyards to build them, Captain. And they've got the ironworks, the factories, and the know-how to arm them. Do you know we have only one major ironworks in the South, the Tredgar Ironworks in Richmond?"

"We'll buy ships from England!"

"Not if the coast is blockaded," Prince replied. "If we're going to win, we'd better win in a hurry."

"I think, sir, our only hope is to be recognized by England." The speaker was a tall man with a crown of silver hair. "If we kill enough Yankees in a hurry, the North will refuse to fight. There's already a strong antiwar party there, and if we won the next two or three battles, I think Lincoln would be forced to declare a peace."

"That is indeed our only chance, sir," Maj. Prince said, nodding. "Without that, we will fight gallantly, and to the last, but in the end we will be worn down by the North's industrial power and sheer weight of numbers."

Several men disagreed with Prince, and the talk grew lively. The food was good, but Jake was humiliated when Rachel had to cut up his meat, a fine steak. "Feel like a blasted baby!" he muttered to her, though she seemed to ignore him. He was glad when she finally said, "Capt. Stuart, thank you for your invitation. I must get my brother to bed now."

The men rose, and Smythe came to take Jake out. When they were outside, Rachel said, "Thank you, Smythe. I can manage now."

"Yes, Miss Franklin. Let me know if you need anything."

The air was cool and fresh after the stale air of the dining room, and Rachel pushed the chair past the churning paddles, coming to the fantail. The night was cloudy, and after a while, Jake said, "Any stars out, Rachel? I still can't see all that clearly."

She gazed at the sky, then said, "No, I don't see any stars."

"Good thing we're not in the middle of the ocean."

Rachel looked up at the dark skies, shook her hair loose, then said, "I wish I knew more about the stars, but they weren't included in my education."

The throbbing of the engines was like the beating of a mighty heart, and as the ship drove into the darkness, Jake said finally, "I always envied sailors, knowing how to find their way by the stars." Then he looked up and added, "But you said there's no stars out now. I guess the fellow who's lost at sea could be a man without a star."

Rachel glanced down at him, saying, "That's a poetic way of putting it, Vince—a man without a star." She reached her hand up as if to touch one of the dark clouds that was racing along overhead, then withdrew it, saying, "That's a sad thought. Every man and every woman ought to have a star, something that doesn't move so they can tell where they are."

Jake listened to the sound of the wind as it whipped over the deck, then turned to see the pilothouse, which emitted only a faint pale and golden glow, and laughed shortly. "Guess that's what I am, Rachel—a man without a star."

She looked at him, a curious light in her eyes. "That's a strange thing for you to say. You've always seemed to know exactly what you wanted."

Suddenly Jake knew he was in danger, for she was studying him carefully. He realized that he'd spoken out of his own feelings, not out of the role he was playing— and what he had said had been out of character. Vince was not a man for philosophical thought. He looked at her and smiled coldly. "Never realized you were one to be fooled by pretty talk, Rachel. If that's all it takes to change your mind about a man—"

Rachel cut him off by grabbing his chair and pushing it toward the cabin. Her voice was tight with anger as she spoke. "You're right, Vince. I should know better than to listen to anything you say." She took him to the cabin and helped him out of the chair onto the bunk. He was wearing only underwear and the long shirt, and was embarrassed as he struggled to get his leg onto the bed. Reaching down, Rachel took careful hold of it, lifted it to the bed, then pulled a sheet up over him. "Are you hurting much?" she asked, though he doubted she cared.

"Not too bad."

She studied him, then made an abrupt decision. "You'd better have something for the pain. I'll fix you a toddy." He lay there as she took the small medicine box from the drawer, poured some whiskey from a small bottle into a glass, then added some liquid from a vial. He took it and drank it down; then she said, "Call if you need something."

He grunted in response.

She moved quickly, drawing the curtain, then got undressed and put on a gown. The lamp threw off enough light for her to see, so she sat on the bunk reading a chapter of the Bible, then put it down and went to bed. She lay there listening to the man's heavy breathing as it grew slow and rhythmic. Finally, fatigue caught up with her, too.

The pounding of the engines beat steadily, and her eyelids grew heavier. In spite of herself, the last thing she thought of before she fell asleep was what Vince had said: *Guess that's what I am, Rachel—a man without a star.*

CHAPTER SEVEN

STORM AT SEA

THE *Jupiter* darted around the Florida Keys, sighting only one Federal ship, which she easily outran. The weather was favorable, but after a quick stop at Savannah, Capt. Stuart told his first mate, Alvin Sears, "We'd better skip Charleston, Sears. I don't like the feel of this weather."

Sears, a saturnine individual with a full black beard and the shoulders of a wrestler, agreed. "Be better, I think, Captain." He studied the horizon, his eyes drawn to slits, then added, "That sky reminds me of a woman. All nice and soft and pretty. But she's likely to change 'fore we can blink, and then we'll feel her claws."

"Not a great admirer of the ladies, are you?"

"Had my hide ripped too often," Sears grunted. "And I got a feeling about that sky. We'd best make the fastest run we can or you'll see the canvas ripped to shreds."

Sears would later have reason to call Capt. Stuart's attention to the accuracy of his prophecy, for as they rounded Cape Hatteras the sun disappeared and the seas began to rise. Soon the waves were so high that the passengers staring through the portholes could see the ripped-up surface of the ocean directly in front of their eyes.

Rachel and Jake became aware of the seriousness of the matter as she pushed him around the deck toward the stern, and the *Jupiter* took a trough coming around, falling into a deep gully between two waves. The ship went into the gully heavily and lay solidly there as a great ridge of water fell into her and buried her. For much too long a moment, Rachel and Jake both felt the inertness of the ship. Then the sea came aboard a second time and the well deck filled, and the port wing of the hurricane deck touched the lifting waves. Rachel grabbed a chair, bracing herself, while Jake sat there clenching the armrest of his chair with his good hand.

In the wheelhouse, Capt. Stuart held the wheel of the *Jupiter* as she plunged and bucked like a half-wild horse. He waited until the ship rose and slowly swung into the seas. He peered through the misty foam and cupped his ears to catch the possible sound of surf breaking. He knew this coast too well—it was a graveyard filled with the bones of ships and men scattered on some rocky point or sucked into a remote reach of sand.

"Take in all sail, Mr. Sears," he commanded, then called down to the engine room, "Give me all you've got, Carl!"

Sears stared at the wild seas, then at the captain. "I told you she was a hussy," he muttered, then left the wheelhouse. When he got to the stern, he saw a woman pushing a man in a wheelchair and cursed under his breath. "Get below! Get below!" he bellowed, shaking his head in disgust as the woman hurriedly moved along the tilting deck and disappeared through one of the doorways. "Woman's got no sense! Acts like we're on a ferryboat!" Then he began yelling commands to the crew, who scurried aloft to take in all the canvas.

Rachel had to brace herself to keep the wheelchair from getting away from her, but finally she made it to the door of their cabin. It was a struggle to open the door while holding on to Jake's chair, but she managed it.

With a sigh she said, "Better get out of this chair and into the bunk."

Jake used his left hand and pulled himself free from the chair to stand on one leg as she moved the chair back. A sudden lurch caught him off balance, and he fell across the edge of the bunk, striking his bad leg and sending a flash of pain along his nerves. As he rolled over onto the bunk, Rachel stooped and lifted his leg. Placing it carefully down, she glanced at his face but said only, "If this gets worse, I'll have to tie you in."

91

"If it gets worse, the ship will go down," he answered tightly. His leg was throbbing like a sore tooth, but he ignored it. "This ship can't take much of this!"

Rachel stared at him, then asked, "Is the *Jupiter* a bad ship?"

"No, but she's made for rivers, not oceans. If this keeps up, she could break in two." Jake had been on riverboats for some time and knew their limitations. As the boat seemed to hesitate, he asked, "Feel that? The paddles came out of the water—they were beating the air. That means that the captain can't get much speed out of her. Not much hope of outrunning this thing."

Rachel was thrown forward suddenly as the ship rolled, and she saved herself only by raising her hands as they slammed against the bulkhead. She stood there, waiting for what seemed like a long time, until the ship recovered. Then she cautiously moved to sit down on her bunk. There was no sign of panic on her face, Jake noted—only an expression of heightened alertness. She said nothing, as did he. The roar of the wild water, which was kept from them only by a thin wall, was joined by the high-pitched keening of the wind. The wind was like a wild animal that prowled around the *Jupiter* seeking entrance, shrieking at times before it subsided into a low moaning sound.

For an hour the two kept to their bunks, Jake lying flat and Rachel sitting up, balancing as if she were in a small boat in tricky waters. Night came and the stygian darkness swallowed the *Jupiter*, seeming to magnify the sounds of the storm.

Rachel got up and managed to light both lamps. The yellow light flickered over the cabin, and she said, "I've never been in anything like this. It's not like a storm on land."

"No. On land you can get under something or run. Not in one of these, though. There's no place to hide."

The amber light gave her face an oriental appearance, and the shadows it cast brought her cheekbones into prominence and emphasized the greenish tint of her eyes, making her look even more Asian. Or perhaps, Hardin thought, it was her stillness, which was a characteristic of the oriental races, that brought that image to mind. But no, he decided, for he had seen Chinese coolies get frantic in a mild storm on the Mississippi.

"Are you afraid?" he asked finally.

She looked at him, wondering at his question, then nodded. "I suppose so."

"You sure don't look it!"

"No sense running and screaming, is there?"

"Well, no. But sometimes in a spot like this, it's hard not to do just that."

"We're in a dangerous storm," she said, and reaching up, she tucked a lock of honey-colored hair under a pin. It was a common enough gesture, but one that was somehow intensely feminine, or so it seemed to Jake. Most women, he reflected, wouldn't be thinking of their hair at such a time. She shrugged, then went on to say, "We may die. That's enough to make anyone afraid."

Jake lay there, wondering at her statement, for it didn't seem to go with her calmness. He thought of what Vince had told him of his sister, that she was very religious. This knowledge had not impressed him greatly, for he had seen some poor samples of Christians from time to time. It suddenly occurred to him as he lay there: *Well, I've been in a poor place to see Christians. Dealing poker in a floating saloon—it's not like I worked in a store in town.*

The thought would not leave him, and he said finally, "I guess you're so calm because you've got religion."

Something about what he had said displeased her. She gave her head a slight negative shake and clamped her lips together. "I'll go get us something to eat," she said, and she left the cabin, balancing herself like a tightrope walker.

Why did that offend her? Jake thought, a puzzled expression wrinkling his brow. *What was wrong with what I said? Maybe it wasn't the sort of thing Vince would say. Got to watch it more closely.*

Rachel came back thirty minutes later with a small sack and a pitcher. "Just sandwiches and milk," she said.

"Not sure it's a good idea to eat, anyway."

"Yes, you must eat." She pulled a sandwich from the sack, handed it to him, then picked up a cup and managed to pour it half-full of milk. She sat there holding it as he ate, despite his request that she eat her own sandwich. The sandwich was dry—cold roast beef flavored with mustard. "Cow must have been a hundred years old," he complained, then took a drink from the cup she handed him. "What's it like outside?"

"I've never seen such waves," Rachel said. "Like mountains. Too dark to see much. It'd be much more frightening in the day, I suppose. Now all a person can do is guess at how high they are."

Jake suddenly gave her a thin grin. "Rather see things than think about them."

Rachel considered his statement, then said, "You don't really think that, Vince."

"Why don't I?"

She spoke evenly, without heat. "Because you've never been a man who'd look at things as they are. Even when you were a boy you'd never look trouble in the face. You'd always run away." A thought touched her, and she gave him a sharp glance. "Remember when you and Les and I rode Daddy's prize yearling?"

"Well—"

"You don't remember?" Rachel lifted her head, surprise in her eyes. "Funny you'd forget that. I was so young I shouldn't be able to remember, but I do." Then she shook her head abruptly. "The calf stepped into a hole and broke his leg. I think we were all about as scared as we'd ever been. But you said, 'Just don't say anything.' And Les said, 'No, Daddy will find out, and I'd rather get it over with.'" The ship lifted, then fell, and she waited until the paddles caught. Then with a slight look of relief on her face, she said quietly, "Les and I went to Daddy and told him. He used the strap on both of us. But you got out of it. When Daddy asked Les if you were in on it, he lied about it. Said it was just the two of us."

Jake fingered the button on his shirt, then remarked, "No one likes a whipping."

"You certainly don't," Rachel said with asperity. "You've never faced up to anything unpleasant in your life! So don't tell me you'd rather watch those big waves, Vince. You know better, or—," she broke off and gave him a glimpse tinged with contempt that she made no attempt to conceal. "Or maybe you've got yourself to believing your own lies. I guess that's what all liars come to in time."

Jake had no idea how to answer but assumed that Vince would have given a bitter reply, so he said, "You're no better! All that religion is just a coat you put on. That's why you got sore when I asked you if it helped, isn't it?"

"Let's drop it." Rachel took the mug, put it down, then sat down on her bunk and ate half of a sandwich. The ship was rolling so badly that she was suddenly conscious of a certain queasiness. "Maybe you were right," she said. "Not the best time to eat."

The storm raged all night. By the next morning, both of them were half sick with the rolling. Rachel said, "We'd better skip the shave today. But I'll change your bandages." She moved about carefully and, finally, after she'd gathered the supplies, came to his bunk. It took considerable art to change his bandages as the deck tilted abruptly, but she finished, then said, "I'll go see if I can find out what's happening."

Jake waited until she left, then managed to get out of his bunk and into the wheelchair. It gave him a perverse pleasure to do something for himself instead of having Rachel do it. He put on his glasses, then rolled himself to the porthole and stood up, balancing on his good leg and bracing his left hand against the wall. The world outside was gray soup, with great, dark waves appearing out of it to slap the *Jupiter* as a man would cuff a small dog, and he felt the awesome force of the blows.

He became so engrossed in watching the seas run over the deck that he didn't notice that his wheelchair had moved toward the door. And then, when the ship gave an unexpected lurch and he reached back to grab the chair, his hand encountered only air. He waved his good arm wildly, then was driven backward, which was a disaster. He twisted his bad leg and cried out with the pain, then fell sideways, his head catching the steel corner of his bunk. At once he felt the hot blood trickle down over his ear as pain tore at him.

When Rachel returned ten minutes later, she found him sitting on the floor, his nightshirt drenched with blood. "What in the world—?!"

Jake, angry at himself and humiliated, snapped, "I fell down."

Rachel shook her head, then bent over. "Get into the bunk," she ordered crossly. He leaned on her, and it took all her strength to help lift him. When he was in the bunk, she got her bandages out, washed the cut in his scalp, then shook her head. "Not quite bad enough for stitches." She put a fiery antiseptic on it, ignoring his involuntary grunt of pain, then bandaged it. "Just what you needed," she muttered. Then as she gathered her supplies, she asked, "How in the world did you manage to cut yourself?"

"Wanted to see out the window," Jake said defiantly. "What's the captain say?"

"I talked to one of the officers. He says if we don't sink before the storm blows itself out, we might make it. He wasn't," she added wryly, "a very optimistic soul."

"Neither am I," Jake admitted. "And it's worse lying here like a sick baby."

She moved to the porthole, looked out for a long time, then sat down on her bunk. When she picked up her Bible and started reading it, he lay there for half an hour, then said with some irritation, "Well, read some of it to me, will you?"

Rachel looked up and the corners of her lips lifted slightly. "You want to hear some of the Bible?"

"Try to find a good part," he said morosely. "I don't need to hear all about how I'm going to hell. I know that already. Isn't there something in there about how to get out of trouble? Daniel in the lions' den, maybe?"

A thought came to Rachel, one that seemed to please her. "The twenty-seventh chapter of the book of Acts," she said, finding the place, and began to read: "'And when it was determined that we should sail into Italy, they delivered Paul and certain other prisoners unto one named Julius, a centurion of Augustus' band. . . .'"

Jake listened as Rachel read the story of Paul's voyage on his way to Rome. He had never read the Bible, but the story was thrilling and Rachel was a fine reader. She read how the voyage was a difficult one, then she read, "'But not long after there arose against it a tempestuous wind, called Euroclydon—'"

"Wait a minute," Jake asked. "You mean that the storm had a name?"

"Yes. Euroclydon."

"Funny, a storm having a name, like a horse or something." He glanced out the window, then said, "If I had to name that one out there, I'd call it *Rita.*"

"*Rita?* Why *Rita?*"

"Because I had a girl once who acted about as cantankerous as that storm." He grinned, then said, "Go on— what happened to the fellows on the ship?"

Rachel read on through the chapter, and when it was finished, he said, "Well, I guess it came out all right, but the ship sank."

"But nobody died," Rachel reminded him. She ran her fingers over the page, then looked up. "I've always liked the part where in the middle of the storm—just when things looked the blackest—Paul told how an angel had come to him and promised that none of them on the ship would die."

"You think that actually happened?" Jake asked. "That there are angels and they talk to people?"

"I believe it happens sometimes, not often," Rachel

said evenly. Then she smiled, "Paul said, 'I believe God, that it shall be even as it was told me.'" The ship rolled, but she smiled, seeming to forget the moaning of the wind and the cracking of the ship itself. "More than anything else, I want to say that I believe God!"

She spoke with such passion that Jake knew she had allowed part of that which she kept hidden to come out. Finally he said, "I guess you do believe it, Rachel. I hope you always do." Then he realized that such a statement from Vince would be unlikely, so he growled, "But I don't think God's going to reach down and pull us out of this storm. That's up to Capt. Stuart and the crew."

"No it's not," Rachel said calmly but then said no more.

Finally, the storm lost its force, fading away like a whipped dog. It was so sudden that the silence seemed hollow somehow. When Rachel took Jake up on deck at three that afternoon, the sun was shining and the water was a sparkling blue.

"Well, it didn't get us that time, did it?" Jake said.

"No."

Her brief reply drew his attention, and he looked up at her. She was facing the bow, and the wind was pulling at her hair. Suddenly she reached up and pulled out some pins, allowing it to fall down her back. There was a smile on her broad lips and a look in her eyes that he couldn't name. Peace, maybe, but more than that.

"Look how still the sea is," she said quietly. "Just like the rolling hills back of the house at Lindwood."

"Well, I'll be glad to get there," Jake answered.

"Will you?" she asked, and it seemed his statement had driven away the lightness of her mood. "What about Duvall? He'll be there, still wanting to shoot you." When he made no reply, she said, "I don't suppose he can shoot a cripple. And that's what you're counting on, isn't it?"

He felt the pressure of her words and the obvious direction of her thoughts but said only, "I guess so, Rachel."

The pleasure of the moment was gone and, though the

weather was fine for the rest of the voyage, there was a barrier between the two of them. Rachel tended to his wounds and saw that he got his meals, but there was no warmth in her.

Going to be a rough homecoming, Jake thought as the ship dropped anchor with a loud rattle at the wharf in Richmond. *If she's this tough, what will the rest of the family be like?*

CHAPTER EIGHT

HOMECOMING

Rᴀᴄʜᴇʟ waited until the hard, bright October sunshine began to fade, then left the *Jupiter*. She went to Harvey Simmons's livery stable to rent a wagon and, as she had expected, was questioned closely by the owner.

Simmons, a talkative man of fifty-five, chatted steadily as he hitched a horse to the buggy, giving her a running commentary on the city until he finally got down to finding out her business. "Heard you went to New Orleans to pick up Vince, Miss Rachel." His eyes were bright as a crow's as he looked up, asking innocently, "He's all right, is he?"

"He got some injuries in a hotel fire, Harvey." Her wry sense of humor came to her aid, and she rattled off the information Harvey was trying to pry out of her, including a summary of the fire itself and the hospital where Vince had stayed. Then she added, "He's got a bad right leg, a bad right hand, some burns on his face, and his eyes are sensitive to light. But with good care, he'll be fine. Just pass that along to anyone who might be interested, Harvey."

Simmons flushed, for he understood the irony in her voice, but he said only, "Well, that's fine. Folks'll be glad to hear it." He stepped back, saying, "Here you are, Miss Rachel. This here mare is real gentle. Won't give you no trouble. Lemme help you up."

Rachel accepted his hand and settled herself in the seat, saying, "Thank you, Harvey. I'll have Tad bring the rig back in the morning."

But Simmons could no more resist speaking of a juicy rumor than he could help breathing. "I heard that Simon

Duvall ain't gonna let the thing drop—about Vince and his wife."

"Did he tell you that?"

"Well, no, but Leo Bates heard him say so. According to Leo, Duvall's going to open up on Vince as soon as he sees him." The man was as avid a gossip as ever drew breath, almost slavering as he probed at Rachel. "Whut you think Vince will do? I mean, he can't live in this county for long without running across Duvall, can he now?"

Rachel took the reins, spoke to the mare, and as the buggy left the stable, she called, "I'll get back to you as soon as I find out what's happening, Harvey!"

Simmons cursed under his breath, then kicked at a stall, startling the gray gelding inside. "Well, ain't she proud now! Like to take a strap to her!" Then he went inside the office and said to a long-legged man who was whittling a piece of cedar into a chain, "Leo, you know what? I think it's gonna be a shootin'—yessiree, I think Vince Franklin is gonna get himself perforated!" He sat down and drew out the possible scenarios for the affair, and within two or three hours he had gotten the word out that Simon Duvall and Vince Franklin were sure enough going to have a gunfight.

As she drove to the wharf, Rachel understood that putting a story of Vince's return in the paper would not get the news around Richmond nearly as fast as the long tongue of Harvey Simmons could manage it. It was, she realized, inevitable, and she turned her thoughts from it as she pulled the buggy up in front of the gangplank of the *Jupiter*. Capt. Stuart was waiting for her on deck and gave her a gallant salute. "Hoped to see you before you left," he said, smiling at her. "I sent Smythe down to get Mr. Franklin all ready, Miss Rachel."

"Why, that was thoughtful of you, Captain," Rachel said with a smile. Stuart was young enough to feel flattered and old enough to be concerned. He had picked up on some of the problems that her brother was likely to bring to her and was sorry to hear it. "It was a nice voyage, storm and all," she said.

"Well, it's going to get a little more tricky as this blockade thing keeps going. You tell your father if he wants anything shipped out or brought back, he'd better take care of it."

"I'll tell him, Captain, and you be careful. Don't let the Yankees get you." She had seen Smythe pushing the wheelchair, with two of the crew following with their luggage, and offered Stuart her hand. "Good-bye, Captain."

"I think we got everything, Miss Franklin," Smythe said. He led the way down the gangplank, then said, "Give me a hand, men." The three of them put the injured man on the seat, then loaded the chair and the rest of the luggage in the back of the buggy. "Good-bye, miss," he said, then began to protest when she held out some bills.

"You've been so good to us, Smythe," she said with a smile. "I couldn't have made it without you!"

As the buggy drove off, Smythe said, "Now there's a real lady, boys! The genuine article!" His eyes filled with admiration. He gave a bill from the cash Rachel had given him to each of the men, then added, "That brother of hers, he's not like her at all. Too bad!"

Rachel put the mare at a fast trot, and by the time they had cleared the city limits and were on the road leading to Lindwood, night had fallen. The stars were out and a silver medallion of a moon began to climb the skies, casting pale bars of light on the back of the mare.

"Good to be off the ship," Rachel said. "It was an adventure for me, but I'm not much of a sailor."

"I think you have to start in early for that," Jake agreed. He was breathing in the odors of the countryside, savoring the smell of rich earth and trees and the sharp, acrid odor of woodsmoke. "I always like fall best," he remarked.

"That's not what you always said," Rachel pointed out.

"How many times have I heard you curse the fall just because it meant winter was coming?"

Jake laughed quickly. "I suppose that's so. But right now, it's pretty nice, especially after that little cabin—and after the hospital."

They spoke little, which was a relief to Jake. He was not on guard enough, and even a small remark such as he had made about preferring a certain season could be dangerous. *Got to keep my mouth shut,* he thought, and he did so for most of the trip.

When they turned off on a side road, Rachel said, "There's the house." When he didn't answer, she asked, "Can't you see it?"

"Well, just blurred, is all."

Rachel said no more, and soon she was pulling the buggy to a halt. As she did so, Les came running out of the house.

"Hey!" he called to Rachel with a grin. "You made it back!"

"Yes, Les," Rachel answered, smiling at him. "And now you can help us. Get that chair out of the back of the buggy, will you? And you'll have to help Vince into it."

"Sure, Rachel." Les lifted the chair and moved it beside the buggy, then, with a powerful grip, he swung Jake to the ground. Jake dropped into the chair with a grimace.

Les looked at him for a moment, then said, "You look like the devil, Vince!"

"Never mind that, Les," Rachel said. "Just bring his things in. Oh, and take the buggy back to Simmons's stable in the morning, will you? Or have Tad do it."

With that, she moved behind the chair and pushed it down the brick walkway that led to the big white house but turned to follow a smaller walk that led around to the side. "I can't manage those front steps," she remarked. "We'll go in by the back." The ground rose slightly, and Jake saw that the back door was on ground level, or almost so. When Rachel called, "Dee! Come and open the door," a woman stepped outside. She held the door open as Rachel lifted the chair wheels up the slight step.

"We done got the downstayuhs bedroom ready," Dee said "We even moved the furniture n'all from his reg'lar room, though I doan know why we done so much." She was a tall, heavy woman of sixty, no longer strong, but knowing everything about Lindwood. "We kin take bettuh keer of 'im there, though."

"That's fine, Dee," Rachel said and moved down a long hall that divided the house. The door at the end was open, and she turned the chair and entered.

It was, Jake saw, a large bedroom, with heavy mahogany furniture and a large bay window opening out onto a garden. "You're probably tired," Rachel said, and she herself had lines of fatigue on her face. "I'll get you ready for bed."

"No, you go on up to yoah momma's room," Dee said. "She's done had a fall."

Rachel whirled to face the tall black woman, exclaiming, "Dee! What happened?"

"You knows that ol' porch on the little house? Miss Amy went out there three days 'go to git somethin', and she forgot about that rotten ol' porch!" Her black face was heavy as she added, "Done gone and broke one laig and twisted t'other one, so she can't no wise git around." Dee saw the alarm on Rachel's face and moved to pat her affectionately on the shoulder. "Now, now, it ain't gonna kill her, but you go on. She's been waitin' for you."

Rachel glanced at Jake, but Dee said impatiently, "I done diapered him plenty of times, so I reckon I can still shove him into a bed! Now git on to yoah momma, chile."

She waited until Rachel hurried out of the room, then turned to Jake, and he saw her eyes harden. "Well, you want somethin' to eat?"

"Just some water, Dee."

She stared at him, asking finally, "Thas all you wants? Jes water?"

"I'm not hungry, but some cool water would be good."

"Fust time you been to bed sober since I kin remember!" She pushed the chair over to the bed and moved to help him, but he shook his head and stood on his good leg, then turned awkwardly and sat down on the bed. "I got you some fresh clothes," she said. "You want me to change you?"

"Just the water, Dee."

Jake changed into the clean nightshirt, then when Dee came back he drank thirstily from the glass she handed him. When he handed it back, he said, "I'm pretty tired. Guess I'll get some sleep."

Standing back, she cocked her head and studied him through a pair of wise old eyes. "You looks like you been drug through a knothole," she announced. "And you sounds funny, all husky like."

"Breathed too much smoke, Dee," Jake said quickly.

She didn't move, and there was something monolithic about her. Vince had said once, *If you can fool Dee, you can fool anybody, Jake. She's as sharp as a tack! And she raised us kids, so she knows every scar on my body—least those I had before I left home.*

"You doan look like yo'self," Dee said, then shrugged. "Nevah thought shavin' off a patch of whiskahs could make so much difference in a man. You want anything, ring dat bell on the table." She moved to the lamp, turned it down until it made only a dimple of yellow light in the large room, then left, moving heavily across the floor. Jake took a deep breath, somewhat unsteadily, then closed his eyes and was asleep almost instantly.

Rachel found her mother sitting up in bed reading her Bible and moved to her at once, exclaiming, "Mama— what an awful thing!"

Amy Franklin, at the age of thirty-nine, was still an attractive woman, but the accident had dimmed her natural vigor and drawn her down. "Fool thing to do!" she said, glaring bitterly at her legs under the blanket. "You'd think a woman would have enough sense to watch where she's going, wouldn't you?"

"I'll bet it hurt like fury," Rachel said, drawing up a chair. She brushed a strand of dark hair from her mother's forehead and listened as the older woman told her about the accident. But soon she said, "That's enough of that. Now tell me about Vince."

Rachel gave her the details, and her mother asked at once, "Has he changed?"

"I—don't know, Mama," Rachel said hesitantly. "It was a close call, you know. He could have died." She tried to put her thoughts together, saying slowly, "He's very quiet—not like himself at all in that way. He's not badly hurt, or not permanently, at least, but I think the whole thing must have scared him."

"What makes you think so?"

"Oh, I don't know—" She shook her head, saying, "He *looks* different. Still like Vince, but not really. There's just something that makes you look twice to be sure it's really him. You'll be shocked, I think." She went into the details—the loss of the beard, the scars on the forehead, the dark glasses. "He even *sounds* different, sort of husky. The doctor at the hospital was afraid it might be permanent, though he never told Vince that."

Amy sat there, thinking hard, then said, "We've got to have more help, Rachel."

"I can take care of the house."

"Not and take care of two invalids. Dee's getting too old to do a lot, and you know what a lot of ninnies the younger ones are. No, I want you to get a woman to come and live here until things get better."

"Who would you like?"

"I've been thinking it over, and it seems the best choice would be Melora, if she'll come."

"Why, yes, that's a good idea, Mama," Rachel said at once. "She's about the most efficient person I know— and nice, too. I'll go in the morning and talk her into coming."

"She may be glad to come," Amy said. "Can't be much of a life for her living out in the middle of the woods. The Yancys are good people, but with Lonnie and Bob gone to the army, and Royal married, it must be pretty hard out there on their place. Cora is there now—the second girl, the one who married the Day boy, and Rose is sixteen. They can take care of the two young ones." She shifted her legs, and her lips tightened at the pain. "Go early, Rachel. I think it'd be good for Melora." She smiled slightly, adding, "Rev. Irons will have to come and visit me pretty often."

Rachel shook her head. "You've been trying to marry them off for a long time, Mama." She hesitated, then asked, "What about Melora and Uncle Clay?"

Amy shook her head firmly. "Clay's married, and Ellen won't ever give him up. Melora is wasted as a single woman. She's what, almost twenty-seven now? And Brother Irons isn't getting any younger."

"He's forty-one," Rachel said, adding what they both knew. "He could have married a dozen times after his wife died—but he loves Melora." Then she laughed, her eyes bright in the lamplight. "We're getting to be worse gossips than Harvey Simmons! But I'll go talk with Melora in the morning. If she agrees, she can come back with me. I hope she'll come, though. It would be good to have her."

The next morning, Jake was awakened by Dee, who came in bearing a tray of eggs, grits, ham, and biscuits. As he ate, she sat down and watched him, her eyes never swerving. Her survey made Jake nervous, and he asked, "Where's Rachel this morning?"

"Gone to git some help wif dis house." Then she said, "They wasn't no need o' dat. I speck dey's enough lazy slaves on de place to take keer of it." She sat there rocking slightly, then added, "But if we gotta have outside folks, I speck Miss Melora Yancy is de' best could be had."

Jake almost asked who Melora Yancy was, then realized abruptly that he probably should know—or rather, that Vince would know. He said no more, and after breakfast, Dee insisted on cleaning him up and changing his bandages. She went at it as if he were a large doll, flopping him about and scrubbing at raw flesh without mercy. Jake hadn't realized how gentle Rachel was but determined either to have her change the dressings or do it himself in the future.

After the ordeal, he said, "Dee, bring me the family pictures."

She looked at him with surprise, but he said, "My eyes are too sensitive to read, but I can look at pictures." He had made a guess that there would be some and was pleased when she returned with quite a collection. "Here dey is," Dee announced. "I got to go to work." She left him, and for the next hour and a half, he studied the tintypes. There were a lot of them, and he enjoyed guessing at the identity of some of the people whose names were not written under the pictures.

One group picture intrigued him—a large family portrait, obviously taken at some sort of a reunion. For a long time he studied the faces, trying to fit them with what Vince had told him. Vince's own family was the easiest, for he knew the two boys beside Rachel had to be Grant and Les, and that the man and woman with them had to be her parents. He knew that the man in the uniform of a Union officer had to be either Gideon or Mason Rocklin, probably Gideon, since he looked too young to be the brother of Thomas. Clay Rocklin he was fairly certain of, for he bore a striking resemblance to his father. The others he could speculate on but realized that in every case he'd have to listen until he heard a name given.

He heard a man's voice in the hall and looked up as the door opened and a Confederate officer came into the room. He was not much older than forty, a wiry man of medium height, with neat features and agreeable brown eyes.

"Hello, Vince," the officer said. "How are you doing?"

"Oh, very well," Jake said, his mind racing, but coming up with nothing. "Sit down," he invited.

The major took a seat, saying, "Your mother is feeling better. That was a nasty break she got." He shook his head, adding, "The doctor still thinks it might give her permanent problems."

"You mean—she might be lame?"

"Well, that's what Dr. Maxwell said, but you know him, always looking on the dark side. I'm believing God will give her a perfect leg."

Suddenly it came to Jake, something that Vince had said:

The preacher is named Jeremiah Irons. Nice enough fellow, I suppose. Falling down in love with a girl named Melora, poor white girl. Funny thing is, my uncle Clay, he's in love with her, too! A good-looking woman, dead gone on my uncle. But she won't get him. He's got a wife—or kind of a wife, I guess. So they're all three miserable!

Jake said carefully, "Can't talk too much, Reverend. Took in too much smoke."

"Rachel told me about it," Irons said, nodding. "From what she said, you're fortunate to be alive." He gave Jake an odd look, adding, "She said you went back into the burning building to pull a man out."

Jake felt a danger here and waved his good hand in a gesture of denial. "I'd like to be a hero, Reverend, but the truth is he had some money he'd won from me, and I wanted to get it back. Sorry to disappoint you."

Irons shrugged, then began asking about how long he expected to be in the wheelchair, but in the middle of Jake's answer, the door opened and Rachel came in with a lovely dark-haired young woman. "I've brought Melora to help for a while, Vince," she said.

"Hello, Melora," Jake said slowly. "I'll try to cause you all the trouble I can. I'm a rotten patient."

"You're rotten when you're *not* a patient," Rachel said sharply, then flushed and laughed uncomfortably.

"Sorry, Brother Irons. I usually try to be good when there's a minister close by."

"So do most other people, Rachel." Irons smiled at her sharp humor, then said, "I'll be moving along. Just wanted to pray with your mother and see how Vince was doing."

Jake said quickly, "You'll notice he didn't pray for me. Rev. Irons knows a hopeless case when he sees one!"

Irons shook his head, saying, "I didn't want to make you angry, like I did the last time I tried to pray for you."

Melora and Rachel exchanged smiles, and Irons added ruefully, "I thought I'd been cussed out by experts, but you made me realize there's a level in profanity far above any I'd ever suspected. But—I sneaked around and prayed for you before I came in. Not much you can do about that, is there?"

"I guess not," Jake murmured.

"Go help Melora carry her things in," Rachel commanded. "I like to see a preacher do a little work once in a while." When they were gone, she turned to Jake, asking, "Did Dee feed you and change your bandages?"

"Yes, and she won't do it again—change my bandages, I mean," Jake said adamantly. "She's got a touch like a blacksmith!"

Rachel laughed out loud, which Jake thought was a delightful sound, then said, "I guess she can feed you and I'll be the nurse. Are you going to let your whiskers grow back?"

"No, they're pretty itchy. But if you'll fix the water and strop the razor, I think I can manage it."

"With your left hand? You can't even throw a rock with your left hand," she said scornfully. She left, coming back with hot water, and as she lathered his face and picked up the razor, she talked about the farm, especially about the horses. He sat very still as she shaved him, her presence stirring him in a way that was becoming more and more familiar—which made it all that much more dangerous.

When she was finished, she carefully removed the bits of dry lather with a moist towel, saying, "I know you don't like horses much. I've bored you talking about them."

Jake loved horses, so he was glad that she'd given him a tip on how he was supposed to react. "Well, you know me and horses."

"I still think you're as much of the problem as the horses, though," she pronounced calmly. "Horses know somehow when a person is afraid of them. If you'd just get over your fear, I think you'd be a good rider."

"How do you figure that?"

"Why, you're strong and you've got good balance," she said.

Disturbed by her gaze, Jake decided to steer the conversation away from himself. He glanced at the door, saying, "The preacher, he's still mooning over Melora, I see." He saw that the remark displeased Rachel and added quickly, "What he ought to do is drag her off by the hair and make her love him. That'd bring her around."

Rachel's eyes darkened with frustration and anger at his callousness. "You're a fool, Vince," she said in a low voice.

"No, just a realist," Jake said, pushing his advantage. "She can't have Clay, so she needs to forget him and take somebody else. The preacher's a nice fellow and he wants her. I don't see what her problem is."

Rachel looked at him with thinly veiled disgust. She noted that the plaster on the cut on his forehead had not been changed and in one motion reached out, gripped it, and ripped it off with a sharp yank.

"Ow!" Jake yelled, clapping his hand to the spot. "You're worse than Dee, Rachel! Next time give a man a little warning, will you?"

Rachel gave him a withering glance. "Vince, you're probably the most unfeeling man I ever met, except, of course, when it comes to your own hide. You've been around enough to know Melora's a woman who's never done a wrong thing in her life. And then there's the good man Uncle Clay has become—and all you can say is they ought to just forget what they feel!"

"Well? What do *you* say?"

She moved away from him toward the door, pausing only long enough to say, "When you love someone, you don't toss that person away—but you'll never understand that." Then she was gone, and Jake lay there rubbing his smooth cheek, a thoughtful look on his face.

Irons carried Melora's shabby suitcase to her room, then the two of them went outside. "I'm glad you're here, Melora," he said, unhitching his horse. "Amy needs you."

"I'm glad to be here, Jeremiah," Melora said, then smiled at him. "Now I can come and hear you preach to the troops in Richmond. I'd like that."

Irons brightened at once. "I'm preaching this Sunday to the whole brigade," he said. "Would you let me come and get you?"

"If I can get away—and if you really want to."

He stood there, at a loss for words, the way he usually was in her presence. She was for Irons the most desirable woman on earth, and he had not taken a wife because he longed to have her. Now he said slowly, "It's a bad time, Melora, but I'm just a simple preacher." He struggled a moment, then shrugged. "I can't think of any way to say it that I haven't already tried. I love you, Melora."

She dropped her eyes for a moment and when she lifted them, he saw they were filled with tears. "Why— Melora!" he said, taking her hands. "I didn't mean to make you cry!"

"It's—all right, Jeremiah," she said quietly. She let her hands rest in his, then said, "You're the most loyal, persistent man in the world, Rev. Jeremiah Irons. You could have married I don't know how many fine women, but you keep on waiting around for me."

"Melora, I know you care for Clay," Irons said abruptly. "Well, so do I. He's the best friend I've ever had. But you'll never have any happiness with him, and I think you know that. He'll never leave Ellen." His grip on her hands tightened, and he urged her, "Love can come to a person, Melora. I can make you love me if you'll just give me a chance."

At that moment, Dee came out of the house, calling, "Miss Melora! Miss Amy she say come to her room soon as you kin!"

"All right, Dee."

The moment between Melora and Irons was broken, but Melora was greatly touched. She looked at the preacher and said, "Perhaps you're right. About learning to love." She paused for a moment, then smiled. "Come and get me Sunday, Jeremiah."

She turned and left, and Irons sprang into the saddle, his face glowing. It was the most encouraging thing she'd ever said to him. In a sudden burst of excitement he kicked his horse with both heels and shot out of the driveway at a dead run.

"Dat preacher, he sho' is feelin' good," Tad said aloud as he watched the minister tear along the road. "Wonder whut got him feeling so good? He don't drink no hard likker and he ain't chasin' no gals!" The slave watched until the horse and rider disappeared, then began to whistle as he moved toward the stable.

CHAPTER NINE

RACHEL'S CHALLENGE

ON THE first day of November, Jake Hardin awoke with a grim determination. He opened his eyes, thinking at once of his resolve of the previous night. It was time to stop being an invalid. At once he threw off the blankets and struggled to a sitting position. The pain in his leg was dull now, rather than sharp as it had been when he had first arrived at Lindwood, and his hand was better—good enough so that he could flex his fingers slowly.

Carefully he swung his left leg to the floor, then used his good hand to lift his bandaged ankle and place it alongside the good one. His wheelchair was beyond his reach, but he pulled himself off the bed and, by hopping on one foot, was able to get to it. He tried to push himself around in the chair, but his right hand was too sensitive to be of much good. "Guess I could go around in a circle," he said after a futile attempt to get across the room. Finally, he figured out how to move the chair by using his good left hand on both wheels—a slow method and one that irritated him, but he managed it.

He spent the next half hour shaving himself. Rachel kept his shaving gear on the dark washstand, and it was a matter of using his right hand to push things around, while using his left for the careful work. Since the wheelchair wasn't high enough, he was forced to stand, using only his good leg. Stropping the blade was beyond him, but he managed to lather up in the cold water, then to scrape off his whiskers using his left hand. When he was finished, he went to sit down, his right leg aching, the left trembling with the unaccustomed exercise.

But he had done it! A sense of satisfaction ran through

him as he maneuvered himself toward the large wardrobe. As he opened the door and looked through Vince's clothing, he thought of how he'd managed to survive his first week. It had been fairly simple, for he'd had no visitors and Brad and Grant were gone with the army. Jake had seen only the family and the house servants, but that had gone well.

He picked out a pair of fawn trousers that were cut rather full and decided he could get them on over his bandaged leg. He chose a white shirt with bone buttons and found fresh underwear next. Then came the monumental struggle of getting the clothes on. The trousers were the hardest, but he managed them by slipping the right trouser leg over his bandaged leg and working it up. The left leg was easy, and after he had slipped on the shirt, he stuffed the tail of it into the pants, then fastened them.

What he'd done so far had been the most exercise he'd had since the fire, but he could sense that he was on the mend. There was some pain and discomfort, but that would pass. He was a stubborn man, and now his whole mind was fixed on getting well. He would push himself hard until he was whole again.

The air was cold in the room, and he looked at the fireplace, longing to put some wood on the coals he knew were hidden under a blanket of gray ash. With a shake of his head, he decided to save that for another day.

Jake moved the chair over to the window. A group of squirrels were chattering just outside, chasing each other around a large oak tree that rose above the house itself. The day was clear, and Jake had a good view of the front yard. He looked at it in surprise—it was huge! The grass was dead and brown, of course, but in the summer he knew that it would be green and lush and clipped like a carpet. This most definitely was the home of a rich man. How different such a life was from his own. He had grown up in poverty, having to make his own way from the time he was only fifteen years old. Vince, he reflected,

had had everything he had not: horses, expensive clothing, a good education. Jake had managed to have some
of those things, but only because he had wrested them
from the world by his wits and his muscles. He wondered what it would be like to have them come without a
struggle but could not imagine it.

Just then, a flash of movement caught his eye, and he
shifted his glance to see Rachel riding across a wide pasture surrounded by a white fence. She was on a sleek
black horse, and as he watched, she took the fence in a
perfectly executed jump. She wheeled her mount
around, and Jake could see the expression of pleasure on
her face as she passed. There was in her, he thought,
more joy than he had found in anyone before. This was a
quality he admired—perhaps because he had even less of
it than most men. The hardness of his life had allowed
for little except survival and had given him a cynical outlook that he could not seem to put away, even when circumstances were pleasant. He always was unconsciously
getting ready for the hard things that he knew lay over
the next hill.

With a sigh, he reached for the photographs, going
through them again. He had studied them for hours and,
by carefully commenting on them to Dee or Melora or
Rachel, had been able to learn the identity of most of the
people pictured.

Dee was his best source. She didn't like him, but she
was proud of the family. All Jake had to do was show her
a picture and ask, "When was this one made, Dee?" and
she would sit down and go over everyone, giving little incidents that helped Jake get them fixed in his mind.
When Jake had showed her the first picture in this way,
she glanced at it and remarked, "Now you see that scar
on Mistuh Paul's face? He got 'dat when he fell in a horse
race in Kentucky." Jake kept her talking, and before long
he discovered that Paul was the oldest son of Marianne,
who was Amy Franklin's aunt and the only sister of Stephen and Thomas Rocklin; that Marianne was married

to Claude Bristol and that they had another son named Austin and a daughter named Marie; and that Claude was not the best husband in the world—that he had, in fact, given his wife much cause for concern through his affairs with other women.

Now Jake flipped through the pictures, including those from the part of the family in the North, and he suddenly thought, *This is a fine family. What a fool Vince is to throw it away!*

Then he became uncomfortable, for he was forced to remember his purpose for being at Lindwood. He was only going to be there long enough for Vince to be eligible for the money—at which time Vince would come back and take over as master of Lindwood. Jake frowned. Though he had not met the owner of Lindwood, he had spent some time with Amy Franklin and knew that she was a fine woman, even noble. He knew as well that when Vince took over, he would be so unbearable that the smooth flow of life at this fine home would be shattered.

Disturbed, Jake moved away from the window, making his way crabwise to the huge rolltop desk. Opening the lower drawer, he was surprised to find a stack of letters. He took them out and began reading them. They were all letters written to Vince, and he managed to piece together something of the man's life from them. Most of the letters were from friends, some of them going back to Vince's youth, and they were rather ordinary. But as Jake went through them chronologically he discovered a pattern, a progressive loss of innocence that told him much about Vincent Franklin. The earliest letters were filled with the things that boys are interested in—hunting, fishing, a play in Richmond. But before long the tenor of the letters changed, as did the correspondents, and Jake could almost date the time that Vince began to dabble in the rougher side of life: wenching, drinking, and gambling. The most recent letters revealed a life that was completely depraved.

Some of the most revealing letters were from women, for Vince catered to women with little—or no—grace. Some of them were merely crude and vulgar; others were married women whose letters contained veiled references to secret meetings and assignations. Finally, Jake had read all he could stomach. He put the letters away and was just closing the drawer when the door opened and Rachel entered.

"Well, now," she said, stopping to stare at him. "I didn't know Dee had come to take care of you." She was wearing a pale rose-colored dress, and her cheeks were flushed from her ride. She looked at him more closely, saying with surprise, "You've had a shave. I'll bet Dee didn't do that!"

"No, I wouldn't risk that. I managed the job myself— and no more food trays in here. I can eat at the table."

Rachel examined him carefully, then said, "You must have had a hard time shaving in cold water. I'll have Jupe bring you shaving water in the morning, and he can help you dress for a time. Are you ready for breakfast?"

"Sure." He put his dark glasses on, which she had picked up from his table and handed to him. As she wheeled him down the hall, he said, "If you could get me a pair of crutches, I think I'll be able to use them pretty soon. My leg's better, and the hand, too."

"Don't rush it," Rachel warned as they moved out of the hall and into the dining room. "Dee, Vince will eat in here from now on."

Dee came through the kitchen door to stare at Jake, then said, "You want eggs?"

"Eggs will be fine," Jake said, and soon he and Rachel were eating breakfast. He had trouble cutting up the large slice of ham on his plate and said ruefully, "Never knew how handy it is to have two hands."

"Let me cut it." Rachel sliced the meat into bite-sized portions, then gave him his plate back. "I forgot to tell you, if you want any letters written, I'll do it, or Melora can."

"Thanks. Guess I'll wait until I can handle the job myself."

"All right." She sat there eating and sipping her coffee, saying little, but finally she said, "I hope Father and Grant will be coming home soon.

Rachel shook her head, and there was a doubtful look on her face. "I thought when the war started that things would go so fast we couldn't keep up with it. But since Manassas back in July, nothing's happened—nothing really big. Except for most of the men being in the army, life's about the same."

"Maybe the North has had enough."

"No, I don't think so," Rachel said slowly. "Rev. Irons spends most of his time with the troops, and he's been around some of the leaders like Col. Chesnut. They all agree that the North had its pride hurt at Manassas. But McClellan's getting an enormous army ready, and in the spring they'll come down on us like a horde of locusts."

"Things look sort of dark, I guess."

Rachel looked at him, seemingly thinking of the war, but she said evenly, "If the Yankees really whip us, we'll all be out in the cold." A smile tugged at her lips and she added, "I know you've been looking forward to tossing us all out for a long time. Now you may be out in the streets with the rest of us."

"You're pretty sure about what I'll do, aren't you, Rachel?"

"You've been quite outspoken about it," she said, then rose and began gathering the dishes. "I'm going to town today. Can I bring you anything?"

"Some newspapers. My eyes are getting better, good enough to read a little."

"All right." She paused, then said, "Ask Melora to read to you. She's the reader around here. Makes any sort of book sound exciting."

Later on in the day, Jake did get to hear Melora read. He had said nothing to her, but she came to his room where Jupe had built him a nice fire. He had almost dozed off when the door opened and he looked up to see Melora enter with some books.

"I've come to read to you, Vincent," she said. Sitting down she added, "Rachel said you might be getting bored."

"Hate to take your time, Melora."

"I'm all caught up. Now what would you like? Poetry or a novel?"

"Read something you like."

She smiled and pulled a book from the stack, saying, "You just made a mistake. Men usually like fiction some, but most would rather read a newspaper. I like poetry."

"Well, it'll be new to me, Melora, since I've not read much."

"Here's one I like. . . ." Melora found her place, then began reading. She had a pleasant voice and, as do most people who read aloud well, she had a lively expression.

ANNABEL LEE

> *"It was many and many a year ago,*
> *In a kingdom by the sea,*
> *That a maiden there lived whom you may know*
> *By the name of Annabel Lee;—*
>
> *And this maiden she lived with no other thought*
> *Than to love and be loved by me.*
> *She was a child and I was a child,*
> *In this kingdom by the sea,*
>
> *But we loved with a love that was more than love—*
> *I and my Annabel Lee—*
> *With a love that the winged seraphs of Heaven*
> *Coveted her and me.*
>
> *And this was the reason that, long ago,*
> *In this kingdom by the sea,*
> *A wind blew out of a cloud by night*
> *Chilling my Annabel Lee;*

So that her highborn kinsmen came
And bore her away from me,
To shut her up in a sepulchre
In this kingdom by the sea.

The angels, not half so happy in Heaven,
Went envying her and me:—
Yes! that was the reason (as all men know,
In this kingdom by the sea)
That the wind came out of the cloud, chilling
And killing my Annabel Lee.

But our love it was stronger by far than the love
Of those who were older than we—
Of many far wiser than we—
And neither the angels in Heaven above
Nor the demons down under the sea,
Can ever dissever my soul from the soul
Of the beautiful Annabel Lee:—

For the moon never beams without bringing me dreams
Of the beautiful Annabel Lee;
And the stars never rise but I see the bright eyes
Of the beautiful Annabel Lee;

And so, all the night-tide, I lie down by the side
Of my darling, my darling, my life and my bride,
In her sepulchre there by the sea—
In her tomb by the side of the sea."

Jake sat still, caught by the beauty of Melora's face as much as by the words she read. "That's very nice, but it's sad. Isn't there enough real sadness in the world without reading about such things?"

Melora let the book fall, and Jake was surprised to see that the expression on her face was not sad, but meditative. She had beautiful eyes, colored a deep green, and her lips were sweetly curved as she said, "There's something about it that isn't sad—at least to me."

"Not sad? But the girl dies and the lovers are parted!"

"Yes, but he still loves her. I guess that's why I like the poem. He says that nothing can take that from him. 'Neither the angels in Heaven above nor the demons down under the sea, can ever dissever my soul from the soul of the beautiful Annabel Lee.'"

Jake studied the woman before him, thinking of what Vince had told him about her love for Clay Rocklin. Finally he said, "But, Melora, if he had married another woman, he at least would have had her. Life's not very good at best, and we just have to take what we can get."

Melora looked at him, saying, "I don't like to think that we should take second best."

"Well, it sounds nice in the poem," he said finally. "Who wrote it?"

"A man named Edgar Allan Poe." She opened the book and gave him a sudden smile, saying, "He wrote some fine stories. I'll try you out on this one. It's not quite as sad as the poem. It's called 'The Purloined Letter,' and it's a detective story."

She read the story, and when she finished, Jake nodded. "Now *that's* a little more in my line, Melora! That Dupin is a sharp operator. Imagine that, hiding a letter by putting it out where everyone can see it!"

"If you ever want to hide something," Melora agreed, "now you know the way to do it. Don't hide it away, but put it right in full view of everyone." She rose and gave a short laugh. "This has been pleasant, Vince."

"I've enjoyed it, too," Jake said. "Maybe you'll even make a poetry reader out of me."

She left the room, and he wondered about her and her love for Clay Rocklin, and the preacher, Jeremiah Irons, who was totally unable to hide his love for this woman. *Looks like God could have put all that together better*, he mused. Then his face grew still as he thought, *'Course, I guess God doesn't really have a lot to do with it. We have to take whatever hand life deals us and either make it work or let it beat us. After all, look at what I've become. God sure hasn't had anything to do with me or my life!*

Leighton Semmes was delighted to meet Rachel as she came into headquarters. He rose at once, moving to greet her, saying, "Well, recruiting is picking up! You're the first volunteer we've had in two days, and the prettiest one, too."

He looked very handsome in his smart uniform, and Rachel was amused at his attention to her. "Nothing I'd like better than joining the Richmond Grays, but there's not much chance of that, Leighton." She was wearing a very pretty brown dress made of fine wool, and she saw the admiration in his dark eyes. "I came down to see if you could tell us anything about Father and Grant. Will they be home soon?"

"As a matter of fact, yes," Semmes answered. "They've been with Jackson in the Valley, but orders went out late yesterday to Col. Benton. They'll be assigned to defend Richmond—and your father and brother will be here next week. They're being sent ahead of the rest of the regiment to take care of any advance preparations."

"Oh, Mama will be glad!" Rachel exclaimed.

"Come along," Semmes said. "It's time I took you to lunch." She began to protest, but he laughed at her. "Come now, if you try to get out of it, I'll denounce you for a Yankee spy!"

They went downtown to the Melton Hotel and, after a fine lunch, they sat there talking for a long time. Semmes was an accomplished conversationalist, and he kept her amused as he related the incidents in Richmond and at the camp. "By the way," he said, "there's to be a ball for the Grays on the fifteenth. I'm taking you to it."

"And I don't have any say in the matter?"

"Not in the least," Semmes said firmly. "Buy yourself a pretty new dress and I'll bring my pistol along to protect you. It'll be fun, Rachel, and I'd like you to come with me."

"All right, Leighton," Rachel agreed. "I can't promise the new dress, though."

"Tell me about your trip to New Orleans—and about the patient."

Rachel gave him the details of the voyage, then spoke of Vince's recovery. "He's doing very well, but it'll be weeks before he's able to get around."

"Did you know Simon Duvall's been making his boasts about what he intends to do?"

"Yes, I've heard about it. But he's not going to shoot a cripple. That wouldn't do his reputation any good."

"With most men, I'd agree. But with a fellow like Duvall, you never can tell," Semmes said doubtfully. "He's got a fiery temper, and if he met Vince at all, he might shoot him without thinking of the consequences. If I were you, I'd talk Vince into staying out of town."

This didn't please Rachel. "He can't stay out of Richmond the rest of his life."

"I guess not, but warn him to be careful. As a matter of fact, I'll be glad to say a word to Duvall myself. I could do it right now. He's always at the Harralson House about this time of day."

Rachel knew this was an offer from Semmes to take up Vince's quarrel, and she understood that he was offering to do it for her, not because of any affection he had for her brother.

"No, Leighton, but you can take me there. I've got something to say to the big bully."

"Now wait a minute—!" Semmes protested, but despite his earnest argument he found himself escorting Rachel to the hotel, which was only a block away. "Now just remember to keep your temper, Rachel," he said as they entered the salon. "There he is over there."

Rachel saw Duvall sitting at a table with several men, playing cards. She straightened her back and marched up to him. "Mr. Duvall, I understand you've been making threats about what you intend to do to my brother."

Her words cut off all conversation, and Duvall came

out of his chair like a scalded cat. He glared at her, saying, "Miss Franklin, you shouldn't interfere. This is between your brother and myself."

"Would you shoot an injured man, Duvall?"

"I won't discuss it with a woman!"

Duvall started to turn but stopped abruptly as Rachel pulled a pistol from her purse and aimed it at him. It was the pistol she'd bought in New Orleans as a gift for Les, a finely designed .36 revolver. It had developed a flaw, and she had taken it to the gunsmith to get it repaired. It was not loaded, but Duvall didn't know that. His face washed pale and he said nervously, "Now, now, that's no way to behave!"

"You think I'll take lessons in how to behave from a sorry bully like you, Duvall?" Rachel said, keeping the gun steadily trained on him. "You're not a man anyone would listen to."

Duvall looked at her, swallowed, then said, "Miss Franklin, this is most unseemly!"

"No, this isn't unseemly," Rachel said. "Let me tell you what will be unseemly. If you harm my brother, I'll shoot you. Not in one of your nice little duels where you have all the advantage. I'll wait for you in a dark alley, and when you pass by, I'll shoot you in the back of the head. Now *that* would be unseemly, don't you agree?"

She looked around the room and contempt dripped from her voice as she said, "I don't suppose any of you have much pride, if you're the friend of a creature like this. But if there's any manhood in any of you, I'd think you'd refuse to listen to this scum when he makes threats against a man who can't defend himself."

She put the pistol back in her purse, saying, "From an alley, Duvall, in the back of the head." Then she turned and walked away.

Semmes gave Duvall a hard look, saying, "I am Miss Franklin's escort. If you resent anything she's said, my man will be glad to wait on you, sir!" Then he moved to Rachel and the two of them left the salon.

"Well, that was fun," Leighton said, and a laugh bubbled up in him. "Rachel, it was wonderful!"

"My father won't think so, nor my mother." Then a giggle came from her unexpectedly. "He did look silly, though, didn't he?"

"He'll keep his mouth shut," Semmes said, nodding. "He's got no choice." Then he asked curiously, "Would you really shoot him, Rachel?"

"No, but don't tell him that."

Duvall turned back to the men at the table, his face ashen. "Well, a man can't fight a woman, can he? The hussy!"

"You'd better keep quiet about your problem with Franklin, Duvall," one of the men said. "It does look bad, threatening a cripple."

Duvall glanced around the table, saw the agreement in the faces, and quickly said, "Of course. I had no intention of fighting Franklin until he's well." But the whole affair had shaken him, and he left the salon shortly afterward. He was fuming inside, and his anger was a black thing that would not be laid to rest easily. As he was walking down the sidewalk, fighting to keep his anger back, someone spoke to him.

"Why, Mr. Duvall, how nice to see you!"

He looked up with a startled expression, nodding then as he said, "Why, good afternoon, Mrs. Rocklin." He knew Ellen Rocklin only slightly but had admired her for a long time. She was hardly young, he thought, at about forty—but she was one of those women who retained her looks and figure. She was wearing a gray dress with a scarlet cape and looked very attractive. "How have you been?"

"Just fine. I'm on my way to look at some jewelry at Mason's." She smiled archly, adding, "You seem like a man who knows what looks good on a woman."

He said instantly, "Allow me to accompany you, Mrs. Rocklin."

"Oh, we're better acquainted than that," she said, smiling. "Let's make it Ellen and Simon."

They moved away and, after they looked at the jewelry, it seemed natural enough to have dinner together. Ellen Rocklin was an enticing woman, and as she listened to Duvall's version of Rachel's actions, she put her hand over his on the table, saying sympathetically, "What a dreadful thing, Simon! Her father ought to whip her. He won't, of course. She knows how to get around him!"

Ellen knew how to get around men, too, and how to get them to do what she wanted. There was a speculative and excited light in her eyes as she spoke to Duvall. She leaned against him, and a startled look appeared in his eyes—and then he smiled. They left the restaurant and moved down the street toward the house where she kept a room. When they arrived, she led him in by a seldom-used side entrance.

CHAPTER TEN

DINNER AT LINDWOOD

DR. KERMIT Maxwell was of the old school of medicine, highly suspicious of any of the newfangled innovations coming out of medical schools. His own training had been brief, at least from an academic point of view, but his practical experience was immense. He had been setting broken bones, administering pills, and bringing babies into the world in Virginia for almost sixty years. And he looked it, too.

He had stopped by to see Amy Franklin and, at her request, had gone to give her son an examination. Jake had been taking a nap on his bed when the door burst open without the formality of a knock. That, added to a booming voice sounding almost in his ear, gave him a leaping start.

"All right, get out of them clothes and let me look you over, boy!"

Jake was pulled to a sitting position before he was completely awake, and he suddenly found himself being stripped of his shirt by a short, thickset man with a round, red face and a pair of sharp blue eyes. Quickly Jake made the connection, for he'd heard Rachel tell Melora that a doctor was coming to see her mother.

But this man looked more like one of the loafers who sat outside City Hall and chewed tobacco than a physician. Still, he more or less *acted* as though he knew what he was doing. He started at the top of Jake's head, checked the gash, which was almost healed; touched the burns, which were forming pink new skin; then grabbed Jake's head and held it still while he peered into his eyes.

"Eyes bother you much?"

"Not so much now. I still wear the dark glasses in bright sunshine."

"Keep on doing it," Maxwell commanded. "Open your mouth." He peered down Jake's throat, then said, "Looks all right. Your mother says you still talk kind of husky."

"That's right, I do."

Maxwell sucked a tooth, thought about it, then shrugged. "Well, you may talk like that the rest of your life. Maybe damaged your vocal cords. But then, you don't sing in no church choirs, anyway."

Jake liked the old man. "But I might want to start, Doc."

"Not likely!" Maxwell had been doctoring the Franklins off and on for years, so he knew quite a bit about the oldest son. His practice was mostly with the hill people, so his visits were sporadic. Still, he had heard of Vince's life, so he knew the sort of man he was dealing with, even though he hadn't treated Vince personally for many years. "Whiskey voice—that's what it sounds like to me," he snapped. "You still on the bottle?"

Jake was amused. "No. I'm waiting for my doctor to tell me it's all right to start."

"You've already drunk enough to do a man for a lifetime." But Maxwell knew that his admonition would have little effect. "Let me see that arm and leg." After checking the limbs, he shrugged. "The devil looks out for his own, I guess. Leave the bandages off the arm, keep a light one on the leg, and don't do too much walking for a couple of weeks."

"Thanks, Dr. Maxwell. How's my mother?"

"Not as well as I'd like." Maxwell frowned and sucked on his tooth again, then added, "That was a bad break. As bad as I've ever seen. Don't tell your mother, but she may be lame for the rest of her life."

"Surely there must be something to do!"

"No, there's not!" Maxwell snapped with irritation. Removing a square of tobacco from his pocket, he bit off a large plug and tucked it into his jaw. "There's not a lot any of us doctors can do, which I reckon you know. People look at us like we're some kind of miracle workers, but mostly it's just common sense. You could send your mother to the finest hospital in New York, and they'd fool with her and charge you all the money you could rake up. But I'm telling you, boy, if God don't heal that break, the finest doctor in the world won't be able to do it!" He whirled and propelled himself to the door, a short, scrappy man with a busy schedule.

Jake put his shirt on, then picked out a pair of lightweight shoes made of the softest leather that could be found. He got them onto his feet, then reached out for his crutches. He had started using them four days earlier, and it had been difficult. His right hand was weak, making him drop the right crutch often so that he had to stoop awkwardly on his good leg to retrieve it, or else call for help. Still, the exercise seemed to have helped, for now he managed to hold on to the crutch with little difficulty. Swinging his right foot, he moved across the room, passed through the door, then turned and made his way to a small room that once had been a study but now had been converted to a bedroom for the mistress of Lindwood. It saved the servants and the two women the climb up to the second floor. Les had done a good job of making the room handy, moving a good bed into it, along with a few pieces of furniture.

Jake knocked on the door, waited until he heard a voice say, "Come in," then opened the door and entered.

"Why, come and sit down, Vince," Amy said quickly. She had been reading a magazine in bed, but put it down and waited until Jake was seated, then asked, "Did the doctor think you're making progress?"

"Yes. Got a clean bill of health." Jake sat there, not as uncomfortable as he had been the first time or two he'd visited. There was nothing frightening about Amy Franklin. On the contrary, she was one of the most gracious women Jake had ever met. Though the knowledge of his secret made him somewhat nervous, he had grown to like the older woman, and several times he had come to her room and sat beside her. She had sensed, he knew, that he didn't want to talk about himself, and she carefully refrained from asking anything personal. But she did talk about her family and about the things of her world—which was a great help to Jake, who soaked up the information.

Now he asked, "What did he say about you?"

Amy smiled at him with a light in her eye. "He didn't tell me what he told you. Maxwell is a blunt old fellow, but he's got some tact. What he wanted to say was that he was afraid I'd be a cripple for the rest of my life. He didn't come out with it, of course, but he's an easy man to read. That is what he told you, isn't it?"

Jake blinked and began to fumble for words, but she cut him off. "Never mind. It was an unfair question. He's wrong, anyway."

"I hope so," Jake said quickly. "You hate being tied down, don't you?"

"Yes, I do. I've always been happy working." A thought came to her, leaving a sudden expression of interest on her face. "It might be that the Lord wanted me to be still and listen." She thought about that, then smiled slightly. "Yes, that could be it. You know, I've spent more time listening to God since I fell through that porch than I have in the last ten years!"

Jake laughed, saying, "Well, that's a pretty rough way of getting your attention. There must have been an easier way."

"No, I don't think there was. We're all about the same, I think. When things are going well, we forget to listen to God. But when the bottom falls out of our world, we start looking up for help. That's the way you were when you were a boy, Vince."

"Calling on God?"

"No, I mean when you were young. You were the most independent little boy I ever saw!" The memory softened her lips, making her look maternal. "But even when you were five years old, you didn't want any help. No sir, not you! You'd yank your hand out of mine and go off on your own. When you'd start falling, you'd go down and scrape your knees. And *then* you'd start holding up your hands and crying out for me."

"I don't remember that."

"No, you were just a baby." A sadness came to her and she said softly, "I guess that was about the last time you reached out and asked me for anything. It grieved me, for I loved you very much."

Jake felt his face grow warm for some reason. He had never known much of a mother's love—none, really—and now he wanted to curse Vince for turning away from this woman. "Well, Dr. Maxwell said it would have to be God who healed you."

"Yes, he's right about that. But even if I do limp, this time has been good for me. For one thing," she said, giving him a sweet smile that reminded him of Rachel, "if I hadn't been here, we wouldn't have had these talks, would we?"

"I—guess not."

She saw his embarrassment, then said, "Your father and Grant will be here for dinner tonight. They got back to Richmond yesterday from the Valley. Rachel went to town and found out that both of them have been assigned to the regiment's advance team."

"Well, that's fine," Jake said quickly. He suddenly felt a surge of panic, for meeting Brad Franklin had been something he'd thought about with apprehension. "Glad I'm on my feet for the big occasion."

"It'll just be family tonight." Amy smiled. "I'm looking forward to it. It's the longest time your father and I have ever been separated since we've been married."

Jake got to his feet awkwardly, got his crutches in place, then smiled. "Well, he'll come home to a beautiful wife," he said and was sorry at once. *Vince would never have said a thing like that!* was the thought that went off like an alarm bell.

Amy Franklin was indeed looking at him with an amazed expression. He halfway expected her to denounce him, but she suddenly smiled, then laughed. "If I'd known that having a burning building fall on you would have made such an improvement, I'd have set fire to the house a long time ago!"

Jake felt a surge of relief. "Well, it did call my attention to a few things, I guess. So if you act up, I can lead you to a rotten porch, and if I don't behave, you can push me into a fire."

After he left her room, Amy sat there thinking of the scene. She was still thinking of it when Rachel came in to bring her fresh water. Rachel looked at her mother's pensive face. "Did Vince upset you, Mama?" she asked quickly.

Amy smiled at her. "No, dear, he didn't. He actually said something quite nice."

"Vince?" Rachel said, raising her eyebrows in doubt. "Don't let him fool you, Mama. He may seem more human lately, but it's just because he's sick. Oh, he's being nice enough, but when he's well, we'll have the same old Vince."

There was a bitter tone in her voice, and Amy said, "You can't let that sort of bitterness stay in you, Rachel. You've been taught better."

Rachel looked at her mother but shook her head stubbornly. "Remember that strawberry horse I had, the one called Prince? Well, he was good, too—until he got a chance to give me a bite or kick me in the ribs! That horse would be good for three months just to get a chance to kick me once!" Her eyes flashed and she said adamantly, "I know you pray for Vince every day of your life, but I just don't—" Then she suddenly broke off. She turned away for a few seconds, then looked at her mother with a weak smile. "Mama, you'd find something good about Judas! And I'm just an old dragon! I wish I were more like you. You never boil over like I do."

"Well, I never pulled a gun on a man," Amy agreed

blandly. Rachel's hand flew to her mouth, and a dull red crept up her neck. Her mother merely pulled her daughter's hand from her embarrassed face and held it. "You have deeper feelings than I do, or maybe I should say *more* feelings."

"You could say 'crazy, wild, unsettling' feelings," Rachel offered with a wry smile. "I try to be cool and lady-like, but then I just pop off, like a volcano. I am trying hard, though, Mama. Really I am!"

"You can't be something you're not, Rachel," Amy said quietly. "You're a woman of strong emotions and, try as you will to repress them, they'll come out eventually. God gave you those feelings and the ability to feel them intensely. So the only thing you can do is ask him to help you . . . and to guide you when the time comes for you to share those emotions with a man."

"Oh, don't worry about me and men, Mama. The spinster of Lindwood isn't going to get carried away."

"Nonsense." She paused, then asked, "Are you serious about Leighton Semmes?"

Rachel stared at her. "How do you know about him? Have you taken up gossiping?" At the twinkle in her mother's eyes, Rachel sighed. "Well, he's handsome and rich and charming. Besides, I'm a challenge to his pride. Just about every woman he's known has practically swooned when he looked at her. Now he's got to have me, but only because he can't have me!"

"He's a worldly man, Rachel. A strong one, to be certain, but not the sort who'd make you happy, I think. He doesn't seem to me to be a man of faith."

Rachel sighed. "Well, maybe you're right, Mama. At any rate, he's taking me to the ball in Richmond. I'll tell you more about how I feel after that." A twinkle sparked in her eyes and she added with a grin, "After I've seen him in his dress uniform." Her mother shook her head indulgently as Rachel rose and left the room, saying, "I'm going to make Vince go with us. I want him to show up in public. I want to give Simon Duvall his chance to shoot him!"

"He won't go," Amy said.

"I'll steal his pants if he doesn't! He'll have to go!"

All day Jake worried about dinner with Vince's father but finally realized that there was no sense in that. *If he sees through me, that's that,* he finally summed it up. The thing was made easier by a short meeting he'd had with the two men earlier. He was reading in the library when he heard horses, and going to the window, he saw two men in uniform dismount and give the reins to Tad, who was grinning broadly at them.

"Might as well get the worst over," Jake said, taking his crutches and making his way down the hall. By the time he arrived, everyone seemed to be gathered in the library. He stood just beyond the doorway, listening as they talked and laughed with Rachel and Les, then swung into the room.

Brad Franklin looked up with shock in his eyes, which Jake had expected. But he said, "Well now, I thought you'd be flat on your back, Vince."

"I'm sure you did," Jake said, a mocking tone in his voice. "But I've had good nursing."

Brad's face reddened a little at the tone in Jake's voice, but he still peered at Jake intently. Grant stared, too, and an uncomfortable silence was filling the room. Quickly Rachel said, "You can talk later, Daddy. Go now and see Mama." Jake threw her a look of gratitude, which only seemed to confuse her.

Blast! he thought. *Out of character again. I've got to be more careful.*

Drawing a breath, he said coldly, "Yes, by all means, go see Mother. That is, of course, if you've had your fill of staring at me. Though I'm sure seeing me like this brings you some pleasure, I don't appreciate being scrutinized like some deformed animal that's going to be destroyed."

"Now, just a minute—!" Grant began to protest at Jake's insulting comments, but his father cut him off, placing a restraining hand on his son's arm and shaking his head. He moved to leave, saying, "I'll see you at dinner, Son."

Jake said nothing in response. Grant threw him an angry look and stepped closer, then said, "You look terrible! But one thing's certain, even if I didn't recognize your face right off, your rotten personality would identify you in a second."

Jake smiled coldly. "What a shame, dear brother, that you weren't there to see me when they first pulled me out from under that building. You might have talked them into just letting me die."

With a muffled exclamation, Grant turned and left the room. Jake glanced at Rachel, noting the tightness of her expression. She merely looked at him for a moment, then shook her head and walked away. Jake sighed, relieved not to have to talk anymore. But he felt a tension growing within himself. *Grant couldn't believe I was Vince—and Mr. Franklin knows Vince better. One slip, and the whole thing's over.*

Later that night at dinner, Brad Franklin was not paying as much attention to his oldest son as he might have. He was being very attentive to his wife, who had been placed at his right hand, her leg bolstered with cushions. She was as beautiful to him as ever and had dressed for the occasion in a dress of light blue silk that set off her complexion.

The two newcomers ate hungrily, and at Les's insistence his father spoke of what had been happening. "Well, we were in the Battle of Ball's Bluff. That was on October 21. Gen. Shanks Evans—the one who held the first of the Yankee charges at Manassas—was in command at Leesburg. The old man drinks like a fish, but he's a fighter, isn't he, Grant?"

"A wildcat," Grant agreed, nodding. "I guess that Union general knows that now!"

"Gen. Stone, that's his name." His father nodded. "He got the idea of crossing the Potomac and attacking us.

Well, Stone managed to stay out of the actual fighting, so he sent Col. Edward D. Baker to make the crossing. He did get across the river, but he ran into four whole brigades, including the Grays." He lifted his glass, took a sip of water, then shook his head. "It was a bloody massacre," he said quietly. "The poor Yankee privates were trapped, and it was like shooting fish in a barrel."

Grant continued the account. "We drove them back to the river, but there was no way for them to cross. So we had them in a crossfire." A shiver passed through Grant's shoulders, and he said, "I did my share of the shooting, but I couldn't help but think what it would be like if our fellows were pinned down like that."

"I read something about it in the paper," Les said. "There's a big public outcry, and Stone is the man they blame. And Evans is the hero around here."

Brad looked up and, seeing that the talk had disturbed Amy and Rachel, said quickly to Jake, "Well, let's hear your report, Son. Tell us about the fire."

Jake was taken off guard but managed to give a brief summary of the event, then said, "It's a good thing you sent Rachel to get me, sir. I was getting pretty low in that hospital."

"Well, to tell the truth, I didn't send her," Brad said. "I was off with the company, and you know Rachel and your mother. They cooked the whole thing up."

"Dr. Maxwell says he's doing fine, Daddy," Rachel said. "I think he's right, don't you, Melora? He's not nearly so much trouble now as he was when he first got here."

Melora had listened to the major's story of the battle, and, after agreeing with Rachel, she asked, "Did you see my brother, Maj. Franklin?"

"He didn't, but I did," Grant said. Grant was a second lieutenant of the Third Platoon of Company D. "Bushrod Aimes is your brother's lieutenant, and we were next to each other on the march and in the line. I even had mess once with the squad your brother is in."

"Is he all right?" Melora asked.

"Sure, he's fine," Grant assured her. "You don't have to worry about him." A smile came to his lips and he added, "That's a tough platoon. Got a sergeant named Waco Smith who was a Texas gunfighter of some sort. Still carries a .44 on his hip, despite regulations. And Uncle Clay, he's in that platoon, too, and you know what a dead shot *he* is!"

A brief silence went over the room, and suddenly Grant's cheeks reddened. He had forgotten about the rumors concerning his uncle and Melora. Now he said quickly, "Clay and your brother Bobby are the best shots in the whole regiment—next to the chaplain, that is." He looked to his father for verification. "Aren't they, sir?"

"Yes, they are. I expect they'll be made sharpshooters as soon as we can get some Whitworth rifles. But Grant's right, Melora. Your brother is in a tough outfit, and they're learning how to take care of each other."

"Is Dent Rocklin back with the Grays?" Rachel asked.

"No, not yet. I think he and his bride are still too much in love for him to do much soldiering," Maj. Franklin said with a smile. "He'd be likely to say to a recruit who was disobeying orders, 'Now don't do that, sweetheart,' instead of bawling him out properly."

"They're back from their honeymoon," Rachel said. "I ran into Raimey a few days ago. They're staying at Gracefield. I expect Raimey will stay there with Susanna until the war's over."

"She's a fine girl," her father said. "From what I hear, she's not let her blindness spoil her life. That's a good thing, isn't it?"

"Very good," his wife said quietly. "It seems to me that God was in that meeting. There was Dent with his terrible wounds, wanting to die, and God sent what you might think would be the very *last* person to save him. But when God does things, he sometimes has to use ways that seem most strange to us."

Rachel said, "Well, if you're all finished with your stories . . . I have an announcement." Everyone looked at her, and she said soberly, "I have a gentleman friend."

"Not you, the spinster of Lindwood!" Grant exclaimed in mock horror.

"Yes, and he's got to be tested. I want to find out if he's serious. Young men can't be trusted these days, you know."

"What sort of test are you giving this young man?" her father asked.

"He's coming to take me to the ball in Richmond. I want all of you to be ready. When he comes to call for me, he'll find he's not only taking me, but my whole family!"

"Oh, come now, Rachel," her father protested with a slight smile at her proposal. "That's too hard a test for any man!"

"No, it's not," Rachel answered coolly, then added, "He's supposed to be an officer and a gentleman, and I'm going to find out if he really is."

"An officer? Which officer?" Franklin demanded.

"Capt. Leighton Semmes."

"Semmes? I know him," Grant said, grinning. "He'll run like a rabbit when he sees this crew!"

"Not if he's serious," Rachel insisted. "Now you're all to come. All except Mama."

"I'd rather stay home with your mother," Brad protested.

"I know you would, but you've got to go. You're the one who has to corner Capt. Semmes and ask if his intentions are honorable."

"And I'm the one who calls him out if he says they aren't," Grant laughed. "Oh, we've got to do it, Father!"

"Yes, you can tell me all about it when you get home," Amy insisted.

"Well, he's definitely serious if he takes this whole bunch on," Brad Franklin said, smiling. "*I'd* have run like a rabbit if the whole Rocklin bunch had ganged up on me when I was courting your mother."

"No, you wouldn't," Rachel said calmly. "You'd have faced up to them, and that's what I want a man to do. I know this one can make nice speeches, but there's more to a man than that." Then she said, "All right, we all go. Agreed?" She looked around the table but paused when she saw Jake.

"You go too, Vince. No shirkers around here."

"Why, I can't dance with this leg, and I look like the devil. Grant said so."

"You go or I'll hide your pants and saw your crutches in two," she said. "It'll do you good."

The others were looking at him, and Jake finally asked, "What about Simon Duvall? Are you going to take a pistol to him again if he threatens me?"

"What's that?" Brad asked in alarm.

"I'll tell you later, dear," Amy said quickly, then added, "You must go. I'll ask it as a favor."

Jake dropped his head in confusion, feeling their eyes on him. Finally he lifted his eyes and met Rachel's direct gaze.

"Well, I guess one ball can't hurt too much."

CHAPTER ELEVEN

A FANCY BALL

THE LETTER from Vince came on Tuesday afternoon. Jake was making his way carefully around the walk that circled the house when a buggy drove up the driveway. "Hey, Vince," the driver called out. "Got some mail for you."

Jake swung himself toward the buggy, and the driver— a short, pudgy man with a set of sweeping Burnside whiskers—reached into a box by his side and brought out a handful of letters. "Got it here somewhere," he said, cheerfully sorting through a few. "Ain't seen you since you got back. Thought maybe you might drop around and we could have a few."

"Been flat on my back most of the time," Jake said cautiously. Obviously the man was a friend. "How've you been?"

"Oh, fine. But did you hear about Grady? No? Well, he got himself in a mess with that Wadsworth girl over in Batesville." The man chattered on about the incident, finally getting a few letters separated. Shoving the bulk of them back into the box, he thrust the rest toward Jake, saying, "That's the lot. You going to the ball in Richmond tonight?"

"Guess so. Won't be doing any dancing, though."

"Well, I'll see you there," the messenger said as he grinned. "Least that bum leg won't keep you from drinking. 'Sides, Mabel Richards will be glad to sit out the dances with you. See you there."

Jake waved, then turned back toward the house as the buggy pulled away. He moved slowly, managing the steps cautiously, then sat down on one of the cane-bottomed chairs. Thumbing through the letters, he found that only one was for Vince. It was addressed in strong, bold strokes—a man's handwriting. He opened it and looked at the signature, then grew still. Bill Underhill! The letter was from Vince! Jake's eyes flew to the top of the page and he began reading.

It was innocuous enough. It began,

> Well, Vince, I've landed down in Memphis for a while. Guess I'll stay here until things get settled. Unless, of course, the Yankees come and take the city. But they'd have to take either New Orleans or Vicksburg to do that, so I'm fine for now. I am running a little low on money. Could you send me the two hundred dollars I loaned you? It would tide me over for a time.

The rest of the letter was a breezy account of Vince's activities, which Jake skimmed through. When he finished the letter, he put it back in the envelope and thought about it. He had to send the money, but it was a touchy subject, for he had no idea how Vince's financial affairs worked. He had less than fifty dollars left of the money that had been in Vince's wallet. Well, he would have to get more.

There was a busy air throughout the house, with the women scurrying around getting ready for the ball. He went to his room and began searching through the large desk, finding almost at once some canceled checks and other receipts in one of the drawers. There were several statements from the Planter's Bank of Richmond, the last one dated in September. The balance showed a figure of $540, and finding some blank checks, Jake was writing a check for $200 when a thought came to him. He then wrote a brief letter:

> Dear Bill,
>
> All seems to be going well with our venture. So far I have been able to do all the things we talked about, though it has been a little touchy at times. By the way,

*you might let me know a little bit more about the
financial end of our partnership, such as income and
how to switch funds, things like that. I am enclosing a
check for $200 as you requested. Let me hear from you
soon, and I'll keep you posted on things here.*

> *Sincerely yours,*
> *Vince Franklin*
> *Richmond, Virginia*

As he put the letter and check in an envelope, he
thought, *Got to get word to the bank that my signature will
be different for a time.* He sealed the envelope with a stick
of sealing wax he had found in the desk. But there were
no stamps, so he put the envelope in his pocket and
went to find Rachel.

"I don't have a stamp," he said when he found her in
the kitchen. "Will you mail this for me?"

Taking the letter she nodded, then commented, "You
write better with your left hand than you do with your
right." She looked at him, that curious light in her eyes
again, as though something was tugging at her awareness
but couldn't quite get through.

"Guess I took more care with it," Jake said, then
added quickly, "I really don't think it's a good idea for
me to go to that ball. Maybe I could stay home with
Mother."

He saw that he had successfully distracted her from the
letter. Her eyes flashed, and she retorted at once, "You
need to go. It'll stop some of the talk that's going around.
And while the talk may not bother you, it definitely
bothers Father."

He had waited for her to tell him of her encounter with
Simon Duvall, but she had never said a word. Now he
asked, a mocking tone in his voice, "You going to take
your pistol in case Duvall comes after me?"

Rachel showed a trace of embarrassment. "He won't
come after you. All he's got is some sort of foolish pride in
his dueling ability. When you get well, he may try to go on

with the thing, but he can't afford to attack an injured man."

"Especially if he's likely to be shot in the back of the head from a dark alley," Jake remarked.

"Oh, I just lost my temper," Rachel said quickly, then changed the subject. "You just be ready on time tonight. Jupe will help you with your clothes."

Jake grinned at her as she turned with a flounce and walked away.

When Leighton Semmes walked up the steps of the mansion at Lindwood, he felt an exhilaration such as he hadn't felt in years. His experience with women had jaded him, but the strong draw he felt to Rachel Franklin was something new. Oh, he had been with women who were more beautiful, but his attraction went beyond her looks, which actually were quite pleasing. What he found most fascinating about her was her resistance to him.

The door opened as he walked up the steps, and a black servant said, "Come in, sir. The family is just getting ready."

Semmes faltered, not knowing exactly what to think of that, but he followed the servant out of the foyer and into a large drawing room that seemed to be rather crowded.

"Ah, Capt. Semmes! Just in time to turn around and go back to town!" Rachel's father came to greet him, a smile on his lean face. "Do you know everyone?"

Semmes looked around, nodding to Grant and Les, both of whom he knew slightly, but said, "All except this lady, I think."

"Melora, may I present Capt. Leighton Semmes of Stuart's cavalry. Captain, this is Miss Melora Yancy."

"My pleasure, Miss Yancy," Semmes said, with a bow. He had heard of her, as had most people in his circle. Now seeing her in a white dress that set off her dark beauty, he didn't wonder that the Rocklin fellow had fallen for her. Just then, Rachel came into the room, and he turned to her at once.

"Well, Captain, you look very dashing," Rachel said, admiring the gray uniform set off by a scarlet sash and a gleaming saber. "You'll dazzle all the young ladies, I'm sure."

Semmes paused uncertainly, for he felt that she was laughing at him, something that had never happened before. Then her brother Les said, with a twinkle in his eye, "You won't have a chance, Sister, not against those good-looking city girls!"

Semmes came up with a smile, saying, "Not at all true! You'll be the belle of the ball, Miss Franklin." His words were more than mere gallantry, too, for she was beautiful tonight. Her ball gown had delicate dove gray and rose stripes, and she had sewn clusters of pink rosebuds to gather the fullness of her billowing skirt into festoons above a silk and lace petticoat that rustled with the slightest motion. With her honey-blonde hair done up in a graceful swirl and her large, blue-green eyes flashing, she was a true beauty.

"Well, we're all here except Vince," Maj. Franklin said, but even as he spoke, Semmes turned to see a man enter on crutches. "This is my oldest son, Vincent," the major said to Semmes. "I don't believe you two have met."

"Happy to meet you," Semmes said. He took in the light gray suit, the ruffled shirt, and the string tie that the young man was wearing, then said, "We did meet once, at a horse race in Savannah."

"I don't think I remember you, Captain," Jake said quickly.

"Well, let's get to that ball," Maj. Franklin said, saving Jake from any further conversation with Semmes. The major led the way to the front of the house, where a large carriage was pulled up with Tad holding the reins. "I think there's room for all of us," Franklin said.

"Oh, let's not crowd ourselves," Semmes remarked. "I'll take Miss Rachel in my buggy."

"That's a good idea," Rachel said, then added innocently, "It'll be an easier ride for you in the buggy, too,

Vince. You won't have to crowd your leg into such a small space." If she saw the irritation on Semmes's face, she ignored it. "Jupe, help Mr. Vince into the buggy."

Jake was amused at the disappointment on the face of Semmes, and also at the tactics of Rachel. However, he said, "You get in first, Rachel. I think the outside would be easier on this leg. Besides, the captain didn't get all dressed up to sit beside me."

Rachel seemed to be the only one who enjoyed the ride to Richmond. The bouncing of the buggy caused Jake's injured leg to ache, and Leighton Semmes found the presence of Rachel's brother an impediment to his plans for the ride. Not that it would have mattered, for the large carriage filled with her relatives followed so closely that he could hear Les's frequent inquiries of, "How's it goin' up there, Captain?"

Semmes put his horses to a fast pace, but when he pulled up in front of the hotel where the ball was to be held, he was disappointed to see that the black driver had kept up. Helping Rachel down, he whispered, "I thought you were a good girl! And here you foist your whole blasted family off on me!"

She smiled, and there was a gleam of humor in her eyes as she said, "Why, Leighton, I do believe you're put out with me!" The two of them went inside, and Les came along to give Jake a hand down.

"You three sure did make a lovely couple," he laughed, handing Jake his crutches. "Bet you ten dollars the captain sneaks off without you."

"No takers." Jake swung across the drive on his crutches, made his way awkwardly up the three steps, then he and Les went into the main ballroom, followed by the rest of the party. Jake's eyes, still sensitive to flashing lights, reacted as he walked inside, for the new, recently installed gaslights were much brighter than anything that had preceded them. He halted abruptly, half blinded, but Melora came to take his arm, saying, "Let's go sit by the wall, Vincent."

As she led him to a line of chairs and saw him seated, he thought of how sensitive she was. "Thanks, Melora. I'm blind as a bat from those lights!" She sat down beside him with an understanding smile. Before long, his eyes had adjusted, and he looked around the ballroom with curiosity.

Lighted prisms dangled below glass shades on the lofty ceiling, casting miniature rainbows upon the dancers who whirled and glided across the glistening parquet floor of the fabulous green and gold ballroom. Around the floor, green velvet draperies framed the scene. Intricately wrought Spanish ironwork decorated a broad staircase that led to the second floor and formed a balcony to accommodate the musicians. It was too late in the year for flowers, but banks of evergreen branches reached to either end of the glistening dance floor and into every available corner, filling the room with their pungent fragrance.

On the bandstand nine musicians worked at sending out the music that floated over the room. Violas and violins sang like great nightingales, a harp tinkled, and flutes and oboes added a liquid accompaniment. Jake took note that there were no vulgar instruments, such as drums, accordions, or banjos.

Shifting his gaze to the dance floor, he saw that the dominant color was the gray of the officers' uniforms, set off by the black sheen of boots and the golden flash of brass buttons. But it was the dresses of the women that caught the eye as they flashed to the strains of a waltz, some of them startlingly décolleté, glowing in flowered and looped gowns of sapphire, yellow, pink, green, and white.

Melora said, "Look, there's Dent Rocklin and his Raimey!" Jake glanced at the couple who were floating by, noting the angry scar on the man's face and remembering what had been said about the two. "I'd never believe she's blind," he murmured. "She's very beautiful, isn't she?"

"Very, and her spirit is beautiful, too." She started to

say something else, but she suddenly halted. Looking quickly in the direction of her glance, Jake saw another couple moving around the floor. He identified the man at once as Clay Rocklin. *That must be his wife, Ellen,* Jake realized. *The woman Vince said was pretty loose.*

He studied the pair, saying nothing, for he remembered the rumors that Clay and Melora were in love. He saw the woman look at him, then say something to her partner, who also glanced in his direction. Then they moved across the floor toward him. Jake braced himself, knowing that they were coming to speak to him, and determined to say as little as possible.

While Ellen and Clay had been dancing, there was little pleasure in it for either of them. When Clay had come home with the Grays, he had gotten a note almost at once from regimental headquarters stating that he was to see his wife immediately, that an urgent message had come from her. When he finally had found her—not at Gracefield but at her room in Richmond—there had been no emergency except for the one in Ellen's mind.

She had demanded money, and when he had tried to explain that there was no money to be given, she had exploded in a rage. He had stood there listening to her raving and the curses that she laid on him but had said only, "Ellen, it's all I can do to pay for your expenses here in Richmond. If you'd stay at home, you'd have more money to spend on clothes."

His words had had no effect, and finally she had released him, but not before extracting a promise that he would take her to the regimental ball. Clay had reluctantly agreed, on the condition that Rena, their fifteen-year-old daughter, would accompany them.

As Clay had expected, though, the evening was a failure. He spent most of the evening talking to Rena, dancing only when practically forced to. When Ellen had pulled him to the floor, both of them were well aware that it was for the sake of form. But then she had said, "Look, there's your nephew Vince."

Clay had glanced toward the side of the room, saying, "I heard he was back. He must not have been hurt as badly as we heard if he's at a dance."

"Come on, let's go speak to him."

Clay was surprised, for Ellen had disliked his nephew for a long time. "All right," he agreed, but when they got to where Vince was seated, he regretted it at once—for Melora was seated beside young Franklin. He shot a glance at Ellen, who wore a cruel smile as she watched his reaction.

"Now you can see your lady friend," she hissed, but as they came to the couple, she said brightly, "Vince Franklin, I don't believe it!" She turned to Melora saying, "Why—Miss Yancy, I didn't see you sitting here."

"How are you, Mrs. Rocklin?" Melora said calmly. She knew Ellen Rocklin had spread vile rumors about her husband and herself, calling her the "white-trash Yancy girl," but she only added, "See how well your nephew is doing, Mister Clay?"

"Yes, indeed. I'm pleased to see you on your feet, Vince, but you look quite different without your beard and moustache."

Jake risked saying, "Well, I'm lucky to be here at all." He knew that both the Rocklins were surprised at his appearance, then added, "Look like a stray alley cat, don't I?"

"Not at all, Vincent," Ellen said at once. "I always thought you should have gotten rid of those whiskers. You look much better without them. Now I'm going to sit here and talk to Vincent, Clay, so you must ask Miss Yancy to dance with you."

It was exactly the cruel sort of thing that Ellen would think of, and she was pleased to see shock run across Clay's face. "You don't mind, do you, Miss Yancy?" she pressed.

Melora was placed in an impossible position by this request, for she was the one about whom tongues would wag for days. Even so, she rose gracefully, saying, "Of course not, Mrs. Rocklin."

Clay was left with no choice, and so he led her to the dance floor. They moved out to the sound of the music, and he said bitterly, "I'm sorry, Melora."

"Why, I think that's awful—that you're sorry to dance with me!" she said and looked up at him with a smile. "I thought you were a more gallant man than that, Mister Clay!"

He admired her tremendously at that moment for her courage and her poise. "'Mister Clay,'" he echoed her use of his name. "That's what you called me when you were a little girl. I still like it. But I'm afraid this will be trouble for you."

"Just enjoy the dance, Mister Clay. I love the color and the music, don't you? The dance will be over in a little while, but there will be many nights that I will lie on my bed and live this moment over again! That's my treasure, you know."

"What's that, Melora?"

She was light in his arms, and he caught the faint odor of lilac, her favorite scent. The lights danced in her eyes, and her lips were curved in a faint smile as she said, "Memories. I keep them in a room in my mind, and when I get sad or lonely, I go there and look at them. Some people do that with paintings, but my treasures have sound and I can smell them and taste them. Do you remember the time we made ice cream and I put blackberries in it? I can still feel how cold the ice cream was on my teeth, making them ache, and how sharp the berries tasted—and how the juice ran down your chin!"

"You still remember that?" he asked, surprised. "Why, you were no more than twelve years old! But I remember it, too. And so many other things about you."

She blinked suddenly and dropped her head, and at once he knew that she was sad. A heaviness came on him and he said, "Melora, I must say something. A hard thing."

"Yes? What is it?"

Clay had trouble getting the words out, but it was a

thing he had to do. It had been on his mind for a long time, and though speaking the thoughts was like a knife in his side, he said, "You've got to say good-bye to me, Melora—you must!" He spoke quickly, cutting off her attempts to speak. "Listen to me! You've got so much to offer, and it's wasted. I know you have feelings for me, and I—I have some for you, too, but we have to forget them."

"How do you do that, Mister Clay?"

Her question was spoken quietly, but it hit him hard. "I know, Melora. I know what you're saying . . . but I've been wrong about this thing. I should have broken it off long ago."

"What have we done that's wrong?"

"Nothing like what the gossip has put on us," he said instantly, but pain pulled his mouth into a tight shape. "But I have done a wrong thing: I have kept you from having the life you deserve, a life with a family and children. Now—right now, Melora—I'm releasing you. We've never made any promises, but the tie is there. From this night on, you're free."

"Free to do what?"

"Free to marry, to have children—to be a wife and a mother, for that's what you were born for, Melora."

She said nothing; she only finished the dance. Then, as the last notes sounded, she nodded. "All right. Let it be so."

As soon as Clay led Melora away, Ellen began probing Jake, asking questions about the fire and about what he'd done since he'd been home. Jake answered briefly, saying at one point, "It still hurts me to talk, thanks to all that smoke I inhaled."

"You sound so different," Ellen commented, and she studied his face carefully. There was a sharp quality in her eyes that disturbed Jake, for it was not a look of ordinary curiosity. He knew how to handle curiosity well enough, but there was some sort of predatory quality in her manner—something strange and unusual that made him tense and ill at ease. She asked so many questions that he finally said in desperation, "The fire seemed to do something to my thinking, too. For instance, I just can't seem to remember some things."

Then she deliberately put her hand on his arm in a caressing manner and leaned forward to say, "You haven't forgotten *everything,* have you?"

Suddenly Jake understood what was happening, and he recoiled from the knowledge. There was no mistaking the way that Ellen Rocklin was touching him, nor the suggestive way she leaned forward so that the full curve of her bosom pressed against him.

She and Vince Franklin must have been lovers! Jake's mind reeled. He sat there almost paralyzed, unable to think at all—but he didn't have to, for at that moment Clay and Melora appeared, and Ellen leaned back. She patted Vince's arm maternally, saying, "Look at this poor hand, dear! It was a frightful burn!"

"Oh, it's much better!" Jake said quickly and attempted to pull his hand free. But Ellen was leaning down, staring at it. "It looks pretty bad," he said uncomfortably, "but the doctor said it'll be as good as new."

"Oh, that's good," Ellen said, but there was a strange gleam in her eyes as she spoke. Then she rose, saying, "You must come to see us at Gracefield. Good night, Miss Yancy."

When the two Rocklins left, Jake drew a shaky breath. He wanted to get up and run out of the ballroom but knew that he could not. "Think I'll go get some of that punch, Melora. Want to come along?"

"Yes, that would be nice."

He got to his feet, and they made their way to the long table groaning with refreshments of all kinds. They found Semmes and Rachel there, and the four of them stood together for a time, Semmes doing most of the talking.

Just when Jake was about to go back to his chair, he saw Rachel's eyes widen, then narrow. "There's Duvall," she said quietly. She looked at Jake, obviously hoping her half brother would do something, but he wanted nothing to do with Duvall. He had long ago decided that his only hope of avoiding a duel—his only chance of not having to kill the man—was to stay away from him. Now he deliberately turned and left the ballroom, turning his back on the startled Duvall. As he swung along, he was aware that he was being watched, and he saw several men curl their lips as he left the room.

Rachel, Semmes noted, had turned pale, but not with anger. "I guess that pretty much removes any doubt that Vince is a coward," she said so quietly that only he heard it.

"Well, after all, he's crippled, Rachel," Semmes offered.

"Would you do such a thing, Leighton? Run from a man like that?"

"Well, I—"

"No, you wouldn't." She looked across the room as Jake passed through the door. "I wish he'd died in that fire," she said, and there was sadness in her eyes. "Vince was never much—but he's *nothing* now!"

When Jake got outside, he found Tad, who had driven the large carriage. "Tad, help me in."

"But the dancin' ain't ovah, Marse Vince."

"It is for me!"

Jake sat there, wishing that he were anyplace in the world but in that carriage. He longed to pick up the lines and drive the carriage as far from Richmond as possible.

But he could not. He sat there until the Franklins came and got into the carriage. No one spoke to him, and the silence was thick all the way back to Lindwood. When Tad pulled the carriage up in front of the house, they all got out and went into the house. After they were gone, Tad asked cautiously, "You want me to hep you down, Marse Vince?"

"Yes."

Jake got to the ground with the servant's help, then

went to his room. He lay down on the bed, fully dressed, not even lighting the lamp. The darkness was a warm blanket that hid him from the world, and he longed for an even blacker night to cover him. But he knew that the morning would come and that he would have to face the world.

Suddenly one thought came to him, but he rejected it at once. It was the thought that he might pray to God.

"No!" he cried out between clenched teeth. "I've done without God this far! I won't whine now, like a whipped puppy!"

He put the thought away and lay there steeling himself for the sunrise, when he would have to go out and face the sneers he knew would be waiting for him.

It was a long night—but not long enough for Jake Hardin.

CHAPTER TWELVE

AN IMPOSSIBLE TASK

"LIKE I said, boy, the devil's going to take care of his own!"

There was a hint of grudging admiration in Dr. Maxwell's tone as he stepped back and watched Jake pull down his pants leg. He had given the young man's injuries a quick inspection, and now his watchful old eyes had a speculative look as he added, "I've seen good people take twice the time to get well that you have. Don't seem fair that a wastrel like you should have such an easy time!"

Jake smiled at the elderly physician, answering, "Sorry to upset your theology, Doctor. But it'll all catch up with me in the end, I guess." He stood and picked up the light cane for which he had traded his crutches. "How's my mother?"

Maxwell scratched his thick jowl, his fingernails making a rasping sound over the stubble he hadn't bothered to shave. "Not doing as well as I'd like." He looked around the room, then asked, "You got any drinking whiskey in here?"

"There's a bottle in the library. Come along." Jake moved ahead of the doctor, favoring his leg, and soon the two men were sharing a drink of whiskey. Jake wanted more details about Amy Franklin's injuries, but there was little that Maxwell could tell him.

"Don't pester me, Vince," he said with a flash of irritation in his voice. "I set the bone and that's all a man can do. Like I said, it's up to God now." He sipped the whiskey, then stared at the younger man. "And you and me, we don't have much influence there, do we?"

"Can't say about you, Doctor, but I don't have any myself."

Maxwell fired a question at him suddenly. "What you going to do about Duvall? You can't run every time you see him. This world's too small for that."

It was the first reference anyone had made about the incident at the ball to Jake himself, although he knew there had been much talk. The Franklin family had not said a word, but there was a coolness toward Jake that had not been there before the ball. Rachel had not smiled at him since that night, and his father had not said more than half a dozen words to him. Amy alone had retained her warmth, and for that reason Jake had spent more time with her than with anyone else.

"They say time heals all wounds, don't they?" he answered Maxwell's question with a question, then added, "Sooner or later Duvall will either get killed in one of his duels or he'll get killed in the war—or maybe he'll just forget it."

"And so you're just going to hide in your little hole, hoping for one of those things?" Maxwell snorted in disgust, finished the whiskey, then slammed the glass down. "You're a fool, boy!" He turned angrily and stomped out of the library. Jake picked up the glasses and, as he made his way to the kitchen, heard the door slam.

"You're right about that, Doc," he murmured. Entering the kitchen, he found Melora shelling peas. She nodded at him but said nothing. She was not, he thought, angry or disappointed in him as was the rest of the household, but she did seem to have lost some of her quickness of spirit lately. He didn't understand why, but he regretted it. "Guess I'll go sit with Mother awhile," he said. "Maybe she'd like some tea."

"She's asleep right now. Wait for an hour or so."

"All right. Can I help you shell peas?"

She did smile then but shook her head. "I'm almost finished. Why don't you go down to the barn and see the new colt? You need to get out more."

"Well, maybe I will." He paused to say, "I miss having you read to me. Maybe I shouldn't have let you know that my eyes are about normal." When she only smiled and shook her head, he turned and left the room. *She's carrying some kind of load,* he thought as he put on his heavy coat and wool cap. *Wouldn't be surprised if it had something to do with Clay Rocklin. She's not been the same since the night of the ball.*

He left the house, blinking at the cold wind that bit at his face. The world seemed dead with all of the grass a dry brown color and the trees looking like skeletons with long bony fingers lifted to a colorless, gray sky. Dry leaves rustled as he walked across the frozen ground, and a gust of wind gathered some of them together in a miniature whirlwind. They lurched at him and seemed to strike at his leg, then they broke apart to go tumbling across the lawn.

The barn was large, with many stalls for horses, a few for milking cows, and a huge loft stuffed with hay. Jake passed by one of the slaves, an elderly man named Delight, who was milking a cow. "Hi, Marse Vince," he said cheerfully. "You come to help me milk dis ol' cow?"

"Guess not, Delight," Jake said, smiling at the slave. "I never could get the hang of milking." He passed along to where the horses were kept and found the new colt with her dam in a walled-off section at the far end. But the leggy creature was not alone. Rachel stood there, stroking his nose. She looked up as Jake entered, saying, "Hello, Vince," in a level tone.

Jake nodded, then put his weight on his good leg, saying, "Good-looking foal." He studied the long slender legs, the wide-spaced eyes, and the fine barrel of the animal, then remarked, "He might win a race or two."

Rachel was wearing her outdoor working clothes—a pair of men's overalls and a worn white shirt. A felt slouch hat was pulled down over her forehead, and she wore a pair of leather boots that were well scuffed and dirty. The old coat she wore was made of wool, but it had lost any color it might have had long ago and had only one button in front.

Even in clothes like that, she's beautiful, Jake thought with a start.

The colt stared wildly at Jake, then moved closer to Rachel, pushing at her with his silky nose. Rachel laughed. "There's your mother over there," she said but stroked the face of the colt, allowing it to nibble at her fingers. She was, Jake thought as he watched her, more attractive in old clothes than most women were in ballroom gowns.

"What's his name?" he asked, wanting to hear her speak. Although he had not admitted it to himself, he had missed his times with Rachel more than he had thought possible. She had been hard, almost cold, but considering his role, he could understand that. Besides, he had come to know that hardness was not what Rachel was really made of; she had a fundamental sweetness that she kept concealed under a rough display of manners—and it was that hidden nature that Jake had grown to like.

"I'd like to call him *Precious,*" she said. "But he'd be embarrassed by that when he's a big stallion. I guess he'll be *Stonewall.*"

"After Jackson?"

"Yes. All colts are flighty, but the first time I came to see this one, he stood there stock-still, and I thought of Jackson and what Gen. Bee said about him at Manassas: 'Rally on the Virginians, men—there stands Jackson, like a stone wall!' "

"Good Southern name for a fine Southern foal," Jake said.

Rachel gave the foal a slap, which made him snort and stagger back to his dam, then she moved away toward the door. "Going back to the house?" he asked quickly, attempting to prolong their moment together.

"No, I'm going to give Crow a workout. He hasn't been ridden in a while, and you know how ornery he gets when that happens." She was at the door and waited as he followed her, hobbling a bit to keep up. When they got to a stall where a tall black horse stared at them over the bars with a pair of wicked eyes, she suddenly turned to Jake saying, "You know, I think your fear of horses started with Crow. From the time he piled you up when you were sixteen, you've stayed away from horses. It's a shame. There are so many fine horses here, and you don't get any pleasure out of them."

Jake said carefully, "Well, maybe you're right, Rachel." He hesitated, not wanting to get too far from Vince's habits, but finally said, "I'd like to ride a little this morning—maybe not on Crow, but on a nice steady horse."

She looked at him, surprise reflected in her eyes. "Well, there's plenty of those around. If you really mean it, I'll have Lady saddled for you."

He agreed, and she called out to one of the slaves to saddle the two horses. When they were ready, Jake moved toward the mare, a smallish horse with a finely shaped head. She turned around to look at him calmly, then snorted once and waited. Tossing his cane onto a bale of hay, Jake took the reins from the slave, grabbed the saddle horn, then put his left foot into the stirrup. "Need some help?" Rachel asked. She had mounted the big stallion in one swift motion and was watching him carefully.

"No, I can make it, I think." Jake shoved off with his good leg, pulling his weight up with both hands, and managed to throw his right leg over the horse, coming to rest in the saddle with a grunt. It had brought a twinge of pain to his leg, but he was happy to know that he was able to ride. He touched Lady with his heels, and she moved obediently, stepping out of the barn into the corral, followed by the big stallion.

Rachel watched him with barely veiled amazement. "You've been on a horse before!"

Jake looked at her quickly. He had forgotten that Vince never rode, and Rachel was too much of a horsewoman for him to try and deny the obvious—that he had mounted the horse and started it out with confidence. Well, the best defense was a good offense, and if there was one thing Jake was learning to do, it was to be offensive.

He smiled mockingly. "Just because I choose not to ride doesn't mean I can't do so, dear sister. Though why that should matter to you is beyond me. Unless, of course, you're afraid that being wrong about me in one area may mean you're wrong about me in others. And that's just too much for you to take, isn't it, Rachel? Being wrong about me?"

For a brief moment, Jake thought Rachel would wheel Crow and ride away from him. Then, suddenly, her expression changed from anger to something he couldn't quite define—but it almost looked as though she was ashamed. She closed her eyes for a second, then spoke in a soft voice.

"I never thought I'd be saying this to you, Vince, but you're probably right . . . and I'm sorry."

Jake looked at her, stunned. When he didn't respond, she lifted her eyes to meet his, and the hurt and confusion he saw in her made him want to reach out and take her in his arms.

"I've had my mind made up about you for a very long time," she said. "And you've never given me any reason to change my opinion—until lately." She shook her head. "There's something different about you, Vince. I'm not sure I can trust it, but I want you to know I'm trying. And I will try to stop making judgments based on the past." She smiled wanly. "Mama says she's been praying for you for years. I guess I need to keep in mind that God just may be answering her prayers."

Jake was dumbfounded, but fortunately Rachel didn't seem to need any response from him.

"Want to ride down to the river?" she asked, and Jake nodded. He had no idea where the river was, but he hoped it was far enough away for him to get his thoughts together. Rachel turned Crow's head toward a low-lying hill with a crop of tall timber at the crest. She kept her horse at a slow walk for Jake's benefit, but with some difficulty, for he wanted to bolt. "He's still rambunctious," Rachel commented. "I remember the day Daddy gave him to you. I cried all night," she said, smiling faintly at the old memory. "I wanted him so much!"

"Well, I guess you got him. I hear you're one of the few who can put up with his meanness," Jake commented. "He was just too much horse for me, I guess." She didn't respond, and he said, "You don't have to plod along with me, Rachel. Give him a run."

"I'll do that coming back. He needs to learn to mind." They wound around a trail that led through a pine forest, then followed it around a small pond that was riffled with the sharp breath of wind. After crossing several fields, all forlorn looking with their dead spikes of old cotton plants, the two riders came to the river. Actually, it was more of a creek than a river, for it was no more than twenty feet across, but it had steep banks, and Jake knew it would be a fine stream when the spring rains came.

It was a cold ride, but Jake enjoyed it. After being cooped up, he relished even the sharp bite of the wind. His face grew stiff and his hands as well. "I like this," he said as they finally turned back. "I wish it would snow."

She looked at him curiously. "You've always hated cold weather. I remember so many times, after it had snowed, how Les and Grant and I would go out and make snowmen and have snowball fights—and you'd stay in the house huddled up to a fireplace."

"I wasn't much fun back then, was I?" he said quietly. When Rachel looked at him uncertainly, he added, "Guess I'm losing my taste for some things in my old age. People always say you do." Then he said idly, "Guess I'd be better off if I did change."

Crow suddenly lunged out, as was his habit from time to time, but Rachel gave the reins a quick jerk, bringing him to a halt. "Stop that!" she commanded and waited until Jake caught up. His remark had caught at her—if only she could believe it! After a silence, she picked up on it. "We all change, don't we? I mean, just getting older means we have to change in some ways. And that's a good thing. I'd hate to be like I was when I was twelve!"

He looked at her quickly, admiring the color the wind had brought to her smooth cheeks. "Why would you hate that?"

She laughed, seemingly embarrassed. "You don't remember what a pain in the neck I was to everyone then? Always crying or laughing—no middle ground. Every day I changed, and the world was either terrible or grand. I wonder why Daddy and Mama didn't have me put to sleep!"

Jake laughed at her outrageous conclusions, saying, "You're still a little along those lines, I think."

"Oh? I thought I was doing better. I wish I was more like Mama. She never gets flustered and bothered over things. Seems as though I cry over dead leaves!"

"Makes you more interesting." Jake grinned at her.

"That's not what you used to say," Rachel retorted. "You'd get so mad at my moods you begged Daddy to whip me."

"He didn't do much of that, did he?"

"Not enough, you'd probably say."

A question came to Jake, surprising him. He tried to put it out of his mind, but it wouldn't leave him alone. Finally, he asked it carefully. "What about Leighton Semmes? You going to get emotional over him?"

"Leighton? Why, I don't know," she said, but his question disturbed her. She fell silent, and the two of them rode without speaking until they got to the crest of the hill overlooking the big house. Pulling Crow to a stop, she said, "He's quite a fellow, isn't he? Money, looks, and all that."

Jake felt an irrational surge of annoyance at this description of the man. "You like him pretty well?" he asked, making his voice casual.

"Oh, I don't know, Vince!" she said with a trace of sudden irritation. The truth was that this question had been much on her mind, and she was upset that she had no clear answer. "Why are you so interested?"

Jake wondered at that himself, but only answered, "Like to see the spinster of Lindwood get a good man. When I get old and broke, it'd be nice to have a rich brother-in-law to sponge off of."

"You're a scoundrel!" she remarked, laughing, surprised by his teasing tone. Then she grew more serious. "We're all going to change, aren't we? Nobody knows what this war will be like, not really. But I think it's going to be worse than the politicians think." She took off her slouch hat and shook her hair free, letting it fall over her shoulders. "I think we're going to lose everything."

"Father doesn't agree," Jake said. "And neither does Semmes, I'd guess. But you'd better keep thoughts like those to yourself. Anyone who speaks badly of the Cause is automatically branded a weakling—or worse."

"I know that, but I can't help what I think. Fortunately, even the war can't take everything away from me. I mean, nothing can take away what matters the most."

"Oh?" Jake looked at her curiously. Rachel returned his look, her eyes serious.

"'Neither death, nor life, nor angels, nor principalities, nor powers, nor things present, nor things to come, nor height, nor depth, nor any other creature, shall be able to separate us from the love of God, which is in Christ Jesus our Lord,'" she quoted, her voice low and confident. "I know you don't believe in that," she said with a shrug, "but I know it's true. And I know that, no matter what happens, God will be there to guide me and sustain me. *That's* what really matters."

Jake found himself strangely moved by what she said and by the confidence with which she said it. If only he could feel that way. . . .

"Anyway," she said, putting on her hat, "Semmes won't be rich if we lose the war, now, will he? Maybe I'd better go North. Lots of rich Yankees, I hear." She slanted a mischievous grin at him.

"Let's both go," he said. "Bound to be some rich Yankee spinsters just waiting for a Southern gentleman to come into their lives."

Rachel giggled, saying, "We're a pair of silly fools, aren't we?"

Jake suddenly grew serious, his wide mouth growing tense. "To tell the truth, Rachel, I'd really like to cut and run. You're right about the war. The South is going to be ruined—no way she can win this war. And I don't want to see it."

Rachel glanced at him quickly. The last two weeks she'd been so ashamed of his cowardice she had avoided him. Now she was seeing something else, and for some reason it troubled her. Without thinking what she was doing, she moved Crow closer to the mare, reached out, and put her hand over his hands as they gripped the pommel. "God has given you so many gifts—and you've wasted them all."

He was acutely conscious of her firm hand on his. "Yes, I have," he said quietly, thinking of all he knew of Vince's past.

"You can change," Rachel said softly, and her voice drew his gaze. "Anybody can change—and down beneath all that anger, I believe there's a very fine man. I'd give anything to see you be that man."

He sat there, aware of her strength, her character—and of how very attractive she was to him. Suddenly he knew that under any other circumstances, he would have pulled her close and kissed her. He longed to do so with a force that startled him—and at that moment he was possessed by a most astounding realization. And that realization, with her hand, so warm and strong, on his, and the planes of her face, so soft and gentle, near his, struck him so hard that it nearly knocked the breath from him.

I love this girl!

It leaped into his mind, and he was so astonished that

he could only sit still and stare at her. *Why, she's all I've ever wanted!* was his next thought, and he suddenly realized that behind all of his restless wandering had been a search for a woman like this. He had known many women, of course, but never before had he met one who stirred him as did Rachel Franklin.

Then, right on the heels of this revelation, came the cold fact of how hopeless his position was. A bleakness formed within him, and he could only say, "I'd like to be that man, Rachel—but it's not that easy."

A shadow came to her face as he said the words, and she drew her hand back. Disappointment pinched her lips together, and she said briefly, "I suppose not," then she kicked Crow in the sides and shot off at a dead run.

Jake followed, slowly. When he got to the barn and carefully dismounted, she was gone. Delight came up to say, "I'll take keer of yoah horse. You have a nice ride, Marse Vince?"

"Very nice," he said evenly and left the barn.

All during November of 1861 both North and South seemed to be caught in some sort of paralysis. After the horrible slaughter of Manassas, both nations had realized that the war was not going to be the quick affair they had expected. On November 6, in the first general election, Jefferson Davis was elected president of the Confederacy for a six-year term. On the first day of that same month, George B. McClellan officially replaced Lt. Gen. Winfield Scott as general in chief of the United States Army. On November 8, two Confederate commissioners, James Mason and John Slidell, took passage aboard the British packet *Trent* out of Havana. Capt. Charles Wilkes of the USS *San Jacinto* intercepted the British vessel in international waters and forced the British captain to surrender his passengers. This action came close to changing the course of the war, for it was an open act of aggression by the United States Navy against England.

There were skirmishes in the eastern sector, but the most significant military movement was the massing of Union troops in the West. An obscure officer named Ulysses S. Grant was assigned to the command of Gen. John Charles Fremont; a red-haired, nervous general named Sherman was attached to that same army. Grant and Sherman would prove to be the most potent forces the North would bring to bear against the Confederacy. On November 13, President Lincoln paid a call on his new army chief, but McClellan kept the president waiting and finally retired for the evening without meeting his superior.

Jake Hardin heard about some of this and knew it was significant to the course of history, but it meant little to him. A much more significant event in his own life was a meeting that he had with Brad Franklin. Jake was sitting in the library reading *Ivanhoe* when Franklin came in and closed the folding doors. There was something in the man's manner that made Jake put the book down with alarm. When the major sat down in a chair and stared at him with a frown, Jake was certain what was coming was something unpleasant.

"Vince, it's time to settle something."

"Yes sir?"

Franklin's fair skin was windburned and rough from his days in the field, and his rather hungry-looking face had none of the good humor to which Jake had grown accustomed. His eyes were pulled down into a squint, and his lips were tense as he said, "Maybe you can guess what I'm going to say."

"No, I don't think I can."

"All right, I'll give it to you as straight as I can. You're a failure in every way. I don't like to say that, especially since for years you've considered me to be unfair, favoring your brothers and sister over you. I'm sorry for that, but I can't change the way you feel—though it's been a grief to me."

Somewhere outside the window, some of the slaves were laughing as they raked the leaves from the oaks, and the cheerful noise of their voices sounded thin and far away, like happy crickets. The clock on the wall ticked solemnly, a ponderous and heavy brass pendulum arching in a uniform cadence from side to side.

Franklin looked down at his hands, sighed heavily, then said, "You've not been a good son. Maybe I've been a bad father—probably so—but my failures were honest ones. Yours were not. I won't lecture you, though. It's too late for that, I know."

He took some papers out of his pocket, opened them, and pressed them flat. "This is a copy of my father's will. You know what it says, or at least you know the part that pertains to you."

"Yes sir."

"Well, my father was a difficult man, and I was a difficult son. He thought I didn't care for him, and he thought I didn't have any love in me, especially not enough to give a son if I ever had one. So he tied the bulk of the estate up in a trust and left it to my eldest son. You've been looking forward to that for a long time. As a matter of fact, it's ruined you! You never felt you had to do anything, because everything would one day be handed to you on a silver platter. You've spent your life on that trust, and I've seen it take every good thing out of you. You've become a womanizer, a drunk, and a coward—in short, Vince, you're a man without honor." He paused to ask, "Care to comment on that?"

"Well, no sir, I guess not." Jake was wishing Vince were sitting in his chair—wishing it hard! He could not defend the life of another man, for he truly didn't know him. But he knew enough to be certain that much of what Franklin said was true.

"You've read the will carefully," Franklin said slowly, as if forcing the words from his lips, "but men have a way of seeing only what they want to see. If I could have found a way to break this will, I'd have done it in a second, but it can't be done. At least—not in the way my father might have expected."

"I don't understand you, sir."

"My father didn't respect me, but he was certain of one thing, and that was my love for the land, for Lindwood. He knew I'd do almost anything a man could do to keep the home place in the hands of Franklins. And he was right—or he was, up until now. But some things are too expensive, and I think holding on to this plantation may cost too much for us to do it."

"You're thinking about selling Lindwood?"

"No. That can't be done. Like most other planters, we live on borrowed money. What Father expected was that my oldest son, when he came into the bulk of the estate at the age of twenty-five, would save the place—pay off the mortgages, invest in new land, or buy more slaves. But you won't do those things."

"Well, it might be—"

"No, you've not shown the slightest interest in this place since you were young—at which time you apparently decided to go to the devil. Well, in a few months you'll be twenty-five, and the will says that you'll get the money." He paused, then shook his head slowly. "For years I've hoped you'd come to yourself, that you'd become a man, but you haven't changed a bit. So, let me read you one little clause in the will you've probably never noticed." He lifted the copy, ran his eyes down it, then read, "'The entire amount of the trust shall go to the eldest son of Bradford Lowell Franklin upon his twenty-fifth birthday, provided that he is at that time living at Lindwood and that my son, Bradford Lowell Franklin, certifies that he is qualified to receive the monies of the trust.'" Brad Franklin lowered the paper slowly, then shook his head. "It never occurred to Father that I'd refuse to certify you, but that's what I'm going to do."

The force of his words hit Jake a heavy blow—but not as heavy as he knew it would be to Vince! "But, sir—," he began, only to have Maj. Franklin cut him off.

"I won't argue this. The will states that if I don't certify that you are fit to receive the trust, it will go to charity.

There are some causes that will be very happy to hear that some large sums are going to fall to them."

Jake had no idea of what to say. If only Vince were here! He finally said, "But that's foolish, isn't it? I mean, I'll be glad to see that the money goes to Lindwood—"

"Vince, you've done nothing but lie to me for years. Why would I take your word for anything?"

Jake sat there stunned, aware that Franklin was watching him with interest. *Probably expects me to start shouting and screaming,* he thought, but he knew that such behavior would have no effect. Brad Franklin was a firm man, and once he had made up his mind no arguments would move him. Jake finally shrugged, saying, "I'm sorry it's come to this. Isn't there some way I could influence you? You may not believe me, but I'd like to see Lindwood prosper."

"Would you? You've never shown such a feeling for your home."

"Well, maybe nearly getting killed changed me some."

"I'd like to believe you. A lot of sweat and tears have gone into this place. I've put my life into it, and it was our dream—your mother's and mine—to grow old here, with our children and grandchildren around us."

"I—I'd like to see that, sir!"

When Jake said this, Franklin stared at him, letting the silence run on. He tried to see beyond the errors of his son's past and look for something that would make him feel that Vince could be honest. Finally he said, "I don't think you mean it—but if you want a chance to prove it—"

"Yes, I would like that. Very much!"

"All right, here it is—" Brad shook his head, interrupting himself long enough to say with a sour smile, "I thought you'd make some kind of offer to reform, to get the money. So if you'll do three things, I'll certify you for the trust."

"Three things?"

"All impossible, Vince, I really believe. But I'll lay them

out, then you can do as you please. First, you'll ride Crow, really master him." He smiled at the expression on Jake's face. "That surprises you? Well, it's a small thing. I gave you that horse knowing that he was half outlaw. You were just starting to rebel, and I had the foolish idea that if you could learn to break a horse to your will, it would teach you something. But he won, didn't he? I saw it happen, and it's been a shame to me that my son is afraid of horses. Do you think men don't know that about you? How many times have I seen you get in a buggy like a woman, when the men were all riding horses?"

Jake had not understood that the matter of Crow was so serious, but now he saw that the horse was a symbol to Brad Franklin of his son's failure as a man. He said quietly, "You know I'm afraid of horses and you know that Crow is a tough one. But I'll do my best with him."

"Will you? I'm thinking it's too late, but that's the easiest of the three. You can guess one of the other things, I would suspect."

Jake nodded, for it had leaped into his mind. "You want me to meet Simon Duvall."

Franklin looked grim. "I think most of this dueling business is wrong—and stupid! But a man sometimes has to choose—and you chose to be branded a coward in front of the world! I won't have it! You can take your chances with Duvall or forget about the trust. Your mother may not agree, but then again I think she will. You may get shot, but if you do, I want to see the wounds in the front!"

Jake nodded slowly. "I agree."

Maj. Franklin was surprised and said so. "I don't think you'll go through with it, but you'll have to if you want the money. Now about the third thing, I had some hope that you might be willing to try a horse and a fight with Duvall. But the last thing—well, I can't see that you'll agree to it."

Jake was thinking hard, and he asked, "Does it have something to do with the war?"

"Yes, it does. You were always a quick thinker. This war, it's not what I wanted. But we didn't have the choice, most of us, so we've had to lay our lives down for our homes. You think it's foolish, this war. You've ridiculed it often enough. But if you want Lindwood, you'll have to fight for it—maybe die for it." He leaned back, studying the face of the young man. "I'm probably asking too much, but I'm convinced that the final ruination of you would be to have great wealth put into your hands. Maybe nothing can change you, but if anything can, I think throwing yourself into a cause might . . . so I want you to join the South in their fight. The men in your regiment will know what you've stood for, and they won't make it any easier."

"No, I don't think they would." Jake felt trapped, and he said, "I'll need a little time. It's not a small thing you're asking, is it?"

"No, but there's no time for thinking. You'll either do it or you won't, Vince. If you're going to do it, I'll need to know pretty soon."

"All right." Jake got to his feet, looked around for his cane, then remembered he'd laid it aside for good the day before. "I'll make a decision as soon as I can."

As Jake left the room, Franklin was suddenly certain that his son would run. "He did before, when it was just one man after his hide," he muttered. "Why wouldn't he do the same thing when he has to face the Union Army?"

CHAPTER THIRTEEN

A VERY TIGHT CORNER

For two days after Brad Franklin laid down his conditions, Jake wandered over the countryside, riding the little mare Lady for long hours. She was a fine little horse, never balking or refusing a command. Then the weather turned bad on the third day, with snow beginning to fall about ten that morning.

As the flakes came down, Jake stopped Lady and watched them with delight. He had always loved snow, but he had spent most of his life where there was little of it. Now the sight of the flakes swirling and dancing in the wind pleased him. Lifting his face, he savored the cold touch of the tiny flakes as they landed on his skin. Finally he moved toward home. By the time he arrived, the ground was white with a thin blanket.

Bob, the youngest of the grooms, unsaddled the mare, and Jake hurried into the house. Going through the front door, he was met by Melora, who said, "Vincent, there's a man to see you. He said his name was Finch."

"Finch? Did he say what he wanted?"

"No, he just said he had to see you. I put him in the library."

"Thanks, Melora." Jake turned and made his way to the library, apprehensive about the man. It had to be a friend of Vince's—and it would be hard to fake the thing knowing no more than he did.

However, that part of it was not difficult, for the tall, rawboned man, who was sitting at the table drinking coffee, rose as he entered and asked, "Are you Vince Franklin?"

"Yes, I'm Franklin."

"Well, I got a message for you. Sort of a private message, I guess, nothing written down." He was a tough-looking man with a scar on his forehead and some teeth missing.

"Well, what is it?"

"Mrs. Rocklin—Mrs. Ellen Rocklin—she wants to see you."

Jake tried to think what she could want. His first thought was that she was trying to stir up her old romance, and he wanted no part of that. "I'll see her pretty soon. You can tell her I'll be visiting at Gracefield later on in the week."

Finch shook his head, saying, "I reckon it's pretty important. She told me to tell you that she *had* to see you—today."

"Today!"

"It's what she said. I dunno what about—," Finch hesitated, sizing up his man, then nodded. "I'd go if I was you, Mr. Franklin. Mrs. Rocklin, she was pretty stout about it. She said that if you wouldn't come, she'd have to come here—and she didn't think you'd like that."

Jake thought rapidly. He certainly didn't want Ellen coming to Lindwood, and he'd had a taste of how vindictive she could be when she'd forced Melora to dance with Clay. *Better get it over with,* he thought, then nodded. "All right. Where'll I find her?"

"She said she'd be in her room, that's in Mrs. Mulligan's boardinghouse, over by the bakery. Said she'd like to see you about one this afternoon." Then he picked up his coat, saying, "Got to get back."

Jake stood there, trying to think of a way out of the meeting, but knowing that he'd have to go. He went to his room, changed to some heavier clothing, then went back to the kitchen, where Rachel was baking a cake. "I've got to go into Richmond, Rachel," he said.

"It'll be too long a trip for you," she said. "You can't ride that far."

"I'll take the buggy."

She tasted the mix, weighed the flavor of it, then put her spoon down and called out, "Melora!" When the girl appeared, she said, "Vince and I have to go to town. We'll be late getting back. Can you take care of everything?"

"Certainly, Rachel. I suppose you want me to finish that cake?"

"Yes, it's going to be a flop, I think. You can take the blame, Vince. Now go tell Tad to hitch up the sleigh while I get some heavier clothes on."

"Wait a minute!" he protested. "I don't have to have a keeper for a little trip to town."

"I need some things at the store," she said, but he saw the wink she gave to Melora. "Go on, now. I'll be quick."

In twenty minutes Jake was driving down the road with Rachel at his side, and despite the fact that he was worried about the meeting with Ellen, he enjoyed the ride. The snow was falling more gently, but it had rounded all the sharp hills to smooth cones and loaves, and the trees glistened like diamonds as the sun came out now and again to touch them.

"I've been looking for an excuse to get out and play in the snow," Rachel confessed. "I love it!"

"It is pretty," Jake agreed. "I like to see it fall like this, but it's a mess afterward."

"You'd complain if they hung you with a new rope!" Her spirits were high because she was pleased to be outside, and the trip to town was a welcome break from the monotony of work. "Everything worthwhile is trouble."

He turned to look at her, noting that the snow had fallen on her hair where it had escaped from her hat, giving it a spangled effect. "What does that mean?"

"Why, just what it says," Rachel said, surprised at his question. "Didn't you know that? I've known it for a long time. For instance, getting married is a lot of fun, so they say. What with the courtship and the wedding dress and the cake. But being married, that's work! Still, you can't just have a wedding without the marriage—so it's worth it, they say. And look at babies, Vince. All nice and cuddly and cute, but they're trouble, too—diapers and colic and Lord knows what else! So you see, everything worthwhile is trouble."

"Never thought of that." He watched the snow as it fell on the backs of the horses and was pleased with their companionable silence as they travelled. The only sound was the soft plopping of the hooves and the slight crunching of the sleigh through the snow. After a while, he asked, "Is the opposite true then? Are things that aren't trouble worthless?"

She thought about it, holding her hand out from under the canopy and letting the flakes settle on her palm. "No, it doesn't work that way," she said. "Look at this snow. And at how nice it is to be out in it. It's no trouble, is it? But it's not worthless. I can remember a lot of times that snow has brought me joy and laughter. Even today, it has brightened my day. Nothing that does that could be worthless."

She fell silent, then said, "It's nice to have good memories, isn't it? Then when the bottom falls out of things, you've got something to think about."

Jake said evenly, "I don't think most people have as many good memories as you do, Rachel. Most of us don't have sense enough to do the little things, and we miss out on memories like this."

They talked all the way to town, and when he pulled up at the store she indicated, she turned her face to him, saying, "What a nice trip! Thanks for insisting that I come!" When he told her she'd invited herself, she stuck her tongue out, then said, "Take your time. I'll be here when you get ready to go back. Or if I'm not here, I'll be over at Grant's Cafe."

He left her and with some difficulty found the boardinghouse Finch had mentioned. It was a respectable enough place, Vince noticed as he tied the horses to the rail then went up on the front porch. When he knocked on the door, a tall, plain woman of fifty opened it. "I'm looking for Mrs. Rocklin," he said.

"Come in." The woman stepped back, adding, "I'm Harriet Mulligan. It's getting colder, isn't it?"

"Not too bad yet, but it could get worse."

"Mrs. Rocklin's room is right at the top of those stairs, second door to your left."

"Thank you, Mrs. Mulligan."

Jake climbed up the stairs, favoring his right leg. When he knocked on the door, it opened at once.

"Hello, Vince," Ellen said, stepping back to let him enter. "You made good time. I didn't know it was going to snow like this or I'd have waited until later." She was wearing a fashionable dress that was cut to flatter her figure, which was somewhat lush. Her hair was done up in what he supposed was the latest style.

He took the chair she offered him, on his guard. "Is something wrong, Ellen?" he asked.

"Have a drink, and we'll talk about it." She took a bottle from a cabinet and started to pour, then said, "But you like bourbon better than scotch, don't you?"

"That's right."

She put the bottle down and looked at him with excitement in her large eyes. "No, you don't like bourbon at all. You always insist on scotch."

Jake looked at her thoughtfully. Now at least he knew why he was there. What he didn't know was if he could fool Ellen. He said in a bored voice, "I'll take either one, Ellen."

Ellen admired the man's poise and poured them two glasses of the scotch. When he picked up his glass, she lifted her own and made a toast. "Here's to a profitable venture."

He stared at her, then drank the liquor. "What's on your mind, Ellen?"

She put the glass down and asked directly, "What's your real name?"

Jake shrugged. "You know my name, Ellen. And you know I don't have time for games."

He got up to go, but she said quickly, "Do you remember coming over to play with my boys when you were twelve years old? The summer that Rena broke her arm?"

"I guess I remember."

"That's odd—because Rena never had a broken arm!" Triumph was in Ellen's eyes, and she went on quickly, "But Vince Franklin did spend most of one summer at Gracefield. And *he* had a little accident. You don't remember that? No, I didn't think you would! But I remember it well enough. Vince and David were jumping off the loft into piles of hay, and Vince hit a sharp piece of wire that someone had left there. It wasn't a bad cut, but it left a small scar." She smiled and asked, "You don't remember what shape the scar was in? No, I didn't think you would. It was in the shape of a heart—a little lopsided, but a heart right between your thumb and forefinger. We joked about it quite a bit. I'm surprised that nobody else noticed it."

As he saw the triumph in the woman's eyes, Jake knew there was no hope. "You're a smart woman, Ellen. Nobody else noticed that, not even Vince's mother or Rachel. I guess they'd forgotten it."

Ellen lowered her voice, even though they were alone. "What did you do to Vince?"

"I don't think I want to talk about it."

"You don't have any choice, don't you see that?" She smiled at him, then said, "Too bad I'm a Rocklin—too bad for you, that is. I've heard about the will leaving the Franklin money to the oldest son when he reached twenty-five years of age. Most people don't know that. When I saw your hand at the ball, I knew you weren't Vince. It took me a little while to figure out the rest of it."

"What have you figured, Ellen?"

"Why, it's the money, of course!" she said with surprise. "Don't take me for a fool—it has to be the money!" She looked at him carefully, then shook her head. "You look enough like him to be his twin. Did you kill him and take his place?"

"No."

Ellen began to grow angry. "Then what's it for, this masquerade?" Suddenly she had a thought, and a look of satisfaction appeared in her eyes. "Of course! That Vince! I know what he's done . . . he found you and hired you to take his place. He's got to be on the plantation to get the money, and he's afraid that Duvall will kill him." She saw his eyes widen as she spoke, then laughed. "I told you not to take me for a fool. Now where's Vince?"

Jake said slowly, "Ellen, I can't tell you anything. I'm just a hired hand."

"Well, you can tell Vince that unless I get a slice of that big pie—there won't *be* any pie!"

"Yes, I thought we'd come to that."

"Sure you did," she said swiftly. "You're a smart boy. I like smart people." She leaned forward and stroked his hand. "I'm going to enjoy doing business with you. What's your real name?"

"Jack Colt," he replied without pausing.

"Well, now, Jack, I think we're at the beginning of a beautiful friendship. How long will it take you to get word to Vince that he has a new partner?"

"He's in New Orleans. I'll have to write him."

"Write today, or send a wire."

"He'll never show his face around here, Ellen."

She studied Jake's face, then nodded. "All right, get the letter off. Tell him I want half."

"You're no piker, are you?"

"Half of something is better than all of nothing, isn't it? I know Vince. He'll pay up."

"Yes, I think he will." Jake got to his feet and started for the door. There was something evil about the woman, and he wanted to have nothing to do with her. "I'll send the letter, but whatever you decide will be between you and him. I'm just a hired hand."

She came out of her chair and put her arms around his neck. "If something happened to Vince," she whispered, "you and I would have *all* the money, Jack!"

There was a heavy air of suggestiveness in the woman,

and it repelled Jake. *I'd as soon kiss a cobra!* he thought as he pulled away, saying, "You'd better do your business with Vince." Then he left the room.

He climbed into the buggy and went at once to the telegraph station. If he could, he would just walk away from the whole situation. There was nothing keeping him at Lindwood, really. Nothing except the fact that he'd given Vince Franklin his word. And if there was one thing that could be counted on about Jake Hardin, it was that he didn't break his word. For whatever reason, he had always stood by the promises or deals that he made. Some men would call it an innate integrity—for Jake, it was just the way things were.

The message he sent to Vince was cryptic, one that the telegrapher could not understand enough to report to anyone. "Come at once. Deal going sour."

He paid for the wire, then left the office and went to find Rachel. She was still at the store and was surprised to see him so soon. "Let's eat before we go back," she said.

They had a good meal, though Jake ate little, and the trip home was a delight to her, if not to Jake. It was dark by the time they pulled the team into the barn, and they made their way through the snow to the house.

"Let's just stand here and enjoy it," she said. "Look, the snow is coming down in slanting lines!"

"Pretty," he said quietly, as she turned to face him.

"You got some bad news in town, didn't you?" she said quietly. "I knew it as soon as you came into the store."

"You're an observant woman, Rachel."

"What is it? Anything I can help you with?" Rachel wasn't sure who was more surprised by her offer, Vince or herself. She still wasn't sure about Vince—whether he was truly changing or if he was up to one of his schemes—but more and more she discovered that she wanted to believe in him. And, as she watched him, an even more amazing realization suddenly came to her.

"No," he said slowly. "I don't think there's much anyone can do."

She stood there, looking at him, still sorting through her own emotions. Finally she said, "Well, if it takes a miracle, there are precedents. I can tell you one that's happened right here at Lindwood."

"A miracle? They've been pretty rare in my life. What is it?"

She turned to watch the snow, and he could tell she was thinking, choosing her words carefully.

"What is it?" Jake asked again.

"I don't hate you anymore." She turned to face him, and shock ran through him as he saw tears in her eyes. "I have for a long time, you know. I just couldn't help it! But since you've come home, I—" She broke off, and he saw that she was trembling, not from the cold, but from sobs.

Without thought he put his arms around her, and she began to cry helplessly. He stood there waiting as an emotion ran through him such as he'd never had in his life. She was warm and desirable, but it wasn't that. It was something more than he'd ever known he could feel about a woman. She thought he was her brother and so surrendered herself to him freely. But he was painfully conscious that this woman—of all the women in the world—was the only one who would do for him!

Finally Rachel's sobs lessened, then ceased. She drew back, her tears making silver tracks on her cheeks in the moonlight. "I'm sorry, but I warned you, didn't I? That I can only hold things in for so long and then it seems I bawl for days. But it's been so awful! I've never wanted to hate anybody—and now it's all gone." The hushed tone of amazement in her voice moved Jake deeply.

"I'm glad of that, Rachel," he said quietly.

She waited, then asked, "There's nothing I can do to help you?"

He stood there looking down into her face, and there was nothing to guide him. He'd been like a cloud all his life, drifting where the wind sent him. Now for the first time, he wanted something, and it didn't look much as though he were likely to get it.

Finally he said, "Maybe you can help."

"What is it?"

He said slowly, "You'll hear about it soon enough, so I may as well tell you myself." He told her of the conditions her father had laid down, then said, "I've got to ride a wild horse, fight a duel, and join the Confederate Army. Almost everybody's going to think I'm a phony and a fraud. I'm going to need all the help I can get."

She suddenly grabbed his coat, her eyes enormous, and there was a great happiness in them. "You can do it, Vince! I know you can!" Then she pulled his head down and kissed him on the cheek. "I'll help you! We can do it together!"

His cheek burned like fire where she had kissed him, and he said no more. For a long time they stood there, watching the snow fall. The flakes were light as air and settled on the white crust soundlessly. She held his arm, and finally they turned and went into the house.

A red fox appeared five minutes later. He trotted up, sniffed the air in a businesslike fashion, then turned and made his way to the henhouse, where nice, fat hens were sleeping without a thought of a visitor.

***

PART THREE
THE BRAVO

***

CHAPTER FOURTEEN

ELLEN'S SECRET

WHEN the rest of the Richmond Grays came back from the Valley to join the defensive forces that ringed Richmond, most of the men were given short leave. This was much simpler in the case of the Grays than for most units, because three-fourths of the men were from the Richmond area and could be recalled quickly in case of emergency. There was a short speech by Col. Benton to the collected regiment, during which he applauded their service. He ended by saying, "It will be up to us to repel the enemy when they come upon us, and I am depending on you to come back determined to keep them from our homes and our land." He called on Maj. Jeremiah Irons to dismiss the regiment with a prayer, and when the chaplain concluded, he dismissed the men, who gave him a rousing cheer.

"Pretty soft, eh?" Lt. Bushrod Aimes said to Capt. Taylor Dewitt. "If we were off in Tennessee with Gen. Johnston, we'd be stuck." Aimes was a happy-go-lucky sort of man, an old crony of Dewitt's, and so he spoke freely. "Most of us will come back with massive hangovers, I expect—but it may be our last chance at relaxing for a while."

Maj. Brad Franklin, who had joined his regiment again for the ceremony, had been standing close enough to hear Aimes's remark and came over to say, "Better not let the chaplain hear you say that, Lieutenant. He's a pretty hard man."

Capt. Dewitt grinned. "Well, I wish the rest of the regiment could shoot as well as Chaplain Irons. It's a toss-up as to whether he or Clay Rocklin is the best shot."

Bushrod said before thinking, "That's for sure, Taylor, and if those two ever got in a fight over Melora Yancy, it'd be a close thing—" Then he saw the displeasure that crossed the faces of both men and realized he'd blundered into a delicate situation. One of the disadvantages of a regiment drawn from the same area was that everybody was aware of the details of the lives of the others. Those who really knew Clay Rocklin had no doubt that his interest in Melora Yancy was free of any immorality, but there was something about the matter that caused talk nonetheless. Perhaps it was because the chaplain of the Grays was a suitor for Melora—and the fact that Melora's brother was in Clay's squad only made the matter even more involved.

Bob Yancy had heard a man from Company A make a remark about his sister and had promptly broken his jaw. It was an indication of the state of the matter that Col. Benton had taken no action. When Aimes had given a slight rebuke to Bob Yancy, the young man had stared at him, saying, "Let another man talk about my sister and he'll get worse than a busted jaw!"

Now Lt. Aimes tried to extricate himself from his unfortunate remark by changing the subject and was aided by Capt. Dewitt, who said quickly, "Well, let's get started on that leave." The three men separated.

Maj. Franklin went at once to speak to Lt. Dent Rocklin, who was giving some final advice to his squad. As he waited, Franklin had a chance to study the young man. He was, the major thought, one of the finest-looking men in the army—or had been before his face had been disfigured by a Yankee saber at the battle of Manassas. He still was handsome from the right side, but the left side of his face was distorted from the wound, the eye drawn down and the mouth drooping in a sinister expression. Like others of the family, Maj. Franklin had feared that the young man would go sour over such a disfiguring injury, but that had not happened. Now as Dent saw him and came over to greet him, there was an ease and contentment in his expression. He smiled, saying, "Well, I get back from a honeymoon just in time to go on leave, Major."

"You're a lucky chap, Dent," Maj. Franklin commented with a nod. He liked the young man enormously and said, "Bring your bride over to our place tomorrow. Amy's invited the whole clan, so you may have to fight over a plate. Where's your father? I want him there with all his bunch. Well, you can tell him his sister said to be there or she'd take a stick to him."

"I'll tell him, sir," Dent assured him. "It'll be good to have the whole family together."

"I'm having one of those picture-taking fellows come over, too. Hard enough to get our tribe together under normal circumstances. Now with this war, this may be our last chance."

Though Franklin didn't say so, Dent Rocklin knew that his uncle was obliquely referring to the fact that some of them might be killed. However, he said only, "I'll give the fellow my best side."

Franklin glanced at him sharply, then smiled. "I'm glad to see you've not let your wounds make you bitter, my boy."

"I've got a lot to be thankful for," Dent said thoughtfully. "I could be in one of those graves out there where so many of our people are. And I've got Raimey." His reference to his new bride brought a light of pride into his eyes and he added, "She's changed the world for me. If I ever amount to anything, it'll be her doing."

"A fine woman! Well, you come prepared to stay at least two or three days." He nodded, then left saying, "See you tomorrow, Denton."

At once Dent went to locate the second platoon and found their sergeant, Waco Smith, giving them a final word of warning. "If any of you think you can get by with gettin' back late," the tall Texan stated acrimoniously, "or so drunk you can't shoot straight, get it out of your mind. The Yankees are headin' this way, and this heah squad is gonna stop 'em." He might have said more, but he glanced around to see Dent and said, "Lieutenant, you want to tie a bell to any of this bunch so's we can find 'em when we need 'em?"

"I don't guess so, Sergeant." Dent grinned, winking at the men. He waited until Smith dismissed them, then went to his father. "I've got a message for you," he said quickly. "Maj. Franklin said to tell you that Aunt Amy commands your presence at Lindwood tomorrow."

Clay grinned suddenly, his bronzed face looking younger. "That sister of mine always did boss me around," he said. "She summoning just me—or the whole crew?"

"It's the whole family. There's even a photographer coming to get a picture."

"Will you and Raimey be there?"

"Oh, sure," Dent said. "And the Bristols, too, I think. The whole clan of Rocklin—or the Southern branch of it, anyway." He hesitated, then spoke his thought aloud, "I think Aunt Amy has the idea that if we're ever going to get a picture of all of us, it better be now."

"She may be right about that," Clay said. "Well, we'll be there." The two men separated, Dent going hurriedly to the small house that Samuel Reed, his father-in-law, had insisted on renting for the new couple. It was a very small white house close to the Reed mansion, but it had been a haven for Dent and Raimey. When he paid the cabdriver and walked toward the house, the door opened and Raimey came flying out, throwing herself into his arms.

"Dent!" she cried out, and even as he crushed her in his arms, he marveled at her movement. *How did she know I'd catch her?* he wondered, but their short time of marriage had taught him that Raimey's loss of vision had not limited her courage or imagination.

"Hey!" he said when he had kissed her, "let's get out of this cold." Keeping his arm around her, he listened as she spoke quickly and with great animation. Dulcie, her maid from childhood, was standing inside with a smile. "Dulcie, how are you?" he said.

"Better than you gonna be if you don't get out of that cold and snow!" she said sharply. She worried him out of his coat, then hustled the two of them into the tiny dining room, where she and Raimey began feeding him at once. She practically shoved her two charges into their chairs. "Now you two set there and eat!"

The two of them ate the tender pork chops, fried squash and onions, boiled snap beans with ham hock, and a plate of thickened, greasy chicken gravy. Afterwards, they topped the meal off with a dish of pickled peaches studded with cloves. Raimey ate little, but told Dent what she had been doing as he ate. She ended by saying, "We're going to Lindwood tomorrow for a few days."

Dent was amused. "I thought I'd give *you* that news. Uncle Brad just told me when we left camp."

Raimey smiled slyly. "Oh, Aunt Amy and I have been planning it for a long time. It's going to be so nice, Dent!" Raimey had never had a large family, and she had claimed the Rocklins as her own family almost as soon as she and Denton were engaged. "We'll go there first thing in the morning so I can help with the work."

Dent leaned back in his chair and studied her as he sipped his coffee. It never ceased to amaze him how this girl had managed to fill his life. He knew himself well enough to realize that if she had not come along and offered her love when he was in the hospital, he would probably not have lived. Their honeymoon had been a revelation to him, for he had learned for the first time to give instead of always taking. It had been mutual, though, for Raimey had given herself so completely in every way that both of them had understood that they had that most rare possession—a marriage that was a union of both flesh and spirit.

Now he said to tease her, "Well, I guess you're tired of me, Raimey. Too bad! I thought our honeymoon would last longer."

"Why—what in the world does *that* mean?" she asked, startled.

"Just that you could have me all to yourself here in this cozy house—but you'd rather go spending time with all those people."

Raimey's quick ears picked up on the teasing note in his voice, and she said instantly, "You're spoiled, that's what you are! I declare, I'm going to have to teach you how to behave, Dent Rocklin!"

Then she came to him and bent over to kiss him. "Now that's a lesson I'd gladly be given again," he said huskily and pulled her into his lap. When Dulcie came to glance in, wondering at the sudden silence, she quickly pulled her head back and nodded with satisfaction.

The next morning they arose late, had a leisurely breakfast, then loaded into the sleigh and started for Lindwood. Dulcie, as a matter of course, was going, for she had been Raimey's eyes for years. She sat in the back, enveloped in a blanket, while Dent and Raimey sat in the front. As they made their way along, Dent found himself describing for his wife the things he saw. In the process, he noted that he was seeing things much more clearly, picking up things that he would have previously ignored. He told her of the red fox that appeared, dapper and neat, with the limp form of a rabbit in its mouth. And he described the sprightly running of a buck and two does as they seemed to float effortlessly on their way. It was a source of happiness to him to be able to bring the world to her. For she had given him so much—his faith, his joy . . . his life.

By the time they reached Lindwood, the snow was falling in tiny crystalline flakes, frozen crumbs actually. The wind blew them so that they stung Raimey's face, and she laughed in delight. "I love snow! Maybe we'll get snowed in and have to stay a week!"

"That'd be rough on Brad and Amy," Dent said, laughing. He glanced around, seeing several sleighs, then added, "Looks like the others are here already." He stopped the team, and several of the slaves were there to take charge of them. Dent, Raimey, and Dulcie hurried inside, where they were met by Rachel. "Hello, Rachel," Dent said, helping Raimey off with her coat. "Beginning to snow."

"Hello, Dent," Rachel said. She smiled and went to Raimey, taking her hands. "Raimey, your hands are frozen! Come along to the fire." She led the two of them through the foyer and into the large living room that faced the front. "Here's Dent and Raimey," she announced. "But Raimey's got to help me—so you get your visiting over quick."

Jake had taken a seat beside one of the large bay windows, saying as little as possible. He watched as the blind girl made herself a part of the group with ease, identifying everyone instantly by their voices. Her beauty was truly striking, and the proud look on Dent Rocklin's face as he watched his wife told him that here was a man who was very much in love.

Everyone greeted Dent and Raimey, and as the small talk ran around the room, Jake let his eyes pass over the group, making sure he knew them all. Vince had drawn a family tree when he'd first drilled Jake, and now it jumped into his mind. The founder of the family, Noah Rocklin, had died, but he'd left four boys and one daughter. Stephen owned a factory in the North, and his brother Mason was a Union officer, so Jake had not tried to fix them in his mind. Mark, Noah's youngest son, was sitting on a horsehide couch talking to his sister, Marianne. Mark had never married, so Jake had been able to remember him easily. Marianne, the only daughter, was fifty-one, and still a striking woman with black hair and blue eyes. Her husband, Claude Bristol, was of French blood and reminded Jake of the things he had heard about French aristocrats—for the man was handsome, smooth, and useless. He was pleasant enough, but there was none of the toughness in him that Jake had seen in the Rocklins. From what Jake had been able to gather, Claude spent his life hunting, raising fast horses, and working as little as possible.

Their three children—Paul, Austin, and Marie—did not favor each other at all. Indeed, they were totally different in appearance. Paul, at thirty, was the oldest and looked like his mother. Austin, who was only one year younger, was short and strongly built, with light hair and brown eyes. His sister, Marie, twenty-four, had curly brown hair and hazel eyes. The two young men were not in the army, which seemed to be somewhat of a matter of embarrassment for their mother—though not for their father. Claude was saying, "Why, the whole thing will be over soon! No need for these two to interrupt their lives for such a short enlistment."

Marianne looked over at Amy and Brad, then at Clay, both of whom she knew had sons in the army. Her blue eyes were filled with what seemed to Jake to be disappointment, and he felt that she was ashamed of her husband for being a weak man. "I don't agree with that, Claude, and I suspect no one else does, either," Marianne said quietly. She glanced at her brother Thomas, who was not well enough for going out in the cold, but had insisted on coming. "Did I tell you I got a letter from Gideon, Thomas?"

Thomas shook his head. "No, Marianne. What's he doing?"

"He's gone to serve with some general called Grant in the West."

"Grant?" Thomas asked with a frown. "Never heard of him. But I don't think we have to worry about that sector. President Davis has appointed Albert Sidney Johnston to serve as commander in the West—which seems to be a mistake, at least to me."

"Why is that, sir?" Clay asked. He was standing at the mantel, looking trim and fit. Jake studied him briefly and thought that, at the age of forty-one, Clay Rocklin was finer looking than most of the younger men in the room.

"Oh, the war is here, in Virginia," Thomas said with a shrug. "This is where they'll hit us with everything they've got. As soon as McClellan gets the Army of the Potomac ready, they'll be knocking at our door. That's where we need to concentrate our armies, not off in the wilderness in Tennessee."

Clay shot a quick look at his brother-in-law, Maj. Franklin. The two of them had talked about this matter earlier, and now Clay said carefully, "Well, no doubt you're right about the Yankees hitting us here. The Northern papers are all calling for it. But they're not foolish, Lincoln and his generals—especially Gen. McClellan. They know they'll have to divide the Southern states to win."

"How can they do that, Clay?" Thomas asked. He had been so disappointed in this tall son of his for years, and now that Clay had come back from a wild youth and had become a strong man of honor, he listened carefully to him.

"Brad thinks they'll try to get control of the rivers."

"Rivers?" Marianne asked with a puzzled frown. "Why would they do that?"

Brad Franklin was wearing his uniform, and there was a soldierly look in his thin face as he answered. "Because you can move armies and material on rivers, Marianne. The North has built up a tremendous railway system, but we have almost no major lines. The only way we can move men and munitions is either by rivers or overland. Some of the food Rachel is cooking came down the Cumberland and the Tennessee rivers—from Kentucky and Tennessee. And if the Yankees get control of those rivers, we'll be cut off here."

Grant Franklin, oldest son of Brad and Amy, said, "I've heard that we've got some forts on those rivers to keep the Yankees away."

"Well," Clay said thoughtfully, "they'd better stand, because if we lose those rivers, we'll probably lose Nashville. Then the Yankees can bring their troops all the way down the river—and they can get a foothold on the Mississippi itself."

"And if they get the Mississippi," Franklin continued, "they'll cut the Confederacy in two."

Thomas Rocklin looked at the two men, then shrugged. "Well, we'll just have to fight them off."

"And any Southern soldier can whip any six Yankee soldiers!" Lowell Rocklin said. He was, at the age of eighteen, a throwback to his great-grandfather Noah Rocklin—determined and stubborn. "Isn't that so, Dent?"

Dent Rocklin, who had gone through the fires of battle at Manassas, shook his head. "Well, Lowell, I know it's popular to say that, but I don't agree. At Bull Run, the Yankees came at us like fury. I suppose there were some who ran away—but some of our fellows ran, too. I wouldn't count on the Yankee army running away."

"But we're fighting for our homes, Dent!" Lowell argued. "That's got to make a difference."

"It does," Dent said quietly. "And I'm praying it'll make enough difference to cause the Yankees to decide that we're not worth the cost. After Manassas, I think both sides looked at the war differently—but after so many men have died, we all know this war's not a little skirmish. The Yankees have it over us in men and munitions. But it's an unpopular war in the North for many people."

"So we just have to kill enough of them to make them call the war off? Is that it, Dent?" Thomas asked. Then he shook his head, adding, "It's a grim business. Here are the three of us—" he nodded toward his brother Mark and his sister, Marianne—"in the South, and Stephen and Mason in the North, with Mason in a Federal uniform. Now all of our sons and grandsons are headed to the battlefield, some on opposite sides."

He looked tired and ill, and Susanna Rocklin, his wife, moved to his side. "God will bring us through it, Thomas. Now let's talk about something besides the war."

"Just one more word—about the war, I mean," Brad said. "Most of you don't know, but Vince is joining the Confederate Army soon."

Jake suddenly felt very exposed, for every person there turned to stare at him. He felt like some sort of strange and exotic animal that someone had suddenly brought into the room! Nothing had shown more clearly how alienated Vince Franklin had become from his family than this moment, when Jake saw incredulity and shock in some of the faces.

Clay said quickly, "Why, that's fine! You'll be enlisting in your father's regiment, I suppose?"

Jake cleared his throat, finding it difficult to think with so many watching him. "Well, probably not. I'm not tough enough for an infantry company."

"Cavalry?" Dent asked, his eyebrows going up. He almost mentioned the fact that Vince had never been a horseman but said instead, "Well, that's not a bad idea. Jeb Stuart's command is looking for men, or Wade Hampton's legion."

Jake knew Dent was being polite, and he also realized that they were all thinking of how he had run from Duvall. His mind worked quickly, and he plunged ahead, saying, "Well, I've got to learn to ride and shoot much better than I do now—and there's the matter of a challenge from a fellow in Richmond. If I can take care of all those things, maybe I'll make a soldier."

Clay exclaimed, "Why, you can do it. If you need any help with shooting, I'll be glad to help. And nobody knows more about horses than your brother Grant."

Jake nodded quickly. "Thanks, Uncle Clay. I'll need all the help I can get—but I've got a pretty fair teacher already where horses are concerned. Rachel's giving me some help there."

His remark brought smiles to most of the faces in the room, and Amy said, "I've tried to make a lady out of that child, but she'd rather ride a horse than dance a reel at a fancy ball!" Despite her words, it was clear she was pleased with the way things were. She added, "You two have been thick as thieves ever since you came home. If you weren't her brother, I'd think that young officer, Leighton Semmes, would have something to worry about."

Jake almost choked on that and barely managed to come up with a smile. "Well, Mother, he needn't even take note of me. Which is a good thing, because I have the matter with Duvall to concentrate on right now."

His remark pleased Vince's father, who smiled. He had given up on Vince long ago. Now, though, there was a stirring of hope within him. Of course, he could not help feeling skeptical, and the long years of disappointment over his son made him frown. Amy, his wife, saw it but held her silence. She had a confident air about her, as though she knew for a certainty that things would work out. And there was something more, too—for at times, she seemed as though she held something in, some knowledge that assured her all was well. Some noticed that about her, but no one questioned it. There was a strong spirit of faith in Amy Franklin. She was still crippled by the leg that refused to heal, but she never had lost hope that one day she would be whole again. Now she applied that same hope to her husband, praying, *Lord, give him your peace. Let him know that you will not let him down. That you are working even now to take care of all of us—even those who do not yet know you.*

Then Amy said, "Let's have some hot coffee and some of that fresh gingerbread I smell." Her eyes were steady as she watched Jake, who stood alone beside the window, looking out at the snow.

The Imperial Hotel was not, in point of fact, imperial in any way. A two-story frame building squeezed in between a row of small businesses on one side and an office building on the other, it was a refuge for those who could not afford to stay in the fine hotels in the center of town, but who were too proud to stay in the shabby rooming houses inhabited by Richmond's working class. In earlier days, the Imperial had held a more exalted status, having housed in one of its rooms no less a guest than George Washington—a fact that was attested to by a large bronze plaque in the lobby.

The paint was freshened at regular intervals, and the carpets changed before the floors showed through. However, the tawdry atmosphere of Simon Duvall's rooms on the second floor kept him grimly aware of his position in Richmond society. He was putting on his second-best coat at ten o'clock in the morning, noting with displeasure that the elbow of one sleeve was noticeably worn. It was a small matter, but he cursed as he pulled it off and threw it with a violent gesture across the room.

Rose Duvall had been asleep, but the sound of his voice awakened her. Poking her head out from under the covers on the heavy mahogany bed, she peered at her husband owlishly, then asked, "Where are you going?"

Duvall gave her an angry glance, then yanked another coat from the wardrobe. "To borrow money," he said shortly. He said no more, and there was a look on his face that brooked no further questions. He pulled the coat on, a fine blue wool model that fit him well. He remembered buying it after a big night at poker. How good it had been, that time! Going into the finest shop in Richmond, picking out the coat, and buying it without even asking the price!

But there had been no purchases like that lately, and the pinch of hard times had soured Duvall. He adjusted his tie and looked at his image in the mirror critically. He saw a lean, olive-skinned man with a fine head of black hair and a set of piercing dark eyes. He touched his moustache with a hand that was almost delicate—a hand he took pride in, for it had done no hard labor and was obviously the hand of a man of circumstance.

He picked up his hat, settled it on his head, then donned his overcoat. As he turned to the door, Rose demanded, "Simon, I've got to have some money. I don't have a penny, even to eat on."

Fishing in his pocket, he came up with a bill and tossed it to her. "Better make it last," he said. "If I don't get a loan, we'll be out of this place on our ear."

"I don't see why you don't enlist in the army," Rose reproached. She was an attractive woman with a full figure, with large brown eyes set off by a beautiful complexion. She had been a dance-hall girl in St. Louis when Simon had met her. He had been intoxicated with her beauty and was still possessive about her, but she was tiresome to him now—especially when she reminded him that he had promised her greater things than a sorry hotel room. Now she gave him a sudden suspicious glance. "You'd better not be going to see some woman!"

Duvall laughed, for he liked to torment her. "That comes ill from you, Rose, after your fling with Vince Franklin."

"I told you there was nothing between us!"

"Yes, you did—and you always tell the truth, don't you, sweetheart?" He studied her with a slight contempt, then left the room. Going down the stairs, he felt a twinge of uneasiness lest the clerk should call him and ask him to pay his bill. But the clerk was busy, and his back was turned as he put up mail. Duvall stepped quickly through the lobby, turning to his left. The air was cold, and he scowled. He hated cold weather. But he had no money for a cab, so he walked quickly until he came to his first stop. He entered the red brick building where a friend of his had an office on the third floor. As he went up the stairs, he went over the speech he planned to make, hating himself for becoming a beggar. But he had reached the end of his rope, possessing only his clothes and a few pieces of jewelry. His gambling losses had been high of late, and now he felt a tinge of fear as the thought of a future with no money rose to his mind.

Pausing before the door of his friend's business office, he straightened his back, put a confident smile on his face, and entered. But fifteen minutes later when he came out, the smile was gone and his back was no longer straight. Though it was cold, he pulled a fine silk handkerchief from his pocket, wiped his forehead with a hand that was not quite steady, then left the building quickly.

Two hours later, at noon, he was going up the stairs to the room of Ellen Rocklin. She answered his knock at once, and her eyes brightened as she saw him. Pulling him into the room, she threw her arms around him, kissing him. He responded as always, with fervor and excitement.

"Now, no more of that—not for now, anyway," she said, pulling away but with a promise in her eyes. "Sit down. Can I fix you a drink?"

"Have one with me, Ellen." He took off his coat and hat, tossing them over a chair, then took a seat. He watched her as she poured two drinks, thinking of how he'd come to need her. They had become lovers weeks ago, and though she was no longer young, there was a hunger in her that he had never found in another woman.

Duvall, however, was a realist. He well knew that his relationship with Ellen was only physical. She would cast him off in a flash if she found another man who pleased her better—and he would do the same with her if circumstances required it. As he took the drink she offered him, he grasped her hand and kissed it, bringing a pleased look into her eyes. "You look beautiful, my dear," he said, glad that he could stir her with so little effort.

Ellen laughed, saying, "You must want something, Simon, coming around at noon telling me how beautiful I am." She sat down, sipping her drink and waiting for him to speak.

"I always want something when I come to you," Duvall said with a smile. He continued to flatter her, and she sat back enjoying it. She had to have the admiration of men, and Duvall was somewhat of an aristocrat, though not much of one. Yet he knew how to say the right things, and, even more important, he was discreet. No matter what else she might do, Ellen would never let her standing as Mrs. Clay Rocklin be endangered.

She did not love Clay, and she was sure that her husband had never loved her—that he was, in fact, in love with Melora Yancy—but the life she led was easy enough. She kept her rooms in Richmond, and she was welcome in many homes due to her marriage into the Rocklin family. From time to time she would go to Gracefield, the family plantation, where she would play the role of wife and mother—fooling nobody at all, but fulfilling what she saw as her role.

Finally she said, "Let's go have lunch, Simon."

Hesitating, he looked confused. Finally he gave a rueful laugh. "Nothing I'd like better, Ellen, but—I've had a bad run of cards."

"Broke? Well, this will be on me." She smiled, then got up and went over to the vanity, where she began arranging her hair carefully. "Let's go to Elliot's."

"Elliot's? That's pretty expensive."

"Just about good enough for us," she laughed. There was an excitement in her that Duvall didn't understand. He felt he knew her well by now and sensed that something was stirring in her. "You have a rich uncle die and leave you a million?" he asked, his eyes narrowing.

"Not quite, but—" she broke off, casting a look at him over her shoulder.

He waited, but she merely shrugged and turned back to the mirror. When he pressed her, she refused to say more—but when they were ready to leave, she kissed him and, stroking his hair, said, "I'm going to buy you a new suit, Simon—a fine one!"

He looked at her, then smiled. "You're *different* today, Ellen. Something's going on in that head of yours. What is it?"

She shook her head, saying, "Let's go eat. But don't let me drink too much. You might get my secret out of me!"

They left, and all through the meal and afterward at her rooms, Duvall said nothing more about it. However, a new anticipation was rising in him.

She's up to something, he thought. *Something big! I'll have to be careful—but I'll find out what she's on to. If I play my cards right, I can get enough to turn things around.*

He stayed with her most of the day, and when he got back to his hotel, he found Rose waiting for him. "Well, did you get the loan?" she demanded.

He pulled a roll of bills out of his pocket, enjoying the surprise that came to her eyes. "Not exactly," he admitted, "but things are going to be better. I'm on to something big this time, and I have a feeling it's going to change everything!"

CHAPTER FIFTEEN

RACHEL'S PUPIL

"ALL right . . . hold as still as you can, please. . . ."

A brilliant light exploded from the elongated pan the photographer held in his left hand, blinding the eyes of the house of Rocklin.

As a mutter of dismay went around, Raimey suddenly giggled, saying, "It didn't bother *me* a bit."

Dent grinned and hugged her, for he had learned that she was not at all sensitive about her handicap. "Come on, let's go see if there's anything left to eat."

The photographer, a thin man named Allen with highly nervous mannerisms, had come to take his pictures at noon, rousting them all away from the table, saying, "We have to get the best light, and with all this snow as a reflector, now is an excellent time." They had risen from the table and followed him outside, where they arranged chairs on a porch that caught the full power of the midday sun. Dent and Clay had picked up Amy's chair and carried her outside, where the older Rocklins joined her sitting in chairs. There was a shuffle when the others were grouped around them, with Amy giving instructions: "Clay, you and Ellen get closer together! And you children, move in closer to them!" She watched as Dent, holding fast to Raimey, was joined by his twin, David; then Lowell and Rena moved in beside them.

"Now," Amy said, "Marianne, you and Claude sit down here with me. Paul and Austin and Marie, stand beside them—get all the Bristols together. Yes, that's nice."

Brad smiled as he came to sit down beside his wife, and she patted his arm, saying, "Now, Grant, you stand there, and, Les, you stand next to him." She waited until they pleased her, then said, "All right, Rachel, you and Vince get beside them." When the pair obeyed, she turned and faced the photographer, saying firmly, "Very well, sir, here are your subjects. Now do your job!"

Allen had fussed with his equipment briefly, then had taken several pictures. When the whole group was captured on his plates, Amy said, "Now get a picture of each family."

"Amy, I'm almost frozen!" Ellen said. She had come only that morning, unannounced and unexpected, and had complained of the weather ever since.

Amy gave her a brief glance. "You can be first," she said evenly. She sat there and watched, fascinated by the processes, pestering Allen with questions until it was time for her own family to be photographed. Then the photographer said with some asperity, "You'll have to stop talking now, Mrs. Franklin. Your lips must be absolutely still."

"I think he's telling you to shut up, my dear," Brad said with a straight face and a teasing look in his blue eyes. He winked at Allen, who at once disappeared under the black cloth that draped him and the camera, then presently surfaced crying, "Hold still, please!" The powder exploded, and then he drew a sigh of relief. "Is that *all*, Mrs. Franklin?"

"No. I want pictures of all the servants. They're waiting, as you can see." She motioned to a large group of the slaves, who were drawn up all dressed in their best, adding, "See you do a good job of them." Then she said, "Let's get inside. My nose is frozen."

The group retired, leaving the poor photographer to deal with his new subjects. When the family was inside, Dent and Clay set Amy down carefully in the dining room. Melora came in from the kitchen, asking, "All through? I took the food off so I could reheat it."

She turned to go, but Clay said quickly, "Melora, I promised your brother Bob I'd have a picture made of you. Come along and I'll have the photographer take yours before he gets started on the servants."

Melora hesitated, obviously reluctant, then said, "Let me get my coat." Clay walked from the room with her, and a small, awkward silence fell on the room.

Ellen glared after the pair, then burst out, "I thought this was a family affair. What's she doing here?"

Amy said instantly, "I asked her to come when I broke my leg, Ellen. I needed help, and you weren't here."

It was a cutting reply, a sharper one than Brad had ever heard his wife give to anyone. But he understood how close Amy had gotten to Melora, and he knew better than anyone else how she resented Ellen's treatment of Clay. He tried to think of something to say to take the sudden chill out of the air but could not.

Ellen sat there, her face flushed with anger, well aware that she dared not lash out at Amy. She had never been close to any of the family, and though that had been her own choice, she resented the bond the others shared. She glanced at her children—Dent, David, Lowell, and Rena—and saw only embarrassment on their faces. It had been years since they had shared much with their mother, and she knew that they all were ashamed of her. She had tried to keep her affairs with men a secret, but in a society as intimate as the one in which she moved, that was impossible. Now, seeing the shame on their faces, she suddenly wished that she had lived a different sort of life. But it was too late, and she could only bite her lip, determining that if she could not strike out at these people, she certainly could do so at Clay!

And she did exactly that the first time she was alone with him. She sought him in his room, lashing out at him as she came in, "Well, did you and your lover have a good time, Clay?" Her face was stiff with anger as she stood there in the middle of the room, cursing him and watching his face. She was hoping that he would show anger, even that he would strike her, for that would show that she still had the power to stir him. But Clay said nothing as he stood there waiting, his face impassive.

When she finally ran out of words, he said, "Ellen, you

know better than that. I've had nothing to do with Melora in that way—ever! She's a fine woman and would not do such a thing."

"Oh, she's a *saint,* is that it?" Ellen's words jabbed at him like knives, and she was infuriated even more because she knew that what Clay said was true. She herself had no more morality than an alley cat, but she somehow sensed that there was a goodness in Melora Yancy— a goodness she herself lacked—and this made her frantic with rage.

Clay stood there, studying his wife as if she were an unusual specimen of animal. She had been a beautiful girl when he had married her, and though she had tricked him into marriage, he had tried for years to love her. Unfortunately, she had done all she could to prevent that.

Now he sighed and broke into her tirade. "Ellen, you're making a fool of yourself. Now leave it alone. Let's try to keep at least the *appearance* of a marriage, for the sake of the children."

"Clay, I'll never divorce you!"

"I know that, Ellen. It doesn't matter. Melora would never marry a divorced man." He hesitated, then added, "I can't say for certain, but I believe Melora is going to be married."

"Married?" Ellen asked, startled. "To whom?"

"That isn't for me to say, but whether she gets married or not, I want no more of your outbursts in front of my family—especially in front of the children."

"You can't tell me what to do, Clay!"

He gave her a considered glance, then said quietly, "I can cut off the money you live on, Ellen. I ought to do it, anyway. Do you think I don't know the way you live? The men you run around with?" Anger began to burn in him, and he fought it down. "Do you think I don't know about you and Simon Duvall?"

"You can't prove anything!"

"Can't I? You've been seen in public with him more

than once. I might just call him out. He might not find it so easy to deal with me as he did with poor Vince!"

"You wouldn't dare!" Ellen gasped. She knew that Clay was deadly with a weapon, that he could probably kill Duvall. Then she was suddenly struck with a frightening thought: *If Simon killed Clay, the Rocklins would throw me out!* It was more than a guess, for she knew that Clay's father was disgusted with her and had said that if it was his decision, he'd lock Clay's wife up at home and cut her off without a penny!

The thought of such a thing brought a stab of fear, and she quickly lost her nerve. "Why, Clay," she said in a milder tone than she had been using. "I guess I'm just afraid of losing you."

"You lost me a long time ago, Ellen," he said quietly. "But we can at least try not to bring pain to others with the mess we've made of our own lives. Now go back to the others and try to act decently."

Ellen glared at him but left his room. Downstairs, she entered the large parlor and saw Jake standing at the window, staring out. Going to stand beside him, she whispered, "Hello, *Vince.*" His expression of distaste amused her, and she added, "Thinking about all the coin we're going to get out of the real Vince?" She laughed at the anger that leaped into his eyes, saying, "Don't worry, I won't tell on you—at least, not if you're good to me."

Clay waited for half an hour after Ellen left, then left the house and walked through the snow. The sunlight striking the crystals sent off flashes that made him blink his eyes, but soon he grew accustomed to it. The scene with Ellen had depressed him, and he walked for nearly an hour, slowly letting the bitterness that she had stirred in him fade. He loved the snow, and he paused once to make a snowball, throwing it with all his force toward a rabbit that dashed frantically away. Clay grinned at the sight and said softly, "Run, you son of a gun! Wish I could run away from my problems as easily as you run away from yours!"

Finally he turned back, taking an old path that led to

the brook north of the house. The field was smooth as a carpet, and he enjoyed leaving his tracks, marring the flawless surface. The brook was lined with large trees, all bare now. As he walked along the bank, a movement caught his eye. He stopped and was surprised to see Melora walking toward him. Her head was down, and she seemed unaware of his presence.

"Hello, Melora," he called out, and the sound of his voice brought her head up. She was startled, and the sight of him brought a strange expression to her face. Clay moved along the bank, coming to stand beside her. "Out for a walk?"

"Yes." She was wearing a green woolen coat but no hat, so that her hair, the blackest he'd ever seen, outlined her against the gleam of the white snow. "I love to walk in the snow."

"You always did." He settled back on his heels and thought of days gone by. "Once it snowed so deep that I had to carry you on my shoulders. You must have been about six years old."

Memory stirred her, and she stood there thinking of that time. "I remember. When we got back to our house, I made you some toasted bread and we put honey on it. Then you read to me out of one of the books you'd given me. I was more than six, though."

They walked along the bank, speaking of time past, but there was a constraint in her, something that kept her from giving him her full attention. She was a woman of warm moods, one who seldom allowed her difficulties to depress her, yet now there was none of the joy and happiness in her that Clay had come to expect.

"What's wrong, Melora?" He stopped, taking her arm, and waited for her to reply.

She said nothing for so long that he thought she would not answer at all. Then she said steadily, "Clay, I'm going to marry Jeremiah."

A sharp pain ran through him, but he allowed none of it to show in his face. He had urged her to marry for a long time . . . but now that it had come, a sense of loss filled him, and he knew time would not dull that feeling. He nodded, then said, "It's the best thing for you and Jeremiah, Melora."

"Is it best for you, Clay?"

"I—guess it is," he stammered. Then taking a deep breath, he summoned up a smile. "God knows I love you, Melora. But there's no way we can ever be together."

Melora's eyes began to fill, and she said in a voice that was not steady, "Clay, I've loved you ever since I was a little girl. First as a little girl loves a big brother. Then later, when I was twelve or thirteen, I had one of those crushes young girls get on older men. But when I became a woman, that changed—and now I love you as a woman."

They stood there, torn apart by the bond that drew them together and by the decision they had made together to never tarnish their love by going against what they knew was right in God's eyes. Suddenly Clay reached out to put his arms around Melora, and as he held her fiercely, she began to weep. It was not something that she did often, but she could not help it. Her body was wracked by a storm, and he could do nothing but hold her.

Finally she drew back, and in a motion as graceful and natural as anything he'd ever seen, she pulled his head down and kissed him. Then she whispered, "Good-bye, Mister Clay!"

Whirling, she ran down the path beside the small creek, leaving him standing there. He knew it was good-bye forever, and the bleakness of the years ahead without her suddenly seemed longer than eternity. When he resumed his walk, his shoulders were stooped, and there was a leaden feeling in his chest that seemed to drag him down. He wanted to run away, to get as far from Gracefield as he could, but he knew he would not. God had saved him from a dreadful life, and now he would see if he could be the kind of man who would trust God when there was nothing to hope for—nothing but the promises of God.

"Vince—Vince! Come on, get out of that bed!"

Jake suddenly came out of a sound sleep, fighting at the hands that were pulling at his shoulders. "W-what—!" he gasped, peering wildly around as if he expected to find his room filled with wild animals. He sat up and threw himself backwards, cracking his head against the solid mahogany headboard. "Ow!" he yelped, and then as his eyes focused, he saw Rachel standing beside his bed. "Rachel! What the devil—!"

"Come on," Rachel said, laughing at his confusion. "It's almost six o'clock."

Jake shook his head, licked his lips, then peered at her asking, "Six o'clock? Well, so what?"

Rachel reached out and pulled the blankets half off Jake, saying, "You're getting your riding lesson, remember? We talked about it last night. Now get out of that bed."

"Wait a minute!" Jake yelled, grabbing at the blankets and pulling them up over his waist. "I'll come—but give me a chance to get dressed first!"

"Well, get dressed then!"

He stared at her as she stood there waiting impatiently, then said, "Do you mind stepping outside while I put my clothes on?"

Rachel lifted her eyebrows. "Aren't we *modest* this morning! Remember me? I'm the one who gave you your bath and helped you put your pants on when you couldn't do it yourself!" Then she laughed and left the room saying, "All right, I'm leaving. But hurry up!"

Jake waited until she closed the door, then got out of the bed and dressed hurriedly. He put on his heavy wool pants and shirt, then pulled on a pair of Vince's boots—which were one size too small—and grabbed a heavy coat off a peg. When he came down the stairs, he smelled coffee and found Rachel just dumping a huge mountain of scrambled eggs into a bowl. "Pour the coffee while I dish out the food," she said. When the food was on the table, they sat down and ate hungrily.

"I'll be glad to get away," Rachel said. "I like to be around relatives, but they sure are pesky after a while!"

"You've done a good job—you and Melora—taking care of them," Jake commented. "Too bad the rest of the family can't be here, the ones from the North." He chewed a piece of toast, adding, "We haven't seen Gideon and Melissa in a long time, have we?"

Rachel gave him a quick glance. "Melissa? Do you mean Melanie?"

Jake's face flamed. Drat his memory! "Of course— Melanie! What's wrong with me?"

Rachel looked at him, concern in her eyes. "You're better physically, but you don't seem to be getting your memory back. And your voice—it's still not like it was."

Jake shrugged, thinking hard of some way to distract her from her present train of thought, but could only say, "Well, the doctor said it might take a long time for my voice to heal. And I guess my memory will take more time, too, to get better."

Rachel had finished her food and sat there considering him thoughtfully. She was a woman of action, and it made Jake nervous when she kept still, for it was out of character for her. Finally she said, "I don't understand the changes in you, Vince. I wish I knew if I could trust them. Sometimes . . . sometimes you seem to be a different man entirely."

Desperate, Jake gulped down his coffee and rose to his feet. "Oh, I guess I'll be about the same when I get all healed up, Rachel. Come on, let's get this riding lesson over with." She rose to follow him, but he could tell she was reluctant to let the subject drop.

They left the kitchen and went directly to the barn, finding Bruno milking. He spoke to them, saying, "I ain't got them horses saddled yet, Miss Rachel. If you jes' wait fo' a minute—"

"We'll do it, Bruno," Rachel replied and walked quickly down to where Crow and a bay mare were in the stalls. "First thing," she said at once, "is for you to get a saddle on Crow."

Jake had watched the big stallion being saddled many times and knew that it took two men to do the job at times—depending on how Crow happened to feel. He liked the big black horse and felt that he could probably handle him, but knew that he had a role to play.

"Rachel," he said as anxiously as he could, "it takes Tad and Bruno both to saddle Crow. And I'm still weak in the leg, and my arm isn't strong."

Rachel gave him a direct look. "It's a little too late to back out now, Vince," she said waspishly. She came to stand directly in front of him, and her brow was wrinkled with a frown. "Besides, this is the easiest thing you've got to do! I mean, the worst that can happen to you is that you'll get kicked or bitten. Crow is tough, but he's not a killer. If you can't face a horse, I don't know how you could ever expect to face a man."

"Well, I guess you're right, Rachel." Jake nodded as though thinking it over. "Duvall can put a bullet in my brain, and anyone can get killed in the army." He hesitated for a few seconds, aware that Rachel was watching him narrowly. "All right! I'll do it!" he announced firmly.

"That's the way!" Rachel said with relief. "Now just remember, a horse knows how you feel. If you're nervous or afraid, he *knows* that, and he'll take advantage of it. So you have to ignore any sort of fear and just let that ol' horse have it! Whap him across the nose if he tries to bite you—show him who's boss!"

"Right!" Jake moved toward the stall, picked up the bridle, then climbed up on the rails of the stall. Crow whirled at once, his mouth open, and all Jake could see was a cavernous mouth and what seemed to be dozens of big teeth! It was so sudden that he reacted by jerking backward—and sprawled full-length on the floor of the stable.

"Oh, well done, Brother!" Rachel laughed from where

she had gone to sit down on a bale of hay and added as he picked himself up. "You sure showed him that time!"

Jake glared at her, then snatched the bridle up. He said in a grating tone, "I hope you're enjoying all this!" Then he climbed up again, but this time he was ready. He'd thrown the bridle up over the top rail, and when Crow swung around to bite him, he drove his fist right into the tender nostrils of the stallion. Crow blinked and let out a surprised neigh, then turned his head back toward the front of the stall. Slowly Jake picked up the bridle and eased it into position. Crow gave one snort and lifted his head, casting a wicked glance at Jake, who said, "Stop that!" Crow shook his head, but Jake managed to slip the bit into place, and fastened the bridle before stepping down. "Now I've got him bridled, but that's not the worst of the thing."

"Maybe we'd better get Bruno to help."

"No!"

Rachel was amazed at the determined light in the man's eyes and got to her feet, ready to help. Crow came out with his head reared high, staring down at Jake. The animal was in one of his bad moods, and for the next half hour Jake struggled with him, trying to get the saddle on. He tied the bridle to the top rail, but Crow still had a large arc to swing in. The saddle was heavy, and full strength had not come back to Jake's hand, so time and time again he would heave the saddle up, only to have the big horse lurch away, sending it to the floor.

Rachel bit her lip after Crow had not only knocked the saddle to the floor but swung around and crushed Jake against the side of the stall. "Vince, let me help!"

"Keep out of this!" Rachel looked at him, taken aback by the fire in his voice. But Jake's blood was up now and he was not about to let any horse beat him. He didn't realize he had spoken so forcefully to Rachel. He had, in fact, forgotten about her—his mind and spirit were caught up in the duel with Crow. He stood there, staring at the animal, thinking. Suddenly Rachel saw him smile, and he went to the tack room and came back with a pair of hobbles. He shortened them until they were only a foot long, then fastened them to the hooves of the horse. Then he picked up the saddle, and though Crow tried to dodge, it was not enough, and the saddle went across his back.

"Now, you black demon," Jake said, breathing hard as he tightened the girth, "we'll see who's boss!"

Rachel smiled. "Well, you've proved you're smarter than he is. But he's still bigger."

Jake stooped and removed the hobbles, then nodded. "I guess he knows that, too. Come on. Get the saddle on that mare."

Rachel saddled the mare and they led the two animals outside. Jake was a good rider, but he had seen the strength and cunning of the horse a few days earlier when Grant had tried to ride him. It had been all that Grant could do to outlast Crow's wild pitches—and Grant was probably the best horseman on the place. Rachel seemed to be the only one who knew how to handle the horse so that he didn't fight being ridden.

"I'll probably get piled up," Jake said, looking up at the high saddle.

"Are you afraid?"

He gave her a quick nod. "Can't help thinking about what he can do. I've been a cripple for a long time. Now if he falls on me or pitches me off and I break a leg, it'll be worse than the first time."

Rachel was suddenly worried, and her hand caught at his sleeve. "Vince, don't do it. Wait for a while. You've made a start. Now do that for a day or two, just until he gets used to you. Then you can ride him."

"No time for that," Jake said. "Just say a little prayer that when I hit the ground I don't break anything." He shook her off and, with a smooth movement that surprised her, swung into the saddle. Crow stood still, caught off guard by the suddenness of Jake's mount—then he began to hunch his back in a sinister fashion.

"Look out—!" Rachel cried out, for she knew the horse well, but it was too late. Crow gave a short hop forward, then leaped high into the air, twisting into a corkscrew shape. When his hooves hit the ground, Jake—who had been thrown off-balance—was flung out of the saddle and hit the ground, landing on his back. He grunted as the air was driven from his lungs and rolled to one side to escape the horse's plunging hooves. But Crow stopped at once, walked a few yards away, then turned and stared at Jake.

"Are you hurt?" Rachel was beside him, sitting in the snow and holding his head on her lap. Her eyes were wide and she was trembling. "Vince—what is it?"

Jake lay there with pain throbbing down his bad leg, unable to speak for a moment. But he wasn't sure which was causing him the most trouble—the pain of having the air knocked out of him, or the feelings that raced through him at Rachel's touch. Then, as some air came back into his lungs, he gasped, "I'm . . . all right." Her face was only inches from his, and he smiled feebly. "Well, it . . . looks like you're . . . back to nursing me!"

He sat up, drew a deep breath, then stared at Crow. "You ornery outfit!" he said softly, then smiled. He liked the horse's spirit and the humor he saw in the way Crow stood there staring at him, almost laughing at him. "Bring him over here, will you, Rachel?" he asked, getting to his feet painfully. "One of us has got to lose this fight—and I'll be blasted if I'll let it be me!"

An hour later, the two horses were making tracks through the snow headed toward the brook. Jake felt as though his head had been driven between his shoulders. He had been thrown four times before he learned to anticipate Crow's movement, and each time he'd gotten up more slowly. Rachel had grown afraid and had begged him to quit, but he had kept it up. Finally, when he had learned how to recognize that Crow was going to jump, he would reach out and strike the animal between the ears with a stick, shouting out "No!" at the same time.

Finally Crow could stand it no more, and all Jake had to do when he felt the huge muscles of the animal bunch was to shout "No!"—and that took care of it.

Now they came to the brook, and Jake said, "Let's have a drink." He stepped off his horse, and they tied the lines of the horses to a low limb, then went down to the creek. He stooped and broke the ice, then, making a cup of his hands, he brought some to his lips. It was so cold it hurt his teeth, but he grinned at her. "Thirsty work, learning how to be a man, Sis."

Rachel shook her head and there was a soberness in her eyes. "I've never seen you act so determined. All your life when something didn't go right, you just walked away."

"Try some of that water," Jake said. He waited until she bent and took a drink, then glanced around. He remembered something that Vince had told him about the place and said, "There's that deep pool, the one where we used to swim."

Rachel nodded, then smiled at the memory. "I remember when I got too old to swim with you boys. I went home and cried all day." Her eyes were soft as she let the memory linger, and she added, "That was the last time you ever did anything with me. You'd hunt with the boys, but you never played with me or took me anyplace after that."

Jake had a bitter thought about Vince but could only say, "Boys are pretty mean sometimes." He hesitated, then added, "Wish I could go back and change it."

"Do you?"

"Why, sure!" Jake paused, suddenly afraid that he might say too much. She was beautiful as she stood in the snow, her cheeks reddened with the cold, and he felt a strange sense of longing run along his nerves. "If I had it to do over again, I'd—"

When he paused, she prompted him. "What would you change, Vince?"

"Well, I guess I'd take my little sister places." He

smiled, then shook his head. "I was watching Dent and Raimey last night. Have you noticed how they stay close together? Oh, I know they're still newlyweds and she's blind and all that—but still, there's something in that pair I haven't seen much of."

Rachel was staring at him. She whispered, "What do you see?"

Jake gave a half-embarrassed laugh and reached out to push a curl of her hair back from where it had fallen on her eyes. "Oh, I don't know, Rachel. It makes me feel like a fool poet talking about it." He struggled with his thoughts, then said slowly, "For a man, women are the only real beauty in this world. A mountain or a sunset— they can be beautiful—but a man can't put his arms around a sunset, can he? There's some sort of an emptiness in a man that the whole sky and sea and all the stars can't fill. Only a woman can."

Rachel was stunned. She had never dreamed such thoughts could be in Vince Franklin. She looked up at him, saying, "How long have you had thoughts like that?"

Jake saw the softness of her lips and knew that here was a woman who could fill the emptiness in him. He started to lean forward, to tell her how he felt, but stopped as though someone had dumped cold water on him. Rachel would never be his, not in the way he wanted . . . she thought he was her brother! Drawing a deep breath, he shrugged and said as casually as he could, "Why, Rachel, I don't know. I guess every man thinks about things like that."

"No, I don't think they do." Rachel bit her lower lip, then shook her head. "Why have you waited so long to—"

She broke off, and Jake said quickly, "I'm the same old Vince, Rachel. Don't let my pretty words fool you again. I'm just not strong enough to be mean yet. Come on now, let's go back to the house."

The pair of them mounted and left the creek. Jake kept up a running conversation, but Rachel could not help thinking of what he had said about loving a woman. She knew his affairs had been shallow, physical involvements; but there seemed to be something deeper in him now. When they got back to the stables and dismounted, Jake said thoughtfully, "Well, I rode the horse—but can I shoot the man?"

"Don't do it! I'll talk to Daddy!"

Jake gave her a curious look. "I have to do it. You know I do. Only question is—*can* I do it?" He stroked the steaming sides of the black horse, then asked a question that was directed more to himself than to her, she thought.

"Can I put a bullet in Simon Duvall? What will it prove if I kill him? Or if he kills me?" Once again, Jake considered just walking away. After all, this wasn't his fight. But the thought of the hurt in Rachel's eyes when she found out that he wasn't what she believed him to be, and the thought of the disgust in Brad Franklin's eyes when he discovered that Jake was a liar and impostor . . . he shook his head. No, he was in this now and he would not back down. Only one thing would stop him, and that was if Vince came back to do these things himself.

Rachel shivered, a quick vision flashing before her eyes of a man on the ground with his life's blood draining out. Suddenly the chill she felt was much more intense than that caused by cold weather. "Why not just go on into the army? That's an honorable thing, and it will satisfy everyone." But even as she spoke, she saw the stubbornness in his jaw. Her next words were spoken in a quiet, sad voice. "You'll face Duvall, won't you? And nothing I can say will stop you."

Jake blinked at her, then suddenly took her hand and blurted out, "Rachel, if I could do anything in the world for you, I'd do it. But this job isn't of my choosing."

She slowly pulled away from him and walked into the stable. Jake thought that it was because she was angry, and he accepted that as right. But he would have been stunned by the truth. For Rachel suddenly had been invaded by strange feelings of tenderness and concern for this man who was her half brother. She knew he had been a wastrel all his life, but that no longer seemed to matter. She thought perhaps it was because she had nursed him back to life, because he had been almost like an infant in her care.

But he was no infant now! And as she left him, she discovered to her consternation that she was filled with fear over what might happen to him. If it had been Grant or Les, that would have been purely natural. But Vince! She had despised him for years, and now, suddenly, she found that impossible. Once again she heard the words he'd spoken by the river. Then the thought came to her, as strongly as anything she'd ever felt: *If I ever fall in love, I want to be for my man what Vince says a woman ought to be!*

As she walked toward the house, she tried to fit the words and the new spirit in Vince to the brother with whom she'd grown up, but it was impossible. He pretty much looked like the Vince she'd always known, as much as he could without his beard. But he certainly didn't act like him. Finally, with a shake of her head, she put away the thoughts of him as much as she could.

But his words, his smile, and his gentleness kept coming back to her, stirring in her emotions that she did not understand.

CHAPTER SIXTEEN

AT THE WHITE HORSE BAR

By THE fourth day of the family reunion, Dee was ready to run the whole bunch of Rocklins and Bristols off. She said as much to her mistress that evening as she was supervising another gargantuan meal.

"Miz Amy, this heah bunch is worse than all them locusts in Egypt!" Stirring a huge bowl filled with batter, she shook her gray head in disgust. "I ain't nevuh *seed* folks eat like they does!"

Amy sat in her wheelchair peeling potatoes. She was still weak but had grown sick of doing nothing. "Now, Dee, it may be the last time we'll have the whole family together for a long time. It's hard on you, with me not able to help, I know—but you've done *so* well!"

The praise caused Dee to sniff, but it pleased her all the same. She gave the batter a few more vigorous slaps with the wooden spoon, then poured it into a black iron skillet. Opening the door of the oven, she inserted it, then closed the door. She wiped her hands on the apron, then stood there thinking. Finally she asked, "Whut you reckon Marse Vince is up to?"

"Up to? What does that mean, Dee?"

"Why, dat young man ain't nuffin' like his ol' self, and you knows it!" Puzzlement grew on her lined black face, and she asked curiously, "Whut's Marse Franklin think dat boy gonna do? He gonna fight with dat man in Richmond? He gonna get hisself killed!"

Amy glanced at the black woman, who was more friend than slave, and shook her head. "I don't know, Dee. I've tried to talk the major out of it, but you know how stubborn he can get when he sets his mind to something. And when I try to talk to Vince—" She broke off abruptly, for the subject disturbed her. "It was fine of him to ride that horse, and I'm proud that he's decided to join the army. But that business with Duvall is terrible!"

"Miss Rachel, she got real close to him," Dee observed. "Maybe she can talk him outta it."

"She's tried, but Vince won't listen." Amy's dark eyes clouded, and there was a mixture of sorrow and anger in them. "This war—you'd think it would be enough! And now this thing with Vince—"

"Well now, don't you get all agrafretted 'bout it, you heah?" Dee came over and patted her mistress on the shoulder, then took the bowl of potatoes from her hands. "You gonna go take a nap befo' supper." She ignored Amy's protests and took her to her room and tucked her in as if she were a child. "You sleep now," she commanded, then shut the door and moved back down toward the kitchen.

When she got there, she saw Jake ride out of the stable on a big black horse. "Whar he goin' now?" she muttered, then shook her head, saying in disgust, "White folks!"

Jake had caught a glimpse of Dee in the window, but his mind was so busy that the sight of her barely registered—just the one quick thought: *I hope she didn't talk to the messenger.*

Looking up at the skies, he saw that the day was ready to fade and knew that he would not be back for supper. The skies were flat and gray with more snow in the offing, but he didn't think of that, for the message that rested in his pocket had driven all other thoughts from his mind the moment he'd received it. He'd been waiting with apprehension for Vince's reply, and when it came it was brief: *Meet me tonight at seven at the White Horse Bar. Underhill.*

The messenger had been a slight young man, no more than seventeen or so, and he had said, "Man who paid me to deliver this, he wants to know will you come?"

"Tell him I'll be there," Jake had said, giving him a dollar. Now as he drove Crow along at an easy gallop, he tried to find some sort of reason in the summons but failed. *If Vince gets spotted by just one person who recognizes him, it's all over*, he thought grimly. And on the heels of that thought came another: *That'd be fine with me!*

All the way to Richmond he thought about what he'd been doing and was not happy with it. No matter how he tried to rationalize it, he still had an edgy feeling. It was a lie, and though he'd done things he'd not been proud of in the past, there was something about the whole thing with Vince Franklin that made him feel dirty. Perhaps it was the way Amy Franklin had shown such love to him. More likely, he thought instantly, there was something about his relationship with Rachel that made him uneasy.

Maybe it's because I never had much of a family, he thought as he reached the outskirts of Richmond. *Always wanted to be part of a big family, and this is about as close as I've ever come. But it's all a lie, and it'll blow up in my face soon enough.*

The streetlights glowed, making yellow points in the darkness, as he rode down the main thoroughfare. The snow was packed down hard, and Crow almost slipped once. "Steady, Crow!" Jake said, patting his shoulder. He asked a man standing in front of a shop, "Friend, where would the White Horse Bar be found?"

"You done passed it," the man replied. "It's back the way you come—look for the sign on yore right."

"Thanks."

When he moved back up the street, he saw the small sign and tied Crow up to the hitching rail. He entered the large room, which was filled with the acrid odor of cigarette smoke and whiskey, and looked swiftly around for Vince. It was a rough place, with a bar along one wall and a few tables and chairs covering the rest of the place. Two of the tables were occupied, but none of the men were Vince. Jake assumed that Vince would have donned some sort of disguise, so he walked to the bar. "I'm supposed to meet a fellow here."

The bartender gave him a steady glance. He was a thickset individual with misshapen ears and scar tissue around his eyes—an old fighter. He nodded toward the door at the rear of the room. "Fellow named Underhill? He's in the back room."

"Thanks."

Jake moved to the door, opened it, and stepped inside to find a single round table with a few chairs. A man was slumped in one of them, wearing a full beard and rough-looking clothes. A limp slouch hat was pulled down over his eyes. Just to make certain, Jake let him speak first.

"Sit down, Jake," Vince said, and when he lifted his head, Jake saw that his face was thin and his eyes were bloodshot. "Have a drink."

"All right." Jake sat down and took the drink Vince pushed toward him but didn't lift it. He was a little shocked at the man's appearance, for he knew Franklin to be a careful dresser. But perhaps that was just part of the disguise. "Nobody would know you in that rig, Vince," Jake said quietly. Then he leaned closer, peering into Vince's face. "You sick?"

"Yes." Vince nodded, then drained the glass in his hand. He braced his feet against the jolt of the liquor and at once began to cough. It was a deep, ragged cough that racked him terribly. When he finally got control of himself, he shook his head, saying, "Been sick three days. Can't seem to shake it off." He peered toward Jake, nodding as he said, "You look good. I told you we could pull it off."

"We didn't pull it off." Jake shook his head, determined to push the matter to a conclusion. "Ellen Rocklin knows I'm a fake."

"How'd she find out?"

Jake related the story, then said, "Vince, it's not going to work. And it's not just the Rocklin woman. I can't keep on forever, not knowing people. I made a stupid mistake just this morning with Rachel." He took a deep breath, then shook his head. "It was a good idea—but it's just too tricky."

"What about my father?"

Jake hesitated, then gave Vince the details—including the three tasks he had to perform.

Vince's eyes lost part of their dullness as he asked eagerly, "Well, Jake, did you ride the horse?"

"Sure, that was easy. But fighting Duvall won't be."

"You won't have to. Join up with the army. Not with a branch around here, but some outfit far away. Ride out and stay there until the time comes. If you stick it out, Father won't force the matter with Duvall."

"What if I get killed?" Jake asked curiously. "That'd put a crimp in your plan, wouldn't it?"

Vince didn't catch the irony in Jake's tone. "Well, in that case, I'd have to find some other way—" Then he saw the slight smile on Jake's lips, and he laughed. "Sorry, Jake! I'm not thinking very straight. But you can wrangle a safe spot away from the action. Maybe in the quartermaster corps."

"That still leaves Ellen."

Vince nodded. "I know, but I can handle her."

"Not without paying her off. She's a greedy woman, and she'll do just what she says if you don't give her the money."

"I can handle her, Jake," Vince insisted stubbornly. "I hope you brought the checkbook with you. I've got to have some cash."

"I brought it." He took the item out of his pocket, stared at it, then remarked, "I think I can go to jail for signing your name to these checks."

"Aw, Jake," Vince protested at once, "you know better than that. Now write a check for a thousand dollars."

Jake looked at him, startled. "Can you cash a check that large here? Won't they ask for identification?"

"I never thought of that." Vince studied the bottle, poured himself another drink, then said, "You'll have to go to the bank in the morning and get the cash. You can bunk in my room tonight."

Jake studied the man, then said, "Let's call it off. We really don't have much chance."

Vince looked startled, then began to plead, "Oh, come now, Jake, it's going to work! And we're both in a hole, and pretty bad, too. Look, let's go get something to eat and we can go over it again."

They left the bar and had a meal, then went back to the bar, where both of them drank too much. Jake was not a man who drank to excess, but he was depressed by the whole thing, and Vince kept insisting they go through with it. In the end he agreed wearily, and after a sleepless night, he went to the bank the next morning and got the cash.

"Now," Vince instructed, "you need to get away as soon as you can, Jake. Write me in care of general delivery in Savannah." He began to cough again, and this time the spasm nearly tore him in two.

"You've got to see a doctor."

"Sure, I'll do that," Vince agreed. He seemed nervous and anxious, saying, "Well, take care of yourself, Jake. Just a little while and you'll be on that island with your pocket full of money."

Jake stared at him but said only, "I'll be glad when it's over, Vince. It's not something I'm going to tell my grandchildren about."

As soon as Jake left, Vince walked out of the hotel and took a cab to the house where Ellen stayed. He felt weak, but there was something he had to do before he left Richmond. The pistol he had slipped inside his belt was uncomfortable, but he ignored it.

Ellen was asleep when the knock came at her door, and it took her several minutes to come out of her slumber. Finally she threw the covers back, drew on a robe, and staggered to the door. "Who is it?"

"Open the door, Ellen!"

She hesitated, then turned the key. Opening the door a crack, she peered outside. "I don't know you," she said to the rough-looking man who stood there. She would have closed the door, except that he put his hand out and stopped her.

"It's me, Ellen—Vince Franklin." As he expected, her eyes opened wide, and she stepped back at once. When he entered and she had carefully shut the door, she exclaimed, "Vince! I don't believe it!"

"Ellen, I'm in a hurry," Vince said. "Let's talk business."

At once her eyes hardened, and she nodded. "I've been expecting you to pay a call. Sit down, Vince."

"No time, Ellen. Just tell me—how much?"

Ellen laughed, letting her robe fall open. "Now that's the way I like to hear you talk! Right down to brass tacks."

"How much, Ellen? Just lay it out, then we can argue over it."

"No argument." Ellen grinned. "I've got you in a box. One word from me and you'll get nothing."

Vince nodded. "I know that. But you've got to be reasonable. I won't get a huge chunk of money. I'll get control of the estate. It'll take me a little time to liquidate it."

"Of course, sweetheart!" Ellen shrugged, her eyes alive with interest. "I know about all that. What I really want is a large bonus—and then a *steady* income, you know what I mean?"

Vince knew well enough. She meant a lifetime of blackmail, but he only shrugged, saying, "I'll make you an offer. Five thousand when I come into the money, and one hundred dollars every month as long as you live."

"Oh, now, Vince, you can do better than that!" Ellen smiled. She was enjoying the thing, he saw, and now she added, "Let's say you double that, and we can do business."

"Double!" Vince exclaimed, pretending to show shock

at her proposal. But after a few minutes he caved in, saying, "Looks like you got the best of the argument, Ellen. Let's shake on it."

She took his hand, laughing at the disappointment on his face. "You and I are a lot alike." She leaned against him. "Maybe this will be more than a business deal—?"

Vince forced a smile, saying, "I'm for that—but now I've got to get out of Richmond."

"How about an advance on that first payment?" Ellen asked quickly.

"Haven't got it. I'll send you two hundred next week."

He left her then and two hours later was on the train headed for Savannah. His meeting with Ellen Rocklin had left a sour taste in his mouth, but he had already made plans for her. There was a man he knew in Savannah, a rough sort of fellow named Elvin Sloan. For five hundred dollars he would shoot his own mother.

A shock ran through Vince at the enormity of what he planned. To have a woman killed! He was truly physically sick, and the thought of doing such a thing raised his gorge.

Still, there was no other way. "She should have stayed out of it!" he muttered as the train clattered over the rails. "No-good tramp!"

He slept fitfully during the trip, but when he finally got off the train, his fever was so high that the conductor took his arm as he stumbled. "Mister, you sick?"

"No . . . all right, I'm . . . all right," he mumbled, shoving the man away. Vince straightened up and forced himself to walk carefully, but by the time he got to the cab stand, a dizziness hit him. The world seemed to reel, and he made a wild grab at the cab—only to fall headlong to the ground.

"Hey—mister—!"

He heard people speaking and felt hands pulling at him, but they could not stop him from sliding into the deep black void that seemed to be waiting for him.

CHAPTER SEVENTEEN

GOD IN THE CAMP

FOUR days before Christmas, Rev. Jeremiah Irons rode into the yard at Lindwood, determination set on his face. He stepped off his horse, quickly tied him to the hitching post, then climbed the steps and knocked on the door. He was met by House Betty, who said, "Lawsy, Rev. Irons, you look plum froze! Come on in and warm yo'self."

Irons stepped inside, took off his mittens and fur cap, then stripped off his coat. "Tell Miss Melora I want to see her, will you, Betty?"

"Yassuh, I sho' will."

The diminutive maid bustled off quickly, saying, "You go on into the parlor, Reverend." Taking her advice, Irons went into the large, high-ceilinged room. He stood in front of the cheerful fire that blazed in the fireplace, clenching his hands nervously and glancing toward the door. Irons was not a man of a nervous temperament; quite the contrary, he was one of the calmest men imaginable under adverse circumstances. But he had slept little for several nights in a row, and now his even features were stretched tightly as he waited for Melora to appear.

Glancing across the room, he caught a glimpse of himself in a beveled mirror and blinked in shock at his own image. *You look like a criminal appearing before a hanging judge for a sentence*, he thought grimly, then at once considered that in a sense, his condition was much the same. He had loved Melora Yancy for years and had waited for her to accept him as her husband. Now he had come to the conclusion that the thing could go on no longer. Either she'll have me—or she won't, he thought grimly, then turned to greet her as she entered the room.

"Hello, Jeremiah," Melora said, coming to stand before him. "Is something wrong?"

"Yes, there is," Irons said abruptly, then gave an embarrassed laugh at his greeting. "Well, no, not really."

Melora relaxed, smiling at him. "You look like someone just died. I was afraid—"

He cut her off, saying, "Melora, I've got to know what you mean to do." He reached out quickly and took her hands, his words rushing forth as if he were afraid to wait. "This isn't sudden, is it, Melora? I guess you know what I want. I've loved you for years, and I've waited for a long time—"

He broke off, and Melora stood there, looking into his direct brown eyes, her hands compressed as he held to them almost desperately. A great surge of pity rose in her as she stood there, thinking of how faithful and patient he had been. No other man she knew would have done such a thing, and she understood that now she had come to a crossroad in her life. She thought of her love for Clay Rocklin—and with one act of will, closed the door on it as firmly as one would close and seal the door of a tomb where the body of the dearest one in all the world had been placed.

Jeremiah had started speaking again, pressing his cause. She waited until he was finished, then answered evenly, "Yes, Jeremiah, I'll marry you."

Irons stood there, stock-still, his face gone pale. He had expected a rejection, and now that she stood there with her hands in his, her eyes confirming her words, he could only stare at her. Finally he reached out, drew her close and kissed her lips, then held her tightly in his arms. They stood there for a long moment, the only sound the ticking of the grandfather clock in the foyer. Then he drew back, saying huskily, "You've made me a happy man, my dear!"

"I must say one thing—"

He put his hand over her lips gently. "I know. It's about Clay, but I know all about that. There is a part of you that belongs to him, and no other man can ever change that. I've always known that, Melora, but you have some feelings for me, too, I believe. And that will be enough." He smiled, adding, "Very seldom do any of us get everything we want, do we? But you and I will have children, and you need them! You were born to have children at your feet. And you'll love me more when they come. Clay is my best friend in this world, and I'll never be jealous of what you feel for him. There must not be anything hidden about this. He must come and go in our home, and he'll be a godfather to our children. Isn't that the way it will be, Melora?"

Tears gathered in Melora's eyes, so that the sight of his face blurred. She whispered, "You're such a good man, Jeremiah!" Then she put her face against his chest, and he let her lie there until, finally, she drew back. She smiled, saying, "Now when will it be?"

"As soon as possible!" Irons said instantly. "I'll have to go ask your father's permission."

"You'll get no argument from him," Melora laughed. "Getting rid of an old-maid daughter will suit him well enough!"

"Not so, but I must talk with Buford anyway." A thought struck him and he said, "Come with me to the meeting at the camp. I'm preaching, and I'll announce it to the regiment."

"Yes! And I'll get up a crowd to go. You go by and talk to my father. Tell him to bring all four of the children to the meeting, and I'll try to get Rachel to bring all the Franklins who can be spared."

"I'll go by and see Clay," Jeremiah said. "I want him to hear it from me—unless you'd rather tell him yourself?"

"No, you're the proper one. I . . . don't think it will come as a great shock to him." She said no more about Clay, and Irons understood. "We'll all be there, so preach a good sermon, Chaplain."

"I probably will be so nervous I won't be able to find my text!" Then he kissed her hand and left the room. She watched from the window as he rode toward Gracefield, and a pain filled her heart as she thought of Clay—but she had made her decision and knew that she had taken a road that led her away from him.

A cavalcade made up of Rocklins, Franklins, and Yancys moved toward the camp of the Richmond Grays early on the afternoon of the twenty-third of December. The roads were packed with snow, forming a hard surface, and the weather was crisp and cold. Buford Yancy led the way with his four youngest children and Melora, followed by the Franklin clan, including Jake, Rachel, Grant, and Les. Dent and Raimey drove another carriage with David, Lowell, and Rena, in addition to Irons's children, Asa and Ann, who were staying with a family from the church. Bringing up the rear was Clay, who drove a small closed carriage with his parents bundled up in the rear.

Clay had said little as he drove with his parents. Susanna finally asked, "Are you all right, Clay?"

"I'm fine, Mother," he had said quickly, but a mile down the road, he said, "You'll hear an announcement tonight. Jeremiah and Melora are getting married." Then he added quickly, "I'm very happy for them. They'll have a fine life together." Thomas had opened his mouth to ask a question, but Susanna nudged him with her elbow, then shook her head firmly.

"Yes, they will," she said quickly. "A pastor needs a wife, and Melora will be a fine one for him."

Melora had told Rachel about her decision, and Rachel had gone at once to Jake, who was reading a book. She told him the news, and he had said, "That'll be hard on Uncle Clay."

"It's best for Melora, though. She needs a home and a family."

Jake had stared at her curiously, remarking, "I thought you were a romantic. All for love and things like that. This looks like a marriage of convenience."

"It'll work out. And you're going to the camp meeting tomorrow."

Jake had argued, but now as Grant drove the team along the icy road, he was glad to be going. Les sat in the front with Grant while Jake occupied the backseat with Rachel. She looked very pretty in a dark wine-colored dress, and the cold air put a sparkle in her eyes. She caught him looking at her and gave him a nudge with her elbow. "You behave yourself in the meeting, you hear me?"

Jake grinned, wondering what Vince had done to occasion such a dire warning, but only said, "You afraid I'll challenge the chaplain's theology?"

"No. But I remember how you sneaked off with that Wilcox girl at the meeting in Oak Grove."

"We were talking about the sermon," Jake said slyly.

Rachel snorted. "I know what you were up to!" Then she smiled, and the dimple in her cheek made her look younger. "One good thing about a camp meeting with the army—there won't be any pretty girls for you to run off to the bushes with!"

"I'd run off with you if you weren't my sister." He smiled at her astonished expression. "You've grown up into a handsome woman, Rachel. I don't know a woman any more attractive."

Rachel blinked at him, taken aback. "Well, that's the first compliment you ever gave me, Vince."

"It's true, though."

A flush appeared on her cheeks, and she gave a short half-laugh of embarrassment. "Well, thank you. Not that it's true—"

"Capt. Semmes will think so."

Rachel protested, but when they got to the camp, it was Jeremiah Irons and Capt. Semmes who were waiting to greet them. Irons went at once to Melora, saying, "You look beautiful!"

Melora looked around quickly, embarrassed at his words, but took his arm, saying, "I had a good talk with

Asa and Ann before we left for the meeting. I hope they'll not think I'll be a wicked stepmother like in the fairy tales." He hastened to assure her that they were delighted with having a mother, and they moved off toward the line of tents stretched out across the open fields.

"Rachel, you're looking more beautiful than ever," Semmes said as he came forward to greet her.

Jake moved to stand beside Rachel, a sly light in his eyes. "See, Rachel? I told you the captain would be here to say that."

Semmes looked up quickly, flushing a little, but then had to laugh. "Vince, you know me too well!"

"We both have bad reputations, Semmes. I've just been doing my brotherly duty in explaining to my sister how little either of us are to be trusted." Rachel covered the smile that rose to her lips as Semmes stood there not knowing what to say. Jake merely smiled at him. "I'm sure you'd have just such a talk with your sister if I came courting her, wouldn't you?"

Semmes had planned a little scene with Rachel, hoping to get her off to one side so that he could press his case. Now the look in Jake's eyes told him that he would have difficulty achieving that. He frowned and said with as much grace as he could muster, "Perhaps so. We do have to protect the ladies."

"Well said!" Jake nodded, then turned to Rachel and gave a wink that only she could see. "Now you see that the captain agrees with me, Rachel."

"Surely I don't need protection at a gospel meeting?" Rachel smiled.

"Oh, the devil is an angel of light!" Jake nodded. "And wolves run about in sheep's clothing. I think I'd better stay at your side, Sister—just in case one of them tries to destroy the solemnity of the meeting by speaking to you improperly."

And stay by Rachel's side he did, to the intense aggravation of Capt. Leighton Semmes! There was a short meeting with the officers, and Jake did not move a foot away from Rachel the entire time.

An officer wearing the stars of a general came into the meeting, and Jake asked Irons, who sat beside him, "Who's that?"

"Stonewall Jackson."

Jake turned a curious gaze on the general, having heard much about him. He was wearing a plain, worn uniform and carried an equally worn forage cap in his hand. He was not a handsome man, but there was something in his features that drew attention. His men, Jake knew, called him "Old Blue Light," referring to his pale blue eyes, which were said to practically glow when Jackson led men onto the field of battle.

Col. Benton said a few words of introduction, then quickly added, "We're privileged to have Gen. Jackson with us this afternoon. General, it would be greatly appreciated if you would say a few words—or even more than a few."

Jackson got to his feet and turned to face the small group. He had a high-pitched voice, pleasant and very clear. "Col. Benton, I am always made happy when the gospel of the Lord Jesus is proclaimed, and I must remark that your command is most fortunate to have a chaplain who does that as well as any minister of my acquaintance." He nodded toward Maj. Irons, adding, "Chaplain Irons and I have enjoyed sweet fellowship, and it is gratifying to know that the Richmond Grays have such a servant of the living God to nourish them in these difficult days."

Jackson spoke briefly. Afterward, when he was introduced to the visitors, he took Clay Rocklin's hand and paused. "I know that name—oh, yes, Manassas." His blue eyes glowed and he remarked, "It was a pleasure for me to sign the recommendation that Col. Benton sent to me, Sergeant."

Clay flushed at the reference to his commendation for bravery, saying only, "It was a small thing that I did, General."

Jackson shook his head. "No, Sergeant, it was not." He moved on and, when introduced by Maj. Franklin to Rachel, bowed slightly, saying, "Your father is a good soldier, Miss Rachel. Are any other members of your family in the army?"

Rachel had never seen a pair of eyes with such power. She suddenly took Jake's arm, saying, "This is my brother, Vincent, General. He's just recovering from a serious injury, but it's his intention to begin his service immediately."

"Indeed?" Jackson put out his hand, and when Jake took it, he held it in a strong grip. "You will be welcome, Mr. Franklin." He hesitated, then added, "Your father will have already given you wise counsel, but may I say just a word?"

Jake was startled and stammered slightly as he answered, "W-why certainly, General!"

Jackson held the young man with his eyes, and Jake felt as though the officer saw deeper than he would have liked. Finally Jackson said, "It is the duty of a soldier to put his life in jeopardy. Many of us will fall in the service of our country. That, sir, is not a tragedy as long as we are right with God. Have you put your trust in Jesus?"

A silence had fallen on those gathered there, and the blood seemed to pound in Jake's veins. He had expected advice, words encouraging him to give his all for the South or a statement of the importance of the war—anything but this! He felt Rachel's presence as she stood so close that her arm brushed his, and he could only give his head a slight shake. "I-I'm afraid not, General."

Jackson smiled then, the severity of his face broken. "There is yet time, Mr. Franklin. I will pray for you." Then he turned to greet the other visitors. Jake's legs were like rubber, for the encounter had been like nothing he had ever experienced.

Rachel was aware of his difficulty, and as they left the meeting to go to the service, she whispered, "Are you all right?"

"Well, not really." Jake swallowed and shook his head. "That fellow really knows how to shake a man up!"

"Rev. Irons says he's always like that," Rachel said quickly. "He attends all the prayer meetings and talks to a lot of the men about God. And he seems as concerned with a Sunday school he started for black children back at his home as he is with the war."

"A strange man," Jake muttered. "A blazing killer on the battlefield—and yet he's got some kind of love in him that I can feel."

Jake escorted Rachel out onto the open field where the Richmond Grays had assembled for the service. There were no chairs, but a small platform had been built for the preacher.

The service got under way when Chaplain Jeremiah Irons stood and welcomed them to the meeting. He paused, then said, "I must introduce one very special guest—the young woman who has agreed to marry me." Melora was forced to stand, blushing but smiling, and then Irons said, "Now we can begin the service."

A lieutenant with a fine singing voice mounted the platform and, after a fervent prayer, began to sing, "All Hail the Power of Jesus' Name." There were no books, but the five hundred or so soldiers filled the field with their lusty singing. They sang "Rock of Ages," "O Happy Day," "On Jordan's Stormy Banks I Stand," and several others.

Rachel noticed that Jake was not singing at all but said nothing to him. She knew her brother had stopped going to church when he was sixteen years old and had begun at that time—or even earlier—to make fun of all that was Christian. Even so, she could see that he had been troubled by Stonewall Jackson's simple question. She began to pray for him.

When the singing was over, Stonewall Jackson, having been asked by Col. Benton to say a few words, rose and greeted the men, then asked them to pay careful attention to the message. "The power of the gospel is the greatest power there is," he declared, his high voice carrying out over the ground. "More powerful than all the guns of our armies, North and South. For guns and cannons destroy, but the gospel of Jesus Christ restores and makes whole. You will soon be facing the enemy on the field of battle, and you may be facing the great Judge of all the earth. On that day, the only question that will have any importance is this, 'Do I belong to Jesus Christ?'"

As Jackson spoke this last appeal, Rachel saw that Vince had clenched his fists so tightly that they were white. His head was bowed, and when Irons stood and began to preach, he didn't lift it at all, but stood there staring down at the ground.

When Irons stood up, he opened his Bible to the nineteenth chapter of Matthew and began to read.

"'And, behold, one came and said unto him, Good Master, what good thing shall I do, that I may have eternal life?

"'And he said unto him, Why callest thou me good? there is none good but one, that is, God: but if thou wilt enter into life, keep the commandments.

"'He saith unto him, Which? Jesus said, Thou shalt do no murder, Thou shalt not commit adultery, Thou shalt not steal, Thou shalt not bear false witness,

"'Honour thy father and thy mother: and, Thou shalt love thy neighbour as thyself.

"'The young man saith unto him, All these things have I kept from my youth up: what lack I yet?

"'Jesus said unto him, If thou wilt be perfect, go and sell that thou hast, and give to the poor, and thou shalt have treasure in heaven: and come and follow me.

"'But when the young man heard that saying, he went away sorrowful: for he had great possessions.'"

Irons closed his Bible, looked out over the upturned faces, then said clearly, "Let me speak to you this day about disguises." A mutter ran through the ranks, and a slight smile came to the lips of the speaker. "Did you hear the story I just read? It's a story about a man who was an impostor. A man who came to Jesus under false colors, wearing a disguise. Oh, not with a false beard or dyed hair! And, to speak honestly, I don't think this impostor was even aware that he *was* wearing a disguise."

Jake discovered that his hands were sweating, even in the biting cold, and he wiped them on his coat. He had the sudden impression that he was standing all alone in the vast field with Irons looking right at him! Unpleasant sensations had begun to work on him from the instant Jackson had asked, "Have you put your trust in Jesus?"

Jake Hardin was not a man of quick emotions; in fact, he had always distrusted emotional reactions. Now, however, he stood there with a weakness such as he had never known, and as Irons continued, he could only stare at the snow and try to conceal what was happening to him.

"This fine young man, the rich ruler who came to Jesus," Irons continued, "would have been a welcome addition to any church in town. I haven't heard of any church in Richmond turning down wealthy young men, have you?" A ripple of laughter went over the crowd, and Irons smiled, waiting for it to pass. "He was a *moral* young chap, much better than I was at his age. Better, in fact, than most of you! He had kept the commandments. Think of that! He had kept the commandments of God from his youth!"

He spoke of how difficult it was for a Jew to keep the multitude of laws and ordinances that made up Judaism, then his voice rose as he called out, "But I show you a greater mystery than that, and it is this: It did not matter that he had kept the rules of his religion—he was not accepted by Jesus Christ as a disciple! What does that mean? It means that not a one of us can come to Jesus because we are good. It doesn't matter that we are church members, that we have not lied or stolen as others. No! That will not do!"

Irons began to relate sections of Scripture to his listeners, using illustration after illustration to show that it was not morality that God required, that there was nothing in any man that could earn him salvation.

"Now about the disguise," he said. "This rich, moral, upstanding young man had done much to appear good. He was, in fact, *disguised* by his good deeds—that is, he had put on robes of public righteousness. His fellowmen saw him as a good young man, one who certainly was right with God. But Jesus saw through his disguise with one look—one look and he saw the heart of the young ruler. And what did he see? Why, he saw a man who loved money more than anything else! The young man had disguised this part of himself from men, but he couldn't hide it from God!"

The congregation was very still as Irons went on. There was an air of strain about them, and more than one soldier, Rachel noticed, was affected by the sermon. Irons said finally, "Some of you are here wearing a disguise. You know that you are not the man you appear to be. Some of you have worn many masks; some of you have played so many roles and been so many things that you no longer know *who* you are!"

Jake started, his shoulders jerking back, and suddenly he lifted his head and stared at the preacher. "But God knows who you are! Yes, he knows, and the glorious thing about it is that, knowing the worst about you—the awful terrible things you wouldn't want your best friends to know—even knowing those things, he loves you! And here is what I've come to tell you today: Don't be afraid of God, for despite what you are, he loves you! *That's* the heart of the gospel. Not what good things you do for God, but what a grand and terrible thing he has done for you. Jesus is the friend of sinners. He came to die for sinners, just like you and me!"

A few cries began to go up, and then as Irons stopped abruptly and looked out over the crowd, he said, "I feel the Spirit of God working right now, and I invite you, no matter who you are or how you may have run from God—come and trust in Jesus! He is your friend, your hope, your salvation. And he is waiting for you to come and accept his love."

At once the song leader began to sing:

"Just as I am, without one plea, But that Thy blood was shed for me, And that Thou bidd'st me come to Thee, O Lamb of God, I come! I come!"

The words seemed to pierce Jake Hardin like swords, and—to his amazement—he felt tears rise to his eyes! He had not wept since he was a child, and now he felt ashamed to show such weakness. He was aware that many men were making their way toward the platform—and he felt an urge to go with them. He was trembling almost violently, and a war was taking place in his spirit, a war that frightened him. He stood there, longing to go forward but filled with fear.

Rachel was aware of the struggle and finally put her hand on Jake's arm. "Why don't you go ask Brother Irons to pray for you?"

Jake could not speak, and Rachel longed to say more but was afraid to. Finally she lifted her head and caught the eye of Irons. He was looking right at her, and she motioned toward the trembling man on her left with a slight gesture of her head.

At once Irons came toward them, making his way through the crowd. He stopped in front of Jake and asked quietly, "You need God, Vince. Will you let me pray for you?"

Jake wanted to say no, but almost without volition, he found himself nodding. He felt Jeremiah's hands on his shoulders and knew that the chaplain was praying—but he could not understand the words because of the fierce battle going on in his mind. It came to this: He knew he was a liar and an impostor, and how could he come to God unless he confessed that, to God and to those he was deceiving?

Finally when Irons asked, "Will you put your trust in Jesus?" Jake shivered like a man who had been hit by a bullet. He longed to agree, to fall on his knees and let God in.

But he did not.

He lifted his head, allowing Irons to read in his eyes the tortured state of his spirit. Then he whispered huskily, "I—can't—do it!" He turned and walked away, making his way as rapidly as he could out of the crowd.

"Rachel," Irons said at once, turning to the woman whose face bore a stricken expression, "I've never seen a man more under conviction. You'll have to be patient. Pray for him, as I will." Irons slapped his hands together sharply, and pain was in his fine eyes. "He came so close!"

Rachel nodded, her own heart filled with sorrow. "Can he—will he find his way, Rev. Irons?"

"I pray he will—but for now, he's running hard. We can only pray that the Lord will catch up to him before it's too late!"

CHAPTER EIGHTEEN

NEW YEAR'S MIRACLE

THE SMELL of pies, cakes, baked meats, barbecue, and other spicy aromas filled the air on Christmas Day at Lindwood. Men and boys were run out of kitchens with dire warnings as the cooks prepared the succulent dishes. At three o'clock the slaves gathered in the barn, where planks had been placed across sawhorses to make tables. Lanterns were hung across the ceiling, and the food was stacked high.

Hams, chickens, ducks, turkeys, and wild game of every sort—all cooked to perfection—covered one table, and a variety of steaming vegetables in huge pots bowed another. Potatoes with thick gravy, yams that dripped syrup, mountains of biscuits, pans of fragrant corn bread, and rolls fresh from the oven added to the feast. And the children swarmed around the desserts: peach cobblers, apple pies, tarts, blackberry muffins, taffy, and candy.

Maj. Franklin asked a brief blessing, then lifted his head and smiled. "All right, let's get at it!"

There was a scramble, and Jake stood back, watching with a slight smile as the slaves piled their plates high with food. When the first rush was over, he moved to the tables and got some of the food, but more for appearance than because he was hungry. Since his experience at the camp meeting, he had eaten little and slept only fitfully. The shock of the emotional impact had faded, but he could not stop thinking about what had occurred.

Rachel was helping Melora bring in the gifts for the slaves, but she looked around for Jake. She had noticed how he had kept to himself since the night of the camp

241

meeting, clear evidence of how the experience had shaken him. There was no time to go to him now, though, for the slaves were waiting with expectant smiles. Each time she handed out a gift, the recipient would cry out "Chris'mas gift!" and there was a constant stream of giggles and shouts of pleasure as the gifts were unwrapped. Most of the gifts were clothing, but candy and other small favors were handed to the smaller children.

When the last of the gifts for the slaves were handed out, Rachel finally went to Jake. She took a small package with her and, when she reached him, said, "Christmas gift!"

Jake looked up, startled, then took the package from her, asking, "What is it?"

"It's a toecover."

Jake stared at her. "It's a *what?*"

Rachel laughed at his expression. She was wearing a red dress with white bows, and her hair gleamed as it caught the yellow rays of the lanterns overhead. "Oh, you've forgotten! A toecover is what we always called a useless sort of gift—something that's pretty, but not good for anything."

He smiled and unwrapped the paper, then looked up to say, "It's not a toecover." He dropped the paper and looked closely at the heavy gold ring with the brilliant red stone. "It's a fine gift," he murmured.

"Well, I didn't really buy it. It belonged to Mother's grandfather, Noah Rocklin. He left it to Mother, but she never did anything with it. I got her to let me give it to you." Her dimples flashed as she added mischievously, "I know how given you are to foppish attire—and it seemed like just the thing for a dandy."

Jake didn't respond to her teasing. He just looked at the ring, then slipped it on the third finger of his right hand. She couldn't know he was thinking, *I'll have to give this to Vince. It's part of the family.* But he was pleased with the thought that had spurred Rachel's gift and said, "That was fine of you to think of such a thing. But it's like you to do a nice thing for someone." He took her hand and, to her complete surprise, kissed it. "Thank you, Rachel."

Rachel's eyes mirrored the confusion that swept over her. She bit her lip, then shook her head, saying, "What has happened to you?"

At once Jake knew he'd made an error and covered himself quickly by saying, "I have a gift for you. It's in my room. Walk to the house with me, and I'll give it to you."

"All right." They left the barn, taking the path to the house. As they walked, Rachel wondered if she should ask him what he thought about the camp meeting. But it was a delicate subject, so she kept the conversation on other things. They entered the house, and when they got to his room, he went at once to the bureau. Opening the top drawer, he drew out a small package and came to hand it to her. "Christmas gift," he said, and watched as she took away the wrapping.

"Why—these are lovely!" She ran her hand over the smooth surface of the silver brush set with mother-of-pearl, then took up the matching comb and ran it through her hair. "How in the world did you know I wanted these? I never said a word to you!"

"Mother told me," Jake said. He had discovered from Amy that Rachel had longed for this particular set, which she'd seen in the finest store in Richmond. He had bought it a week earlier, and now he stood there delighting in the sight of her obvious pleasure in the gift. He had given presents to women before but could not remember so enjoying the act. "A woman with hair like yours deserves the best in combs and brushes," he commented, then again realized that such a speech was out of character for Vince. "After all, if you're going to marry Leighton Semmes, you'll have to get used to fancy things. He's rich, isn't he?"

Rachel seemed uncomfortable with the question. She ran the comb through her hair, then turned abruptly and walked over to the window. "Oh, I don't know."

He came over to stand beside her, noting how her skin was translucent as the bright bars of brilliant sunlight bathed her. She had a few freckles across her nose, something he'd never noticed, and there was an inner well of energy about her that threatened to spill over. "What's to know? He's rich, healthy, and good-looking." When she didn't respond he pulled her around, adding, "That's better than being poor, sick, and ugly, isn't it?"

She giggled and reached up to give his hair a tug. "You fool! Let me alone about Semmes." Then she dropped her hand, asking curiously, "Why are you so anxious about my love life? You never gave a thought to it before."

He shrugged, thinking of the days that had passed since she had come to him as he lay in the hospital. "I guess being helpless and dependent changes a man. I always thought I was a pretty tough fellow, but then when I was flat on my back, not even able to wash my face—" He hesitated, and a shadow came to his eyes. "If you hadn't come to me, I think I'd have given it all up."

They stood there, facing one another, and the sunlight fell across the room, filled with millions of motes swarming in the beams. Far off they heard the muted singing of the slaves, a happy sound that floated on the air like a far-off melody. He studied her face, noting that she had the prettiest blue-green eyes imaginable, admiring how the sweep of her jaw was smooth and silky, yet strong—made more so by the cleft in her chin. He was shaken again by the realization of how much she had come to mean to him, and something of his feelings came into his expression, so that she asked at once, "What is it?"

His feelings washed over him, surprising him with their intensity. He had never thought to tie himself to one woman—but that was exactly what he longed to do with Rachel Franklin. The impossibility of his situation came to him, and he forced himself to smile before she could read the pain that shot through him. "You know the cuckoo bird never builds a nest," he said, forcing his voice to be light. "She lays her eggs in the nests of other birds, leaving her chicks for the other bird to raise. Sometimes the baby cuckoo is large, so he just pushes the real chicks of the mother bird out to die."

Rachel was confused. "Why are you telling me about a cuckoo?"

"Because you've had to take care of me—and I'm just like that big overgrown cuckoo. Taking everything and giving nothing."

Her eyes grew soft and she shook her head. "Maybe it was a little like that at first," she admitted. "I didn't like you at all, but now you're another man."

Her words seemed to strike him hard, though she didn't understand why they should. She had meant them as a compliment and added, "I'll tell you something amazing, Vince. I've decided that if I ever do get married, it'll be to somebody like you!"

Pain once again streaked through Jake, and he shook his head, a bitter light glowing dully in his eyes. "No, Rachel, you deserve better than that," he said. "I guess we better join the others." Turning, he left the room, and she followed, hurt a little by his abrupt words and by the curt dismissal in his voice. They found Amy in the parlor looking out the window at the children who were having a snowball fight.

Looking up, she said in a strange voice, "I want to tell you two something."

"What is it, Mother?" Rachel asked. She was still thinking of Vince's strange behavior but went to stand beside the wheelchair.

Amy said without a trace of emotion or excitement, "I'm going to get a gift from the Lord. A belated Christmas present." She smiled at the bewilderment that crossed Rachel's face and added, "I'm going to get out of this wheelchair and walk."

Rachel blinked with surprise, then said quickly, "I hope so!"

"It's not hope anymore," Amy insisted. " 'Hope deferred maketh the heart sick,' " she quoted. Then she nodded firmly, adding, "That's what I've been doing ever since the accident—hoping. But last night I had an all-night session with God. It was like Jacob wrestling with the angel at Peniel!" A rueful smile came to her lips, and she shook her head with wonder. "I behaved in a very—well, *unusual* way with the Lord. I just *demanded* that he touch my leg and heal it!"

Rachel could not resist a glance down at her mother's leg, still propped up and looking swollen. "Oh, it's no better, Rachel," Amy said quickly. "But God gave me a promise last night. He said I'd be walking before the old year ended."

Jake was staring at Amy, disbelief on his face. Amy looked at him, then said, "I think part of my healing is for your benefit, Son." When Jake looked startled, she said, "You've got a long way to go, and you need God. But you don't know if you can trust him. Isn't that right?"

"Why—I guess most men feel like that, Mother."

"Yes, they do. But you've watched for weeks as I lay in that bed and in this chair, getting worse. And you've talked with Dr. Maxwell, and he told you I'd probably never walk again, or at best I'd be limited to using crutches, didn't he?"

"Well—"

"Of course he did! I'm not a fool, and neither are you." Amy suddenly smiled, then said, "But when you see me walk as well as I ever did, you'll know that God is able to do anything! Now go on about your business!"

Dismissed with a wave of Amy's hand, the two walked back out into the cold air. "Is she losing her mind?" Jake asked, stunned by what he had heard. "I've never heard of anything like that!"

Rachel didn't answer at once. They walked along the packed snow, in silence, each considering what Amy had told them. Finally Rachel said quietly, "Vince, Mama has always been able to hear from God. You know that, too, even though you always laughed at such things. Now I think we're going to see God do something very wonderful." Then it seemed to her that the moment had come, and she said quietly, "And I believe that it's all part of what God began when Gen. Jackson asked you if you'd ever trusted in Jesus."

She said no more and just walked on down the path, but Jake was shaken. He'd never seen God as he'd seen him reflected in the life of Amy Franklin, and now he felt that he was being moved along a road, directed by a power he could not see or hear. Somehow, he knew, there'd come a point on that road when he'd have to make a decision about God, and the thought of it made him clench his fists. He said nothing, but he knew the clock was ticking off seconds and, sooner or later, the rendezvous with what he feared most would be at hand.

All over the South, the threat of invasion by the Federal Army was in the air. It was in Richmond that it was strongest. Everyone knew that Gen. George McClellan was building the largest army that had ever marched on the planet—over two hundred thousand men, it was reported. Sooner or later that force would cross the Potomac, and there was no doubt in a single mind about its objective: it would head straight for Richmond, the symbol of the Confederacy.

Perhaps because of the imminence of this threat, parties were given almost nightly in the city. There was something of the Epicurean philosophy—"Eat, drink, and be merry, for tomorrow we may die"—about the constant holiday air that prevailed. That there should be several large New Year's Eve parties, therefore, was a foregone conclusion, and Rachel had agreed to accompany Leighton to the largest of them all, which would take place at the Elliot Hotel.

She was ready when he came for her, looking quite beautiful in a pink and gold brocade gown. As they drove into town, he made all the proper gestures of gallantry, and Rachel listened to his talk, weighing it carefully. When they reached the hotel, early darkness had fallen. When he pulled the horse up, he wrapped the lines firmly around the brake and turned to her instead of getting out.

She watched him carefully, aware that he was going to kiss her. When he put his arms around her, her curiosity rose and she allowed him to pull her close. The kiss was expert, and there was, to be sure, a certain stirring in her, for Semmes was a handsome man. She had been kissed before by him, and for one moment, she let herself believe that the response she felt was love. Then she suddenly let her lips slide away and drew back.

Semmes was thrown off-balance and tried to draw her into another embrace, but she smiled and shook her head. "I think we'd better go inside, Leighton."

He stared at her, then said, "You've heard that I've been a womanizer, I take it?"

"It's the common talk."

"Well, I've told other women how beautiful they are," he admitted. "I've even told some of them I loved them. I've said those things not entirely meaning them. Now I want to say them to you because I mean them—and I wish I'd never used those words before."

"At least you're honest."

"Is there a chance for me, Rachel?"

Rachel smiled quickly, then shook her head. "I don't know, Leighton. I really don't know. Now let's go inside."

He took her into the ballroom, his temper ruffled by her lack of response to him, but he was an optimistic man. *She's a woman, therefore she can be had* was his thought, and he spent the next two hours pleasantly enough, enjoying her company and not pressing her in the least.

The room was crowded, and Rachel saw that Jake had come along with her father. They came to speak with her, her father saying, "You look lovely, Rachel. Good thing you took after your mother and not me!"

Rachel laughed and patted him on the shoulder, then turned to Jake. "You can give that leg some practice, Vince. I've seen several young ladies waiting for you to ask them to dance, but your first one is mine."

Jake grinned at Semmes and stepped forward at once. As they moved out onto the floor, he asked as casually as he could, "Did the captain make his offer yet?"

"Oh, he made an offer, all right," Rachel laughed. "I'm not sure, though, just what kind of offer it was."

"Little girls need to beware of tall handsome strangers with long teeth."

He seemed in better spirits than he had been for several days, and she enjoyed her dance with him. But when he took her back to where Leighton stood, he said, "Captain, be careful. This woman is dangerous!"

"Will you dance with me again?" Rachel asked him, surprising both herself and Jake. He struggled with the desire to claim all of her dances—regardless of how it might look—then sighed in surrender to common sense.

"No, my leg is growing sore again. I think I'll join the cardplayers," he said, trying to ignore the disappointment that crossed Rachel's face. He smiled at her and Semmes. "You two look very handsome together," he said, forcing himself to play his role. But the words left a bitter taste in his mouth as he walked away.

As he left, Semmes frowned. "I can't figure that fellow out. He's not much what I expected. The word I got was that he was a pretty sorry specimen."

"He's—changed a lot since he was injured," Rachel said, watching Jake walk away, wishing she understood herself and her reactions to him . . . then she changed the subject.

The time went by, with everyone looking at the big clock from time to time. At eleven-thirty Rachel said, "Come along, Leighton. Let's go get Vince away from that old card game."

Semmes was reluctant but had little choice. Rachel moved ahead of him, and when they entered the room used for cards, they found themselves in the middle of a drama.

There were at least fifteen men in the room, but there was almost no sound. Everyone was standing silent, gathered loosely around a table where Rachel saw her father and Jake sitting. Right across from Jake sat Simon Duvall.

He was drunk, Rachel saw at once, and seeing her brother Grant, she moved to him, whispering, "Grant—what is it?"

"Duvall came in thirty minutes ago—drunk. He forced his way into the card game, and he's been trying to get a fight out of Vince." His face was dark with anger and he said, "If he doesn't shut his mouth, I'm going to shut it for him!"

Rachel felt a streak of fear but could only stand and watch. This was a man's world, and she knew that Vince would get no help from anyone.

Duvall threw his cards down, having lost yet another hand, and glared across the table, saying, "You been taking lessons, Franklin?"

Jake could have beaten Duvall blindfolded, for the man was a poor player. He had been taken off guard when Duvall had walked in, and alarms had gone off in his mind at once when he heard others mention Duvall's name and saw that the man was drunk and spoiling for trouble.

"Do you want to play another hand, Duvall?" he asked evenly.

Duvall cursed, saying, "Come on, you whelp! I can beat you at cards—or anything else!"

Jake dealt the cards, and the stakes rose rapidly. The other two players dropped out, and Duvall, obviously with a good hand, raised the bet again. "Now we'll see what kind of nerve you got!" he said. When Jake met his raise, he tossed his cards down with a harsh laugh. "Three aces!" he said, and he started to pull the chips in.

Jake laid his cards down, saying nothing. A full house.

A mutter went around the table, and Duvall's face flared with anger. He shouted, "You cheated, Franklin."

Jake said evenly, "Careful, Duvall."

But Simon Duvall had just lost the stake he'd been waiting for for weeks, and rage washed over him. "You're a cheat and a coward! I'm taking that pot!"

He reached out, but Jake said, "Take your hands away, Duvall. Either bet or get out of the game."

Duvall stared at him, then his voice grated as he said, "I'll fight you for it."

"It's mine already," Jake said.

"You dirty little coward!" Duvall almost screamed. "I've been waiting for this. Now come on out and we'll see if you can act like a man!"

A silence fell over the room. Brad Franklin wanted to order Duvall to leave the room. In fact, he *would* have told any other man at any other time to do just that—but this time his son was on trial. One glance around showed him that every man in the room expected Vince to run. He was expecting it himself, and he steeled himself for the shame that he felt certain was coming.

Rachel closed her eyes, knowing that if Vince ran away, he was finished. She was trembling and wanted to leave but could not. When she opened her eyes, she saw that Jake was studying Duvall with a steady gaze.

The silence ran on and it got to Duvall, who yelled, "Are you going to fight me, or not?"

Jake said softly, "Yes, Duvall, I believe I am."

Duvall was shocked. He started to rise, a smile on his face. "Come along, then. We'll find a place—"

"This place is good as any," Jake said.

"Here?" Duvall said in a startled voice.

Jake reached into his pocket and pulled out a fine linen handkerchief. He unfolded it, then, holding one end, flipped it out, saying, "Take hold of that end, Duvall."

Duvall, acting on instinct, took the end of the handkerchief. Then he growled, "You crazy? We going to fight with handkerchiefs?"

Jake moved so smoothly that few even saw the .32 revolver that appeared in his hand. A gasp went around the room, and Duvall blinked, his sodden mind suddenly much clearer in the one instant that he saw the gun.

"You've got a gun under your coat, Duvall," Jake said. "Take it out. Then we'll hold on to the handkerchief and on the count of three we'll start shooting."

A gasp went around the room, and Brad Franklin, fighting man that he was, could not help but grow pale. He knew it was one thing to stand twenty feet away and take a shot at a man, but to face his fire only inches away, with no chance in the world that he would miss—!

Duvall's face was a study. His lips puckered as though he had tasted something bitter, and his olive complexion grew gray as old paper. He stared at the gun that Jake had now placed on the table but made no move to go for his own.

"This—this isn't the proper way to fight a duel!" he protested.

Jake's eyes were cold as polar ice, Rachel saw, and his voice was steady. "You've been running around calling me a coward for months, Duvall. Well, here's your chance to prove it. Now—*get your gun out!*"

Duvall flinched at the harsh command. He hunched his shoulders and squeezed his eyes together. Slowly he lifted his hand and reached inside his coat—but stopped abruptly.

"No! I won't fight you like this!" he gasped. Dropping the handkerchief, he got to his feet and would have left, but Jake's voice caught him.

"Hold it, Duvall!"

The man turned to find that Jake had picked up his gun, and he shouted, "I'm not drawing on you, Franklin!"

Jake stood up, putting his gun inside the shoulder holster. Then he said, "All right, we've both got an even chance. Pull that gun, Duvall. Let's see if you're a man or not!"

But Duvall had seen how the other had conjured the .32 out of the holster. He shook his head, saying, "I won't fight—"

Jake cut him off, moving around the table quickly despite his limp. He came to Duvall, raised his hand, and cracked him across the cheek. "Come on! Are you a man? Pull that gun!"

Duvall suddenly ducked and, shoving men to one side, ran out of the room. The sound of his short, labored breathing faded as he passed through the doors, and there was a sudden babble of voices. Men were coming to Jake and patting him on the shoulder. Rachel glanced at her father and saw tears on his cheeks.

"I want to go home, Leighton," she whispered. "But I want to go with my father and my brother."

Later she could remember little of the ride back. Jake said almost nothing. Once her father said, "My boy, I believe I'm going to have to tell you how very proud of you I am!"

They got out of the buggy and went into the house. A light was on in the parlor, and Brad said, "I'd better turn that out. Betty must have forgotten it."

Then they all heard Amy call. "Come into the parlor, all of you."

Brad looked at the others with surprise. "Why, I guess she's waited up for us." He led the way, and as they entered, he saw Amy sitting on the couch, her wheelchair across the room. "Amy—!" he said, concerned, and started toward her, but she stopped him by crying out.

"No, stay there, Brad!" Her dark eyes picked up the reflection of the lamps, and there was a look on her face that none of them could understand.

"Amy, are you all right?" Brad asked with some confusion.

"Yes, dear, I'm all right."

She spoke quietly enough—then she suddenly gave herself a push against the arm of the horsehide sofa, coming to her feet awkwardly.

"Mother!" Rachel cried out, then pressed her fist against her lips, for her mother took two short steps, paused for one moment to gain her balance, then with a happy cry walked across the floor. Brad leaped to grab her in his arms, crying out, "Amy!"

Jake did not move but stood transfixed as Rachel ran to her mother. They were all laughing and crying at the same time, and finally Rachel asked, "Mother, did you walk before twelve o'clock?"

"It was just as God promised me," Amy said, tears gleaming in her eyes. "I waited until it was five minutes until twelve. Then I reminded the Lord of his promise . . . and then—I got up and walked!"

"It's a miracle!" Brad whispered. "Does your leg hurt?"

"Like fury!" Amy laughed. "But God didn't promise me it wouldn't hurt or that I would run around the house—just that I'd walk."

Then she turned to Jake and held out her hand. In a soft voice, filled with triumph, she asked, "Now, my dear boy, do you see what God is able to do?"

Jake Hardin stood there unable to speak for a moment. Then he smiled and said, "Yes, I do see."

In a flash, the others were all talking at once—but Jake was quiet, for he knew that God had spoken to him again, this time in a manner he could neither deny nor ever forget!

CHAPTER NINETEEN

A LONG, LONG HONEYMOON!

A WARM wind swept across the South, melting the snow and thawing the streams. It was exactly in the middle of January, the fifteenth, when Jake remarked to Rachel, "This weather can't last, can it? It seems too good to be true."

They had left Lindwood at noon and ridden to the foothills, stopping to water Crow and Lady at a small stream. Rachel was wearing a pair of Grant's old jeans, a worn blue blouse, and a thin sweater. Her hair crept out from beneath a wide-brimmed slouch hat, and she poked it back as she said, "I don't think so, but we can enjoy it while it lasts."

The ride had put color in her cheeks, and her clear eyes sparkled in the sunlight. "Let's race to that old pine," she said with a smile and, before he could even nod, kicked her horse into action. Jake yelled, "Hey—no fair!" then Crow shot out of the creek in pursuit of the mare. It was less than a quarter mile to the tree, and the mare was a quicker starter. But the long legs and powerful frame of the stallion began to tell, and he shot past Lady, winning the race by a length.

"You lose," Jake said, grinning. "Now pay up!"

"We didn't bet," Rachel said.

"I always get something for winning. You'll have to make me some of those fried pies."

"No. You always eat too many of them. You'll get fat."

Jake grinned wickedly, then, before Rachel could react, he brought the stallion closer, reached out to throw his arm around Rachel, and kicked Crow in the ribs, neatly picking Rachel off her horse. "Vince—!" she yelled. "You put me down!"

He kept Crow at a trot, squeezing Rachel close and ignoring her indignant cries. He came to a small depression in the ground that was filled with water. He stopped the horse and smiled down at her. "Either I get my pies or you get a bath. Which will it be?"

Rachel squirmed in his grasp, but his arm was like steel. "You wouldn't dare!" she cried, trying to hit at him.

"No? Well, let's see—"

He loosened his grip and Rachel felt herself slipping. She screamed and grabbed at his arm. "No! Don't drop me!"

"Do I get the pies?"

"Yes!" she exclaimed breathlessly, somewhere between laughter and tears. "You beast!"

Jake laughed, tightened his grip, then moved Crow to dry earth. "Sticks and stones . . . ," he said, amused at her anger. He abruptly reached over with his left hand and lifted her easily in front of him, holding her like a child. "Now if I was one of your gentleman callers—say, Capt. Leighton Semmes—I'd get more than a fried pie out of you in a situation like this."

Rachel reached up, grabbed his hair, and gave a tremendous yank. Jake yelled, "Hey!" and shook his head to free himself. "Let me go! You're pulling my hair out!" When she persisted, he suddenly constricted his grip, holding her so tightly that she gave a gasp and released him. She looked up at him, and he thought she was angry, but then he saw she was laughing.

Rachel said saucily, "It's a good thing it's me you're hugging instead of one of those dreadful women you like to chase around with!"

As she laughed up at him, he was suddenly painfully conscious of her soft form pressed against his chest and of the gentle curve of her lips only inches away. Something in his face made her stop laughing, and then she too was conscious of the intimacy of his grip. For some reason she could not fathom, the touch of his iron arm around her disturbed her. She waited, trying to understand, confusion flooding her face with color. They stared at each other until she finally said, "Put me down, Vince."

At once he swung her to the ground, then dismounted and handed her Crow's reins. "I'll get Lady for you," he said and walked away, glad to have something to do. He took his time bringing the horse back, handed her the reins, then said, "Sorry for the horseplay."

"It's all right." A restless discontent had been stirring in Rachel for days, driving her to feverish activity at times, at other times bringing a desire of solitude so strong that she had gone on long rides alone. Now she was disturbed anew by the swirl of emotions struggling within her breast. Most disturbing of all was the fact that she did not understand what was making her discontented.

Suddenly she spoke. "Let's walk for a while," she said, and as they moved across the thawing ground, she struggled to put her feelings into words. "Things are so—so *fragile!*" The word didn't seem right, and she shook her head impatiently. "That doesn't make any sense, I know, but I've been so confused lately."

"I've noticed."

She looked at him with surprise, then said, "I thought I was keeping it to myself. I guess we all feel the pressure of the war. I'm afraid for Daddy and Grant—and now you'll be going to fight. I try to think that it'll be all right, but every day we get news that one of the boys we grew up with has been killed—like Bobby Felton. Remember how nice he was?"

"Fine fellow." Jake nodded.

"Now he's dead. Killed in a meaningless battle in Kentucky." Her lips drew tightly together, and she walked along silently, then said, "I saw Jenny Prescott last week. She and Bobby were engaged. Now he's dead and she's lost him. And his mother—you know how she doted on Bobby! She's a broken woman."

A cloud of blackbirds rose, filling the skies, and their raucous cries drifted back to the two people walking side by side. "I always hated blackbirds," Rachel said suddenly. "They remind me of darkness, of bad news." Then she shook her head, going back to her thoughts. "Last night I had an awful nightmare. I was all dressed in white, in a wedding gown. All the people were there, and I was coming down the aisle. I could see Rev. Irons there waiting to marry me—but I couldn't see the groom, not his face anyway." She gave a sudden shiver and fell silent.

Strangely disturbed, Jake asked, "Was that all of it?"

"No. I got to the front of the church, and the man I was marrying turned around—and he was dead!" Rachel stopped, her head lowered and her voice a whisper. "He—didn't have a face. Just a skull. And I woke up screaming. I've never done that before!"

"It was just a bad dream, Rachel."

She gave her shoulders a shake, as if to throw off the memory, then turned to him. "I know, but it's happening all around us. The best of our young men are going off, the most courageous boys, those who really love the South. What's going to happen when they die? Who'll take their place?"

Jake saw that she was terribly disturbed, and he spoke in a soothing voice. "Best not to think of those things, Rachel."

"How can you not think of them?" she demanded. "When I look at Daddy or Grant—or at you—I can't help but think you could die." She paused again, then asked, "Don't you ever think about it? About Daddy and Grant and all our friends?"

"Yes, I think of it. I think of myself, too. A man's a fool who doesn't think of that." He had not intended to speak of it, but said, "What Gen. Jackson said was true. It hit me like a bullet, Rachel!"

"Vince—do you believe in God?"

"Yes. But that's not enough, is it? I've seen some pretty sorry specimens who claimed to be Christians. Guess that's what I've been hiding behind for a long time. But then, I've also seen the real thing. Mother and Jeremiah Irons—and you, of course."

"More than anything in the world, I want you to find peace with God. You have so much to live for!"

Jake stopped and gave her a strange look but said only, "You really mean that, don't you? Well, I'm a hard case. Never did have much use for people who used religion as a trade with God. 'If you'll do this for me, God, then I'll do something for you.'" He shook his head, a faint sadness in his eyes. "I can't seem to do that, Rachel."

She said only, "I'm glad you can't. Any religion that worked like that wouldn't hold up. Real faith is like the sermon Brother Irons preached at the camp meeting—Jesus asks for all we are, especially whatever it is we love most."

He turned to face her, started to speak, then changed his mind and fell silent. Finally he said, "We'd better get back."

When they arrived at the house, Rachel said, "Look, there's the gelding Brother Irons rides."

"Came to visit Mother, I guess."

When they entered the house, they found Irons talking to Amy in the parlor. He rose and greeted them, and Jake would have left but was detained when Irons said, "I've been waiting to talk to you, Vince."

Amy rose, saying, "Come along, Rachel. We'll make some coffee."

When the two women had left, Irons said, "Vince, I've got to go to Fort Donelson." He seemed unhappy but shook it off saying, "My brother is there with the army. I just got word that he's very ill, critically maybe."

"Fort Donelson? Where's that?"

"In Tennessee, way up in the northern part, almost in Kentucky. Fort Henry is on the Tennessee River, and Fort Donelson is just a few miles away on the Cumberland River." Irons shook his head, his mouth drawn up tight. "If the Federals take those two forts, they can use the rivers and pin us down."

"I've heard my father say so."

"Well, I've got to go. Baxter is my younger brother, and he may be dying. I'm leaving as soon as I can—probably tomorrow."

"I hope he makes it, Chaplain."

"I pray so, but that's not why I wanted to talk to you. You've made up your mind to join the army, and I thought this might be an opportunity for you."

Jake stared at him. "Me, Chaplain?"

Irons seemed reluctant and said, "Well, I'm probably out of line, but it occurred to me you might like to go with a troop of cavalry that's being raised to go to the defense of Donelson. Jeb Stuart's sending an officer and a few men. Everybody knows that Gen. Johnston's spread thin, so there's an attempt to send reinforcements. Melora told me you had decided against the infantry because of your leg. All you'd have to have to join the Sixth is a horse."

Jake stood there, thinking—and the more he thought of it, the better it sounded. He had come to realize that joining the war was not just something he was doing for Vince, or to fulfill Brad's requirements—he wanted to join because he felt it was the right thing for any Southern man to do. "I'd really like to go, Chaplain. But would they take me?"

"Like a shot!" Irons said with a grim smile. "They need every man they can get. The enlistment is for ninety days, so when that's over, you might want to join the Grays—or perhaps stay in Stuart's cavalry."

Jake made up his mind on the spot. "I'll do it. How do I sign up?"

"The troop will leave day after tomorrow. I'll go along, so we'll be together. Capt. Wainwright will be in command of the troop. I'll tell him about you, and I know he'll be glad to have you. Bring a rifle and a sidearm. I don't think there's much in the way of arms."

Jake nodded. "I'll be ready. Where should I report?"

"Be at the camp tomorrow at eight." Irons rose to go,

then paused to say, "Well, that was the easy thing. Now I've got to go tell Melora we'll have to put the wedding off until I've taken care of my brother."

"That's tough on both of you, Chaplain."

"Can't be helped." When Irons nodded and left the room, Jake went to find Amy and Rachel, who were just getting the coffee ready. "The preacher is gone," he said, then he hesitated. "I'll be leaving tomorrow."

Rachel gasped, "The army?"

"Yes. I'll be going with a troop of cavalry to Tennessee."

Amy said, "I know you think this is something you have to do, Vince—but be sure it's right. Your father and I don't agree on this thing. You've proven yourself by riding the stallion and facing Duvall down."

Jake said, "I guess I'll have to go." He wanted to explain, but knew that he never would. Amy turned suddenly and left the room, and Rachel went over to stare out the window. There was a rigidity in her back, and Jake felt she was angry for some reason. "Rachel, don't be angry," he said, going to stand beside her.

She turned to face him, and he saw that tears had gathered in her eyes. The sight of her tears hit him hard, almost as if someone had struck him in the pit of the stomach. From his earliest memories, Jake Hardin could not recall anyone shedding a tear over him. Then another thought hit him even harder than the sight of her tears: Rachel was not crying for him, but for the man she thought he was. And this was a bitter thing to him.

Her voice was husky, tightly controlled, as she said, "I—wish you didn't have to go! I'm afraid!" She reached out, touching his cheek gently, her fingers tracing the line of his jaw. "I know I ought to smile and talk about how glorious it is for you to serve in the army—but I just can't!" Without another word, she abruptly whirled and ran blindly out of the room, leaving him standing there. She ran up to her room, threw herself on the bed and wept. She didn't understand what was happening inside her. All she knew was that there was a dull, hollow dread in her—a void such as she had never known and that wasn't going away. After some time, she rose, washed her face, and sat down in the rocker beside her bed. For a long time she sat there, staring out the window. And then she closed her eyes and began to rock.

"Melora, I'll be back soon," Irons said. "If my brother is able to be moved, I intend to bring him back with me to Richmond."

"I hope so, Jeremiah. I could help you nurse him."

The pair was standing in front of Melora's house. It was late in the afternoon, and they had just come back from a long walk down the lane. He had told her of his brother, and she had listened quietly. Finally, when he finished, she smiled at him and said, "That's like you, Jeremiah. You couldn't do anything else—being the man you are."

They had reached the house, and he had said, "I've got to go, but oh, I hate it so!"

Melora said, "I'll be here when you come back, Jeremiah."

Irons smiled and put his arms around her. "I'm the luckiest man in the world! You've made me so happy, Melora!" He kissed her then, and she responded. He drew back, smiled and said, "You go right on planning the wedding. The day after I get back—that's the day we get married!"

"All right." She smiled, and there was a softness in her eyes as she said quickly, "We'll have a short honeymoon, I suppose, since you're in the army."

A boyish smile lifted the corner of Irons's lips, and he suddenly grabbed her around the waist, lifted her, and spun her around. When he put her down he said, "We'll have a honeymoon for the next thirty or forty years, Melora Yancy! I promise you that." Then he kissed her again, turned, and mounted his gelding. He was still smiling, and there was a happiness in his fine brown eyes such as she'd never seen. "Good-bye, my dear! I'll be back soon—and you must get ready for that long, long honeymoon!"

He wheeled the horse, touched its sides with his spurs, and sent it galloping down the road. Melora stood and watched him, and just before he went out of sight, she saw him turn, pull his hat off, and wave it. He called out, his voice coming to her thin and clear: "A long honeymoon, Melora!"

And then he was gone, hidden by the line of straight, dead trees that reached up with lifeless fingers that seemed to be reaching to heaven.

CHAPTER TWENTY
A LATE VISITOR

JAKE had always been a light sleeper, able to awaken with all his faculties sharp, and the sound of footsteps coming toward his room woke him instantly. He lay there listening, expecting them to continue down the hallway, but when they stopped and a faint tapping came at his door, he was out of the bed at once. The room was illuminated by silver moonlight flooding in through the window as he went to the door quickly and opened it. He half expected to see Tad, for one of the mares was due to foal at any moment, and he'd told the slave to come for him when it was time.

The hallway was dark, and the figure seemed too bulky to be the slave. "Tad?" Jake asked, but then the man pushed himself forward, shoving Jake backward. Jake reacted instinctively, grabbing the coat of the intruder and swinging him around.

"Easy, Jake! It's me—Vince!"

Jake had drawn his fist back to drive a blow at the intruder but halted abruptly. Keeping his grip on the rough coat, he leaned closer trying to see the features of the man, but it was too dark.

"Light the lamp," Vince ordered and stood there as Jake got a match and did so. When Jake turned around, shock widened his eyes, and Vince said, "It's me, Jake. Look like something the cat dragged in, don't I?"

Vince walked over and sat down in the rocker beside the window. Jake was shocked at his appearance, for he had lost so much weight that his clothing hung on him. Vince had always kept his beard trimmed neatly, but now it was bushy and ragged, hiding most of his face.

The broad-brimmed slouch hat he wore shaded his eyes, and when he took it off Jake saw that Vince's eyes were sunken and his cheeks had lost their fullness.

"What's going on, Vince?"

Vince looked at him carefully, then said, "I don't expect you to understand this, but here's the story."

Jake listened as Vince spoke, and his eyes narrowed as he heard how Vince had gone to Savannah to hire a man to kill Ellen. He said nothing, but his eyes were hard. Vince did not try to excuse himself but went on with the narrative.

"I got off the train at Savannah and keeled right over. Woke up in a hospital. I was so sick it was like a dream. Guess I never did really come out of it, not for a few days, anyway. When I did finally come around enough to know where I was, there was a man in the same room on a cot just across from me. He was dying, Jake, and I've never seen a more bitter man!" Vince's eyes hardened at the memory, and he waited for a moment before going on. "He cursed me, he cursed the doctors, and he cursed God! Then he told me I was going to die, too."

Jake studied Vince, then asked, "Did you believe him?"

"Yes!" Vince nodded emphatically. "And it was bad, Jake. There I was, in town to hire a killer—and dying alone in a room next to a crazy man!"

"What happened?"

"The fellow died. Went out cursing God. When they took his body out, I was alone, still sicker than I'd ever been. Then I started flickering out, Jake. My mind was gone, and all I had was crazy dreams . . . then something happened—I got scared!" At the memory, Vince took out his handkerchief and wiped his brow, his hands trembling slightly. When he put the handkerchief away, though, he managed a smile. It wasn't much of a smile, but it was the best he could do.

"I was there for a week, thinking every day that I was going to die. And finally all I could think of was . . . what a mess I'd made of everything! I thought I could handle anything—but I found out different."

Jake saw there was something in Vince's face that hadn't been there before and asked, "What happened?"

"I don't really know, Jake. I hit bottom—and when I did I made myself one promise: if I lived, I'd do things differently. And then I prayed. Felt like a fool! Jake, I don't think I ever prayed in my life, but when a man's staring into his own grave, it makes him do strange things!"

"You found God?" Jake asked.

"N-no, I can't say that I did." Vince bit his lower lip, seeming to have trouble with his words. Finally he said, "It was like God was giving me some time, Jake. And I guess that's what I'm doing here. Sooner or later, I'll have to decide about God—but the time hasn't come just yet."

His words startled Jake, for they were what he had said of his own condition. He smiled grimly, shaking his head. "So you came back home?"

"Yes! I had plenty of money, but I had to stay a week in a boardinghouse to get my strength back enough to make the trip."

Jake stared at Vince, doubt in his face as plain as if it were a printed sheet. "I don't believe you. You're up to something tricky. What have you got up your sleeve now?"

Vince shook his head. "Nothing, Jake. I got all the trick shook out of me in that hospital. I walked out of there weak as a sick cat. I'm stronger now, but I'm out to win or lose." Vince's face was set, and suddenly Jake knew he was telling the truth. "I don't know how to work it out, Jake, but I'm letting you off the hook. You've done your job—more than I ever should have asked of anyone. You've faced down Crow and Duvall for me . . . I wish I could have done that myself. . . ." His voice trailed off for a moment, then a fresh determination settled on Vince's face. "At any rate, now the rest is mine. And if I make it— get the money, that is—you'll sure get your share."

Jake asked curiously, "What about the army? That's the last of the requirements your father laid down before he'd let you inherit the estate."

Vince shook his head, fatigue drawing his mouth downward. He rubbed his forehead wearily, saying, "I dunno, Jake. Guess I'll join up with the Grays."

"That won't work. In the first place, we may have looked alike once, but you've lost weight and I've gained. You show up for breakfast in the morning and it'll be all over. In the second place, even if that didn't happen, you'd never make it with an infantry company."

Vince stared at him, but his lips drew together stubbornly. "I don't know how to do it any differently. Maybe I could leave a note saying I'm leaving to join up with an outfit someplace else."

Jake thought quickly, then said, "Listen, Vince—" and rapidly told him of the plan to send a troop of cavalry to Tennessee, including his own intention of going along. "You go away and stay hid out," he ended. "I'll put in the three months, then you'll be able to come back and I'll fade away."

Vince stared at him for a long moment, then laughed ruefully. "I really *have* changed, Jake," he said. "If I hadn't, I'd take you up on that like a shot! But I won't let you do it. I'll leave here now and catch up with that troop someplace between here and Tennessee. That way nobody here will see me. You skedaddle out of here, Jake."

The room was quiet, and the two men studied each other, a smile on Vince's lips and doubt in Jake's eyes. Finally Jake said, "I guess you mean it, which I'm glad to hear. But I'll go along with you to Tennessee." A smile touched his wide mouth and he added, "You can join up as Jake Hardin."

"You mean it, Jake?" Vince was obviously relieved. "I'd try it on my own, but I'd feel a lot better if you were there with me until I get back to full strength."

"You get out of here," Jake said. "The troop will take the Miller Road for sure. You let us pass, then catch up with us. Tell the captain you just came in from the country." Then he added, "A man can get killed where we're going. You sure you want to do it?"

"I'm not too sure of anything, Jake," Vince said tentatively. Then he added strongly, "But I guess one thing is pretty clear—I'm not going to go back to what I was!" He got to his feet, saying, "I'd better get out of here, Jake. But I'll see you on the road. Bring along a good, well-mannered horse for me, will you? Say you want him for a spare mount." He didn't wait for a reply but moved across the room and stepped through the door, closing it after him.

Vince left as quietly as he could, but the floor squeaked loudly. When he stepped out onto the back porch, he took a deep breath and was about to let it go with relief when a voice broke the silence.

"Stay right where you are or I'll shoot you dead!"

A violent jerk twisted Vince, but he held himself upright. Turning slowly he saw Rachel standing in the moonlight. She was wearing a dark robe, and in her hand was a pistol aimed right at his stomach.

"Go back inside," Rachel said. "You're going to jail."

"Wait a minute—"

"Shut up and go inside! I'm going to get my brother up, and if you move, well, I'm a good shot and I can't miss at this distance. Now go inside!"

Vince said slowly, "Put the gun down, Rachel."

The sound of his voice startled her, he saw, for the gun in her hand wavered. "It's me—Vince," he said quietly. "Don't be afraid."

Rachel's lips were dry, for she was not as free from fear as she'd tried to seem. The moonlight was bright, but his back was to it so she could not see his face clearly. "Vince? You can't be Vince!"

Taking off his hat, Vince stood before her. "It's me, all right. I know it's a shock—but just let me explain."

"You can explain to my brother and to the sheriff, whoever you are!"

Vince said, "Rachel, it's me. I've lost twenty pounds and I'm hiding behind this wild beard. I've had to hide out, but now I've come back."

It *was* Vince's voice! Rachel moved closer, looked carefully into his face, then began to tremble. She lowered the pistol, then cried, "I don't understand!"

At once Vince began to speak, explaining the ruse he had engineered. He told it all, leaving out only his intention to have Ellen killed, thinking that would have to come later. But he told her of his brush with death and how it had brought him to something new.

"I don't know how to explain it, Rachel," he said finally, "but when I thought I was going to die, I met myself for the first time—and I didn't like what I saw. Now I'm going to finish what Jake started. I'm going with that cavalry troop to Tennessee. I'll either get killed or find out if there's any good in me at all."

Rachel glanced upstairs, then back at Vince. "Who is that man?" she asked in a harsh voice.

"Like I told you, his name is Jake Hardin," Vince answered. He told her a little of how the two of them had met, then said, "He's going with me to Tennessee."

"A gambler," Rachel whispered brokenly, and there was an expression on her face that Vince didn't understand. "A fortune hunter out to make money from us!"

Vince started, then said, "Now wait, Rachel—I talked Jake into this!"

"I'll bet it wasn't hard when you promised him money, was it?"

She turned to go, but Vince caught her arm, asking, "Where are you going?"

"To tell that—that charlatan to get off the place!"

Vince held her arm, saying urgently, "Wait now, Rachel—don't do that!"

"Why shouldn't I?"

"Well, I need him, to tell the truth. I'm still pretty weak, and Jake's a pretty tough hairpin. He's going with me to the army. He'll be out of the house tomorrow." His tone assumed a pleading tone as he continued, "Rachel, you don't think much of me, and I can't blame you a bit. I know I don't deserve any breaks—especially from you—but I'm asking for one."

"What do you want?" Her voice was as cold as the winter air itself.

"Time. Just time. Don't tell anyone about this. You may not believe it, but I've got some kind of hope that I can be the kind of son my father's always wanted. But I need the chance to prove it—by going to the army. I'm asking you for that chance, Rachel." Vince's thin face was clearly outlined by the moonlight as he added, "If you call out, it's all over before I've even had a chance to try. I'll never know what sort of man I *could* be."

Rachel stood there, her lips drawn together tightly, her eyes hooded. Just when Vince had decided she would never listen to him, she started speaking so quietly that he had to lean forward to catch her words. "You're right, I don't believe it. All you've ever done was try to hurt us all. You're a coward, a liar, and a cheat. I'm ashamed to be related to you at all!"

As she spoke, her voice low with fury, Vince felt shame and remorse wash over him—but he held her angry gaze. He knew she was right and that there was no reason for her to give him any kind of consideration, but he hoped against hope that she would give him this one last chance.

She stood looking at him for a moment, then said in that same low, angry voice, "All right. Get out of here."

"Thanks, Rachel!" Vince said, relief washing over him. He would have touched her, but she drew back sharply. "Can't blame you," he said instantly. Then he turned and disappeared into the darkness.

She waited until the sound of his horse's hooves had faded, then went back into the house. Going to her room, she put the gun in the drawer of her nightstand, then stood at the window, looking out, seeing nothing at all.

At breakfast, there was a cheerful note, for Amy determined to send Vince away with a happy memory. Rachel said little and ate almost nothing, but no one seemed to notice.

After breakfast, Jake went to his room, coming back with two rifles and two Colts in holsters. "Always carry two of everything," he said, smiling, then went outside saying, "I'll have Tad saddle up, then I'll come back."

"Have him saddle Lady," Rachel said. "I'll ride as far as Hardee's store with you."

Jake looked at her, surprised. His mind raced for a moment, wondering how he would explain the extra horse he'd promised Vince he would bring. Then he decided they would just have to find a horse for Vince later.

"All right," he said.

He left the house but was back in a few minutes. "Guess it's time for me to go."

Amy went to him and drew his head down. "I'll pray for you—and I'm very proud of you, my son!"

Jake took her kiss, then awkwardly patted her shoulder. "Be back before you know it," he said, smiling at her. Then he asked, "Ready, Rachel?"

"Yes."

They mounted their horses, and Jake leaned down and handed some cash to Tad, saying, "Buy something real nice for everyone, Tad. Have a party on me!"

"Yassuh!" Tad grinned. "You watch out dem Yankees doan put nuffin over you, Marse Vince!"

"Do my best!" Jake laughed, then pulled his horse around, and he and Rachel rode out of the yard. When they were out of sight of the house, Jake said, "Wish I didn't have to go."

Rachel made no reply. He turned to her, noting how pale her face was. Her hair was tied back, and he thought she looked very tired.

"I caught Vince going out of the house last night," she said suddenly, her voice even, as though she were remarking on the weather.

Her words seemed to explode in Jake's mind, and he stopped his horse instantly. She paused as well and turned to stare at him, her lips a thin line.

He looked down at his hands, squeezing the horn of his saddle. "Well, I told Vince it would never work."

She waited for him to continue but saw that he was silent. "Oh, don't worry, Mr. Hardin," she said bitterly. "I'm not going to turn you in." Still he didn't speak, and she cried out, "You must have enjoyed it a lot—making fools out of us all!"

Jake sat in the saddle, studying the ring on his hand. A thought came to him and he took it off. He turned to face her, saying, "You can give this to Vince when he comes back—"

"Give it to him yourself!" Her eyes flared with shame, and she said, "I'll never look at that comb and brush you gave me without thinking what a fool I was! And you know what? That's good!" She threw her head back, fighting against the tears that were misting her eyes. "It'll teach me never to trust anyone again as long as I live!" She started to turn her horse's head, but he reached out and held her arm.

"Just a minute—"

She jerked her head back to look at him, fury in her eyes.

"What for? So you can have some more fun?"

His hand was clasped around her arm tightly, and his face was tense. "Rachel, you have a right to think the worst of me, but before I go, you're going to listen to me, just for a moment."

"Of course I will. You've learned how to handle women, Mr. Hardin." A bitterness hardened her lips, and she wanted to strike him. "I think you've proved that—the way you've led me around by the nose!"

Jake saw that it was no good. He released her arm, then said, "All right, Rachel, you win."

She stared at him, thinking he would speak, but he did not. There was an air of fatalism about him, and she suddenly longed to be done with the whole thing. Drawing her horse's head around, she gave Jake one last bitter look. Then as she drove her heels into Lady's flanks she cried out, "Never come here again! Never!"

Jake watched her as she rode away, then turned Crow's head toward Richmond, as certain as he had ever been of anything that he would never see Rachel Franklin again.

And with that certainty, something inside him seemed to die.

✵ ✵ ✵

PART FOUR
THE RETURN

✵ ✵ ✵

CHAPTER TWENTY-ONE

A PERFECT TRAP

STEPHEN gave his wife a look of cynical humor, saying, "Ruth, don't get so excited. It's only the president of the United States." He knew, however, that it was a lost cause, for his wife had spent the last several months swimming in the huge pond that made up Washington society, and tonight the apogee of her career as a hostess had come—Abraham Lincoln and his wife were coming to her home.

True, it was not a major function, but it was a triumph, nonetheless, and Ruth Rocklin could hardly enjoy the evening for planning how she would casually drop the information to her circle of acquaintances in days to come: *What? Oh, dear me, yes, Doris! The president did drop by for my little reception last night. Of course, he and Stephen are rather close and went off to the library to talk about the war, so I had to spend most of my time with Mary—*

"Come away from the window, Ruth," Stephen said, grinning at her. "It's only the president—not the Second Coming!" He looked over her shoulder to catch sight of the tall man helping a short woman out of the carriage, then said, "Let's go greet them. I don't think they'll stay long."

His remark offended Ruth, and she gave him an angry look but was too nervous to argue. "Come along, then," she said, "and don't go dragging the president off to your study to look at your old guns!"

Stephen grinned behind her back, for he well knew that the reason Lincoln had agreed to come was to get a look at his new rifle. When he had issued the invitation, he had said, "My wife wants you to come to a reception at our house, Mr. President. It'll be a bore, as all such things are, but I've got the bugs worked out of that new eight-shot musket we've talked about producing. . . . "

Now as Stephen came forward to shake hands with the president, he smiled and received an answering smile from the tall man before him. When Lincoln had agreed to come, Rocklin had said, "Now, Mr. President, we'll both have to endure some social life, but I'll kidnap you as soon as possible, and we'll go to my study."

An hour later, the two men were in the large study alone, the president holding a musket, speaking with great animation about its potential. Rocklin's Ironworks had grown into one of the largest producers of muskets in the North, and Stephen had met with the president on matters of firearms several times. They were interrupted by a knock on the door, and when Rocklin answered it, an attractive young woman came in with a sheaf of papers.

"Ah yes, here they are!" Rocklin said, taking the papers eagerly. "These are the drawings of the musket." Then he said, "This is my granddaughter, Deborah Steele."

Lincoln smiled and put out his hand. "I met you at your uncle's office in the War Department, didn't I, Miss Steele?"

Deborah was amazed at the man's memory. "Yes, Mr. President," she answered, thinking as she did so how much the president's smile added to his homely face. She noted that he had a pair of warm brown eyes and that his mobile lips smiled easily.

"Gen. Scott appreciated Maj. Rocklin," Lincoln said, nodding, speaking of Gideon Rocklin, Stephen's son. "He could never find another aide to put up with his ways." His brow wrinkled and he asked, "Didn't your uncle mention something about the young soldier who's been doing some writing?"

"Oh, that's Noel Kojak," Rocklin said, nodding. "He's a private in my son's company. Have you seen the stories that he's been writing about army life?"

"Yes, I have. They're the real article!" Lincoln nodded with approval. "Most of the stories I read about army life would be better found in a romance novel—Kojak's are so real you can almost *smell* the camps he describes."

"Pvt. Kojak is a protégé of my granddaughter's here," Stephen said. "He was working in the mill, and she encouraged him to enlist. Then she found out he was a natural-born writer and introduced him to an editor."

"You've done the country a service, Miss Steele," Lincoln said, then frowned. "Most of the country thought this war was a nice little adventure, but they need to know the truth about it—and that's what your young man gives them, and very well."

Deborah said with some hesitation, "He's been criticized for being too realistic. Some say he takes all the glory out of war."

"Good! The sooner we get rid of that idea the better! War is a nasty, dirty business, as your uncle or any professional soldier will tell you. That last story I read by young Kojak, about men dying of measles—it was terrible, and not in the least *romantic!* And it was exactly the way it is. Tell him to keep writing, if you would, Miss Steele—and that, if he pleases no one else, he pleases his commander in chief!"

"I'll tell him, Mr. President," Deborah said quickly. "He'll be very proud."

"I suppose you get a love letter from him now and then?" the president inquired with a smile. "In between his more intimate remarks, does he say how things are in the area he's stationed?"

Deborah flushed at his teasing but said at once, "He's very happy to be with Uncle Gideon—Maj. Rocklin, I mean. He says that all the men like a general called Grant because he's a fighter and the rest are not."

Lincoln's head snapped back, and a light blazed in his deep-set eyes. "Tell Kojak to put *that* in one of his stories for the country to read, Miss Steele! This man Grant, he's not one of our top men, but he *fights!* Did you read how he attacked a Confederate force in Belmont? Got into a real fight, had to cut his way out, but he *did* something!"

"My son thinks he's like a bulldog," Stephen put in. "Says he doesn't spend too much time worrying about what the enemy's going to do to him—he's too busy worrying about how to hurt the army in front of him."

Lincoln started to speak, but the door opened and Ruth Rocklin entered, a reproachful look on her face. "Now, Mr. President, I've given you and my husband plenty of time to look at guns. You *must* come out and meet my guests!"

Lincoln asked, "Did my wife send you, Mrs. Rocklin?" He grinned at her flustered expression, adding, "I knew as soon as Miss Steele came in that Mrs. Lincoln would send for me. Would you believe as homely as I am, she's still jealous of attractive young women?" He sighed and nodded to Deborah, saying, "Tell that young man of yours to keep writing, Miss Steele—and if Grant gives your son a chance to fight, Rocklin, tell him to pour it on! I can't get McClellan to use the Army of the Potomac in Virginia."

"I heard," Stephen said with a straight face, "that you wrote him a letter saying if he didn't plan to use the army, you'd like to borrow it for a little while!"

Lincoln laughed, saying as he left the room, "It sounds like something I might say, doesn't it?"

Ruth followed the president, but Stephen detained his granddaughter, asking her, "Are you worried about Noel?"

Deborah smiled at him, saying, "Of course. You're worried about Uncle Gideon, aren't you?" Then she shook her head, adding, "I think of him a great deal— but I think of Great-Uncle Thomas's family in the Confederate Army, too. I'm sad for all of them, Grandfather!"

"It's a sad time," Rocklin agreed, his face lined with concern. "Like the hymn says, 'We're dwelling in a grand and awful time.'" Then he gave her a hug, and they left the study to join the others.

Rachel and her mother had been knitting socks for the Richmond Grays when Melora came into the room. "Why, Melora," Rachel said, "I didn't expect to see you today." Melora had gone back to her home after Amy's leg had grown strong enough for her to get around, and both women had missed her. "Let me fix you something to drink."

Melora shook her head. "No, thank you, Rachel. I only have a few minutes." She seemed a little upset—which was unusual for her, Rachel thought—but when she took an envelope out of her purse, saying, "I have a letter from Jeremiah," both Rachel and her mother grew still.

"Is it bad news, Melora?" Amy asked quietly. "Is it Vince?"

"Oh, no," Melora said quickly. "It's nothing like that. As a matter of fact, I came because when the messenger brought me the letter from Jeremiah, he had one for you, too. He was in a rush, so I offered to bring it to you."

Amy took the letter, opened it, and began to read. "How is Jeremiah's brother, Melora?" Rachel asked.

"Very sick, he says. I don't think Jeremiah expects him to live. He says disease is terrible at Fort Donelson. Five of the men who went with him and Vince have died, and a dozen more are down with one illness or another— mostly malaria."

"How did the letters come? We haven't heard a word from Vince."

"Gen. Floyd sent a courier back asking President Davis for reinforcements. When Jeremiah heard about it, he asked the lieutenant to bring a letter for me, then he told Vince. From what he says, it's not likely any mail will get back here again very soon."

Amy said, "Let me read Vince's letter to you. It's not very long—:

> "*Dear Mother and Father,*
> "*I write this in haste, for the courier is waiting right now. We made the journey to Tennessee with some*

difficulty. I was under the weather, but a new friend of mine named Jake Hardin nursed me along. When we arrived here, we were attached to the cavalry under Gen. Nathan Bedford Forrest. He is a striking man indeed—a former slave trader and a wealthy man with no military training whatsoever. But he has, Jake says, a natural military genius. We have been on patrols constantly, fighting skirmishes with the Yankees every day. They are thick as fleas around Donelson! Sometimes I am so tired when we get back to the fort it's all I can do to fall off my horse and get to my cot. But Jake always rousts me out and makes me eat.

"Neither of us likes what we see here, nor do any of the men—or the officers, either. Fort Donelson is perched on the banks of the Cumberland River, and the Yankee gunboats, they say, are right up the river, ready to come and shell us. So there will be no escape by the river, and if the Yankees close in our front, we will be caught in a perfect trap—perfect for them, I mean.

"Both Jake and I feel the battle will come soon, so I will not be able to write again. If I fall, remember these last days and try to forget and forgive the rest.

"Rachel, thank you for your favor. I'll try not to let you down.

"Love,
"Vince"

Amy looked up to see tears in Rachel's eyes. She asked gently, "What favor does he mean, Rachel? Taking care of him when he was injured?"

Rachel shook her head, then, dashing the tears from her eyes, whispered, "No, Mama. It was something else."

The Tennessee River overflowed its banks, the swift current bringing down an immense quantity of heavy driftwood, lumber, fences, and large trees. As the serpentine line of Gen. Nathan Bedford Forrest's cavalry pulled up to the river's muddy banks at noon on February 6, the entire troop had a clear view of the gunboats that were headed for Fort Henry. Downstream they could see the fort, and beyond the fort itself there seemed to be troops moving.

"Dismount!" Gen. Forrest yelled, and the men all got off to rest their horses.

"Look at that!" Jake said in awe. "They're going to squeeze those poor fellows in a vise!"

Vince was so tired he could hardly sit on his horse, but the sight of the flotilla of ships steaming toward the fort made him forget his fatigue. "Maybe the guns in Henry will do for those ships. Sure do hope so."

They watched as four large gunboats—the *Cincinnati*, *Carondolet*, *Essex*, and *St. Louis*—formed on a line abreast. The wooden gunboats formed another line abreast about one-half mile astern of the ironclads and fired over them. A roaring filled the air as the *Cincinnati* opened fire. The fleet edged closer to the fort, which seemed to be a blaze of fire, and the roar of the cannons was almost deafening. Soon the guns from Henry opened fire and made hits almost at once on the gunboats. Jake saw the ship with *Essex* on the bow struck so hard that she reared out of the water, then drifted helplessly downstream. Men were wildly throwing themselves into the swollen river, trying to escape the flames and destruction. It seemed a Confederate victory was coming. But it was not to be so.

The short-lived battle turned soon after it started, for, as was later revealed, Fort Henry was built too low on the water, and most of her best guns were flooded and totally useless.

"There's the surrender," Forrest muttered to his adjutant, when a white flag was raised at the fort. "Let's get back to Donelson. They'll be coming our way pretty soon." He swung to his horse, making an imposing figure. A big man, six feet and two inches tall and strong as a blacksmith, he exuded an air of leadership. He called out, "Mount up, men!" and drove his horse on a fast trot down the winding path that led to the river. As soon as they were on the Fort Donelson road, he stepped up the pace to a fast gallop. The distance was only twelve miles, but by the time the troop arrived, Vince was hanging on by sheer nerve.

Jake pulled up, took a quick look at Vince, then dismounted and grabbed the reins of Vince's horse. "You go see about some grub," he said. "I'll take care of the horses."

Vince slid wearily out of the saddle, giving Jake a wry look. "You don't have to take care of me like you was my mama," he said. "But I guess I'll take you up on that deal."

Jake watched as Vince plodded toward the fort, then unsaddled the horses, rubbed them down, and saw that they got their fair share of the forage from the soldier in charge. As he turned toward the fort, he was thinking of Vince. *He's come a long way. Didn't think he'd make it here to Donelson, but he hung in there.* He knew that without his help, Vince probably wouldn't have made it, for he was still weak from his sickness and was not used to the hard life of a soldier. But they'd done it, Jake thought. They'd managed to join up under each other's names and to carry off the masquerade successfully. It was almost a kind of game, responding to Vince's name in public and using his own name when he and Vince were alone. It was a strain, at times, but they had pulled it off. And no matter what happened now, Jake knew that Vince would never be the same. There was an element of pride in him now, and Jake could see that Vince was determined to go through whatever lay ahead of them.

He entered the fort, noting that all the guns pointed landward were in firing position. Glancing toward the side facing the Cumberland River, he saw the same condition applied there. *Guess they know what's coming,* he thought, then made his way to the long, low building where he and the rest of the troop from Virginia were quartered. As he entered, he saw Vince talking to Jeremiah Irons and went at once to where they stood.

There was a hard set to Irons's mouth, and when Jake looked at the chaplain inquiringly, he shook his head. "My brother's no better. I don't think he can make it for long."

"What about taking him to a hospital?" Jake asked. He had grown fond of Irons, and of his brother, too.

"He'd never make the trip," Irons said. "Anyway, we're pretty well ringed in by Federals, I think. Gen. Forrest offered to send a small squad, which was fine of him. But every man is needed here, and we couldn't get through anyway."

"When we give these Yankees a thrashing," Vince said, "maybe we can rent a boat and get to the Mississippi."

"Well, we'd run right into Grant if we tried that," Jake said. "His command post is in Cairo. No Confederate ship can get past that spot."

"That's right, I'm afraid," Irons said. He seemed low in spirits, which was not strange, since he had nursed his brother almost constantly since arriving at Donelson.

"Let me sit with him, Chaplain," Jake said quickly. "I think we'll get sent out in the morning to screen the Yanks, but you need a little rest."

Irons nodded wearily. "Maybe for a couple of hours. Thank you."

He moved away, and Vince said, "You've got to be worn out yourself, Jake."

"I'm OK. Let's get a bite, then you rest. I'll grab some sleep later."

They each got a plate of beans and bacon and some coffee, then sat down to eat. "This Gen. Forrest is a tough hairpin, isn't he, Jake?" Vince said, chewing slowly. "And those men of his are hard as nails."

"They're a tough bunch, and that's what we'll need." Jake swallowed a cup of scalding coffee, then added, "I was talking to Capt. Wainwright this morning. He thinks we're in a box. Told me that Gen. Johnston ordered a first-class fort built here, but it was never done. Johnston found out at the last minute that there was practically nothing here and had some engineers throw up this fort along with Fort Henry. But they're not much as forts go. Those big gunboats can pound them to pieces. And with the Yankees coming in Grant's army, we've got no place to retreat."

"Some of the officers say we ought to pull out now, while we can. Can't say I'd object, but I guess we came to fight."

Jake looked at Vince, a light of approval in his eyes. "If I forget to say this later, I've been proud of the way you've handled this. Your family will be proud, too."

Vince colored and drank some coffee to cover his embarrassment. "Well, I'm coming to this a little late in my life, Jake, and I couldn't have done it without you." He ate slowly, then asked, "How'd you make it with my family? You've never really said. Was it hard to fool them?"

Jake didn't like to speak of it, Vince saw, but he did say, "God's blessed you with a fine family, Vince. I envy you."

"Well, you can come and see us after all this is over."

"Not likely." Jake hesitated, then went on. "Rachel told me never to come back again."

Something in his tone—something wistful that wasn't really like Jake—caused Vince to look up quickly. "Rachel said that? Well, she's just sore right now. "

Jake rose to his feet, shaking his head. "I guess it's more than that. I deceived her. She can't ever forget that." He turned away then, saying, "Better get some sleep," and trudged off to the small room where Baxter Irons lay.

Jake's conversation with Vince had depressed him, for it reminded him of Rachel's hatred—and it was that which cut him more than anything else. He shook his head, trying to get her out of his mind, and found Irons with a higher fever than usual. He got some water and began sponging the wan face, and suddenly the sick man opened his eyes. "Jerry?" he whispered through chapped lips.

"No, it's Vince. How do you feel, Bax?"

"Can't complain."

"You never do," Jake said. He poured some water into a glass and Irons drank a little of it.

"What's going on out there?"

"Yankees took Fort Henry this afternoon."

"That means they'll be headed for here, don't it?"

"Expect so, Bax, but we'll hold them off."

Irons shook his head weakly, his eyes sunk back into his skull. "I—tried to get Jerry to leave—but he won't do it."

"We'll be all right."

The sick man stared at him, then closed his eyes. He had an alarming habit of dropping off like this, and it was happening more often. Jake sat beside him, angered by his helplessness. Bax Irons was no more than twenty-three, and his life was over. Many others had died of sickness in this place, but Jake had taken Bax's hand more than once, and he was the only one Jake had watched slip slowly away.

An hour later, Jake awoke when Bax said, "Vince—"

"Yes—you want something, Bax?"

Bax was burning up with fever, his eyes glazed with pain. "Vince, are you a man of God?"

Jake said slowly, "No, Bax, I'm not."

"Too . . . bad! Wish you were . . . !" He labored for breath, then said with terrible effort, "I'm glad I . . . got that settled!" Then he whispered, "Vince . . . go get Jerry—"

Jake leaped up and ran full speed to where Irons slept. "Jeremiah, come quick!" he said, and Irons got to his feet at once. "I—I think he's going!"

Irons left at a run, and Jake followed. He didn't go close, but let the two men have their moment together. It was dark, with only a few lanterns glowing in the long room, so he could barely see the outline of Jeremiah's body leaning over the bed.

The time ran on, and Jake closed his eyes, but he was too aware of what was going on a few feet away to sleep.

Finally he heard steps and opened his eyes to see Jeremiah Irons standing there, tears running down his cheeks.

"He's gone?"

"Yes." There was pain in Irons's eyes, but his voice was even and his lips were relaxed. There was a peace about him, Jake saw with wonder, and he waited for the chaplain to speak. "He was longing to go, Vince," Irons said softly. "He gave me some messages to pass on, and then he just slipped away."

Jake blinked and bit his lips. "He was such a fine young fellow. I'm sorry, Jeremiah."

"No, don't be. 'Precious in the sight of the Lord is the death of his saints.' " Irons hesitated, then said, "He spoke of you, Vince."

"He did?"

"Yes. He said to tell you that Jesus loves you."

Tears burned at Jake's eyes, and he couldn't speak. Finally he got control and said, "That's not easy for me to believe."

"No, you think you've got to earn God's favor. Most people do. But the New Testament denies that on almost every page. That's what grace is. We can't help God. Either the blood of Jesus is enough—or it isn't."

Jake said quietly, "Well, it was enough for Bax."

Irons said, "It's enough for you, too, my boy. It's enough for all of us!"

CHAPTER TWENTY-TWO

ESCAPE FROM FORT DONELSON

THE FUNERAL for Baxter Irons took place at sunset, just after Jake and Vince came in from a patrol. Exhausted, they all but fell off their horses and went at once to the sector outside the fort that had been set apart for the burial ground, finding two dozen or so men there, with Jeremiah Irons standing at the head of the grave. Irons looked up as they hurried to join the group, nodded at them, then began the service.

It was a brief service, consisting mostly of readings from the Scriptures. Jeremiah Irons's voice was clear on the cold air, and when he had read from the Bible, he closed it, then stood there looking down at the pine coffin. He spoke for a few moments about his brother, stressing that Baxter had put his trust in Jesus Christ, then nodded to the men beside the coffin. They picked up the ropes and lowered the coffin, then stepped aside. Irons picked up a handful of the red dirt, tossed it into the grave, then turned away. He stood there silently as the men filled the grave, then he walked away.

Jake and Vince fell into step with him, not certain of what they should say. Finally Jake said, "I guess you'll be pulling out pretty soon."

Irons shook his head. "Not for a while. We've got a lot of sick men—and lots of those who are well are pretty scared about the battle. I'll stay for a few more days."

Vince glanced in the direction of Fort Henry, saying, "You don't have a lot of time, Jeremiah. We ran into Yankee pickets today. Grant's headed this way for sure. Capt.

Wainwright says the generals think Commodore Foote will bring his gunboats up the river any time."

"I guess that's right," Irons agreed. "But we've had lots of reinforcements. Heiman's troops from Fort Henry and the Second Kentucky under Bushrod Johnson. And Gen. Buckner's division."

Jake offered, "I heard that the Yankee general Lew Wallace was on his way by river transport with his division—as many as ten thousand men. We've only got eighteen thousand men at most, so we'll be facing at least three-to-one odds, and that's not counting the fire from the ironclads."

The three men spoke of the difficulties faced by the Southern forces, and it was Vince who said, "Well, we'll just have to stand up to them, I guess. But I think you should leave now, Chaplain."

But Irons refused to go, and for the next few days he found plenty to do, working with the sick and encouraging the fainthearted. He preached every night to large groups, and more often than not Jake and Vince were there to listen. Many men professed faith in Christ, and early one morning, a large number of them braved the cold waters of the Cumberland as Chaplain Irons baptized them.

Jake stood on the bank with Vince, silently watching, wondering at the sight. There was something impressive in the way the men lined up, dressed in their oldest clothes, waiting their turn. One of the candidates, a tall soldier from Arkansas named Opie Dennis, caught everyone's attention. He stood quietly as Irons said, "Upon your profession of faith, I baptize you, my brother, in the name of the Father, the Son, and the Holy Ghost." He was so tall that Irons was forced to take a step back to lower him, and when he came up, he began to shout, "Glory to God! Glory to God!"

Vince whispered, "I guess Opie's happy enough." Then he turned to face Jake. "Kind of makes me wish I was in there, Jake. How about you?"

Jake said, "It makes a man think. I guess I hope my time will come. Your mother would be real happy if you found God—and Rachel, too."

Vince said nothing, and after the service, they were called out by Capt. Wainwright for a patrol. "Gen. Forrest wants to find out what the Yankees are up to," he said laconically. "Guess we know, but the other generals, Floyd and Pillow, are gettin' nervous."

Gen. Forrest led a force of nearly one hundred men out on the patrol, and they rode through the bottoms for several miles. Jake saw the general suddenly throw up his hand, halting the line of troopers. Forrest was staring through the line of trees; following his glance, Jake saw the flash of the sun on metal. "There they come," he murmured to Vince, who was on his left. "The show's about to start."

He was correct, for the patrol followed the progress of the ironclads and watched them pitch into Fort Donelson at once. It was three-thirty when, at a range of less than two thousand yards, the *St. Louis* opened fire. The other ironclads followed suit, and shells exploded against the thick earthworks of the fort. Gen. Forrest passed down the line, and Jake heard him say to his aide, "Nothing but God Almighty can save that fort!"

But Foote had made a serious mistake. He had taken Fort Henry by bringing his fleet to point-blank range and blasting away—but he had either ignored, forgotten, or not known that the lower guns at Henry had been flooded, which had made his task there easy.

When the gunners at Donelson opened fire with its biggest guns—a ten-inch smoothbore Columbiad and a 32-pounder rifled gun—they practically blew the *Carondelet* out of the water, smashing the anchor and knocking the plating to pieces. All of the ships came in for a hard battering, and Foote, on board the *St. Louis*, was wounded in the foot by a shell that crashed into the pilothouse, killing the pilot and carrying away the wheel. Out of control, the ship drifted downstream after the

Louisville. The *Pittsburg* was sinking, and all the while not a single man in the waterside batteries had been hurt.

Still, the resounding victory over the gunboats did little to lighten the gloom that had settled on Donelson's three generals. They were convinced that they could not save the fort, and that night they met and planned the breakout. Basically, they intended to slam Grant with a sudden hammer blow, then break out to the south toward a road that led to Nashville. Gen. Gideon Pillow's men, on the Confederate left facing Gen. McClernand's division, would attack at dawn. Gen. Simon Buckner would leave a single regiment, the Thirteenth Tennessee Infantry, in the trenches to the right, facing Gen. Smith's division, and move the bulk of his men to the center. Once Pillow had rolled over the Federal troops, Buckner would strike the hinge and hold the door open while Pillow's division marched out to safety. Then Buckner would follow, fighting a rear-guard action to make sure that the bulk of the army escaped intact to fight again on more opportune ground.

It was a good plan, and later on Capt. Wainwright explained it to his sergeant and a few of the men, including Jake and Vince. Wainwright laid a sheet of paper on a table in the mess hall, saying, "Here's a map of the area."

"Gen. Forrest says we'll go with Gen. Pillow, fighting on foot. When we've rolled McClernand back, Buckner will pull his division from the right to the center and take Smith out, shoving him back. Then Pillow's men can get away through the gap in the center. We'll mount up and help Buckner fight the rear-guard action to make sure the whole army gets out. Get your muskets ready, because we'll move out to the attack at dawn."

All night long the men worked frantically, the cooks preparing three days' rations, the sergeants making certain that the men had ammunition and that their muskets were in firing order. Jake and Vince, along with the rest of the cavalrymen, saw to their horses as well, for, as Jake said, "We'll be needing mounts if this thing works."

A winter storm spread misery that night, and a howling wind covered the noise of the Confederates as they made their preparations. By morning the ground was covered with fresh snow, and tree limbs were sheathed in ice.

As daylight brought a thin line of light in the east, the order came to leave the fort. As soon as they were outside, a line of battle was formed two lines deep. Jake and Vince were in the second line, near the left, and at once the order came to advance. The officers moved back and forth checking the lines, and the sergeants were like hunting dogs, hounding the men and shoving them into position.

The line struck the picket line of the Federals, catching them completely off guard. When two or three of the Union soldiers fell, the rest scurried away, yelling, and a cry went up from the Confederate officer, "Charge, men!" At once the entire line began to run, and Jake smelled the acrid odor of gunpowder as they rushed into the Union lines firing. The firing of the muskets reminded him of corn popping over a fire, the sound being magnified many times, and from the left came the thunder of artillery.

A shrill yelling—a yipping noise like high-pitched voices of dogs—arose from the men, and Jake found himself joining in. To his surprise, he felt no fear. He found himself eager to stay up with the line, and glancing over to his right, he saw that Vince was yelling, too. The trooper to his left, a small man named Davis, coughed suddenly then fell on his face, not moving. Jake's first impulse was to stop and help him, but Sgt. Prince yelled, "Go on! Go on!" and he picked up the pace at once.

The smoke was getting thicker, and suddenly they ran into a small camp where three of the enemy were trying to reload their muskets. They had been cooking breakfast, and as Jake watched, one of them was struck by a bullet and driven into the fire, knocking the coffeepot down. One of the other Federals threw his musket down and started to run, but a minié ball took the top of his head off before he got ten steps away.

The other soldier stood there, his empty musket in his hand, his eyes wide with shock and focused on Jake. He was no more than eighteen years old, and Jake lowered his musket, intending to tell him to surrender, but another Confederate ran at the boy and with a savage yell thrust his bayonet into his stomach. The two stood there for one moment, the Confederate grinning, the boy staring at him with a look of reproach. Then the Confederate yanked his bayonet free and, when the boy fell, lifted his musket and stabbed the helpless soldier in the chest, screeching wildly.

Jake stared at the scene, noting that Vince had stopped as well, his face pale as paste. "Come on!" Jake yelled, and the two of them rushed to catch up with the line. As they advanced, shadowy figures were moving ahead of them, and soon they encountered a line of solid fire. Jake fired at them, then fell to the ground to reload. He saw Vince standing upright, reloading, and yelled over the crash of musketry, "Vince! Get down!" They moved forward slowly, for the Yankees had stiffened their line.

For the next three hours they were surrounded by smoke, confusion, and death. The battle was not one line against another. Instead, it was broken up into hundreds of small fights as units got separated from their brigades. But the Federals were shoved back, and a cry of victory went up from the Confederates as they gave way.

"Now's the time for Gen. Pillow to get this army out of here," Jake panted. "The door's wide open!"

Capt. Wainwright's hand had been wounded, and he was wrapping it in a handkerchief. "Yes, but it won't stay open long. Grant's going to find out pretty soon what's going on. He'll not stand to lose, not Grant!"

An hour later, the firing on the left had picked up, and Wainwright nodded. "Hear that? We've missed our chance. Some stupid general thought we could take on the whole Federal Army! Now we—"

The firing was heavy, and Jake could not hear the rest of Wainwright's words. He turned around and saw that the captain was facedown on the ground. When he rolled him over, he saw a small black hole in his temple. Jake put the officer's head down, moved down the line to Sgt. Prince, saying, "Capt. Wainwright's been killed."

Prince stared at him, then said, "This thing's gone sour. No way we can get out of here."

His words were prophetic, for an hour later the Confederates were retreating. As they fell back, Vince yelled, "Look, Jake—!"

Jake turned to see Jeremiah Irons bending over a soldier. Jake glanced at the Yankee lines, which were driving toward them. "Come on!" He ran, bent over, to grab Irons by the arm. "Come on! The Yanks are right behind us!"

Irons got to his feet and looked at the advancing line of Federals, then the three of them moved back. Jake fired, sending one of the enemy down, then, as he was reloading, he heard Vince cry out. He whirled, expecting to see Vince down, but it was Irons who was lying on the ground and Vince running to him. Jake leaped to the wounded man's side, looking for his injury.

"It's in his chest, Jake," Vince cried. "We've got to get him out of here."

"Grab his legs," Jake said, and the two of them dropped their muskets and picked Irons up. His eyes were open, glazed with shock, and as the two men carried him across the field, he fainted. A sergeant yelled at them to leave him, but when he saw that it was an officer they were carrying, he said no more.

They got Irons back to the field hospital, where a busy surgeon came to look at him. The air was loud with the sound of muskets and artillery, but the cries of the wounded men could be heard over everything. "He's hit bad, I'm afraid," the doctor said. "If I go in for that bullet, it may kill him."

"What if you don't?" Jake demanded.

The doctor, a fat man with thick hands, gave them a hard look, then said, "He'll die, would be my guess."

"Take it out!" Jake said at once. "Any chance is better than none."

In the end, the doctor finally did just that. He was a rough man, and Jake cringed at the operation, but when it was over, the doctor said, "He may make it. Keep him warm and give him plenty to drink when he can take it." Then he turned back to the growing crowd of wounded men.

"Let's get him to bed," Vince said, and the two of them soon had Irons in a bed, wrapped with blankets. When they had done all they could, Vince asked, "Think we ought to go back to the fight, Jake?"

"No. We're penned in now. No way out." His face was grim in the dim light, and he added, "I hope the prison camp we wind up in isn't as bad as I know they can be— because that's where we're going to spend the rest of the war!"

Vince stared at him, then shook his head. He got up without a word and disappeared from the room.

The three Confederate brigadiers gathered to compare notes. Buckner considered the army's position desperate. "You should have marched out as we planned, Gen. Pillow!" he said grimly.

"We'll still get out, as soon as it gets dark," Pillow snapped. Pillow was a sharp-faced man who had earned a reputation for incompetence during the Mexican War. On one occasion, he had mistakenly ordered his men to build their breastworks on the wrong side of the trench, leaving them exposed to the enemy.

Gen. John Floyd had fear on his face, for he had been accused of having misappropriated $870,000 as President Buchanan's secretary of war. He was certain that the Union would try him on those charges, and he had no thought except getting away.

The three men argued until one o'clock, when Nathan Bedford Forrest came to report. Forrest was shocked to discover that the generals were discussing the surrender of the army. His eyes blazed, and he exclaimed, "The Federals haven't occupied the extreme right. We can still march out. My scouts have found an old river road. It's under water—no more than three feet—but only for one hundred yards."

But Floyd said, "My medical director says our troops can't take any more punishment."

"Have you thought how much punishment they'll take in a prison camp, General?" Forrest snapped. He argued for over an hour, but finally the generals took a vote. They all agreed to surrender the men, but Gen. Floyd spoke out and said he would not surrender himself, and Pillow at once said the same.

"I'll share the fate of the army," Gen. Buckner said.

"If I place you in command, Gen. Buckner," Gen. Floyd said, "will you allow me to get out as many of my brigade as I can?"

"Yes, I will."

Floyd turned to Gen. Pillow and said, "I turn the command over, sir."

Gen. Pillow replied just as promptly, "I pass it on."

Gen. Buckner said, "I assume it."

At that, Forrest snorted angrily. "I didn't come here for the purpose of surrendering my command!" he said with contempt dripping from his voice. He stomped out and in a short time had gathered his officers. He told them of the generals' decision, then said, "I'm going out. Anyone who wants to go with me is welcome. I'll get out—or die!"

Vince had been wandering around the camp in despair. He'd seen one of Forrest's lieutenants, a man named Sloan, whom he knew slightly. "Lieutenant, what's Gen. Forrest going to do?"

"Get out of this rat trap!" Sloan spat out. "We've found

a way. If you want to go, be ready in half an hour. We're pulling out then."

Vince whirled and raced back to where Jake was sitting beside Irons. "Jake! We've got a way out of this place!" He quickly informed him of Forrest's plan, adding, "It's the only hope we've got. I'm going to get the rest of the troop."

"Wait a minute!" Jake indicated the motionless form of Irons. "I can't leave him here to be captured."

Vince had always been a clever enough man. His brain was working fast now, and he said, "We'll hitch our horses to a wagon. We can put him in the bed. We've got to cross some water, but I don't think it'll get as high as the bed. You get him ready, while I go steal a wagon and get the horses hitched to it."

"Watch out for Crow," Jake called out as Vince left at a dead run. "It might hurt his feelings some to pull a wagon." But Vince was gone, and Jake began his own preparations. Irons was unconscious and could be left, so he took care of provisions. He made a raid on the commissary, taking as much as he could carry in two large burlap bags. By the time he got back, Vince was there with the wagon hitched up and most of the men of the troop who'd come from Virginia with him. He was telling them, "We're getting out of here. I didn't enlist to die in a prison camp! Little, you and Poteet go bring the chaplain out. He's taken a bullet, and we're taking him out with us!"

Jake was surprised to see the two men jump at Vince's command, and as they loaded the injured man onto the bed of the wagon, he said so quietly that only Vince could hear, "You make a pretty good officer, Vince. Any orders for me?"

Vince grinned at him, saying only, "Shut up, will you!" The two of them got into the wagon, and Jake took the lines. "Let's get out of this place, Jake," Vince said, and they moved out, followed by the mounted men.

They met Forrest with his command outside the fort,

and by daylight the horses were belly-deep in freezing water. Many of the infantrymen had gotten word of the breakout and were wading waist-deep, but there was no complaining. At the head of the column rode Gen. Forrest, ever alert for Federals.

"Pretty hard on a wounded man," Vince said, looking back at Irons. He got out of the seat, going back to put more blankets over the still-unconscious man. When he came back to sit beside Jake, he shook his head, saying, "He's in poor shape, Jake. I don't see how he can make it."

Jake didn't answer, but his own spirit was gloomy. Finally he shook his head, saying, "Times like this I wish I was a praying man. But all I can count on is what I can do. And I'm thinking that won't be enough."

CHAPTER TWENTY-THREE

RETURN TO VIRGINIA

GRANT'S victory over Fort Donelson touched off celebrations all across the North. At the Union Merchants' Exchange in St. Louis, speculators stopped work to sing patriotic songs; in Cincinnati, everybody was shaking hands with everybody else, and bewhiskered men embraced each other as if they were long-lost brothers.

In the South, many believed that they had lost the war at Donelson, for the fall of the fort opened the way south and led to the fatal splitting of the Confederacy, which had been the Union plan all along.

The editor of the *Richmond Examiner* did not underrate the importance of the North's victories over Fort Henry and Fort Donelson. He saw in it the beginning of future disasters.

Rachel came into her mother's room with a copy of that paper, saying, "Mother, listen to what the *Examiner* says about Donelson:

> "'The fall of Fort Donelson was the heaviest blow that has yet fallen on the Confederacy. It opened up the whole of West Tennessee to Federal occupation, and it developed the crisis which had long existed in the west. Gen. Johnston had previously ordered the evacuation of Bowling Green, and it was executed while the battle was fought at Donelson. Nashville was utterly indefensible; by the sixth of April surrender of Island No. 10 had become a military necessity. The Confederates had been compelled to abandon what had been entitled 'The Little Gibraltar of the Mississippi,' and

experienced a loss in heavy artillery, which was nigh irreparable.

"The Confederate loss was 12,000 to 15,000 prisoners, 20,000 stands of arms, 48 pieces of artillery, 17 heavy guns, from 2000 to 4000 horses, and large quantities of commissary stores. The Confederates lost more than 450 killed and 1500 wounded, while the Union loss was 500 men killed and 2100 wounded.'"

Rachel threw the paper on the floor with an impetuous anger, saying, "These newspapers! Can't they *ever* say anything good about our side?"

Amy picked up the paper, read through it, then said, "Well, it *was* a terrible loss for the Confederacy. Your father says it'll take a miracle for us to recover."

Rachel shook her head, anger glinting in her eyes. "Fifteen thousand of our men prisoners!" She walked around the room, unable to curb the impatience that welled up in her. Since news had come of the fall of Donelson, she had been on the rack, unable to sleep for worrying about her brother. Every night she prayed that he was a prisoner and not in an unmarked grave outside the fort. Regret worked on her, cutting like a keen knife at the memory of how she'd sent him away so coldly. And she couldn't even bear to think of Jake and the last words she'd spoken to him.

Her mother had been anxious over Vince, of course, but she had noted Rachel's almost frantic activity since the news arrived. Now she said, "Rachel, you mustn't go on like this. I'm believing and praying that Vince is a prisoner. You've got to do the same."

"I know, Mother," Rachel said, forcing herself to be calm. She took a seat and began to knit a sock, her face pale and her lips tight. The two women sat there for only a few minutes, and finally Rachel said, "I'm going for a ride over to Melora's, Mother."

"Take the Yancys some of the potatoes," Amy said. "I'm sure they're getting low on food."

"I will."

Two hours later she pulled her horse up in front of the Yancy house. Buford came out, his lean form bent but his eyes bright. "Well, now, Miss Rachel! Come a'callin', did you?"

"Brought you some potatoes," Rachel said. As he took the sack, she slipped to the ground and walked with him to the door, asking, "Have you heard from Bobby?"

"No. He ain't much fer writing," Buford said. Opening the door, he called out, "Melora! Company!" He tossed the potatoes on the table, saying, "Got a nice fat doe this morning. I'll go cut a quarter off for you," and left the room.

"It's so good to see you, Rachel," Melora said, coming over and kissing the younger woman. "You sit down and I'll make some tea. Have to be sassafras, I'm afraid. Unless a ship breaks through the blockade, we'll be drinking that for a time."

"That's fine, Melora." Rachel sat at the table, listening as Melora talked and made the tea. As always, she admired Melora, thinking her one of the most beautiful women she'd ever seen. She was tall with raven black hair and striking green eyes. At twenty-seven she possessed a slim figure, yet was rounded by a womanly grace. Finally she sat down and the two women began talking.

After a short time, Rachel asked bluntly, "Melora, aren't you worried about Brother Irons?"

Melora put her slim fingers around the mug, took a sip of the tea, then nodded. "I am, a little. I wish they'd release the names of the prisoners—but they're in no hurry for that."

"I—I'm almost sick over Vince," Rachel said haltingly. She hesitated, then blurted out, "I was angry with him when he went away. I said terrible things! Oh, I could cut my tongue out!"

Melora leaned forward, put her hand on Rachel's, waiting for the girl to get control. Finally she said, "You know, Rachel, God gave each of us a spirit all our own, none of us the same. He's like an artist, wanting to make all of his creations special. That's part of the glory of God. Remember how some of the psalms talk about how varied his creation is, about all the kinds of birds and the wonderful creatures that are in the ocean?"

Rachel was caught up with the words—Melora had always spoken poetically, and wrote so, too, she suspected—but now she asked, "What does all that have to do with my being a beast to my brother?"

"Oh, I'm sure you weren't a beast, Rachel!" Melora laughed. "But you're different from other people. You've got powerful emotions that just won't be still. You're like a boiler full of steam, and you've got to let off some at times or explode."

"Full of hot air, am I?" Rachel said, amused at Melora's words.

"Full of love, full of hate, full of every kind of emotion," Melora insisted. "I wish I had more of that in me!"

Rachel stared at the older woman. "But—I've always wished I was more like *you!*" she exclaimed. "So cool and collected, you never lose your temper!"

Melora sipped her tea, then shook her head. "I'm the way God made me—and so are you. Neither of us should complain or be unhappy with the job God did on us."

Rachel put her chin in her hand, thinking about what Melora was saying. Finally she said, "Well, at least Brother Irons won't have to worry about fits of temper."

"And the man who gets you won't have to worry about being bored!" Melora giggled surprisingly. "He'll get his head skinned at times, I suppose, but he'll get something else, too."

"What will he get?"

"He'll get a woman who'll give him such love as men dream of but few find."

Rachel's face turned scarlet, and she hid it with her hands. "Melora! You make me sound bold and wanton!"

"No, because your love will be strong in all areas: physical, emotional, and spiritual. That's just it—you have a tremendous capacity for love in all its facets." Melora came out of her chair to stand beside the girl. Putting her hands on her shoulders, she said, "You often remind me of Mary Magdalene. Not the early Mary—but the one who loved Jesus so much that she washed his feet with her tears and dried them with her hair. I don't think anyone on earth ever loved him so much. And that's the kind of love that's in you, Rachel. All you need is a fine man to give it to."

The two women were still, and finally Melora went back to her chair, saying, "Let's pray for our men. For Vince and Jeremiah. For all of them, even the poor Northern boys who are suffering."

Rachel bowed her head and they prayed . . . and before the final "Amen," she whispered a prayer in her heart, without really understanding why she did so, that God would watch over one reckless, deceitful gambler.

A spring wind, brisk but with a hint of April warmth, brushed against Vince's face, and he lifted his head, sniffing the breeze. He turned to Jake, who was dozing beside him in the seat. He nudged him with an elbow, saying, "Jake, wake up!"

Jake woke instantly, looked around, then spotted the buildings making a smudge against the sky down the road. "Richmond?" he questioned.

"We made it, Jake!" Vince said with excitement in his voice. "By heaven, we made it!"

Jake smiled, thinking that both of them had had doubts about getting back to Virginia. First they'd had to get permission to leave the Army of Tennessee. Gen. Forrest had listened to Vince's plea, then had given them extended leave to get back to Richmond.

He had waved off their thanks, giving Vince a pass and wishing them well. "Hope the preacher makes it," he said as they left, but there was doubt in his voice, for he'd talked to his own medical officer about Irons and had received little hope.

Getting permission to leave had been relatively easy—reaching their destination was far from that. The weather had turned even worse, so they'd had to travel between icy rainstorms and frequent snow flurries. The two of them could have forced their way through, but with Irons running a fever, they'd had to hole up in whatever shelter they could get, which meant slow progress.

Now at last, they were at Richmond, and Vince turned to look at Irons, then said, "I hope we're not too late." Jake made no answer, for he had little hope that the minister would recover. He was convinced that Irons was hanging on to life by an act of will so that he could see his children one more time. It had been a hard time for Jake, for when Irons was conscious, he'd talked about God and had repeatedly urged both men to let Christ come into their lives. It had not been a pushy thing, which would have repelled both Vince and Jake—it was simply an outgrowth of the love in Irons that was always visible. Both men knew the minister could no more help sharing his faith than he could help breathing.

As they came into the outskirts of town, Vince said, "Jake, it's time to make a switch."

Jake stared at him with a puzzled look. "A switch?"

"Right. You've been Vince Franklin too long, my friend. Today, I step back into my own shoes! But we've got some adjustments to make."

"I'd better cut out now," Jake said. "If they see the two of us together, it's all over."

"Just trust your Uncle Vince!" he said with a grin.

Jake said no more, but he decided that as soon as they got the chaplain to a hospital, he was leaving. "Think I'll go keep Jeremiah company," he said, and Vince pulled the wagon to a stop.

Jake got in the back and sat with Irons, seeing to it that he was comfortable.

"Where are we?" the sick man whispered.

"Richmond, Jerry," Jake said. "You'll be with your family real soon."

Irons looked up, his eyes glazed, but managed a smile. "I—knew you two—would do it!"

Jake sat beside him, not talking much. He had learned that Irons liked to have someone there when he woke up from his fitful sleep. They made their way to the camp, where they were directed to the military hospital. Less than thirty minutes later, Irons was in a bed, between white sheets, and two doctors were hovering over him.

"Looks like Irons is in good hands for now," Vince said to Jake. He nodded.

"You'll want to find your father—," Jake started to say, but Vince shook his head, cutting him off.

"No, not just yet. We haven't really officially reported in, and there's something I want to take care of before we do. Come on!"

Jake started to argue, but Vince just took his arm and urged him back out to the wagon, then headed into town. Soon Vince pulled the wagon over, saying, "I'll be back in an hour, Jake. Then we can go on to the camp and report." He grinned broadly, then disappeared.

Jake went around to the back of the wagon, stretching out, weary to the bone. He wondered about Vince, what sort of scheme he was up to, but was too exhausted to care. It was over as far as he was concerned. *Just let me get rested and I'll pull out,* he thought.

He grew sleepy and was dozing when he felt the wagon give and heard Vince say, "Wake up there, Private! You look like a sloppy soldier to me!"

Glancing toward the sound of Vince's voice, Jake was shocked at what he saw. Vince stood there, dressed in a spotless gray uniform, and he had been carefully barbered. His beard was neat and trim, the way it'd been when Jake had first seen him, and his hair was cut in his old fashionable style.

"What do you think, old buddy? The old Vince, eh?" He grinned. "By George, it's good to be myself again."

Jake said with an admiring glance, "You're some sight to behold! You look like a hero." He got to his feet, adding, "I'll leave you here—"

"You'll do nothing of the sort!" Vince said sharply, cutting him off. "I know you think you'll be recognized, but come along and let me show you something." Jake jumped to the ground and followed him to a store window, where Vince waved at their reflections, saying, "Take a look at yourself, Jake."

Hardin squinted into the glass and received a shock. He'd let his beard grow since leaving Richmond, and now it was a bushy mask. He'd never been able to grow a neat beard, which was one reason he'd always shaved closely. His clothes, he saw, were in tatters—not a single garment was whole. "I look like a bum," he said, studying his reflection. "But what do you need me for?"

"I don't know," Vince said honestly. "But we've gone through some rough times." He hesitated, then said quietly, "I don't have a friend in the world, Jake, except you. I need you. Isn't that enough?"

Jake looked at Vince quickly, seeing that there was none of the old cynicism in his eyes. He thought hard, then shrugged. "OK, I'll go along, Vince."

"Fine! Now we report to the adjutant."

They drove to the camp again, and Vince went into the office at once, asking the sergeant, "Is Maj. Franklin here?"

"Sure is," the sergeant said, nodding. "He's over at the drill field."

Vince turned and went back to say to Jake, "He's at the drill field. Let's go find him." He got into the wagon and, when they got to the field, he said, "There he is, Jake."

Maj. Franklin had seen the wagon but had turned to speak with one of the sergeants. Vince had advanced to within ten feet of him before he turned back. He took one look at Vince and his face grew pale. Vince said, "Sir, I've come back to report."

Brad Franklin seemed to be frozen. He ignored Vince's salute, his arms hanging down at his sides for a moment, then he lurched forward unsteadily, crying out, "Vince—!" He grabbed the younger man, holding him with all his might, and the soldiers who were drilling watched with amazement. Until, that is, Sgt. Clay Rocklin said, "About face, ladies! On the double, march!" Then he turned to Cpl. Royston. "Pete, take care of them. I'm going to welcome my nephew home!"

Maj. Franklin had released Vince, but his voice was unsteady. He wiped his eyes, saying, "Well, you ought to be shot for giving an old man such a shock!"

Vince's voice was husky, and he had to clear his throat before he could answer. "I—couldn't get word to you, sir." Then he handed Gen. Forrest's pass to him, saying, "I'm on extended leave. Chaplain Irons—he's at the hospital. I'm afraid he's in bad shape."

Franklin saw Clay waiting and said, "Sergeant, come here."

Clay came at once, his face happy. "Vince, I'm happy to see you."

"Uncle Clay," Vince said abruptly, "I've brought the chaplain home. He was wounded in the battle. I—I don't see how he's lived this long."

Clay's face clouded with sadness. "I want to see him. And someone ought to go to Melora. She can tell his children. I believe they are staying with one of the parish families."

Franklin said instantly, "Clay, you're on leave. Take care of Jeremiah. Do whatever seems best. Use my name."

"Yes sir." Clay moved quickly to the wagon, and Maj. Franklin said, "Son, go at once to the house. I can't leave right now, but the family needs to know you're safe." He drew his shoulders back and said proudly, "By heaven, you're home! Thank God!"

Vince echoed his father, saying, "Thank God!" then turned and went to the wagon. Clay, he saw, was already in the wagon, waiting. As Vince approached, Jake said, "Shall I drive you to the hospital to see the chaplain?"

Vince watched with alarm as Clay looked up at the driver, but there was not a flicker of recognition in his uncle's face. "Yes, we'll go there first."

It only took a few minutes for them to reach the hospital. Vince followed Clay inside to talk with the doctors briefly and get an update on Irons's condition before talking with Melora. Then he said, "Uncle Clay, I've got to get home and tell everyone I'm all right."

"Yes, go right now. And have Rachel go with you to get Melora."

"Yes, sir, I will."

Jake was sitting on the porch but rose as Vince came out. "Come on, Jake. We've got chores to do."

Jake hesitated. "Maybe I'd better stay with the chaplain."

"No, I'll need you. Come on."

Jake followed him to the wagon, and the two of them drove off at a fast trot. Soon they were clear of town, yet Vince said nothing. He was thinking of the love he'd seen in his father's eyes when he had greeted him—something he'd wanted to see all his life!

Jake, however, was thinking of Rachel, wishing that he was anywhere in the world other than on his way back to Lindwood. But he was committed to Vince and so, as the wagon rolled along, he sat there, dreading the moment when he'd have to face her.

All he could think of was the contempt in her voice as she'd said, "Never come here again!"

Tad came stumbling into the kitchen, where Amy was helping Dee fix potato salad. His eyes were wide and he was bawling out his words so rapidly that Dee said, "You gone crazy? Whut you yellin' about?"

"Marse Vince!" Tad finally shouted, pointing with a wavering hand. "It's Marse Vince come home!"

"Glory to God in de highest!" Dee screamed, and the two women ran out the door. Rachel was hanging clothes out on the line in the back and, when she heard the screaming, she dropped her best nightgown in the mud and ran around the house. She stopped dead still when she saw Vince leaping off of a wagon only to be engulfed by Dee and her mother.

Suddenly Rachel couldn't breathe, and the earth seemed to spin around, forcing her to stagger toward the house. She leaned against the wall until the dizziness passed, then walked unsteadily toward the three. Vince, seeing her coming, pulled away from his mother and Dee and turned to meet her. He seemed to be waiting for a sign, and Rachel saw in his eyes that he was uncertain. Remembering her anger when she'd sent him away, her heart smote her and she began to run, tears coming into her eyes. "Vince! Oh, Vince!" she cried as he caught her up in his arms.

He held her tightly, then said, "Rachel—!" His voice was choked with emotion.

She pulled back and looked at him, saying, "You're back! You're not dead!"

"Not a bit of it," he said, then turned to his mother and Dee, saying, "Could a man get a bite to eat around this place?"

This was what the women needed, something to do to take the strain off of the moment. Amy came to him, hugging him again, then said, "You come in the house right now, Vince Franklin! I'm going to feed you until you pop."

Vince stopped, then turned to the wagon and said, "Come on, Jake. I want to introduce you to my family."

Jake, feeling like a complete fool and a total fake, wrapped the lines around the seat, stepped to the ground, and advanced reluctantly a couple of steps as Vince said easily, "This is my best friend, Jake Hardin.

Jake, I want you to meet my mother, Amy, and my other mother, Dee. And this is my sister, Rachel."

Amy smiled and came to offer her hand, saying, "I'm so glad you've come with Vince, Mr. Hardin!"

Jake pulled off his hat and muttered a brief thank you, giving Amy's hand a quick shake and nodding toward the black woman. Then he looked at Rachel. She was staring at him, her face pale. He would not have been surprised if she had denounced him on the spot. But she only glanced at Vince, then said, "I'm glad to meet you, Mr. Hardin."

Vince didn't miss the awkward exchange, and he spoke quickly to relieve the strain. "I've got bad news, I'm afraid. Jeremiah Irons was wounded at Donelson. We managed to get him out—but he's in a bad way!"

Amy said at once, "We have to tell Melora!"

"That's what Father said," Vince agreed, nodding. "Rachel, he thought you might go after her, take her to get the children, then go to the hospital at the camp."

"Oh, yes!" Rachel said. "I'll go right now!" She turned to Tad, who was standing ten feet away, saying, "Tad, hitch the grays to the buggy."

"Yas'um, Miss Rachel!"

"Both of you come inside," Amy insisted to the two men as Rachel ran to change clothes. "You both look so tired!" She led them into the house, and soon they were eating the best meal they'd had in weeks. Vince told the story of their escape, making little of his own part in the effort.

Jake ate very little, but when Vince was finished with his story, he said, "Mrs. Franklin, your son is the worst storyteller I've ever heard. It was his doing that got us out of Donelson. If it hadn't been for him, Chaplain Irons and I would both be in a Yankee prison right now!" He told the story again, ignoring Vince's protests.

When he finished, Amy said quietly, "Your father will be very proud, Vincent."

Vince flushed and started to protest, but Jake said,

"Vince, I need to go back to camp. Could I borrow a horse?"

"Certainly you can!" Amy nodded, then had a thought and added, "But would you go with Rachel to get Miss Yancy? It'll be dark by the time she can get to Richmond, and I'd feel better if a man went along with her."

"Why—yes, Mrs. Franklin," Jake said hesitantly, seeing no way out. At just that moment, Rachel came in wearing a dark brown dress and a coat to match.

"I'll stay in town with Melora and the children, Mother. Don't worry about me."

"I'll be in tomorrow, dear," Amy said, nodding. "Mr. Hardin's going to town, too, so I asked him to go with you and Melora."

Rachel shot a strange glance at Jake, but said, "That's nice of you, though I doubt we'll have any trouble."

Vince said, "I'll have Tad saddle a good horse for you, Jake. Come along." When they were clear of the house on the way to the barn, he said, "You'll have to talk to Rachel, Jake. Don't let her give us away."

"Nothing I can do about that."

"Just talk to her, and I'll talk to her tomorrow. She's hot-tempered, but she's got a good heart."

Ten minutes later, Jake drove the buggy down the road, a fine chestnut gelding tied to the rear. Rachel didn't say a word, nor did he—not for over a mile. Finally he said, "This wasn't my idea, Rachel."

"It wasn't mine, either."

Jake shifted uncomfortably on the seat, not knowing how to talk to her. Her face was stiff and there was a rigidity in her spine as she sat beside him. Finally he said, "I can't change what you think about me, but you shouldn't be angry with your brother. He grew up while we were in Donelson." Still she said nothing, and he felt his own anger rising within him. "It's good that you've never made a mistake, Miss Franklin. Makes it real easy for you to come down hard on us poor mortals who have!"

Rachel had been sitting there, trying desperately to find a way to speak to the man beside her. She had decided that he was not the rogue she'd taken him for—and she could no longer deny that his presence, even the very sight of him, did strange things to her heart. The feelings that had so confused and troubled her when she thought Jake to be her brother now came back in a flood, and she felt her face grow warm. She longed to look at him, to drink in the sight of his face, to feel again the camaraderie they had established during their time together as "brother" and sister . . . but her pride was too great.

Then, when he lashed out at her, her answering anger brought a fierce halt to any efforts she might have made to break through the walls that surrounded her. The buggy moved steadily down the road, both of them bound into silence. Rachel kept her head turned to one side, determined not to let Jake see on her face the mortification that she was sure was showing. She knew there was something mean about the way she was acting, something small and despicable. Here a man had come out of a death trap, a man who had, she sensed, brought her brother through a hard time—and all she could do was stare ahead, refusing to look at him or offer a word of thanks.

The longer it went on, the worse it got for her. She longed to turn, to ask Jake about Vince, to give him a chance to explain the strange events of the past—to tell her if everything between them had been an act. Instead, memories came to taunt her and fear told her that he'd made a fool out of her, had probably even laughed at her. Her cheeks flamed, and finally she set her lips.

Jake Hardin might perhaps be better than she'd thought at first, she told herself, but he still was a man she'd like to see out of her life forever!

CHAPTER TWENTY-FOUR

AT ANY COST

Cʟᴀʏ and Melora brought Irons to Lindwood three days after his being admitted to the hospital in Richmond. Both of them had stayed with him constantly, taking turns sitting up at night, and the Irons children, Asa and Ann, clung to them for assurance. Irons had rallied for two days, glad to be with his children and among friends, but then the deadly fever that had racked his frame all the way from Tennessee rose. And nothing would bring it down.

"You may as well take him home," Dr. Evans said on the third day, his long face showing regret. "He doesn't want to be here—and there's nothing I can do for him."

"We'll take him to Lindwood," Amy said at once, for the parsonage used by Irons for so many years was occupied by his successor. "We have plenty of room for everyone."

So Clay had driven the sick man home in a closed army ambulance, commandeered in the name of Maj. Franklin, arriving at Lindwood late in the afternoon. Irons wanted to try to walk, but Clay said, "You've been bossing me around from the pulpit for years, Brother Irons. This time *I'm* giving the orders. You can run around all you like after we get you on your feet."

Irons smiled up at him, his face so thin that the skull was plainly outlined. "I'll be running through the green pastures soon enough, my brother."

Clay blinked—he didn't miss the allusion to the psalm—but turned and called to Jake and Vince, who were standing a short distance away. "You two, make yourselves useful!"

As the two men carried the sick man inside on the stretcher, Irons said, "You two have carried me many a mile, brothers—but I guess I won't trouble you after this trip." He lay down with a sigh of relief, and his eyes closed when they put him into the bed. But he opened them to say, "I can't get to a church or a pulpit—so you two will have to be my congregation." A smile turned the corners of his lips up, and he whispered as he dropped off into a comalike sleep: "The sermon . . . will start when . . . I wake. . . ."

Melora came over and arranged the covers around Irons, then sat down beside him. Clay hesitated, then asked, "Will you see that the ambulance gets back to the regiment, Vince? I don't want to leave."

"Sure, Uncle Clay." Vince left the room, followed by Jake. When they were outside the house, Vince walked slowly to the wagon, biting his lip nervously. "He's not going to make it, Jake." Shaking his head with an angry gesture, he suddenly struck the side of the wagon with the heel of his fist, saying angrily, "After all the misery we went through getting here—to lose him now—!"

Jake felt even lower than Vince, so low that he made no answer. He had not been hopeful from the time he had seen the wound, for he knew how rarely a man lived through such a thing. He had begun to respect Irons as a man long ago; now he had grown to reverence him as a man among men. Never once had Irons complained and, even when the pain must have been terrible, Irons's sole concern seemed to be for the souls of his friends.

"Guess I'll take the wagon back," Jake said heavily.

"It's too late, almost dark now. I'll take it back. I've got to go to town tomorrow morning, anyway." Vince paused, then added, "Got to go see Ellen." When he caught the sudden look Jake laid on him, he shrugged. "Got to be done, Jake. Might as well get it over with."

The next morning Vince was on his way to Richmond shortly after dawn, his horse tied to the rear of the ambulance. After dropping the ambulance off at the hospital, he rode straight to Ellen's boardinghouse. He was met by Mrs. Mulligan at the door, who said, "Mrs. Rocklin has moved." There was a tight set to her lips, and Vince was aware that she was upset.

"Is something wrong, Mrs. Mulligan?"

"Yes, there is—" She hesitated, then said firmly, "I had to ask Mrs. Rocklin to look for other quarters." Her lips drew together, and she shook her head. "Times are hard, with the war and all, and I need all the boarders I can get. But to be plain with you, sir, Mrs. Rocklin isn't a careful woman, as far as men are concerned, I mean. And I'll ask you not to come here again."

"Of course. Did she leave an address?"

"No—but you might try the Cosmopolitan Hotel. I've heard she was there."

"Thank you," Vince said. He left at once and made his way to the hotel she had mentioned. It was located in an older section of Richmond, one that was going to seed. As he dismounted and went inside, Vince noted that the Cosmopolitan had little left of pretension. The lobby smelled rank with age and odors of the years, and the clerk, a thin young man with grimy hands and hair slicked down with grease, merely nodded when Vince asked for Mrs. Rocklin.

"Number 206."

Vince ascended the stairs, took a left, and knocked on the door lightly. At first there was no answer, so he knocked louder. This time he heard a muffled voice but couldn't make out the words. Finally the door opened a crack, and Ellen peered out. Her eyes were bleary, but they opened wide when she recognized him, and she asked, "What are you doing here?"

"I have to talk to you, Ellen."

She hesitated, then opened the door. Vince entered, taking in the dilapidated condition of the room, but said only, "How have you been?"

Ellen was wearing a purple robe over her nightdress, and her hair was tangled. "I heard you were back," she said. A speculative light came into her eyes and she asked suspiciously, "What about the money you were going to send me? I never got a dime!"

Vince said carefully, "Ellen, I think you'd better get something straight. The last time we talked you made all kinds of crazy accusations."

Ellen stiffened and started to say something, but Vince cut her off.

"I didn't come to argue with you," he said evenly. He was disgusted with himself for ever having had anything to do with this woman. Now he wanted only to get his business done and get away from her. "I didn't think too clearly after the accident, Ellen. Maybe I was confused when we talked last time. But I'm myself now, so there'll be no money for you."

"And when I tell them about *this*—!" Ellen cried and reached out to snatch his hand with her own. "Your mother and Dee will remember the real Vince had a scar—"

"But there *is* a scar," Vince said. "Look for yourself."

Ellen stared at his hand, saw the heart-shaped scar, and the color fled from her florid face. She stood there speechless, then threw his hand away, crying, "You had it fixed! But there are other ways! You're a phony, and you know it!"

"Ellen, you've got a fine husband and fine children," Vince said quietly. "Why don't you quit all this and be a wife and a mother?"

A wildness surged into Ellen Rocklin and, lifting her hands, she clawed for his face, but Vince caught her wrists and held her easily. She struggled but could not break free. She cursed him horribly, threatening him with everything she could think of, but finally he said, "I'm going, Ellen. Don't go any further with this thing. You'll only hurt yourself and humiliate your family." Dropping her wrists, he turned and left the room.

The sound of her cursing came through the door, and he walked swiftly away, his lips set in an expression of disgust, as he left the hotel.

Thanks to Vince's father, Jake and Vince were granted indefinite leave. Even so, Jake would have left Lindwood despite his promise to Vince but for the fact that, twice during the next three days, Irons asked for him. He had gone at once to sit beside the dying man, and both times Irons had whispered, "Jesus loves you, my brother!" He was so weak that he could say little more, and Jake longed to give him some assurance—but had none to give.

When he wasn't with Irons, Jake kept to himself, riding a tall roan named Dancer over the dead fields and through the evergreen timber. He had seen Rachel five times but had not spoken to her at all. Melora was friendly but absorbed in taking care of the sick man and comforting his children. Jake longed to talk with Amy Franklin, but she seemed preoccupied. Besides, he knew they couldn't talk as they had before, when she had believed him to be her son. . . .

It was on a Friday morning that Amy surprised him by coming to join him, sitting down with him and asking about his family, as he ate a piece of bread with honey. It gave him an odd feeling, talking with her, as if he were a ghost come back from oblivion—a ghost that no one even noticed.

He gave her the bare details of his history, leaving out the worst parts, and then she said, "Brother Irons is very fond of you." A frown crossed her brow, and she added quietly, "I sometimes think he's only keeping himself alive for the hope of seeing you and Vince come to God."

Jake felt a painful stab of regret. He looked down at his hands on the table, clasped them together, then said, "I—I wish it would happen, Mrs. Franklin."

She looked across the table and on impulse reached out and put her hand over his. He glanced up, startled by the gesture, and memories of the times she had talked with him came flooding back. "Vince has told me a little of how you've been such a help to him. Not many details, but he thinks you helped him find himself. And I've wanted to thank you for that." Jake shook his head, but she refused his protest. "I won't burden you with it, Jake, but if you would, Maj. Franklin and I would like it if you'd look on us as your family."

Jake looked up, startled—but he had no chance to respond, for just then Rachel came into the room. She stopped abruptly and stared at the two sitting there, their hands together. At once Jake rose, saying, "Thank you, Mrs. Franklin. Miss Rachel—" He nodded and left the room.

"What a fine young man!" Amy said, sadness in her tone. "What do you make of him, Rachel?"

"I don't make anything of him, Mother. After all, I really don't know him."

Amy looked up, surprised by the coldness in her daughter's voice. "Why, Rachel—what's the matter?"

Rachel bit her lip but said only, "Nothing. I'm just upset. Brother Irons is slipping away, and there's nothing we can do."

"There's one thing," Amy said at once. "We can pray for Vince and Jake Hardin. That's what is on Jeremiah's heart now. I just told Jake I believe Brother Irons is hanging on just to see the two of them saved."

Rachel shook her head. "People don't find God just because somebody wants them to," she said flatly. "If that were so, Christians wouldn't have lost relatives, would they?"

"Rachel, you sound cynical," Amy said sharply. "You were taught better!" She caught herself, then came to stand beside Rachel. "I'm sorry, dear. I suppose all of us are upset. But I believe God answers prayers—and I've been praying for Vince for a long time. Now I'll pray for Jake Hardin. You'll join me, won't you?"

Rachel gave her an agonized look, for she was emotionally a ruin. Ever since her clash with Jake Hardin she had been tossed by doubt and self-loathing. Now as her mother asked her to pray for Hardin, she knew that she was empty inside; she had never felt so spiritually dry since she had become a Christian. She had tried to pray, but it was no use; the heavens were brass and God seemed so far away that she even began to doubt if she herself was a believer.

"I—I *can't*, Mother!" she said, getting the words out with difficulty. "Please don't ask me to explain!" She turned and walked from the room just in time to hide the tears of frustration that sprang to her eyes.

Amy spoke to Melora about what had happened. Melora said, "Rachel's going through some sort of a crisis, Amy. She needs our prayers almost as much as Jeremiah. He's at peace—but all you have to do is look at Rachel and see that she's in misery."

The next day Jake and Vince were sitting in the library when Melora came in to say, "I think he's going. He wants to see both of you. I'm going to get the children."

Both men rose and went at once to the sickroom. Jake saw a dreadful pallor on Vince's face and felt a weakness come into his own legs. When Jeremiah held up his hand, Jake took it at once. It was cold and had no strength.

"Jake . . . Vince . . . ," Irons whispered, "want to . . . thank you both . . . for bringing me home!"

Jake suddenly could not see, and he dashed the tears away from his eyes with his free hand. His throat was thick and it ached, but he managed to say, "Wish I could do more, Jeremiah! Lord, I wish I could!"

Vince had gone to the other side of the bed. He had taken Irons's other hand, and the tears were running down his face, an expression of grief contorting his features. He kept himself from sobbing only by an effort.

Irons lay there quietly, and he seemed to be listening to something. Suddenly both Jake and Vince felt that there was a strange stillness in the room—and a *presence* somehow—that neither of them could understand.

"God is here," Irons said, and his voice was suddenly strong, not the weak whisper they had grown accustomed to. He looked up at them, his eyes clear, and as he spoke, Jake felt the cold hand tighten on his with a sudden power.

"I've wondered why God brought me back here," Irons said, speaking distinctly. "I was ready to go to him at Donelson. All the way here, I kept asking God why he didn't call me home. Now I know! He's given me some things to say."

He lay there for a time, and Jake asked, "What is it?"

Irons looked up and tightened his hand. "It's you, Jake—and you, Vince. God is waiting for you. That's why you brought me here, not just so I could tell my family good-bye, but so you both would let God find you. That's why, boys, I've been telling you that Jesus loves you."

As Jake listened to the words, which he had heard so many times from Irons over the past days, something came to him. It was like fear, for he began to tremble—and yet it was not that exactly.

Jesus loves you!

Suddenly he knew what it was! He had heard of Jesus Christ since his boyhood. He knew the stories in the Bible about Jesus, but Jesus had always been a dim figure, a picture in a book with a halo around his head—a man like George Washington or Alexander the Great, someone about whom he had heard and in whom he had believed.

But now he was somehow aware that here, in the very room where he stood holding the hand of a dying man, someone had entered—and he knew that it was Jesus! He saw no visions, indeed, could not have seen if a physical form had been there, for his tears blinded him. But he *knew* he was not alone!

And he'd always been alone—that was what came to him as he stood there weeping. He'd had friends, but he'd been alone in every other sense. He'd become so accustomed to it that he'd even forgotten to be sad about it. But now as Irons said, "Jesus loves you," he knew that he was being asked to give up his aloneness. It was as if someone were saying, *Let me come into your very being. Let me share your grief and your fears. Please, just allow me to come in, and you'll never be alone again!*

Jake stood there, trembling like a man with fever, and then Irons prayed, "Lord Jesus, these men need you. They're afraid, but take away their fear. Show them how much you love them—let them know you died for them! Let your blood cover their sins, O Jesus!"

Jake never was able to remember exactly what happened. He knew that Irons asked him to pray, to call upon God, and he knew that he did. It was an awkward prayer, more of a cry for help than anything else—but he never forgot the peace that came into the room . . . and into his heart.

And then Irons said, "Thank you, God, for these two men!" He released Jake's hand and reached up to pull his head down, then held him there, against his chest, whispering, "My brother, love God always!"

Then he released Jake, who turned from the bed, conscious that Irons was now holding Vince in an embrace. He stumbled out of the room, made his way blindly through the house, and walked away toward the grove of trees where he would be hidden from all eyes. There he threw himself flat on the ground and began weeping with great tearing sobs, praying and calling out to God.

He never told anybody what took place during that secret meeting with God—but when he came out, Jake Hardin was a new man.

As soon as Jake and Vince left the room, Irons called for his children. He spoke with them quietly, blessing them and asking them to follow God always. Finally he appeared to grow weaker.

Melora was there, and he smiled at her.

"Clay?" he asked.

"I'll get him," she said, hurrying to the door and calling his name. Clay entered at once and came to kneel at the bedside; Melora knelt on the other side. They held his hands, and he seemed to be gone. Only the slight rise and fall of his chest told them he was still there.

Then he opened his eyes and looked first at Clay and then at Melora. His lips curved in a smile and he said, "I have loved you, Melora." Then he turned to Clay, saying, "My brother, you have been faithful. God has told me he will reward you—"

He lay there for a moment, then his eyes closed. "God—is—faithful!" he said haltingly, then smiled and, with a sigh, expelled his breath.

Melora reached up and pushed a lock of hair from his forehead. Her eyes were brimming with tears, and when she looked at Clay, she said, "Now we know how a child of the King goes home!"

CHAPTER TWENTY-FIVE

A FINE CASE OF REVENGE

JEREMIAH Irons was buried with full military honors, and one of the speakers to pay tribute was President Jefferson Davis. Melora said later, "Jeremiah would have hated all that fuss!"

After the funeral, a reporter from the *Richmond Inquirer* cornered Jake, having discovered that he had been one of the two men who'd brought Irons back all the way from Fort Donelson. Jake tried to make his escape, but when he realized that the reporter, a heavyset young man with bulging eyes and a heavy moustache, intended to make him the hero of the story, he said, "Let me give you the real story about our escape." Then he proceeded to relate how Vince Franklin had been the real leader. He told the truth, though he minimized his own efforts and expanded Vince's.

The reporter, whose name was Jarius McGonigle, scribbled madly, his eyes popping with excitement. "This is a real story, soldier! You'll read it in the paper tomorrow."

"Remember, you promised to leave me out of it."

"Sure, I'll do that," McGonigle said and scurried off, mumbling to himself.

The next day when Jake came back from a ride, Amy called to him from the porch. He tied the horse and found the family there, with Maj. Franklin standing in front of them. Rachel, he saw, gave him one quick look, then dropped her eyes. She looked pale, and there was little of the vivacious quality he'd always seen in her.

"Jake, I want you to hear this, too!" Maj. Franklin said and unfolded a newspaper with a flourish. Holding it up, he said, "Col. Benton brought it to me, and as soon as I read it, I got on my horse and nearly ran him into the ground getting here."

"What in the world is it, dear?" Amy asked. She had never seen Brad so excited—or rarely so—and tried to read the headline, but he was holding the paper up before his eyes as he began to read.

> *"'Many brave men have taken up arms for our beloved Cause, and we honor them. It is only fitting that one of our own be mentioned here, and we pay tribute to the hero of Fort Donelson—Pvt. Vincent Franklin.'"*

A cry of astonishment ran around the group, and Vince turned pale. His father gave him a proud look, saying, "Listen to this!" He continued to read the story, and Jake smiled despite himself, for McGonigle reached the heights of oratorical splendor in describing the hair-raising escape out of the fort, led by Vince.

Brad read on,

> *"'No less a man than Gen. Nathan Bedford Forrest himself said, "This young man is the epitome of our fine Southern aristocrats! With soldiers like Pvt. Vincent Franklin under our banners, we need not fear for the future!"'"*

Vince saw the smile on Jake's face and burst out, "Blast you, Jake Hardin! You're behind all this!"

"Just told it as I saw it," Jake protested.

As her father read the account, savoring every word, Rachel was watching Vince. By now she knew him well enough to understand that he was embarrassed over the article. She also could tell from his dour looks at Jake— and from Hardin's bland looks in return—that the truth had been stretched. But her father was so pleased that she could not be sorry. Her mother, too, she saw, was leaning forward to catch every word, as were Grant and Les.

Finally Brad finished reading, and then the paper was passed around so that each of them could read for himself. Vince refused to look at it, going to stand at the window. Jake went to him, asking slyly, "May I have your autograph?"

"You snake in the grass!" Vince snapped. "I'd like to punch your head! Why'd you tell that reporter all those lies?"

"They weren't lies, most of them. If it hadn't been for you, we'd be in a Yankee prison camp. I owe you for that, so just consider this my first payment!"

Maj. Franklin called for attention, saying, "Tomorrow there's going to be a special presentation ceremony. Several of the men are going to be decorated, and Col. Benton insists on your being there, Vince. I wouldn't be surprised if you didn't come away with some kind of a decoration."

Vince protested, but his father said, "You've made it clear that you don't like such things, but it's really for the others, for those who've been at home, praying for their soldiers. Not very many good things have happened to our armies lately, and it'll be good for people to see that some fine things are taking place. You'll have to go, I'm afraid."

Vince argued but in the end agreed. Jake slipped away while the family was talking, took Dancer's reins, and led him to the barn. He stripped off the saddle and began rubbing him down, thinking with a smile of the way Vince had been taken off guard. When he was almost finished, he heard a sound and turned to see Rachel, who had walked in through the doors at the far end of the barn.

She stopped as he turned to face her, almost as if she were afraid of him. "I—came to ask you something," she said with an obvious effort.

"Sure." Jake put Dancer in the stall, filled his box with feed, then turned to say, "What is it?"

Rachel looked around to where Bruno was cleaning

out a stall a few feet away. "Could we go outside?" She turned and he followed her through the door. She glanced toward the house, then turned and walked along the path that led to a small pasture surrounded by a rail fence. Inside were five grown sheep happily nibbling at the brown grass. Rachel looked at them, and Jake came to lean on the fence a few steps away from her.

A brisk wind blew her fine hair over her face and she reached up to tie it back with a ribbon from her pocket. Her fingers, Jake noticed, were long and tapered, and her wrists looked strong. She had fine skin, made rosy by the breeze, clear and smooth with a few freckles across her nose. As Jake studied her silently, he thought that she had always impressed him as one of the strongest women he'd ever met, determined and firm. Now, however, she seemed undecided. She picked at the top rail of the fence, stripped off a flexible splinter, held it between thumb and forefinger, then tossed it to the ground and turned to face him.

"Was that true, what the paper said about Vince?"

"Most of it. All the important parts were true."

"It was really Vince who found the way out?"

"He found Gen. Forrest, who was leading the escape. Forrest's scouts had found the old road earlier, but it was Vince who got the men from our regiment together and persuaded them to get out while there was still time. The wagon for Jeremiah was his idea, too."

Rachel listened to him carefully, weighing his words. Her lips looked soft and vulnerable, rather than firm and almost harsh as Hardin had seen them more than once lately. She stood there, her eyes looking serious, and then some sort of embarrassment came to them and she let them fall. "I-I'm glad it was true," she said. "Daddy and Mother are so proud!"

Jake nodded but said nothing. In truth, he didn't know what to say. Just the sight of Rachel fired strong emotions within him, but he couldn't say anything. He thought, suddenly, that she seemed to be waiting for him to speak, for she lifted her eyes and her lips parted, seemingly with expectancy. His breath caught in his chest and he struggled for control. He wanted to tell her that he loved her, that there was no other woman in the world for him, nor ever would be. He wanted to take her in his arms and kiss her, to hold her with all the strength that was in him and never let her go. He did none of these things.

Rachel saw something of the struggle going on in the tall man who stood before her, but when he remained silent, she stiffened her back and said evenly, "Thank you for telling me. I'm glad for Vince."

She moved away then, and Jake wanted to run after her. But for what? What could he say? She hated him, and with good reason. He was guilty! Even if that didn't loom before him, he was a penniless man, a gambler with no future. What could he offer any woman?

So he let her go and stood there watching her walk slowly back to the house. When she disappeared through the door, he turned and walked toward the grove of pines that crested the small hill. He found the place where he'd come to pray on the day that Jeremiah Irons had died—and discovered that it was still a good spot for meeting with the Lord.

The Richmond Grays made an impressive sight as they marched onto the field, rank on rank. The president sat with his wife on the platform, along with most of the members of his cabinet, applauding the men as they went through their maneuvers smartly. After the drill exhibition, President Davis descended and met Col. Benton, and the two of them presented decorations to several of the soldiers.

Finally when all the expected awards were made, Col. Benton said, "We have one more award to give to a fine soldier who is not a member of the Richmond Grays. Pvt. Vincent Franklin—front and center!"

As Vince came to stand in front of the two men, Brad

Franklin rose to his feet stiffly, his face under tight control. As the president read the commendation, giving the details of Vince's exploit, Brad turned and his eyes met those of his wife—and the two of them smiled.

The president, after reading the commendation, smiled, too. An austere man with chiseled features, he had been accused of being cold and unfeeling, but there was a warm light in his gray eyes as he said, "Your family is well represented in the army, Pvt. Franklin. Both your father and your brother are in the Richmond Grays. I am wondering if you would like to join them in this fine regiment?"

"Yes, Mr. President!" Vince exclaimed at once.

Davis smiled more broadly, saying, "The powers of the president are strictly limited, but I think in this case there will be no protest if I use my office to make your request official. And I feel certain that Col. Benton will welcome my request that you be appointed sergeant as of this moment!"

"Certainly, Mr. President!" Col. Benton said instantly. "Congratulations, Sgt. Franklin!"

The ceremonies were concluded, and Vince was surrounded by many people—including some of his friends who were in the Grays, as well as by his family. He smiled and shook his head when Clay came to him, saying, "You'll have to give me lessons, Uncle Clay. I don't know a thing about being a sergeant!"

"Just yell as loud as you can," Clay said, shaking Vince's hand. "Now we're all going to the hotel for a reception, I hear."

"I guess so," Vince said. "Father insisted on it."

"He's very proud of you. We all are. God has brought you to a place of true honor."

The reception was held in the dining room of the Edwards Hotel, which was soon crowded to the walls. "We should have gotten a larger room, Amy," Brad said as he brought her a glass of lemonade after shoving his way through the crowd. "I never dreamed there'd be this many people here."

Amy took the glass, sipped the tart liquid, then looked across the room, pleased to see Vince surrounded by friends. "It's wonderful, isn't it, Brad?"

"Miraculous, I'd say," he answered. "I don't think I'll ever doubt God again, Amy. Just a short time ago Vince was going to hell as fast as he could manage it. Now it's all different!" He glanced at her, asking, "Did he tell you about what happened to him when Jeremiah died?"

"Yes! And he wants to go all the way with the Lord, Brad. He told me he wants to be baptized as soon as possible." Her eyes grew sad for a moment as she said, "I'll miss Jeremiah so much, but he died doing what he loved most—winning men to Jesus!"

"Vince says he thinks Jake Hardin was converted, too."

"We've got to help that young man, Brad! He seems so alone. You must get close to him."

"I will," Brad promised, nodding. "I'm going to try to get him transferred to the Grays so he'll be with Vince. You know, Vince told me that the worst thing about all this today is that Jake got none of the credit. He says he'd never have made it if it weren't for Jake. But we'll make it up to him!"

After an hour and a half the crowd thinned out, and Vince saw Rachel sitting alone, looking rather forlorn. He went to her, took a seat, then said, "Well, this will be over soon. It's been fine, but I wish Jake had gotten something." He saw a shadow cross her face and asked, "What's wrong, Rachel?"

"I guess I'm just feeling a bit of a letdown," Rachel said, and then she reached over and patted his hand. "I've just got the mullygrubs."

He smiled at the word, a carryover from their childhood days that signified a case of depression. "You need a sweetheart, Rachel. What's become of Semmes? I thought there was a promising romance budding there."

Rachel smiled slightly. "Haven't you heard? He's engaged to Marianne Huger."

"Well! He caught a big one, didn't he? Her father's the biggest planter in Mississippi, I hear." He studied his sister carefully, searching for a sign that she was grieving the loss of Semmes, but could tell nothing from her face. "But how does that make you feel?"

"Leighton was never in love with me," Rachel said with a shrug. "He was just challenged. I was the only girl he'd courted who didn't fall all over herself to get him." She suddenly smiled, adding, "Now it looks as though I'm the spinster of Lindwood for good."

"Don't be ridiculous," Vince said sharply. "And don't call yourself that anymore. I don't like it."

Rachel shook her head, then changed the subject, "The talk is that McClellan is about ready to move against Richmond—" She suddenly paused, and he saw her eyes widen as she looked across the room.

He followed her gaze and saw Simon Duvall standing in the double doors leading into the dining room. "That's trouble," he said, and he got to his feet. Rachel rose and followed him, noting that Duvall's face was flushed and that he was weaving. She paused as Vince came to a halt close to Clay and Ellen. She got one glimpse of Ellen's face and saw that she was pale beneath her makeup. She was clutching at Clay's arm, trying to pull him away, but Clay stood firm, his eyes fixed on Duvall.

"What do you want, Duvall?" Vince called out, his voice carrying over the room.

Duvall blinked and with an effort focused his bloodshot eyes on Vince. He licked his lips, and when he spoke his speech was slurred. "Gonna have—it out with you . . . Franklin!" He was so drunk he could hardly stand, but there was a mad look in his eyes.

"You're drunk," Vince said steadily.

"Yes, I'm drunk! But I'm no coward, which is what you are!"

Maj. Franklin roared, "Get out of here, Duvall!"

"Whas' matter, Major? I'm not good enough for you?" Duvall sneered, then when Maj. Franklin took a step, he yelled out, "Stay where you are!" His hand dipped inside his coat, and when it came out, he flourished a large pistol. "S'none of your business!"

Jake had been standing along the wall, but when Duvall had walked in, he grew alert. He had watched and listened, moving away from the wall and coming to stand a few feet away from Vince and Rachel. He wished he had a gun, but there'd been no reason to carry one. None of the other men had guns, either, he was sure. When Duvall pulled the revolver, he thought rapidly, *Too far to make a jump at him—maybe I can get around behind him.*

But there was no time, for at that moment one of the soldiers lunged at Duvall, intending to get the gun away. Duvall turned and shot the man. The bullet struck him in the shoulder and drove him back. A woman screamed, and some of the men yelled, and Duvall in his confusion simply lifted his gun and fired.

Jake saw a woman go down and, without thought, launched himself to where Rachel was standing in the line of fire. He threw his body between her and Duvall, catching a glimpse of her eyes staring at him in amazement—and something more—but before he could decipher her look, he suddenly heard the explosion of Duvall's gun and pain ripped at his head as a slug plowed along over his ear. Agony raced through him and he began to fall.

The last thing he heard as he slipped into darkness was Rachel's voice, calling his name.

CHAPTER TWENTY-SIX

THE WORLD IN HIS ARMS

THE WAITING room of Mercy Hospital was small, merely a cubicle of ten feet square, with an assortment of chairs scattered about. Cigar smoke hung in the air, making it stuffy, and after a time Clay Rocklin rose and opened the single window that looked out on Charter Street. He stood there, staring out but not really seeing the traffic that passed or the pedestrians that ambled by on the walk.

The scene kept coming back to him—Duvall firing blindly, Ellen falling with a cry, and his own failure to do anything. The suddenness of it had caught him unaware, as it had all the others. He had seen Bushrod Aimes bring Duvall down by cracking him on the skull with a heavy lamp and had gone at once to Ellen, who was lying on her face, moaning softly. The back of her dress was soaked in blood, for the bullet had caught her in the small of the back as she had turned to run away.

There had been confusion then, and he had seen that Jake Hardin was lying on the floor, utterly still. His bloody head rested in Rachel's lap, while she stared at him with a pale face that was wet with tears. The lieutenant who had set Duvall's rampage off—a tall man named Smith—had gotten to his feet and walked to the carriage without help. Clay had carried Ellen to a carriage, and Vince, along with three others, had carried Jake to another.

The doctors had gone to work at once, but to those assembled in the waiting room it seemed an eternity since they had first arrived. Once a doctor had come out to speak to the friend of Lt. Smith, saying, "Come along.

He's all right now. Got the bullet out without much trouble."

Later another doctor, a younger man with a fresh round face, emerged, asking, "Who's waiting for the head wound?"

Rachel stood up to ask, "How is he, doctor?"

"Well, we've got the wound all sewed up, but he hasn't come to yet." A frown pulled his lips down, and he shook his head doubtfully. "Bad case of concussion, I'd say."

"But he'll be all right, won't he?" Amy asked.

Like all doctors, this one hated to be wrong. He figured it was better to put the worst face on a situation, then if something went wrong there would be no way for the family to accuse. "I hope so—but you can never be sure with these cases. I'd say take him home and watch him. Keep him warm and even if he wakes up, you make sure he stays put in bed."

"We'll take him with us," Maj. Franklin said firmly. "Vince, let's go get an ambulance. It'll be easier on him."

Amy stayed with Clay when they left, but Rachel walked out of the waiting room and caught up with the young doctor. "May I sit with him?"

"Certainly! Right this way." He led her to a room where Jake lay in a bed, his head bandaged and his eyes closed. "Your husband?"

"Oh, no!" Rachel said quickly.

The doctor gave her an odd look, then decided, *Must be a sweetheart. He'll be a lucky fella, if he lives. That's one good-looking filly!* "Just keep him warm, even if you have to use hot-water bottles," he said, then left her.

Rachel sat down beside the bed, her face on a level with Jake's, and stared at his profile steadily. As the time moved slowly, she thought of the first time she'd seen him, in another hospital. And she thought of how she'd cared for him, almost as if he were a baby. The memories of their time together came clearly and, looking back, she saw that she had been vulnerable with him while she thought of him as her brother. Now, though, she realized that all the time there had been something more to her feelings than sisterly concern. Something in her had responded to Jake's masculinity, to the tenderness and closeness he had shown her. She was sure he had known that, and yet . . . he had not capitalized on it as some men might have done. Instead, he had treated her as a sister. And a friend.

She sat there quietly, her hands clenched tightly, watching his still face. A question kept surfacing in her, formless and wordless, but insistent. It had something to do, she understood, with her feelings for the man lying there, feelings she'd never been able to express. She was a woman born to love, but never had she found a man who stirred deep emotions in her. Until she had met Jake Hardin. But her feelings for him were complicated and confusing, particularly because she'd been convinced that all her affection had been a natural outgrowth of the fact that Jake was her half brother.

But he was not her brother, and the memory of how betrayed she'd felt when she'd suddenly discovered the masquerade came to her. Now in the still darkness of the small room, looking at Jake's face, she found herself understanding that her anger had been tied up somehow with the loss—and relief—she had felt at the discovery that this man was *not* her brother.

Slowly she reached out and laid her hand softly on his cheek. It was a caress, yet it was more than that. *Why do I feel this pain?* she cried out wordlessly. *I've never felt this way about any man!* She let her hand linger on his face, feeling the rough beard and tracing the firm line of his jaw. Then he stirred and she quickly pulled away.

"Are you awake?" she whispered, but he kept his eyes closed, and she sat back waiting for the ambulance.

Her life had always been full and busy, but now for some reason that wasn't clear to her, she felt a terrible emptiness—a void that needed a fulfillment that she craved, but could not even pray for—because she didn't know what she really desired.

Back in the waiting room, Clay and Amy sat together, saying little. There was a heaviness in Clay's expression, and when Dr. Carver came into the room, Clay got up at once and faced him. "How is she, Doctor?"

Carver, a muscular man of forty with a heavy black beard, nodded sparely. "She's alive, Sgt. Rocklin. The bullet tore through some large muscles—but I'm afraid it touched the spine."

"Will she be all right?"

Dr. Carver bit his full lower lip, then stroked his heavy beard before answering. "I'm concerned about the bullet. It's too close to the spine for me to remove."

"Can you leave it in?"

"Yes, but I must tell you, she's got no feeling in her lower body."

"She's paralyzed?" Clay asked sharply.

"I'm afraid so," Carver admitted. "It may be a temporary thing—or later we may decide to try to remove the bullet. But even if we did that, if the spine is damaged, she may be crippled permanently." He shook his head, adding, "I wish I could give you better news."

"May I see her?"

"She's still groggy from the chloroform, but you can go in." He hesitated, then said, "Let me give you one caution, Sergeant. In cases like this—I mean, if she is actually paralyzed—it's important to be very positive. She'll be frightened and confused. Try to encourage her all you can. She'll need all your support."

"Yes, Dr. Carver." Clay nodded. "Take me to her, please."

Amy watched as the two men left, depressed by the news. She thought of how Clay had been tied to a loveless marriage with Ellen for years. She thought of his love for Melora, understanding how empty his life was without her—and she thought of Melora's love for Clay. Now, if Ellen were truly paralyzed, she'd be clinging to Clay like a leech, draining him of every possible ounce of strength.

Amy closed her eyes, thinking, *And he'll stay with her! Even if she turns out to be a helpless cripple, nagging at him constantly—Clay will never leave her.*

It should have pleased her to know that there were men like Clay Rocklin who were faithful to their commitments—but she sat there heavyhearted, thinking of the long parade of empty years that her brother faced.

Clay found Ellen awake and almost crazy with fear. She was crying wildly, and when she saw him, she groped for his hands, crying out, "Clay! I can't move my legs!"

"Don't be afraid, Ellen," he said quietly, taking her hands. "It'll be all right."

But she clung to him with a fierce strength, fear pouring out of her. "Clay! Help me . . . I can't move—my legs won't work."

He stood there, trying to comfort her, to ease the fear, but she was out of control. For years she had thrust him away, but now she clung to him gasping, "Don't leave me! You can't leave me, Clay!"

He stood there, looking down into her face, which was contorted with fear. He had long ago lost any feelings of love for her; she had given him little choice. She had gone her own way, often with other men, a fact he well knew. Now as she clung to him, all the years of abuse and cruelty from her seemed to come back. And a harsh anger that Clay had thought long buried, even forgotten, rose within him.

Then an insidious voice, thin and small, seemed to say, *If she would only die!* There was a savage pleasure in the thought, and he found himself forming a picture of how it would be: *I'd not have to put up with this intolerable thing any longer—and I could have Melora!*

Immediately on the heels of that thought came another: *Lord, forgive me!* He shook his shoulders and, in a voluntary act of will, forced himself to pray for Ellen.

And then Clay Rocklin—who had risked his life in wild, bloody action on the battlefield—did the most difficult and courageous thing he'd ever done or would ever do. He leaned down and touched Ellen on the cheek, then said quietly, "I'll never leave you, Ellen. I'll stay with you as long as I live."

There was nothing but an ebony sky, a total darkness without a single gleam of a star, a silent world except for thin voices that came floating over the void like the distant cries of yesterday's ghosts. And there was no time, for there was neither sun nor moon to mark it. He felt he could have been floating through the velvet blackness for centuries, all the while that the pyramids were being put together or the great canyons of the earth were being dredged, a pebble at a time.

The voices came from time to time, and with them—at times—he felt hands touching him. One of the voices he came to know, for it came more often, and the touch that accompanied it was more gentle and soothing than the rest. There was a firmness in the touch, yet at the same time he sensed a gentleness such as he had never known.

Finally the darkness began to be broken by streaks of light that hurt his eyes, and with the light came a sense of earthiness. He felt the rough texture of a blanket against his skin, and the pungent odor of alcohol made him wrinkle his nose. A fly buzzed in his ear, lit on his cheek, then made a tickling sensation as it walked across his skin.

He lifted his hand to brush the fly away and instantly heard a voice. "Jake?" The sound of his name recalled him to the world, and he opened his eyes to see a face looming over him in the dimness cloaking the room.

"Jake? Are you awake?"

His thoughts rushed through his brain, ill-assorted and without order. He knew this woman who leaned over him—yet for his life could not remember her name. It bothered him and he licked his lips, trying to speak. The face disappeared and then came back. "Here—drink this."

A coolness was at his lips, and he was aware of a raging thirst. Clumsily he gulped the water, knocking against the glass so that some of it spilled and ran down on his neck. When it was gone, he coughed and put his head back. As he lay there, some of the disorder resolved itself, and he waited until a name came to him.

"Rachel?" he whispered.

"Yes, Jake. It's Rachel." She took a cloth, dipped it into the basin of water and bathed his face. It was cool, and her touch was soft. "How do you feel?"

There was an interval between her question and his answer, for his mind was working very slowly. "All right." He looked around the room and then back at her, trying to think about why he was here. Finally he remembered a little of it and asked, "There was a shooting—?"

"Don't try to remember," Rachel said quickly. "Just lie still. It'll all come to you soon enough."

He found that he was very sleepy but didn't want to go back into the darkness. Still, no matter how hard he tried, his lids closed, and he cried out, "Rachel—!" as the darkness closed in, like a dark ocean pulling him down into fearsome depths.

But she took his hand and put her lips close to his ear. "Go to sleep, Jake. Don't worry, I'll be right here."

Then he felt the strength of her hands and knew that he could trust her. He smiled and called her name faintly, then dropped off into a sound, normal sleep.

When he next awoke, bright sunshine was pouring in through a window, and he heard the sound of birds chirruping. He lifted his head, which brought a stab of pain, and quickly he lay back down. Lifting his hand, he touched the bandage around his temple, and then it all came rushing back to him. He remembered Duvall's twisted face and seeing a bullet striking a woman. He remembered moving in front of Rachel and the blow of the bullet.

The door opened and Dee came in with a tray. She took one look at him and surprise came to her wrinkled black face. "Well! You done decided to cheat the debil, has you?" She moved across the room, put the tray down on a table, then bent over, peering into his eyes. What she saw pleased her, for she grunted with approval then said, "I gotta' go git Miz Amy. You lay right there, you heah me?"

She whirled and left, and Jake took time to inspect the room, realizing suddenly that it was the room he'd occupied when he had stayed at Lindwood during his masquerade. Then the door opened and Amy Franklin entered. She came to him at once, her eyes bright with expectation, exclaiming, "Praise the Lord! You're all right!"

Jake nodded, which was a mistake, for the motion sent pain streaking through his head. He blinked, waited for a moment until it passed, then asked, "How long have I been here?"

"Two days," Amy said. "You had a very bad case of concussion." She came closer and peered into his eyes. "All clear now," she announced. "We were very concerned for a time." Then she asked, "Do you want anything?"

"Something to eat!"

She laughed at his urgency, turned to Dee and said, "Make this man some strong turkey broth and some scrambled eggs." When Dee left the room, Amy sat down beside him, a pleased look on her face. "I'll send word to Maj. Franklin and the boys at once. They were all called back to duty. An emergency, I believe."

The war seemed far away, having nothing to do with this pleasant room with the blue wallpaper covered with pictures of deer leaping over fences. Jake thought for a moment, then asked, "Who else got shot besides me?"

"A young lieutenant named Smith. He got hit in the shoulder but is doing fine."

She hesitated, and Jake felt a jolt of fear. "Rachel! Did Rachel get hurt?"

Amy peered at him in surprise. "What a funny thing to

ask! No, she's all right. Don't you remember her at all? Her taking care of you, I mean?"

It came back to him then, how she'd been there when he'd first come out of the coma. Nodding, he said, "Why yes, I remember now."

Amy was looking at him with a puzzled expression. "You threw yourself in front of her when Duvall started firing. Do you remember that, Jake?"

He dropped his eyes but made no answer. He did remember it, but it sounded pompous to admit doing such a thing—like something out of one of those penny romance novels! Quickly he avoided the question, asking another. "Anybody else hurt?"

Amy was curious about his refusal to admit to shielding Rachel. They had all seen him do it and had tried to reason why he would do such a thing. All but Rachel, that was. She had refused to speak of it at all. Finally Vince had gotten irritated with her, saying, "Well, Rachel, if a man risks his life for you, the least you can do is seem a little grateful!"

Now, seeing Jake's reticence to discuss his action, Amy said, "Ellen Rocklin was wounded—very seriously."

Jake glanced at her with a question in his eyes. "Is she dying?"

"She was shot in the back. The bullet lodged near her spine, too close for the doctors to operate. She'll live, but she's totally paralyzed below the waist."

He lay there for a long time, then said, "That's a tough break. I'd rather die, I think."

"Well, you almost did," Amy chided gently. "One inch to the right, the doctor said, and that bullet would have killed you." She hesitated, then said, "I must ask you, Jake—please don't get angry with me—!"

She looked agitated, and Jake was puzzled. "Go ahead. What is it?"

"When you and Vince went in to Brother Irons when he was dying, Vince gave his heart to Christ. Jake, did anything like that happen to you?"

He saw the kindness on her face and at once said, "Yes, it did." He lay there trying to find the words to express what had happened to him. "Ever since that moment, Mrs. Franklin, I've been different. Can't really explain, but for the first time in my life, I've got peace. And all the time I've got the feeling that, well, that I'm not alone." He looked at her, his eyes open with a hopeful expression. "Is that what it means—being a Christian?"

"Oh, yes, Jake! That's part of it!" Amy exclaimed. Then she began to speak of the Christian life, and he lay there listening carefully. The things she said seemed impossible, but then, the peace that had come to him had seemed impossible, too! And it was far from that.

Finally Amy laughed, saying, "You're just like a baby, Jake! Oh, you're a strong man, but all of us are like babies when we first are born into the family of God!" She reached out and touched his forehead, soothing it. "I always wanted another boy to raise. Now it seems the Lord has given me one." Then she blinked her eyes and said with a short laugh, "And a *hungry* one, too! I almost forgot! I'll go help Dee with your dinner." She rose and walked to the door but turned to say before she left, "I'll go tell Rachel that Lazarus is up and about. She's hardly left your side these past two days, Jake. She'll be mad as a wet hen that I was here when you awoke instead of her!"

But though Jake waited, Rachel didn't come. Not all that day, though he heard her voice out in the hall once or twice. Dee came, and Amy was with him often, but he caught no glimpse of Rachel—and he could not bring himself to ask about her—not until Amy came in to wish him good night.

She brought him some fresh water, smiled at him as she wished him good night, and then he asked, "Is Rachel sick or gone?"

Amy gave him an odd look, then said, "Why, no, Jake. She's here, not sick at all." She started to say more, but something kept her silent. She said, "Good night. You'll feel better tomorrow."

Then she was gone, and he lay there wondering why he had expected a woman who hated him to come and visit him.

He did see Rachel again, of course, several times over the next three days. She never came to his room, but when he was able to get up and go to the table for meals, she was there.

The first time they met, she stopped dead still. Then, after an awkward silence, she said, "I'm glad to see you up and about, Jake."

"Thanks." There was something unpleasant about the meeting to him, for he felt that he was putting her into an impossible position. *She despises me, and she's forced to be polite because I protected her and I'm in her home.*

This thought grew until, five days after the accident, he got dressed, gathered his few belongings, and made his way downstairs. Amy and Rachel had gone to visit a neighbor. Dee saw him, though, and exclaimed, "Where you think you're going?"

"Time to move on, Dee," he said. He went over to her and, to her astonishment, gave her a hard hug. "Thanks for taking care of me," he said with a smile.

She sputtered and followed him, saying, "You ain't strong enough to go faunchin' around yet!"

Jake turned and smiled at her. "Tell Mrs. Franklin I'll be back to thank her properly pretty soon." He ignored her protests and walked out of the house toward the stable. He found Tad shoeing one of the horses and said, "Tad, would you hitch up the buggy for me? I need to go to town."

"Shore, I will, Marse Jake," Tad agreed at once. But when he had the team hitched and Jake got up on the seat, he said, "I bettah go along, Marse Jake. You ain't got yo' strength back."

"All I have to do is sit here, Tad." Jake grinned. "Tell Mrs. Franklin I'll leave the buggy at the livery stable. Take care of yourself—"

He drove the buggy out, and Tad stood there scratching his head. Finally Tad went to the house and found Dee, who glared at him, saying, "Well? You jest *had* to hitch up dat buggy, didn't you?" When Tad began to sputter with indignation, she shook her head with exasperation, adding, "You ain't got a lick of sense!" But she knew she was really angry at herself for letting the man go, knowing that Amy would be upset.

She was exactly right, too. When the two women came in not long after Jake had left and Dee told them what had happened, Amy exclaimed, "You shouldn't have let him go, Dee!"

"Dat's right!" Dee moaned. "Everything's always *my* fault, ain't it now? Anything goes wrong, it's Dee who done it! Well, you jest tell me dis—how I'm gonna stop him? You tell me *dat!*"

Amy, feeling remorse, for she knew that Dee could have done nothing, began to comfort her. By the time she got the indignant woman pacified, she found that Rachel had disappeared. She went upstairs, but as she passed Rachel's room on her way down the hall, she stopped abruptly—for she heard a muffled sound. She hesitated, thinking of how strangely Rachel had behaved since Jake had recovered. While Jake was unconscious, nothing could induce Rachel to leave his side. Once he had regained consciousness, however, she had refused to go near him!

Amy knocked on the door, and Rachel said in a muffled tone, "Go away!" At once Amy opened the door and saw Rachel lying across the bed, her face buried on her arms and her body jerking as she sobbed wildly.

"Rachel! What in the world is wrong?" Amy cried. Going over to the bed, she ignored Rachel's wails of protest and pulled her upright.

"Oh, Mother—leave me alone!" she gasped but then gave a great cry and fell into Amy's arms.

Amy had long known of the depth of passion that lay in this daughter of hers, but this was the most dramatic evidence she'd seen of it. Great sobs tore through the girl, and her breath came in gasps. Amy made no attempt to speak but held the weeping girl until the sobs began to subside. Finally they stopped, and Rachel pulled away and began searching for a handkerchief. Finding one in her pocket, she wiped her eyes.

"Rachel, all of this must have something to do with Jake," Amy said quietly. "Can't you tell me about it?"

Rachel bit her lip, then threw her head back, tragedy in her blue-green eyes. "You'll think I'm crazy, Mama."

"Well, even if you're crazy, you're still my daughter."

Rachel gave her a desperate look, then began to speak. "Mama, you've got to promise me not to tell. It's not my secret!"

"Whatever it is, Rachel, I'll never tell a living soul."

Rachel knew her mother would allow herself to be torn to pieces before betraying a confidence, so she at once spilled out the story of Vince and Jake, their scheme to get hold of the inheritance. When she stopped, she looked at her mother, who had not shown one flash of emotion. "Mama—aren't you angry?"

Amy smiled, then said, "I was when I first discovered that Jake wasn't Vince, which was about twenty-four hours after you brought him home."

"You knew?" Rachel gasped, shock in her eyes.

"Of course I did," Amy said. "Am I such a ninny I can't recognize a boy who is like my own son? He looked like Vince, but he wasn't in the least *like* Vince. I can't see why the rest of you didn't see through him right off." She smiled at Rachel's confusion and said, "Why didn't I tell anyone? Because when I prayed about it, God told me to hold my peace, to sit still and see what he would do. And we have seen, haven't we? Both Vince and Jake are men of God now. What if I'd rushed in and exposed them? They both might well have been lost forever. Rachel, all of us have a time when God deals with us very directly, and this was the time for Vince and Jake."

"Mama . . . I never knew! I was so mad because he *deceived* me! He made a fool out of me!"

Amy studied the girl, then asked gently, "I think I begin to see. When you were nursing Jake, thinking he was your brother, you began to feel rather peculiarly toward him, didn't you, Rachel?"

Rachel gave a great start, her eyes flying open with shock. She had thought no one would ever find that out! "He—made me feel—"

When she broke off, unable to finish, Amy inserted, "Like a woman?"

Rachel's face flamed and she tried to get up, to run from the room, but Amy pulled her down and asked, "Rachel, do you love Jake?"

"No! How could I love a man who—"

"Who hurt your pride?" Amy broke in. "Is that it?" Amy studied the face of her daughter, then said, "Pride's a fine thing, I suppose. But lots of Southerners have too much of it, I think. Men fight duels and kill each other because they're too proud to say I'm sorry. And that's foolishness, child!"

"Mama, I can't forget the way—"

"Rachel!" Amy spoke severely. "Can pride take the place of having a man beside you? Can it keep you warm or hold you when you cry—or give you children to love?"

"Mother!"

"Rachel, I haven't known Jake very long, but I know he's been an instrument that God has used to make Vince into a man. And I know that whatever kind of man he used to be, he has changed since he first came to our home. He became a new man when he gave his heart to Jesus. Don't you believe that God can wash out the old and make us new?"

Rachel sat there staring at her mother, the words piercing her like swords. For days she had been torn by a struggle between her pride and her love, and now her own mother was calling her a fool. And she was right!

"Mother—I love him so!" she burst out and, jumping up from the bed, she began to wring her hands. "What can I do!"

"Do? Why, you absurd girl! Get on that horse of yours and ride like the wind. And when you catch up to him, tell him you've been wrong!"

"But—what if he laughs at me?"

Amy rose and, with a smile, kissed Rachel. "You're a silly child—but you're a desirable woman. Men aren't very smart sometimes. If he gives you any trouble, just let the tears well up—and fall into his arms!"

Rachel's face flushed, but she gave her mother a fierce hug. "Thank you, Mama!" she cried out, then ran out of the room. Amy went to the window and watched as Rachel ran to the barn. In a surprisingly short time, Lady came flying out of the barn with Rachel leaning low over her neck. Then, with a wave at the window where she knew her mother was standing, Rachel was gone, the horse low to the ground at a dead run.

Jake was slumped on the seat of the buggy, his face set doggedly, when he heard the sound of a horse approaching. It occurred to him that whoever it was was in a big hurry, so he pulled the buggy over to the edge of the road to give him plenty of room.

The sound of the hoofbeats grew louder, and then—

"Jake! Wait for me!"

Jake abruptly hauled up on the reins, nearly upsetting the team, which reared up and snorted with indignation. As he calmed them, he watched in amazement as Rachel pulled Lady to a stop, slid off, and ran toward the wagon. Taking one look at her face, Jake fell out of the wagon, ignoring the pain in his head as he struck the ground, and moved toward her. "Rachel—is somebody hurt?"

Then he saw that she was crying, and without a word she threw herself against him. Shock ran through him and he stood there, holding her as she clung to him fiercely. Her arms were around his neck, her face was pressed against his chest, and he was intensely conscious of her warmth and softness.

Finally she drew back and looked up at him, her eyes moist. "What is it, Rachel?" he asked, his voice hoarse.

"Jake," she whispered. "I've been such a fool! I'm still a fool, because I came to tell you—"

When she faltered, he urged her, "Tell me what, Rachel?"

"To tell you . . . that no matter what happens, I love you!"

The instant she spoke the words, something inside of her relaxed and she smiled through her tears, stunning Jake with her beauty. "You may not love me, Jake Hardin, and you can laugh at me and ride away—but that won't change anything. I love you!"

Jake was completely astonished by her statement—but not so astonished that he lost all of his senses, for he drew her to him with an urgency that startled them both. She was warm and yielding in his arms, and her lips were soft and willing. He kissed her, holding her closely, drinking in the sweetness and goodness that he had known was in her, that he had long desired. He could scarcely believe that she was here, in his arms. Yet she was, giving herself to him, and he sensed the promise in her and was humbled that she had come to offer herself so courageously.

Then she drew back, and he said at once, "Rachel, I never thought I had a chance!" He took a deep breath, then let it out slowly. He began to smile. "I've got nothing to offer you—"

She put her fingers over his lips, saying firmly, "Don't ever say that! Not ever!"

He kissed her fingers, then suddenly laughed, a laugh of pure joy such as he would never have thought he could give. "What a shock your father and mother are in for! A penniless beggar asking for their daughter's hand in marriage."

"Don't worry about that!" Rachel said instantly. "I may have chased you all over the county, but that's over. Now you can come courting me just like any other lovesick young man!"

Jake took her in his arms again and, when she protested, tightened his grasp. "A man in love will do any fool thing," he said, with a gleam of humor in his eyes. "So you can expect me to come with my guitar, serenading you with love songs and offering to shoot any dandy who dares look at you. Think that'll answer?"

"Yes," she said with a twinkle in her eyes. "Yes, I believe that will do quite nicely!"

Then she kissed him, and when he drew back, he said, "Rachel, do you realize that I've got the world . . . right here in my arms?" A fierce gladness filled them both—a gladness that they were certain would not lessen, no matter what the years might bring them.

Jake held Rachel close for a moment longer, then lifted her onto the buggy seat, climbed up beside her, and turned back to Lindwood. There was a lot to be discussed, to be settled. But they had plenty of time to work it out. A lifetime, in fact.

As they drove away, Lady stood there, not understanding what had happened to her rider. Finally she snorted, gave an impatient leap, and trotted smartly after the buggy that was growing smaller in the distance as it moved down the lane.

THE END

GILBERT MORRIS is the author of many best-selling books, including the popular House of Winslow series and the Reno Western Saga.

He spent ten years as a pastor before becoming professor of English at Ouachita Baptist University in Arkansas and earning a Ph.D. at the University of Arkansas. Morris has had more than twenty-five scholarly articles and two hundred poems published. Currently, he is writing full-time.

His family includes three grown children, and he and his wife live in Baton Rouge, Louisiana.